Brave New World

Firmin Murakami

ISBN: 979-8-7442-4141-4

DEDICATION

This book is dedicated to my wife, Gael Baxley Murakami, who helped a one-eyed, aging, almost completely blind man, learn how to use a modern computer. I would never have been able to get my computer going again each time it quit working without her help. But after much struggling, I managed to write this book for whatever it may be worth.

CONTENTS

1 THIRTEEN YEARS LATER

No one ever returned to Old San Luis de Colorado and even the roads were no longer maintained. Rose continued to grow vegetables in her garden and the guards came to deliver the vegetables to the old Engineering compound where very few people lived there anymore.

People quit referring to Matt as a young man because he was now thirteen years older. This suited Matt just fine. Sierra never found anyone that she wanted to marry so she was just fine as she was. She was now thirty something and no longer a young girl.

In long Island Savana stopped having any more children after her fifth child and was still home schooling her kids winch was much safer.

The world population dropped from somewhere close to twelve billion people to less than eight billion world-wide. Of course, these were just estimates, because it was impossible for most countries to count how many people were still alive. The hardest hit were the poor countries because they didn't have the resources to handle a Pandemic.

The stock market ceased to exist because people weren't manufacturing anything anymore.

In Okinawa, Thor and Mitoko also got older, and Thor quit going to Ume island anymore. Their youngest daughter took over the cooking for Thor and Mitoko. As time went on, she became better at cooking.

Thor still had a huge amount of money in the bank, so he kept all the people who were still left in the lumber mill. Thor made Shinzo the manager of the lumber mill because he worked for Thor so long that he knew every aspect of the business. The mill was only open from eleven in the morning to three in the afternoon because no one was doing any more building in Okinawa anymore. Thor could have closed his lumber mill, but the few people that still worked for him would then starve if he didn't keep the mill open and pay them some kind of a wage.

Thor closed the other lumber mill on the new volcano and only a skeleton crew was stationed there to guard the large amount of valuable cousin to the tungsten carbide that he still had. A shallow grave was dug for the precious metal and it was buried there, and the workers planted some Ume trees over place where it was buried. The tree was only planed over the precious metal in case there was ever a need to start manufacturing more products from the metal.

All the new help was let go and only the three engineers were left at the mill at the new volcano. Thor continued to pay them the same wages as they earned when they were manufacturing products, but now it was just a place for the engineers to stay and be comfortable.

The Korean restaurant had no customers anymore, so they closed shop. Thor's engineers hired the cook to cook for them along with his assistant.

Yuki hired a housekeeper for Thor and Tomiko to do all the hard work for them so their kids can learn how to run their family businesses. Yuki kept bringing Ume fruit to Thor's house in hopes that he would start to eat some of the fruit. Thor wasn't in any pain but didn't have the energy that he had when he was younger which would only be natural.

Mitoko on the other hand developed a sharp pain in her lower back and was now willing to try anything to relieve some of the pain so she took Yuki's advice and started to eat some Ume fruit.

In Mexico, Sierra learned how to fly Matt's Cessna 180 and got better at it as time went on. Matt worried about her but she was a careful pilot and Charlie always made sure that the plane was always in perfect flying condition before Sierra took the plane out.

2 INTRUDER

Sargent Major Sant Anna was still alive and had his guards continued perimeter patrol around the old motorhome. One day \ one of his guards noticed that a small cabin was now built over the handy flat spot where Sierra harvested Diamonds. The perimeter guard reported this to the Sargent Major, so a squad of armed guards were sent out to apprehend the intruder.

The guards shot the hinges off the door and smashed the door down. The man inside was a young man and he came out with his hands up and looked scared. All the guards had their riffles pointed at the young man's head and was ready to kill him on the spot. The guard with the walkie talkie called his Sargent Major and told him that we have an intruder and asked him if him if he should be shot on the spot.

The young man was now convinced that he was going to be killed immediately. The Sargent Major said just wait until I call the boss. He called Matt and they talked for a short time. Matt told the Sargent Major to bring him into the guardhouse because Matt wanted to personally ask him some questions.

They brought the prisoner back into the guardhouse and Matt was already there. The guard went through the regular routine of taking his photograph and taking his fingerprints and put all the formation on the computer. His name just happened to be Winston Smith just like in the story by the name in BIG BROTHER 1984.

Matt said he might have information on how he got here and could tell us what the real outside world is like now. The Sargent Major had a lot of questions for him and so did Matt. He was strapped in a metal chair and handcuffed with bright lights sinning on him. Cameras were rolling as he was being interrogated.

Winston said that he avoided all the big cities and was looking for a safe place to live. He said that he saw the barbed wire about ten miles to the north of where he finally decided to build a safe cabin but the fence looked like it was not being kept up so he just walked over the downed fence and he said that there were no signs saying that the place was all private property so that was the reason that he continued to walk south until he found a nice flat spot where he started to build a safe cabin.

Matt was now convinced that he was not a real criminal but just unfortunate wonderer that ended up on his property. Matt told the man that he was still the Mayor of San Luis de Colorado, but the town was destroyed by a small earthquake and the town was now deserted. Matt said that he had electricity restored to where the old town once stood and also had a sewer system put in and he can have water piped into for anyone one willing to start a new town.

Matt said he will give the young man ten thousand dollars to build a small restaurant and even supply him with guard protection if he wanted it.

The young man was glad that he was not going to be executed but instead given a chance to start all over with the generous help from the Mayor. Winston said I will work very hard to build the best restaurant in the whole area with the money that you offered me, and I can start to work immediately.

Matt said that he will bring some heavy equipment to the site and you are welcome to use it whenever you need it.

3 NEW DEVELOPMENTS

Eighteen months later San Luis de Colorado looked much different now. There was a superhighway right through the middle of the town and the three Engineers moved back from Okinawa and built a seven-story hotel and named it the Hotel San Luis de Colorado just like the old hotel-restaurant that was destroyed by the earthquake so many years ago. The front of the hotel faced South and had a large, curved reeving area for busses and limousines to park and let their customers off there three were attendants to take the cars of customers that came by car and parked it for the customers.

Off course this building being designed by the three engineers had a lot of steel rebar that the original Ritz Hotel didn't have and was rated to withstand an earthquake with a magnitude greater than seven on the Richter scale. All the windows on the hotel bedrooms were large plate glass windows every customer had a great view of the entire new town still being built.

There was a new post office in one of the side streets that went South from the main highway and many small shops that sold their wares. There were many small eating places scattered all over the small new town. Many people came from neighboring small towns just to see the new town. The superhighway extended all the way to Monterrey and many people could come by car be in San Luis in less than an hour and a half. The original town hall was converted into a police station and also run by the Sargent Major.

The young man that built the first building in San Luis had a truck stop on the South side of the main drag and had a modern gas station where truckers could pay by credit card without coming into the building to pay their bills. There was one island for Diesel Fuel and another island for Gasoline. If you didn't have a credit card a customer can come into the building and pre-pay by cash and a pump will be activated for the amount of gas that the customer already paid for.

The building had a cafe where truckers or anyone else can get a meal for a reasonable price and all the waitresses were young and friendly. There was a team of good cooks in the kitchen that could cook a meal quickly and the dining room was always lbusy 24-7.

Winston Smith started to pay Matt back all the money that Matt loaned him in the beginning to get started and in a few years, he will be debt free and maybe even up a rich man.

Matt found the truck stop diner too busy most of the time so during the day he always liked to look for a new small eating place away from the main drag and found them more to his liking. It seemed that a new eating shop would pop up every week and it was hard for Matt to keep up with all the new eating places.

Mathew the Mechanical Engineer grabbed a nice spot on the main drag before all the good places got taken up and started up a car dealership. The lot was huge, and he managed to have five different car makers give him the exclusive rights to sell their cars in San Luis and no one else could sell any of these cars that he now owned the franchise for. He hired a team of good car salesmen and they managed to make enough money to be happy.

Maria moved back from Monterey and set up shop in the new Ritz San Luis. It was similar to the original shop that she had before the Earthquake but now it was bigger and a lot fancier. The place was big enough to have two permanent sales ladies work full time at the counter.

Matt was still the Mayor of San Luis, but he now had two assistants that handled all the Mayor's duties for him. Sometimes Sierra would stop in and help out but that was not necessary.

4 A NEW CABIN

Back in Okinawa, Mitoko's pains were now all gone, and she can bounce around like a teenager. She looked and felt twenty years younger. Thor developed a pain in his left leg and finally agreed to start to eat some Ume fruit. He didn't like the small sour ones, so his son went to Ume Island to get him some of big ripe ones that were sweet.

After he started to eat the ripe ones, he liked it so much that he started to accompany his son to Ume Island and harvest his own Ume fruit. At first, he got on the cherry picker and used a Styrofoam box to harvest them and eat them right there. But before long he got more particular and started to sample the Ume fruit in different stages of ripeness right in the basket of the cherry picker and only picked the ones that he liked the most for the day.

Sometimes he will stay in the basket half a day sampling the fruits in different stages of ripeness and gradually migrated to the sourer ones. He visited Ume Island at least once a week and stayed there the whole day. His son spent his time harvesting saplings that were growing under the taller trees to take them back to Shinzo so he can sell them in his lumber yard.

When Thor's son Nidangun got married, Thor gave him his boat as a wedding present. Nidangun married a nice girl by the name of Kiyoko just like his grandmother who was such a great businesswoman. Kiyoko was an energetic young girl and liked to go to the farmer's market and sell soft shelled crabs and the small ume saplings. People always liked the crabs and the baby trees, so she sold out long before anyone else at the market. She started to make a lot of friends at the market so instead of rushing back home after she sold all her goods she visited with her friends at the market and bought some vegetables from her friends.

Nakanogun and Kiyoko didn't have any kids yet, so they had a lot of time to visit different places after dinner and even meet with their friends at night.

Techiko married her boss Assaimoto who was an only child and Thor cut off a big chunk of Platinum from the watermelon sized ball and gave it to her as a wedding present and she put it in the bank vault for safe keeping. Assaimoto parents were from Tokyo and had a nice home.

They had a big wedding for their son and his bride and had a big reception for them at fancy restaurant in Tokyo. Techiko had no idea what the reception cost Assaimoto parents but she knew that it wasn't cheap because they served Sashimi as the main course.

For their honeymoon Thor bought first class tickets for them to go to San Luis de Colorado in Mexico for two weeks.

Thor continued to go to Ume Island pick his own fruit and ate a lot of them while on the island. He gradually switched to the sourer ones and found them not that bad. He lost a lot of weight and started to look younger each time that he went to Ume island. He had to buy new clothes that fit him better. He had a lot more energy and felt like a young man again.

He had his son take him to the South side of the new volcano where no one lived and built a small cabin near a hot water Onsen for himself and Tomiko to live in and let his son have his old house. The South side of the new volcano was like a tropical paradise and things grew there quickly.

There was a lot of thumb sized eggplants growing there so Tomiko learned how to cook them as well as pickle them and they ate a lot of them with hot white rice. Thor noticed a lot of beautiful fish on the South side of the volcano, so he frequently walked out on the wooden wharf and fished for their dinner.

Tomiko was a great cook so she loved to cook the beautiful fish for dinner every night. Each night it was a different fish and Thor had a surprise dinner every night. They were happy and had no plans to return to their old place which was too large for them now and if his son started to have kids, they would need a big house like Thor and Tomiko had to raise fifteen kids themselves.

5 REUNION

When Thor's daughter and her husband reached San Luis de Colorado, she called her dad and told him what a beautiful place it was now. Thor decided to fly there and see for himself what the new town now looked like. When Thor arrived in San Luis, the engineers that used to work for him put him in the Penthouse of the hotel in San Luis. Thor thanked them for the nice penthouse and stayed there for a few days but decided to move to the old gated compound where he still owned a great house and stayed there.

He hired a housekeeper, a cook, and some maids because it was such a big house. Thor found the handy restaurant still run by Sarge to be a handy place to have his dinners and he found out how Matt built up the old San Luis after the earthquake and that Matt was still the Mayor.

Matt told Sierra that Thor was now in San Luis and he looked twenty years younger and that he came to see how the town has changed. Matt told Sierra that her friend Techiko got married and was on her honeymoon and staying at the Ritz San Luis.

Shinjiro always called Sierra to let her know how he was doing and to let her know that her room was always ready for her to come back anytime and visit again. Sierra asked Shinjiro if he ever took a vacation from his fishing job. Shinjiro said that he bought another boat and now he had two fishing boats, and everything was now running just fine. Shinjiro said that he found a great Captain for his second boat and he was now running the whole show.

Sierra asked him how his wife Isabella was. Shinjiro said that we now have seven kids a nanny, a cook and maids so she doesn't have to any work taking care of the house or the kids either. Sierra asked him to put Isabella on the phone and they talked for over an hour

After the long phone conversation Isabella told her husband that she was flying back to San Luis to join her old friends for a while and asked her husband if he wanted to come with her. Shinjiro told Isabella to go first, and he will come later. Isabella flew back to Mexico on a Delta flight on first class, and she was looking forward to seeing her old boss Matt.

Matt called Savana in long Island and told her that everyone was now in San Luis and that we were going to have a reunion. Savana said that all her kids were now in school and they were old enough so she will come and join the party. Matt said I will send a jet to pick you up in Long Island and to be ready to fly in two days.

Three days later everyone was in the large dining hall of the Ritz San Luis and all having a big party. The east corner of the dining hall was closed off with shoji's so they can have their own party and have more privacy. Everyone was talking at the same time and everyone wanted to know what everyone else was now doing so there was a lot of noise.

The three Engineers who owned the hotel-restaurant were also there and even thinking about building a special section in the dining hall for private parties.

Kasha and Franky heard about the big reunion, so they decided to join the party also. There were no auctions coming up in Okinawa, so they closed up their shop and flew to Mexico to join the party.

Madam Madrid heard that her niece was now in in San Luis, so she flew back to see her.

Sierra put Kasha and Franky in the Ritz San Luis so they could be close to Savana and they could talk about art.

6 FLIGHT BACK FROM SPAIN

The next night they all went to the penthouse and watched world news. The penthouse was a huge place so there was enough room for everyone. The news started by saying that they world population was now reduced by more than a third of what it was before the pandemic started. The commentator said that there were whole towns that were abandoned, and no one lived there except rodents and bats that seemed to be immune to the deadly virus.

The television showed whole towns being burned to kill the rodents and the bats in hope of getting rid of the last remaining strains of the deadly virus. All the people watching the news were happy that they didn't live in such a deadly place.

Madam Madrid told everybody that Isabella's grandfather died, and she was the only living relative left to inherit the large estate and suggested that Isabella return to Spain with her to claim the estate. Everyone in the penthouse agreed with Madam Madrid and told Isabella to go to Spain and claim the estate.

Matt flew Kasha, Franky, and Savana flew back to

Long Island and they stayed in the large studio that Savana hadn't used in a long time because she was busy homeschooling her kids at home. But now that the schools opened up again, she no longer had to home school her kids. Savana put Kasha and Franky up in her old art studio that was not used in quite some time. Even her husband Sam joined them in the art studio and took part in some of the meetings. They decided to restart EDHOP industries and there was still a lot of money in the old account. They decided to start small and just make some great paintings and maybe even have an auction.

Madam Madrid and Isabella found the estate that Isabella inherited and there were some back taxes on the property, so Madam Madrid paid the back taxes. The estate was only one property away from Madam Madrid's estate. The property in between the two properties was a small piece of land and had no buildings on the property but there was a young man that lived there in a shack and was just scrapping by selling some trees for lumber.

Madam Madrid approached the young man and asked him if he was willing to sell his small piece of land. The young man said that it was the only place that he can afford to live in and that he already owed some taxes on the property. He said that he was an artist but so far, he has never sold a single painting and that was why he was selling the fine old oak trees for money.

Madam Madrid invited the young man to have dinner in her grand house and they can discuss several options. The young man was happy to be invited to dinner and he looked like he hadn't had a good meat in quite some time. Isabella said that she had some friends who lived on Long Island that were successful artists and suggested that the young man visit them to see how they were able to make a lot of money.

Madam Madrid said that she will She pay for him to go the Western hemisphere and a friend will take him to Long Island. She had an old passport and changed the photograph on the passport with the young man's picture and it looked good enough for the trip to Mexico. She alerted Matt that she was sending a young man on a Delta flight 203 and that he will arrive in Yuma International tomorrow morning.

Buy this time Captain Tsukinoue retired and his co-pilot Takashi Kato was promoted to be the new Captain and Matt hired a newly graduated pilot to be the co-pilot by the name of Ricardo Montauban.

Matt personally met the plane from Spain and picked up the young man and brought him back to San Luis. He asked Sierra to accompany the young man on his plane to Long Island and make sure that he that he didn't get lost.

On the one-hour flight to Long Island Sierra had time to talk to the young man and found out that he could speak some English.

The jet landed on Long Island and Savana was there to pick them up and brought them to Savana's art studio. Savana introduced Manuel to all the artists at the studio and Savana showed him where his bedroom was. The cook made some food and they all had lunch.

7 REVERIE

There was an old Castle on the estate that Isabella inherited but there were no modern conveniences in the old castle. But the estate was huge and covered three small hills. In between Isabella's estate and Madam Madrid's estate there was a small piece of land that Madam Madrid wanted to acquire. Madam Madrid went to the city hall and paid the back taxes of both properties and converted all three properties into one large estate.

Madam Madrid asked Isabella how many children she now had, and she said that she had seven. Madrid asked if any of them would like to come to Spain and live with her in her large estate. Isabella said that the oldest two boys who were now teenagers and soon they will be taking over the family business of fishing for tuna and selling them to the Tokyo fish market but maybe the youngest daughter might be willing to go to Spain and learn how to speak Spanish. Madam Madrid couldn't speak Japanese so she couldn't come to Japan to pick up the young girl, so she called Sierra and asked her to go to Mikame visit her old house and bring the youngest daughter Shitanoko back to Spain.

Sierra said I will do that for you, and she said that she will be in Mikame in a week. Madrid was a big modern city so there will be no problem with just speaking English. After Sierra arrived in Mikame she spent ten days in her old house and enjoyed being treated like royalty. During her stay in Mikame she got to gradually know Shitanoko, and they became good friends. Shitanoko was young enough that she can learn to speak a new language as she grew up in Spain.

When Sierra and Shitanoko got to Madam Madrid's mansion Shitanoko was treated like an only child and got a lot of attention and she loved living in Madam Madrid's beautiful Mansion. She was too young to go to school yet, so she spent all of her time with Madam Madrid.

She was a bright child and started to learn how to speak Spanish quickly and Madam Madrid considered Shitanoko as her own daughter even if she was more like her granddaughter.

Madam Madrid took her to museums and fine restaurants and the child loved all the attention. Before long the child could easily get around Madrid all by herself but being so cute, she could be kidnapped so Madam Madrid never allowed her to be on her own in a big city like Madrid.

After Sierra spent a week in Spain her father asked her if she was done with all the business in Spain and told her to come back to Mexico. Sierra saw enough of Madrid, so she returned home.

Everyone who came to San Luis for the reunion already went somewhere else like Kasha and Franky or were now ready to return to Japan. Matt asked Sierra if she realized that he has spent more time with her than

with anyone else in the world. Sierra thought about that and realized that her father was right.
They were back in their motorhome now and it was the most private place that they had. Matt said I think that I am going to keep the motorhome just the way it is and there no need to make any new changes. He said if anything breaks off course, I will fix it or hire someone to do that but for other than that I'm happy to leave things just the way it is. Sierra didn't say anything because she was just thinking about what her father just said.

The sun was starting to settle down in the west and Sierra was just looking at it slowly went below the horizon. She didn't turn the lights on in the motorhome because she was just enjoying the day come to an end.

Matt came back into the living room after he took a shower and changed his clothes and sat down by the dining room table with her. Finally, he said why are you sitting in the dark. Sierra snapped out of her reverie and realized that her father was now sitting at the table. Sierra said I just realized how lucky we are to have this motorhome be able to live here in quiet and not be bothered by anybody else. Matt was now quiet as well and they sat in the dark just looked at the lights coming on in the guard's complex down below.

8 AKITAS

Next morning Sierra got up early and had only corn flakes and orange juice and was thinking about what she and her father talked about in the dark as the sun went down in the West.

She thought how nice it would be to have a dog living in the trailer with her. Her father Matt got up and came into the living room and asked what she had for breakfast and she said that she only had cornflakes and some orange juice.

Sierra asked her father what he thought about getting a dog as a pet to live in the motorhome with us. Matt said that might be fun and asked what kind of a dog Sierra wanted. Sierra asked her dad if he ever heard of the story about Hachiko. Matt said I remember seeing a movie about that story and said I wouldn't mind having a great dog like that myself.

Sierra said let's go to Japan and find a dog like Hachiko. Matt said great and leave tomorrow then. They first got busy and emptied their refrigerator put all the perishable in a box. Matt called the guardhouse and told them to send someone to the motorhome to pick up some food. Next, he called Captain Takashi Kato and told him to get the jet ready to fly to Japan.

Sierra wanted to know more about Akita dogs, so she got on the internet typed in Akita dogs for sale. The first one was in Connecticut there was a lot of photographs beautiful Akita dogs. She sent an email to the Akita farm and a message came back saying that the farm went out of business and they no longer had any Akitas for sale. She found another one in Alaska and they had some photographs of the different Akitas that they had a for sale, but she didn't like any of the dogs that they had for sale. She kept looking then she took a break to have some coffee.

The guard came to the motorhome to pick up the box of food and Matt gave the box to the guard. Matt asked what Sierra was doing and she said that she was just looking on the internet to look for Akitas that were available for sale. Matt got on the computer and did some searching as well.

He found one in Ciudad Victoria which was just below Monterey. Matt e-mailed them and asked if they had any Akitas for sale. The lady who picked up the phone said we have too many and we are trying to reduce our inventory.

Matt asked if she had any photographs that she can put on the screen. She showed many beautiful Akitas. Matt noticed that there was one large Akita that was mostly white and had a dark black area around his eyes that made him look like a Panda bear. Matt liked that one and asked about it. The lady said that she didn't have his full lineage and so she couldn't sell it as a genuine Akita. Matt said how many do you have, and the lady said that she had a litter of them sired by the big Akita, but she didn't want to euthanize them because they were so cute. Matt said that he will be right down to look at the Akitas today.

Matt told Sierra that he found some Akitas, and they are in Ciudad Victoria and I want to go look at them. Sierra asked how far Ciudad Victoria was and Matt said that it was just below Monterey. Matt said I might buy all of them because they are so cute. Sierra asked which car .should take then. Matt said we can just take my GMC and I'm sure that the place sells cages there if they sell dogs there.

Matt asked Sierra to grab a bag of silver amalgam and maybe we can make a trade for the dogs with it in Ciudad Victoria.

Two and a half hours later they were in Ciudad Victoria and looking at the dogs. The lady came out and said you must be the person who called about the large white Akita and Matt said that he was. The lady walked Matt all the way back to the part of the yard that didn't look like it was well taken care of and she said there they are.

There was the big Akita that looked like it weighed about a hundred and fifty pounds and there were five pups with a mother dog. There was no food in the pen but there was a large bowl fresh water. Sierra went into the pen and picked up the biggest pup and hugged him. Sierra said that this pup must weigh about twenty pounds and Matt agreed that it was aa big pup.

Matt said I would like to buy all of them and asked how much she wanted for the lot. She said that they were all vaccinated for rabies and other shots that they give for pups that were five months old so you can just reimburse me for all my costs that I put in them already.

Matt said how much would that be then. Th lady said since you are taking all of them a thousand dollars should cover all the costs then. Matt reached into his wallet and pulled out ten one-hundred-dollar bills and asked if American money was O.K.

The lady said that she has a lot of customers from the states, and she was used to working with American money. Matt said I have some silver amalgam with me and handed the lady a handful of the heavy metal. The lady was an amateur jeweler herself and new some things about silver and other precious metals. She looked at the amalgam and said that these were not pure silver and some of them weighed more than silver. She picked up the heavy one and showed it to Matt. Matt picked it up and said maybe there was some that had more gold in them and that was why they weigh a little more. The lady asked Matt if he wanted the heavy ones back. Matt said I have plenty more of these silver amalgam so doesn't worry about it.

Matt asked if she sold any handy cages for the pups. The lady said I have a whole yard full of them and I can show you some. Matt was glad that he brought his GMC truck because it had a lot of room for the cages. Matt said I will probably need a lot of fencing and asked if she had some fencing as well. The lady noticed that Matt had a big truck and asked him if he wanted the all the old fencing where she kept the Akitas you can have all of it. The lady called on her cell phone and called Rodriguez. Rodriguez came out and asked what she wanted. The lady's name was Elizabeth and told Matt that she just goes by Liz around here. Liz told Rodriguez to take the old fencing down and put it in Matt's truck and Rodriguez said I will get some tools and be right back.

Matt said I don't want to drive in the dark, so he asked Liz if there was a motel or a hotel in Ciudad Victoria. Liz said that there was a small motel nearby and they don't charge too much. Matt said I will check it out and be right back.

The motel was close by and the place was clean, so he rented one of the rooms. And came back to the Liz's Akita ranch. Matt said I rented a room at the motel and I want to take you out to dinner if you have time. Liz said I haven't been out to dinner in a long time so let's go find a place to eat. Matt told Liz to get into his truck and they drove to the main part of Ciudad Victoria and he found a fancy restaurant. They tried to walk in, and the head waiter said that in the evenings a suit and tie was required to enter the restaurant. Matt said fine and left the restaurant with Liz and Sierra and got back into the truck.

Matt asked where else should we go then. Liz said continue South and we might find something. Soon they were in Tampico and found a nice restaurant and went in and found a seat inside. The place was clean and had a good choice of things to eat.

As they waited for their dinner Matt asked Liz if she ever went to San Luis de Colorado. Liz said isn't that where the town was destroyed by an earthquake and Matt said that it was, but it was completely rebuilt, and it is a fine modern city now. Matt said I would like to invite you to visit San Luis one of these days.

9 AKITA PUPPIES

Takashi Kato the newly promoted Captain of Matt's jet was disappointed to hear Matt tell him that the trip to Japan was cancelled. Matt said that he found some cute little Akita puppies right here in Mexico and they are now all being taken care of by his guards at the guard compound.

Kato wanted to see what the puppies looked like, so he went to the guard compound and found the place over-run by curious people wanting to look at the cute little puppies. All the puppies in a fenced in compound with wood chips on the ground. A guard stood watch over the fenced in area to make sure that no one got too close to the puppies.

Sierra took the biggest puppy and brought him in her motorhome. She named the healthy puppy Shogun and he soon started to know his name. Shogun was still in its growing stage where it drank a lot of fresh water liked to eat so he always took a nap after he had his fill. Sierra made sure that the puppy didn't wet in the motorhome by taking the puppy outside to pee frequently. Matt made a small enclosure in the motorhome for the puppy so he can have his own space where there was always fresh water and some high-quality dog food.

Sometimes he will pick the puppy up and hold the puppy in his arms. But at the rate how fast the puppy was growing it won't be long before Shogun be too heavy for Matt to hold him in his lap. But for the time being the puppy was happy to be held tightly and be loved. Whenever Matt had to pee himself, he would take the puppy outside the motorhome and show Shogun where to pee.

Matt always took the puppy where the old outhouse used to be and let him pee and poop there. Pretty soon Shogun learned that was where he was supposed to relieve himself. After only one week all Matt had to do was to open the motorhome door and the puppy will go directly to the same spot and pee and poop there.

By the second week Shogun would let Matt or Sierra know when he had to pee and all they had to do was to open the door and the puppy will go directly to the same spot and pee.

Meanwhile the guards were training the other puppies where to pee and poop as well. The guards built individual dog houses for each puppy with fresh straw for them to sleep in and be comfortable at night.

Before long word got out that there were a lot of cute puppies at the guard compound and people came in droves just to have peek at the cute little puppies.

Captain Santa Anna decided to allow the people to hold the puppies for a dollar a minute to offset the cost of all the expensive dog food that the guards bought for the puppies. Young children especially loved to hold the puppies. Before long they made enough money from allowing the people to hold the puppies that it paid for all the dog food and they even made some profit.

An animal vet from Monterey heard about all the cute puppies and he opened a small shop to provide health care for the dogs that were now getting so popular. The vet hired his oldest daughter to operate the store to sell high grade dog food and he made appointments for anyone wanting to have a dog or cat looked at for any problems that they developed. His daughter loved cats, so she brought a few cats and displayed them in the front window for sale.

Cats were easier to take care of, so some older people bought a few of them. Cats were also known to be good hunters, so some farmers bought some to protect their grain storage rooms.

Some people who came to the Ritz San Luis heard about the beautiful Akita puppies and wanted to buy one. Captain Santa Anna talked to this boss Matt and asked him what he thought about selling an Akita dog to a tourist.

Matt told Captain Santa Anna not to sell the original dogs that produced the cute little puppies but to go ahead and let them produce a new litter as soon as you build a facility hold a new litter of pups. The Captain said the guards will have ball starting a new litter then.

Matt said I will have Sierra start a web site to advertise Akita Puppies and in time you may have a thriving business selling Akita puppies.

10 JEROME

At the Ritz San Luis restaurant there was cook who was born in Jerome Arkansas and remembered the tasty soups that his mother made when he was a child. Sometimes childhood memories get enhanced as we get older and we long for the food that that we grew up with.

He was named Jerome after the small town that he was born in. When he was in the military he was stationed in a small town in Germany and his military base was not close to any large cities, so he spent time working for an old farmer whose kids were all grown up and his grown kids didn't like working on a small farm. Basically, Jerome was bored just staying on the insignificant military base so instead of doing drugs like many of his buddies did just to keep them from going out of their minds he started to take walks away from the base and noticed the old farmer who was growing a lot of vegetables that they sold to the military base and made a living doing that.

The farmer's name was Hans Schmitt, and his wife was a great cook. One day after Jerome worked for the farmer for several hours he was invited to stay for dinner.

It was a warm day, so they told him to take a shower and get cleaned up. The dinner was a simple dinner with a fine soup and some freshly baked rye bread. The bread tasted the best when it was just removed from the oven and Jerome ate a lot of the bread and the fine soup.

The soup reminded him of the soups that his mother made when he was kid still living in the small town of Jerome. Of course, the concentration camp at Jerome where they kept Japanese Americans prisoner during WWII was now torn down and only an insignificant concrete monument was still left there. WWII was such a long time ago that very few people even remembered that there was a concentration camp at Jerome.

Also, the American people wanted to forget that they incarcerated Japanese American citizens in concentration camps, so it was never brought up in any of the American schools. Already many adults didn't even know that they put American citizens in Concentration camp during WWII.

Meanwhile Jerome was treated like a son and just stayed at the farmhouse with the Schmitt's. Gretchen always made the fine soup on weekends. Jerome even borrowed the old truck from the firm to go to town to buy the soup bones and he selected the best bones that the butcher had and even paid for the soup bones which was basically a by-product of the meat business, so it was cheap. Sometimes he would splurge and buy some lamb chops or other cheaper cut of meat for Gretchen to cook for the weekend. This became a regular thing for Jerome until he was transferred back to the states and finally discharged from military service with a rank of Sargent which was unusual for anyone stationed at the small base. Jerome wasn't spending money on illegal drugs, so he had more money than his other military buddies. During the two years that he spent helping the Schmidt's he helped Gretchen in the kitchen to make the tasty soups. Sometimes he even came on a Friday just to start cooking the soup bones to get it ready for the weekend dinner. Jerome learned that Gretchen always used some white vinegar when she cooked the soup bones which made the bones softer after they were slow cooked for twelve hours or more.

When Jerome applied for his discharge from Military service, he didn't want to get discharged from Fort Shelby in Mississippi because there was nothing in the old town of Jerome anymore and his mother passed away several years ago.

Instead, he asked to be discharged from Fort Dix in New Jersey because he wanted to see the bid city of New York.

11 THE NEW COOK

Matt made his yearly trip to visit his daughter Savana who now had seven kids and he didn't want his grandkids to not know him. He had Captain Takashi Kato fly him to Long Island and he stayed at Savana's art studio where it was always comfortable. Matt asked how her art business was getting along and she said that they had one auction recently and made a lot of money.

Matt said I should go see my grandkids, so they won't forget who he was. Howard Senior heard that Matt was back in Long Island, so he invited him to go have dinner in a new popular restaurant called Wolf Run which was a fancy new restaurant and usually you had to have a reservation to even get in. Howard was a friend with the owner of the Wolf Run so Sebastian got him in the restaurant even if it was a Friday night.

Howard was seated at a nice table in the middle of the restaurant, and they were ready to order. Everyone else ordered something with red meat in it but Matt was now more health conscious, so he ordered the soup with the fresh loaves of Minnie bread.

When Matt started eating the soup, he noticed that the soup was the best soup that he ever had. He mentioned this to Howard, and he said I will call the cook who made the soup, and you can talk to him.

The cook couldn't come out right away because he had to wait until his break to leave the kitchen. After Howard paid the bill and they all went into the parking lot to return home the cook who made the soup came out to the parking lot and apologized because he was required to wait until his break to come out and talk to Howard. Howard introduced Matt to the young cook and said that Matt was the one who really wanted to talk to him.

The young cook said that his break was only fifteen minutes long, but he can talk for a while. Matt asked the young man how much he was getting paid for working here. The young cook said that he gets paid $750 a month which was a great pay, but he had to find a place to live in Chinatown where he could afford to pay for a cheap place to live. He said I like the work here, but he didn't like that four hours that he had to spend just to get to work and back and sometimes after work he had to take a taxi because all public transportation closed by midnight.

Matt suggested that he quit now and don't even bother to get his pay because Matt said I will give you a thousand dollars right now and I will take you to my daughter's art studio tonight and tomorrow I will fly you out of Long Island and give you a job paying a thousand a month and I can give you a free place to live and also buy you a car so you can drive yourself to go wherever you want to go.

The young man said I only have a half an hour

more to finish my shift and today it was payday so I can collect my pay and I can go with you to your daughter's studio for the nigh. Matt said I will be back here by midnight to pick you up then and left with Howard.

Howard drove back to his home and discussed what Matt offered the young man and they all agreed that the young man will be happier in Mexico. Savana's Husband said I had a nice nap this afternoon and I'm all rested up so I can drive back to the restaurant and pick up the young cook and I will just wait until he finishes his shift. Matt said thanks and stayed with the Johnson family to have coffee until Sam came back.

Forty minutes later Sam was back with the young cook who went by Jimmy and he told everybody that he got his paycheck for the month and the boss gave him a week without pay to attend to his business and asked him to make sure that he returned because he might get a raise. So now the young cook was leaving on good terms and can even come back if he wanted to come back. Everyone was happy for the young man.

Sam said why don't I drive Jimmy back to his room in Chinatown because the traffic after midnight is much easier this time of night and I can be back here in an hour. Everyone said that sounds like a great idea and Matt said I will go with you to Sam to keep him company while Jimmy clears out of his room in Chinatown.

12 AN OLD TRUCK

The Ritz San Luis restaurant now had a bunkhouse for any employee that wanted to stay there because it was just behind the restaurant and it was free. Jimmy liked the place because it was clean and didn't have cockroaches like the room in Chinatown that he had before.

After Jimmy was introduced to all the kitchen staff the chef said take a few days off to see the whole town and get familiar with San Luis and you can start on Monday morning start work then. Jimmy thought what an easy going place this hotel was. Matt drove Jimmy to Mathew's car dealership and asked him if he had any used cars for sale today. Mathew the Mechanical Engineer who owned part of the hotel as well said we have several used cars and walked them to look at the used cars. Jimmy owned a car when he was a kid but never when he was in the military because of all the regulations with the military.

There was an older Mercedes Bens and a Buick sedan and an older truck with a tailgate lift, but it had a few dents on the truck and Mathew said take your pick. Jimmy said why Is this truck so cheap. Mathew the car dealership owner said that it was a stick shift, and no one knows how to drive a stick shift anymore.

Jimmy actually learned how to drive a car back in Arkansas when he was a kid using a stick shift truck. Jimmy liked them because the transmission on them last forever and they are usually trouble free.

He told Mathew the car dealership owner that he would like to buy the stick shift truck and pulled out five hundred dollars as a down payment. The actual price tag on the truck was written on the windshield and said $2500. Mathew the owner of the dealership knew that Jimmy was with Matt who was his boss and said I will drop the price of this truck to a grand because it is a stick shift and I want to get it out of here anyway.

Matt pulled out five one-hundred-dollar bills and handed to Mathew. Mathew said we have a new paint department now and I can have the red truck repainted for you for free because we bought up a lot of old Acrylic automotive paint.

Jimmy did some painting on old cars before he went into the Military and said I can paint the truck myself. Mathew showed Jimmy the new paint shop and told him to have at it. But he said if you are not done by Monday the paint crew will be back and they can help you then. Jimmy said thanks to Mathew and they all went to the new paint shop. There was a kid there who was looking for a job working in the paint shop and asked Jimmy if he needed some help. Jimmy said sure and asked Mathew if that was O. K.

Mathew told the kid if you do a good job, I may even give you a job in my paint shop. The kid said thanks boss and said that he wanted to get started on the red truck right away. Mathew called one of his mechanics and told him to show the kid where everything was. The paint shop was brand new, and everything needed to paint a car was already stored there. The mechanic said I'm going to lunch now and will be back to see if you needed anything else today. The kid's name was Johnny and said thank you sir.

Matt asked Jimmy if he was O. K. just staying here for now and handed Jimmy a hundred-dollar bill and said if you get hungry take a break and get something to eat and left. Jimmy said I will find some bondo and started to fill out some of these larger dents. Then Johnny said we should first take out the big dents by heating the dented area and push out the dent first before we even start to use bondo. Jimmy knew that the kid was right, so he found an Oxy-acetylene torch and started to heat the largest dented area first.

Johnny said stop and he got under the large fender kicked the depressed area and the dent popped right out. He then got some old towels and soaked it with water and held it over the bulged-out spot and the area shrunk and it was now perfectly smooth with rest of the fender. Jimmy was surprised how fast the big dent disappeared and complimented Johnny on doing what he did.

Then he asked Jonny if he was hungry, and he said let's go find some Tamales. Jimmy liked Tamales also, so they went to a Tamale shop and had some Tamales.

13 CLEAN UP

Monday morning Jimmy reported to work at the Ritz kitchen, and he was given some things to do. The head chef called Alberto his assistant to go to the butcher shop and buy some soup bones to start to make some soup for tonight and told Jimmy to go with him. They bought a lot of soup bones and came back to the kitchen and the chef told them to put some in the large pressure cooker and cook them for two hours. The assistant cook did that and after two hours they let the pressure cool down and he saved the new broth.

Alberto put the still warm soup bones into a paper box and told Jimmy to take it outside throw it out. Jimmy took the box outside but didn't throw the soup bones out into the dumpster but just put it in a shady spot because he was going to try something later with the discarded soup bones. The chef told Jimmy that it was enough for him and come back tonight if he wanted to see how the soup was made for the evening customers. Jimmy said that he will be back tonight to see how the soup was made.

Jimmy went to the Car dealership to see how his red truck was coming along. When he got there Johnny was just leaving for lunch and asked Jimmy if he wanted to go with him. Jimmy said sure and they walked to the Tamale shop again and sat down. A waitress came by and dropped them a menu and they ordered some Tamales. Before the tamales came Johnny went to the salsa table and filled a large bowl with fresh salsa and started to eat the salsa with a spoon. Jimmy looked at Johnny enjoying the salsa, so he went to get himself some salsa also. When they finished eating the salsa their Tamales arrived and they started to eat the Tamales. Johnny got up and got himself more salsa, so Jimmy did the same.

After they finished their Tamales, Jimmy asked where he was staying. Johnny said he was living with his uncle about twenty miles north of San Luis and his Uncle had a spare car and he lets him use the car whenever he wants to use the car. Jimmy said then you are comfortable then. And he said I am fine, and his uncle makes good tortillas and some refried beans, and we have that every night. Johnny said the only thing that he didn't like was the cockroaches that come into the kitchen at night and floor is full of cockroaches and you have to put boots on just to get to the outhouse to take a crap.

This didn't sound too good to Jimmy and he told Johnny that he had a large bedroom with a bathroom attached to the bedroom and I also have great T.V. And we can get a lot of different channels. Jimmy said I have a small bed and a couch, but we can exchange the couch for a bed, and you can sleep there if you like. Johnny said I will try that tonight then. Jimmy said I have a night shift at night, and I will be all done by midnight so you can stay in my room after you finish work and stay there until I get off work. Johnny said that sounds great, so I'll see you at midnight. Johnny went back to work at the paint shop and Jimmy took a nap before he had to report to work for the night shift.

That night after Jimmy finished his shift, he volunteered to clean up the kitchen and all the kitchen staff left for the night. He swept the floor and put everything away and turned the pressure cooker off for the night where he put some vinegar into the pressure cooker before he put the previously cooked bones into the pressure cooker.

He turned the lights off and went back into his large bedroom and found Johnny watching T.V. Johnny looked all cleaned up and he said I took a hot bath, and it was the first time that he took a hot bath. Johnny asked Jimmy if he was through working for the night. He said he was bur he still wanted to go back and check the soup bones. Johnny I'll come with you then. They walked twenty feet to the back of the kitchen and Jimmy got his keys out and opened the kitchen to check his soup bones. Johnny said that smell great and asked if it was ready to eat.

Jimmy said I wanted to put some vegetable into the broth, but you can try the broth if you like. Jimmy got a bowl and gave it to Johnny, and he ate the whole bowl quickly and asked if there was more left. Jimmy said if you are still hungry, I have some sirloin steaks that we didn't get to finish cooking tonight so let me put it in the microwave and you can have some of that as well. Johnny said I heard of sirloin steaks but never had any before and it was really wonderful. Johnny said why don't I come here every night and help you clean up the kitchen every night. Jimmy wasn't really wasn't thinking about volunteering to clean up the kitchen every night but thought if Johnny was willing to help him why not.

14 PRESSURE COOKING

Next morning when Johnny showed up for work at the paint shop the shop foreman asked Johnny if he would like to be in charge of removing the dents from the cars that we get into the shop because you are so good at it. Johnny said what if I finish all the dent removal jobs and end up with nothing to do. The shop foreman said we can start to train you to do some of paint mixing jobs then and even promote you to do some painting if you get good at it.

Johnny said I will like that then. The foreman said we can even switch your working hours to suit your new job better for you if you like. Johnny said thanks boss and went back to removing more dents.

When Jimmy showed up for his morning shift at the kitchen the chef said you did such a good job of cleaning up the kitchen how would you like to be in charge of the clean-up every night from now on. You might even get a raise as well.

Jimmy said that will love to do that, but I would still like to continue be in charge of making the broth every day and I can come in early just to take care of that because I have some ideas that I would like to try in the making of the daily soups. The chef said you sound pretty ambitious but if you really want to try your own recipe on making the daily soup you can try it out for a while until it gets to be too much for you.

Jimmy said I would like to start today, and he immediately started to make the soup broth by putting some big bones into the big pressure cooker with some white vinegar in with the soup bones. Jimmy said after three hours I will come back to check on the soup bones again and left.

Johnny finished his dent removal job for the day and the foreman took him to the paint shed and showed him all the acrylic paints that they had in the paint room. He said I want you to organize all the paint cans in this room and make a list of everything that we have. Johnny said I will get right on it.

When Jimmy returned to the kitchen, he turned the heat off under the pressure cooker off and let it cool off. He then went into the cooler and brought out some carrots and some parsnips and cut them into large chunks then put them into the pressure cooker and let it start rocking for two minutes and then turned the heat pressure off again. After that he turned the heat off under the pressure cooker and let it cool again. All the cooks were watching him and after all the pressure died down in the pressure cooker and after it cooled down enough, he opened the lid of the pressure cooker and served some of the new soup to the other cooks that were watching him.

The chef looked at the soup and said the carrots looked bright red and the parsnips looked a bright yellow and said that I have never seen such brilliant-colored vegetables ever before. Everyone took a taste of the new soup and agreed that it was the best soup that they ever tasted. The Chef said serve some of the new soup to our customers for lunch and see how they take to the bright colors. The soup was written in as a special for the lunch menu and it was not expensive.

After some of the lunch customers finished their new soup, the Chef personally went into the dining room and asked the customers how they liked the new soup. They all said that they loved the soup and was going to tell their friends about the wonderful new soup. The chef went back into the kitchen and asked Jimmy to make more of the wonderful soup for tonight. Jimmy said I'll make as much as I can, but we don't have that much broth left anymore. The chef said then make more broth for tonight. Jimmy said I'll do the best that I can, and I will make even more of the broth and asked if there was another large pressure cooker. One of the assistant cooks said that we only have one large pressure cooker. The Chef told the assistant cook to go buy two more pressure cookers then and assistant cook immediately left the kitchen.

15 BONES

Matt knew that the Ritz restaurant always made soup and they used soup bones to make the broth. He walked into the kitchen and found Jimmy emptying a large pressure cooker of the spent soup bones into a large cardboard box and they were still hot. Matt asked what you do these old soup bones. Jimmy said all the flavor from these bones were all boiled out, so we just throw them out.

Matt said in that case you probably wouldn't mind if I take all the old bones then. Jimmy said you will be doing us favor by not having to wait for the garbage man to take them away. Matt noticed five large cardboard boxes full of old bones and loaded them all in his GMC truck and said thanks to Jimmy and left.

Johnny finished organizing the paint storage room, so he called his foreman to come look at the room. The shop foreman was man about fifty years old with greying hair and everyone called him Mr. Max because Maximilian was too long to use in an automotive repair shop.

Max looked at all the one-gallon cans of acrylic paint neatly stored on three levels of shelves with the front of each can all facing forward so anyone can immediately see what color the paint was. Max told Johnny that he did a great job.

Max turned around and noticed a lower shelf of mismatched old paint some of them had part of their labels torn off the cans. Max said I remember when we bought these cans at an auction and at the time, I thought that they were a good buy but most of these colors are no longer available and even the company that manufactured them are now out of business. Max picked up one can and said this can is empty so it should be tossed. Johnny said I opened that can and there is still an inch paint on the bottom of the can.

Max asked if your old truck was ever painted. Johnny said not yet because he was saving up some money to have it painted. Max asked Johnny how much he paid for the truck and Johnny said that Matt talked the salesman to drop the price all the way down to nine hundred dollars.

Max told Johnny if he realized that you couldn't even buy one can of Automotive acrylic paint today for less than five hundred dollars. Johnny said that he knew that acrylic paint was expensive, but he didn't realize that it was that expensive.

Max said let me call Clifford who retired last year and see if hie is still around. Max had his cell phone with him and called Clifford's old number and Clifford answered right away. Max said it's me Max and you are the only guy that knows anything about old acrylic paints and wanted to know what you are doing now. Clifford said I'm fishing for Marlin here in the Caribbean and having a ball.

Max said in that case you probably won't be interested in giving me some advice on some very old acrylic paints. Clifford said I heard the old paint shop was bought out by some rich guy and it was now a fancy modern paint shop. Clifford said I wouldn't mind coming to San Luis to see what kind of a place you have now. Max said we are always here so come down here whenever you have time to kill.

Matt brought the four boxes of boiled out soup bones to Captain Santa Anna and showed him the bones. Santa Anna picked one up and smelled it and said it has no Oder like real soup bones. Santa Anna said bring one of the older pups in here and see if he likes to chew on these old bones. The guard said yes Captain and came back with a dog about seven months old.

The Captain told the dog to sit, and the dog sat like he was told to. Santa Anna tossed the bone in the air and the dog caught the bone in his mouth and started to chew on the bone. They all watched the dog chew on the bone and marveled at how the dog could grind off pieces of the hard bone. The captain picked up the bone again and said these bones may be useful for keeping the dog's teeth clean like a toothbrush.

Santa Anna asked how many bones Matt had. Matt said I have four and a half large boxes full of these bones. Santa Anna noticed that some of the bones were still damp and said we should sun dry them to ensure that they don't have any moisture left in them so they can be safely stored in a dry place. Matt said great idea go ahead and take care of that then. The captain called a couple of his guards and told them what to do with the bones.

Matt said I will take the partially empty box with him and see how Shogun likes the bones and left.

16 MARLIN DINNER

Clifford showed up to the newly remodeled paint shop and found Max. Clifford said I brought you somc frozen Marlin and wanted to know if Max knew how to cook the fish. Max said I have no idea so let me call the Ritz Hotel and asked them if they knew anything about how to cook a Marlin.

Matt was at the Ritz hotel talking to the two former engineers that were now in the restaurant business. Matt picked up the phone and asked Max what he had. Max said I have a friend who brought me a frozen Marlin and I have no idea how to cook the big fish. Matt said I will send some cooks to come and look at the fish and they should be there in a few minutes.

Max introduced Johnny to Clifford and told him that Johnny was in charge of the paint storage department. They all walked to the paint room and looked at all the paint stored in the room. Max picked up one of the old paint cans and asked Clifford if he ever worked with this brand. Clifford said this is really old paint and asked where he got the paint and Max said that it came with some other paints that they bought at an auction.

Just then a couple of cooks arrived and asked where the Marlin was. Clifford said it is in the back of my truck and it is covered up to protect it from the sun. One of the cooks looked at the big fish and said it looks like it was getting thawed out. The cook touched the fish and said it looks like the fish is still frozen inside and maybe it is still usable. The cooks said we should bring this back and put it back in a freezer until we can figure out how to cook a fish like this. Clifford said actually I don't even know if people eat Marlins. One of the cooks said we will let you know and call you what we can find out and left with the fish.

Clifford asked Max if he had a computer that he can use and showed Clifford into the room where there was IMAC desktop computer. Clifford said I never used an Apple computer and asked the young girl in the room if she was familiar with this computer.

The girl's name was Sonja and she said that it was the newest desktop that Apple makes, and it is a great computer. Clifford asked Sonja if she had time to help me with this computer. Sonja said I would be happy to help you.

Matt brought the box of boiled soup bones and showed it to Sierra. Sierra said they looked like soup bones and asked Matt if we should give one to Shogun. Shogun was on his comfortable bed in the motorhome and taking a nap. Matt put all the soup bones in the freezer and left only one of them put for Shogun and put it on the dining room table. Sierra picked it up and smelled it and said it didn't have any fragrance to it. Matt said that is probably because they were pressure cooked several times and all the flavor was now gone from these bones. Matt picked it up and smelled it also and agreed with Sierra that it had no small left on the bone. Matt put the bone in Shogun's food dish and said maybe when Shogun wakes up, he might chew on it.

Meanwhile Matt made some tea with the frozen Ume pit in it and asked Sierra if she wanted some. Sierra said I've been making some tea with the frozen Ume pits and I am starting to like it.

Shogun finally woke up and he saw the soup bone and started to gnaw on the bone and Matt and Sierra could hear him gnawing on the bone. Sierra said I think that Shogun really likes the to chew on the soup bone and let him continue to chew on the bone.

Matt got a call on his cell phone and one of the engineers that used to work for him said we are going to cook up some of the Marlin and wanted to know if Matt wanted to come to the restaurant to taste the Marlin. Conan the Chemical engineer said how about at five before the dinner crowd starts to come in. Matt said O.K. And said that he will be there at five.

Max got a call from the restaurant and he was told that they were going to try out the Marlin and asked if he was game to try out the Marlin tonight at five in the evening. Max said I will bring Clifford with me who actually caught the big fish, and we will be there at five tonight.

At the restaurant everyone was seated and the cook drought in the cooked Marlin for everyone to see how they liked it. Clifford said that the fish was too tough. Someone else said it doesn't have any flavor. No one had any favorable comments for the fish. The waiters came in and removed their plates with a of fish still on the plates. The evening wasn't a total loss because the waiters brought all of them the new soup that Jimmy perfected and everyone there had enjoyed eating the soup.

17 CLEAN-UP

/Clifford told Johnny all he knew about the paints stilt stored in the paint room. Clifford said he had Sonja look up as much information as she could find on the old acrylic paints but most of were so old, she couldn't find anything that would help us. He asked Johnny if his old truck was ready to be painted now. Johnny said that we put two coats on grey primer on the truck and it was sanded with 6-0 sandpaper and it was as smooth as we can get it

Clifford said you won't mind if we did some experimenting on your old truck then. Johnny said any kind of finish paint would be better than just leaving it with the grey Primer that didn't look too exciting. Clifford said let's go back into the paint storage room and see if can figure out which cans still looked good enough to use. Clifford said why don't you just try experimenting by starting with the can that have the least amount of paint left in them and make sure that you use enough thinner so that you won't have to spend too much time sanding out any lump that you may end up using such old paints.

Clifford said I'm going back to Monterey do some more fishing now and I will be back in a couple of weeks to see how your paint job came out. Johnny said thanks for all you help. Clifford said I don't think that I was too much help to you at all but have fun trying new techniques and left.

At the restaurant Jimmy tried using vinegar to cook the tough Marlin and it made the fish more tender but even the dogs didn't like it. Jimmy brought some of it to the Pet food store and asked the vet if she thought that the cats would like to eat the Marlin. By this time even the bones were soft and when she gave some to the cats, they seemed to like it and she told Jimmy to bring more of it and put it into airtight glass canning jars and maybe she can sell some to the cat owners. Jimmy said I will do that bring you some tomorrow.

Back at the car dealership that Mathew owned Johnny's assistant finished all his dent removal job for the week and came into paint room to see what Johnny was doing. Johnny told Chris his assistant, what he was doing, and Chris said let me help you. Johnny told Chris what Clifford told him about keeping the paint thin so they wouldn't have to spend as much time sanding the bumps out when it fried it would be a bigger job trying to sand acrylic paint because it was so much tougher than the grey primer that was traditionally used all the time.

Johnny said I want to go visit my roommate and see if he needed any help and left Chris all by himself to experiment with the paint job.

When Johnny walked into the kitchen all the cooks were helping Jimmy pressure cook all the Marin and putting them into glass canning jars and the place looked like an assembly plant. After Johnny saw what they were doing he said I'm going back to our bedroom to take a nap and he will be available to help Jimmy tonight to clean up the kitchen after midnight. Jimmy said thanks and said I'll see you at midnight then.

When Johnny returned to the paint shop Chris was all done with his first coat of paining Jimmy's old truck. Johnny said you did a great job and said I want to treat you to some dinner. Johnny first stopped at the restaurant to see if Jimmy wanted anything. Jimmy said we made a mistake, and we cooked a couple of New York Strip Sirloin steaks too long and the customer refused to accept it, so we had to cook him another one.

Jimmy asked Johnny if he wanted to try the overcooked steaks and asked Johnny if he wanted to have it. Johnny said sure of course so Jimmy sat them down in a kitchen table and added baked potatoes and fresh vegetable to the steaks and both Johnny and Chris finished it off in no time at all.

Johnny said we will be back at midnight to help you clean up the kitchen. Jimmy said I can take care of that myself but if you came to help me with the job will go faster. At exactly at midnight the only person still in the kitchen was Jimmy and he was eating some ice cream. Johnny and Chris came into the kitchen and started to clean up the kitchen. Twenty minute later the kitchen was all cleaned up. They carried all the garbage outside and there was nothing left to do. Jimmy told them to sit at the metal kitchen table and made both of them a huge strawberry shortcake. There was so much ice cream on the shortcake that they almost couldn't finish it all butt they managed to eat all of it.

Johnny said what if we come here every night at

midnight you just watch us do the clean-up work. Jimmy said O.K. And I can make you a late-night dinner while you do that so that was now new what they will do at night from now on.

18 TRUCK SALE

With all the help that Jimmy was getting from Johnny and Chris every night the kitchen was sparkling clean every morning when the rest if the cooks came to work. They mentioned this to head Chef who went by Hernandez. All the rest of the cooks already knew how to make the fine soup that Jimmy thought them how to make so Hernandez asked the rest of the cooks if they can handle all the tasks that Jimmy was currently doing while Hernandez rewarded Jimmy with a one-week vacation. All the rest of the cooks liked Jimmy, so they agreed to let Jimmy go on a week's vacation.

Johnny and Chris were also doing such a good job that Mathew the Mechanical Engineer who owned the car dealership gave them a week's vacation as well. In the meantime, Johnny and Chris came in on weekends and finished painting Jimmy's old truck with five coats of left-over acrylic paints found some old metallic flakes and the final paint job looked better than a brand-new truck coasting more than seventy-five thousand dollars.

The first day of their vacation they all just slept in

took it easy. At midnight the day before they all ate a lot of left-over food in the kitchen, and they were still pretty full. They drove all over San Luis in the newly painted truck and finally returned to the car dealership and just parked in the Used car section of the lot. They couldn't overhear the big boss talking to customer dressed in a suit with a teenaged boy.

The boy looked like a spoiled kid and it looked like so far, they didn't find what the boy really wanted. The big boss was tired of talking to the customer with the impossible kid so when he noticed Johnny in Jimmy's newly painted truck, he called Johnny over and asked Johnny to talk to the customer.

Johnny was always happy to help his big boss who was so generous anyway and walked up to the customer and started to talk to him. The kid noticed the gleaming fuchsia colored truck and said I want that one. Johnny told the customer to take his kid to the truck let him sit in the truck and he will be right back.

Johnny, Jimmy, and Chris all went into the big boss's office and told him what just happened. The big boss said I know that you all put a lot of work into that truck but if you are willing to part with your big prize, I will give each of you any used car that I have in my lot because I want to keep my reputation of having the best cars in the area.

Johnny said O.K. I will go talk to the customer then. Johnny said his boss gave me permission to sell this truck to you, but do you realize that this a stick shift truck and not too many people even know how to drive a Manual transmission truck anymore. The customer said that he learned how to drive on a stick shift, and he really liked them. He continued to say that manual transmissions outlast automatics transmissions ten to one. They all agreed. The customer said I own a string of fine hotels all over the Southern part of the U.S. so I don't have the time to teach my boy how to drive a manual transmission so if you promise to do that, I will give you a hundred thousand in cash right now. All three of them immediately agreed to the offer and said we will be happy to teach you son how to drive this truck then.

The customer said follow me to Yuma and we can go to the Yuma First National Banks and I will give you the cash at the bank. Johnny, Chris, and jimmy followed the customer to Uma in the big truck parked at the bank. Johnny followed the customer into the bank where the customer withdrew a hundred thousand in cash and handed it to Johnny.

The customer said follow me to my hotel and I will treat you all to a fine dinner. As the three of them followed the customer to the hotel Jonny gave the cash to Jimmy and said this is yours because the truck was your truck. Jimmy reached into the bag and gave Johnny twenty grand and said take this. Jimmy then took ten grand and gave it to Chris. They all thanked Jimmy for being so generous and after they parked the truck, they all followed the customer into the Hotel-restaurant and sat at a round table.

The customer' said my name is Samuel Goldman and I have to be on the road a lot to check all my hotels all over the country so I will put you all up in my hotel here in Yuma and you can start to show my sone how to drive a stick shift starting tomorrow. They all said fine as they sat at the table and waited for a waitress to come to their table.

19 CAR SALESMEN

Captain Santa Anna and his guards had a litter nine pups and they all looked just like Shogun. Thc pups were too young to let people come and hold the cute puppies, but they were allowed to put their name on a list to buy one of the puppies when they are three months old soon there were more names than they had puppies. Santa Anna called Matt and told him of this fact. Matt said I will stop in today to talk to you.

In Yuma the Chris had no trouble teaching the young boy how to drive a stick shift. The boy wanted to drive the truck to school so Chris said you can do that, and I will drive the truck back home so no one will scratch the beautiful truck. The boy agreed that that was the best solution. Chris did this for three days until the boy's father came home again for dinner. Chris told the father that his boy was now fully trained to drive the car safely now but Chris said the car was too pretty just to leave it in the school parking lot without having someone stand guard over the truck in the parking where so many Jealous boys can walk by and scratch the beautiful paint job.

The father asked Chris if he can stay a few more days until he can come up with a good solution. Chris said sure, I will be happy to do that.

Johnny and Jimmy took a bus and returned to San Luis and told their boss that Chris stayed there longer to teach the boy how to drive the truck safely. Mathew the boss said that was good news. The boss said I know that you are on your vacation, but he was short a good salesman for his franchise of all the beautiful new cars and wanted to know if Johnny would want to try his hand at selling cars.

Johnny said I would like to try that. Mathew, the boss, explained how most successful car salesman prefer to sell cars on a commission basis because they make more money that way and they can make a quick sale by even reducing the price of any vehicle that they sell without having to keep coming in to get permission from their supervisor just to do that.

The boss gave Johnny five one-hundred-dollar bills and told him to take the rest of the day off to buy himself some decent clothes.

Johnny went to see Jimmy and told him that he was going to be a car salesman and the boss gave him some money to buy better clothes. Jimmy said he knows a Taylor shop that sells good clothes.

When they got there was a man trying to have his grey suit made bigger because he gained a lot of weight. The lady who ran the Taylor shop said instead of adding a lot of material to your old suit which would make your suit look like patch work I have a nice suit that a customer didn't want because he couldn't afford the alteration cost for the suit, so she accepted the suit to help him out. The man tried the suit and it fit him perfectly and said I'll take it. The lady said how about a hundred dollars and the deal was closed.

The man said do you want to buy my old suit that is too small for me now. Johnny stepped up and asked the man how much he wanted for the suit. The man said this is a fine Italian silk suit and is a very expensive suit, but I'll take a hundred dollars for the suit because it no longer fits me anymore.

Johnny said let me try it on and see if it fits me. Johnny came out of the dressing room and it did fit him perfectly. He spun around and the lady said there are some worn spots under your arm and when Johnny raised his arms everyone could see holes under his arm pits. The man said I'm sorry I didn't know that so you can have the suit for free.

Johnny asked the lady if there was any way to fix the suit. The lady said this material is very a hard to duplicate because it is silk so there is no way to fix the suit. Johnny had a ten-dollar bill in his pocket so tried to give it to the man who gave him the silk suit and the man said you look like you need the money more than I do so just take the suit and just don't raise your arms and everybody laughed.

After the man left the Taylor shop Johnny asked the lady if she sold some white dress shirts. She looked at Johnny and came back with two white cotton shirts. She said how does ten bucks apiece sound to you and Johnny said fine and Johnny gave her two ten-dollar bills. The lady said wait a minute and came back with three polyester cheap tires and said take these for free because you might need them. Johnny said thanks and left.

Jimmy looked at Johnny's shoes and said you need some shoes other than those tennis shoes with paint on them, so they went to a second hand store and they found some cheap patent leather shoes for seven dollars that fit Johnny good enough.

After that they went back to Jimmy's free room because he worked for the hotel restaurant and put all the days acquisitions of clothes on top of Johnny's bed. They took a shower and went to bed early. At eleven thirty in the evening Jimmy got up and told Johnny that he was hungry.

There would be very few restaurants open at this time of night, so they walked across the lot and walked into the back door of the hotel kitchen and everyone was now gone except for a new hire who was trying to clean up the kitchen. Jimmy said let me give you a hand and in fifteen minutes the kitchen was cleaned up. There were some pressure-cooked soup bones in a box, so Jimmy showed the new hire where to put the box of soup bones outside behind the kitchen.

After that the new hire said I normally fix myself something to eat after I finish cleaning up the kitchen so let me fix you guys something to eat as well. Jimmy said I can help you and he was a better cook than the new hire. Jimmy went into the refrigerator and found some roast beef and made some great sandwiches for all of them. After that the new hire went into the cooler and made three Banana splits and they were now all stuffed.

Jimmy said we may come and help you tomorrow night after we get off work then Jimmy and Johnny left the kitchen and went back to their rooms and slept like babies.

20 CASH

In Yuma it was decided that the best thing to do for now, was for the kid to park his truck in an secure parking lot a block away from his high school and walk to school from there. The father told Chris that he did a fine job and asked him how he was going to get back to San Luis. Chris said I can always hitch hike and it will be free. The father said I have an old car outside my garage, and I don't need it anymore so you can have it and ride it back to San Luis. The father came back with a title to the old car and gave it to Chris. Chris said thanks and said maybe I'll come back someday and see how your boy is doing with his new truck. The father gave Chris twenty bucks for gas and told him goodbye.

When Chris drove into the car lot, he saw Johnny all dressed up in a suit so he asked him what he was doing in a suit. Johnny said I'm a car salesman now so that is why I have on a suit. The Chris said who's in charge of the paint shop now and Johnny said maybe you are now because I am outside in the car lot.

Just then a man in a suit came to the car lot and

asked Johnny if he had any new Mercedes Bens on the lot. Johnny said we keep our new cars indoors so follow me. Johnny showed the man the most expensive Mercedes and the man looked it over and said this is cheaper than the same car that he looked at in Monterey, so he said I'll take it. Johnny said just follow me and asked the man to have a seat at a desk gave him some paperwork. Johnny asked if the man wanted to get a loan and the man said I don't need a loan and said I will just give you cash. Johnny said I will be right back and got his supervisor. The supervisor said we rarely have any customers who want to pay cash for a brand-new car and asked hm if he would prefer to pay by a personal check or even a cashier's check. The man said I have the cash in my car now and I can give you the cash instead. The supervisor said let me get my secretary and she come and count your cash for you. The man said can we go somewhere more private where we can count the cash. And the supervisor said we can come into my office and it will be more private there. Chris was listening to all this and paying a lot of attention.

The supervisor called is secretary to come to his office to help me count some money. All the money was in different denominations of money. The man said go ahead and count all the money and I will be back in half an hour. Chris followed he man to his car and asked him where he was going next. The man said I'm going to find a place to get something to eat and invited Chris if he wanted to join him. Chris said I'm a little short on cash so I will skip the lunch. The man said don't worry I will pay for the lunch. Chris said in that case I would definitely like to join you. The man said I am not too familiar with this town so can you tell me where we can get a good lunch. Chris asked the man fancy or just simple. The man said simple would be better. Chris asked the man if he liked Tamales because he was dark complected and might be Mexican. The man said simple would be better. Chris knew a Tamale shop that made great Tamales and showed the man where to go in his beat-up looking old truck. As they were eating the man asked Chris what he did for a living and Chris said I paint cars. Chris didn't ask the man what he did for a living because he could even be a gangster.

The man paid for the Tamales and gave the old lady who looked like she owned the place a fifty-dollar tip. The lady said "MUCHISIMAS GRACUIOUS EL SENIOR" . The man said Vaya con Dios, and they left the Tamale shop.

When they returned to the car dealership all the money was counted and strapped together in different piles neatly. The secretary handed the man a sheet of paper showing all the denominations of money and it came out to be $78, 345.00. The Mercedes had a price tag of $65,000.

The man took three thousand and put the cash in his fat wallet and said the $ 345 was for all the work you did to count the money.

When the man walked outside, he asked Chris if he could use a beat-up old truck and Chris asked how much he wanted for the truck and he said it yours if you want it and there is no charge. Chris could see no problem in accepting something for free, so he said thank you sir.

21 JUNK YARD

When Chris drove his newly acquired truck to the back lot, he noticed that license plates were ten years out of date. He even wondered if the truck was a stolen car. The tires looked brand new, and the engine sounded great. He walked back to the building where he found Johnny and found him free. He told Johnny that the man that bought the Mercedes gave him this truck and it runs great, but he thought that that the truck might be a stolen truck.

Johnny said just sell parts from the truck but don't try and fix it up because the VIN number is hard to change. Chris said I think that you are right. Johnny said go talk to the boss because he promised all of us a free used car when we agreed to give up our vacation to start our new jobs.

Chris said I'll go see him right now. Mathew was looking at some new cars that just came into the display room. The boss saw Chris and asked him if he picked out a car for himself yet and Chris said not yet. Chris said not yet and that was what he wanted to ask you about. Mathew said we have too many junk cars in the back lot and was thinking about taking some to the worst ones to a land fill and get rid of the worst looking ones. Chris said I can take care of that for you.

When Jimmy and Chris delivered some soup bones to Captain Santa Anna, Chris said I want to start a junk yard for old cars and sell them to people who wanted to buy old junk cars or we can even sell parts of the cars and maybe make a few dollars from our business. The Captain said the boss has a lot of land all the way to the fence ten miles to the south and no one comes that way very often. He said also Josefina has some land right on Highway No. 2 that she may be willing to sell you so go see her at the old factory where the guarded compound is.

Jimmy and Chris found Josefina art a desk sorting some papers. Jimmy asked Josefina if she wanted to sell her father's property. She said sure why not and asked how much you were willing to give me for the land. Chris asked how large the property was. Josefina said that never had it surveyed but it stars from the highway and extends South where no one lives in that area. Jimmy asked what it has on the land.

Josefina said there is a broken-down house with t an outhouse in the back and we don't have any well. Chris said in that case the house isn't worth too much money. Josefina said you can use some of the boards from the old house and you can design whatever you like. Jimmy asked if they could look at the place. Josefina said you can't miss it it's the only place on Highway No,2 and it's only a mile West of here. Chris said we will go look at it and get back to you later.

Jimmy and Chris went back to Jimmy's small room and took a shower. Jimmy's room was so close to the hotel kitchen that they could smell all the great flavors of what they were preparing for the evening meat. They walked across the parking lot and walked into the back of the kitchen and the new hire saw them and told them to wait outside and sit at the table there and he will bring them something to eat. A few minutes later the new hire brought them a huge bowl of soup with some fresh bread. Jimmy and Chris ate all the soup and the fresh bread and bought them to the sink and started to wash the bowls.

The kitchen now looked clean enough, so they went back their room tried to figure out what to do next. Chris said let's go see Josefina and talk to her again.

When they got to her office she was gone. Sarge's restaurant was just a stone's throw from here, so they went there and found place was also not busy. Matt walked in the restaurant and saw Jimmy and sat by them. Matt asked Jimmy if he was hungry, and he said we had a bite to eat already but maybe we can order some desert. Matt ordered a big meal and asked Chris how things were coming along with him. Chris said his boss wanted all the junk cars removed from the car dealership and taken to the land fill but Chris thought that they may still be useful to some people, so he wanted to start a junk yard.

Mat said that was a good idea and that he will finance the project for Chris. Chris told Matt that he talked to Josefina and she agreed to sell him her old place. Matt said that would be a perfect place for a junk yard and he may have some old vehicles to give Chris to start to his junk yard.

Matt said I will talk to Camacho to build you a nice office in front of the new junk yard and the place will look better.

Matt's order came and he started to eat his dinner.

Jimmy and Chris ordered vanilla ice cream. Matt stopped eating for a minute and said Josefina's property is not defined so you should claim as much of the land as you can and go ten miles back from the road, I will put up a fence for you so you will never run out of space. Matt said I will take you to an auction soon and I will show you how to bid on old junk and you can sell it for profit, and you will make a lot of money.

Matt was telling Chris so many things so fast that Chris couldn't imagine how any of this could be done.

22 GETTING READY FOR BUSINESS

Camacho was happy to be back in business working for Matt again. Chris was officially still on his vacation, but his boss told him that he needed two cars painted right away. It took Chris the rest of the week to get the two cars ready for the paint job. The official painter had to leave because his mother needed help in Monterey, so he got permission to take care of his mother.

Mathew approached Chris if he wanted to work over the weekend to get the two cars painted and Chris knew that this was good chance to get promoted if he did a good job. He asked Johnny if he had to work over the weekend and he said nor really. Chris said the boss gave him an opportunity to paint two cars over the weekend and could use some help.

Johnny said I made enough money for this month so I'll let the other salesman have a chance to sell a few cars so I can help you this weekend. On Saturday, they finish the first car and went back to the kitchen to help the new hire clan up the kitchen and get their late-night dinner. Next morning, they slept in a little longer and when they reported to the paint shop the other salesman was having trouble with a customer.

Johnny stepped in and talked to the customer. The customer said I want to buy a Hearst, but you don't have any in this lot. Johnny said I think that I have the perfect car for you and called Chris and asked him if he wanted to sell the huge black limousine that he got from Yuma. Chris said sure because no one wants an old relic like that and walked the customer to the back of the lot where there were a lot of used cars.

Chris pointed to his shiny limousine and asked the customer how he liked the Limo. The customer said that it was perfect for his needs and asked how much Chris wanted for the limousines. Chris got the car for free but just to see what the customer would say he said a new car like this would cost more than a hundred thousand dollars today, but you can have it for sixty-five grand.

The customer said I will take it and gave Chris fifty grand in cash and said I will be back with the rest next week with fifteen grand more. Chris was surprised that the customer didn't even try to talk him into lowering his price, so he said fine just take the Limousine and I'll see you next week.

After the customer left, Johnny asked Chris if the customer will ever come back with the fifteen grand and Chris said it doesn't matter to me now because I have fifty grand that I didn't have before and got rid of the old relic.

Chris said let's go celebrate and have a great meal. Johnny asked weren't you supposed to still paint the other car and Chris said I almost forget so let's get on it now. Two hours later they had the first coat of paint done on the second car. And it was in the drying room with where there were a lot of bright lights to get the first coat dry. Now, they were ready for a good lunch, so they went to the Tamale shop and had some Tamales.

Camacho and his crew finished a good-looking steel fence in front of the junk yard, and it was more than a mile long. There was a fine gate and the driveway led to an office and Matt had Josefina already sitting in the office. Off course there were no customers yet because there was nothing to sell yet.

But Josefina was happy to have her old job back when she worked for her father before he retired and went away and left her the property. The office was not a shack like it was when her father had a junk yard but was now a gleaming new building with wide windows, new filing cabinets, tables a few lounge chairs for customers when the office opened for business.

Matt always seemed to run his businesses this way and the people who worked for him liked his easy-going style. He even told Josefina to start interviewing someone to help her in the office so she wouldn't get lonely with no customers coming in.

23 PAINT SHOP

Mathew complimented Chris for getting both cars painted over the weekend and told him to take a few days off. Johnny was working on commission so he could take off anytime as long as there was another salesman on the lot'

Chris said let's go see Josefina and see if she still wants to sell me land. When they got to the new junk yard, they were surprised that there was long steel fence already up in the front of the junk yard. The gate was open so they drove through the fancy gate and came to a modern looking office building.

The sign in the front window said open as it was blinking. Josefina was on the phone talking to someone. When she was off the phone Chris asked her, what happened here. Josefina explained that Matt never did like to waste time getting a new enterprise started so he hired a construction company to get a lot of work done last week.

Chris said I don't see anything in the yard for sale yet so why are you even open. Josefina said we have more than ten thousand acres here now and it's all fenced in, so we have a lot of room to put a lot of stuff here.

Both Chris and Johnny were amazed how fast Matt worked. Josefina said if you have any old cars that you no longer need bring them here and I will sell them for you. Chris said you know how to do that then. Josefina said I used to work for my father until he retired, and I have a lot of experience selling all sorts of used equipment. Chris said I have some old cars so I will bring them here today and left.

Chris and Johnny went back to the car dealership and asked bis boss Mathew which cars he wanted to take out of the back lot. Mathew said I have some bad news for you so sit down and I will explain what happened.

Matthew said I now have a chance to have exclusive franchise rights to sell a lot more of the popular Japanese car and I need more space. He said when I first started this business, I bought more land than I ever thought I would ever need but I was wrong. San Luis is getting to be such a popular place to run a business that there is no land that I can now buy because all the land next to me is now all new thriving new businesses.

The boss said the only way that I can handle the new Japanese car business is to remove the old paint shop and everything that goes with it. He added off course this will mean you will be out of a job but I can start to train you in selling Japanese cars and in a year or so you might become a good salesman.

Chris said what are you going to do with all the old paint stuff. Mathew said I might have an auction sell it all and I might get some money for it. Chris said I have a better idea just sell it to me and I will find a place to move it to and I will pay you back as I soon as I start to make some money.

Mathew said you're a young man and I owe you a lot of favors so just take the entire paint business, and I can give you some money so you can get started more quickly. Chris said I don't need money I have some friends and they will help me get the job done quickly and left by driving a couple of the old junk cars out of the back lot.

When he got to the new junk yard Matt was there talking to Josefina. Chris explained what Mathew told him about getting into the new business of selling Japanese cars and said that his boss gave him all the entire painting business to him and wants me to get all of that out of there as soon as possible.

Matt said I'm thinking about getting into selling old heavy equipment and having a painting shop right here in this junk yard and it would be a great advantage for me so I will talk to Captain Santa Anna and have him round up all available guards to help you get the entire paint shop moved from the car dealership and we can start out own paint shop here.

24 NEW PAINT SHOP

One week later the paint shop from the car dealership as now moved to Chris's new junk yard and Chris was in charge of doing all the paint jobs. Mathew started to design a new show room for his Japanese cars and the place was buzzing with new activity.

Everyone was now happy with all the new progress. Matt rewarded all his guards by letting them purchase new cars for themselves from Mathew his old friend and Mathew gave Matt a huge discount for any car that his guards wanted to buy.

Johnny was learning a lot about the Japanese. cars and he was told to promote them first.

The nursery man that sold different trees and plants wanted to retire so h contacted Matt asked Matt if he was interested in buying his property. Matt said you have a very large place here and asked the man what he wanted for the land. The man said how about a hundred thousand dollars. Matt said how about a hundred and ten thousand dollars and you can help m land scaping the lot to make it look beautiful. The man said I will be happy to do that for you.

Matt talked to Camacho again and told him that he had another job for him so don't furlough his workers yet. He showed Camacho the hundred-acre plot of land and told him what he wanted to be built here. Matt said I want the usual sewer and water system also and I want a large building built fifty feet back from the fence where he wanted to paint cars.

Matt called Thor in Okinawa if he was still making things with the new tungsten carbide material. Thor said we cut back our hours, but we still make a few cutting rings for Thermodynamics because they started to order a few rings from us again.

Matt asked Thor if he remember what his old claw bucket excavator looked like. Thor said I used that machine, and I couldn't get any traction with the machine because the tracks were worn out smooth. Matt said I wonder if you could build me a new set of tracks for the machine with the magic tungsten carbide material. Thor said that would an easy job and I will make one plate first and send it to you so you can make sure that it will be the same as the tracks that are on your machine. Matt said great and after I get the track put on and make sure that it works, you can finish making the rest of them.

Camacho and his team finished building the front and part of the East side of the property for the new paint shop and it looked similar to what he built for the junk yard with the same design for the entry gate.

The nursery man planted beautiful flowers just outside the fence all around the lot.

After the paint shop was mostly completed Chris started to move some of the automotive paint equipment into the shop. An older man walked into Chris's paint shop and said this looks like it was going to be fancy paint shop. He said he had a paint shop, but he had to quit because his eyes got bad, and he could no longer see what color to paint a car anymore. Chris asked the old man if was interested in having a job as a prepper before the paint is put on. The old man said I don't need good eyes to that job so I will love to have some income.

25 NEW HIRES

Johnny had a lot to learn about the new Japanese cars, so he studied all their new features whenever he had time. Eventually he became the office manager for all the Japanese cars. He had a young girl as his assistant, and he let her take a shot at selling a Japanese car. Her name was Clementina and she turned out to be a great salesperson. She also wanted to work on a commission basis because her father was a car salesman. She knew that weekends were the best time for selling new cars so she asked Johnny if she can work weekends.

Johnny said after you sell your first car, I will alternate with you and let you try one of the weekends.

Jimmy continued working at the restaurant and he was promoted to assistant first cook and got a small raise. His shift was changed to the evening shift where most of the high-end customers came to the restaurant.

The new hire became faster at cleaning up the kitchen after the restaurant closed so sometimes, he would let him go as soon as he finished most of hard work and he could go home earlier.

Johnny and Chris still bunked with him in his room next to the restaurant, so they usually came at midnight to finish up the final clean-up and have a late-night dinner. The dinner always depended on what was left in the refrigerator that night. But beggars can't be choosy, so they always helped in the kitchen after midnight.

Matt decided to have his GMC repainted, so he brought it into the new paint shop and told Chris to repaint his truck. Chris asked if he wanted to have it painted a different color and Matt said no because he will then have to re-register the truck at the guard house. Chris asked Matt if there was any hurry and Matt said I have other vehicles so take your time. After Sierra heard about Matt having his truck re-painted, she decided to do the same with her beat up red truck.

Chris put an add in the San Luis daily newspaper for a helper to prepare cars for painting and figured that if someone sees it, they will call. Meanwhile he had the man with bad eyes to start to take the dents out of Sierra's red truck. You didn't have to have great eyesight to remove dents from an old truck because you can do it by touch. When he got the dents taken care of Chris only had to use very little bondo to make the surface perfectly smooth. He got some primer and painted the truck with the grey primer. He had Sanchez sand it again to smooth the surface. He gave it a second coat and Sanchez sanded it again and it was as smooth as it could be. He opened a brand-new can of red Acrylic paint and gave it its first coat of red paint. He left the truck overnight in the drying room with bright lights to make sure that it will be perfectly dry by morning.

Meanwhile Sanchez started to sand Matt's black

GMC. There were no dents on the GMC, so he didn't have to take any dents out of Matt's truck. There was no need to use primer on Matt's truck because Sanchez didn't have to use any bondo on the GMC. Chris gave the truck its first coat of black paint and put the truck in the trying room as well.

Matt brought the giant claw excavator to the paint shop, but it was too large to fit in the shop, so he told Chris to figure out how to paint the excavator. Chris said I'll work on that.

That morning two young men showed up at the paint shop and reported to Chris. Chris showed them how to sand the giant excavator and told them to sand the giant machine outside where there was more fresh air. Chris provided them with protective masks and as well as ear protection devices because he gave them portable grinding machines to grind out the rust spots.

The young me were clever so they built scaffolding to get to the higher parts of the excavator. It was close to lunch time so he told the young me to stop and he will take them to lunch. Chris took them to the same Tamale shop that was close to his new shop and treated them to lunch. Chris complimented them for building a clever scaffold. He told them that this was hard work so take it easy and rest frequently.

After lunch he told the young men to go home get some rest you can start again tomorrow and wear some old cloths because there was no need for good clothes. Chris said we start at eight in the morning every day. The two were happy to get the rest of the day off.

The next day was Saturday so Chris said you can work today, and I will pay you time and a half because it was a weekend. The two me were happy to hear about the time and a half pay. After five hours Chris came out and said I will pay you for this week and you can come back on Monday morning and finish the job then. Chris gave them more than what was promised because it was hard work, and they were happy because they were flat broke.

26 SPY WORK

Jimmy carried three boxes of used soup bones to the guard house and noticed that they had another litter of pups. Matt stopped in to check in on the pups. He asked one of the guards how many Akitas were left from the last litter. The guard said we still have five and they are getting pretty big. Matt said most dog lovers prefer pups no older than three months so you may have a hard time getting rid of the older ones. He saw Jimmy and asked him how his job was coming along. Jimmy said he got promoted and now works during the evening shift so that is why I came this morning to deliver these soup bones.

Matt asked how his GMC was coming along. Jimmy said we just finished painting it this weekend and it is ready to be picked up along with Sierra's red truck. Matt said thanks I'll try and pick them up today. Then he said why don't you take a couple of the older pups and train them as guard dogs for the paint shop. Jimmy said Johnny would love to have them took them with hm in his van.

Matt went back to his motorhome and told Sierra

that her truck was ready to be picked up. Sierra said let's go pick them up today.

Jimmy drove to the paint shop and told Johnny that he talked to Matt and told him that his truck was ready so he may come by to pick it up. Johnny said it's a nice day so I will have the new hires give the GMC a good coat of Simonizing to make the paint job last longer. He called the new hires and told them simonizes the black GMC. The new hires got right on it with heavy circular sanding wheels covered with soft sheepskin pads and made short order of the simonizing job. They saw the red truck, so they did the same with Sierra's truck as well. They finished the final simonizing job by taking soft, clean rags and gave it the final touch and both trucks sparkled in the bright sun.

Johnny said you did a great job of simonizing the trucks so take an extra hour off and go get some lunch. The new hires said thanks boss and took off.

Matt and Sierra showed up to pick up their trucks and saw their trucks sparkling in the bright sun. Matt said I've never seen such a great paint job like this ever before except in a new car dealership. Johnny said that's because we just simonized it and if you simonize it every once and a while the paint job will last forever.

Matt asked how big of a job is it to simonizes a truck. Johnny said it's pretty easy if you do only a small section at a time and he said I'll be right back with a can and show you how to do it.

Johnny came back with a small can and a soft rag and demonstrated how it was done. Sierra said let me try to do that and she did a small section and agreed that it was easy. Matt said give me five cans of simonize and I'll have the guards do it one their new cars. Johnny said

I will be right back. When he came back, he had a whole carton of simonize cans inside and gave the whole box to Matt. Matt said we will have the best-looking cars in all of San Luis. Matt said thanks and then you need a raise soon and said goodbye.

Johnny's new hires came back from lunch and said we had the best lunch that we ever had in a long time. Matt asked where you went, and the boys said we went just around the corner to the small Tamale shop. Matt said I may visit them soon.

The boys said we should simonize the big excavator so the paint will last longer. Johnny said good idea and told them to give it a try. The boys got right on it and they looked like they were having fun.

An hour later Johnny came out and told them that you were working too hard so take the rest of the day off and gave them both a twenty-dollar bill and told them to go by themselves something.

Now Johnny was all alone and just admiring the big excavator. A big truck pulled up and there were two older men in the truck. The two men got out of the truck and asked if the excavator was for sale. Johnny said we just ordered new tracks for the excavator and just waiting for it to arrive. The older man said we can fix the track for you if you let us borrow the excavator for a short time. Johnny asked who they were. The older man pulled out his business card and gave it to Johnny and he looked at it carefully. The card read Ajax construction company. Johnny said let me call my boss. Matt picked up immediately and said II will be right over. Meanwhile the men were looking over the excavator talking between themselves.

Matt arrived talked to Johnny and Matt walked

over to the men looking at the excavator. Matt walked over to them and Johnny could see them talking for more than ten minutes. Matt came back and talked to Johnny again and asked him what he thought about letting them borrow the excavator. Johnny said as long as they keep the excavator right here in San Luis it may be O.K. Matt said I will ask them where they were planning to use the excavator and follow them to their site. Johnny said I will go with you.

Half an hour later they were close to a small hill and they saw three small backhoes working at the site. Matt said I can see why they want to borrow the big excavator now.

Matt asked what his new hires were working on now and Johnny said that they were all done for the moment and just taking a break. Mat said I want to use them as armature spies and have them watch what they are working on and report back to you or me and we will keep an eye on them for a while. Johnny said they would probably like to do that.

Matt told the older man that he had a lot of money invested in his excavator and asked if minded if he hired couple of guards to watch the excavator overnight so that kids didn't come around and mess with any of the equipment.

The older man said that was a good idea and that he will help pay for the guards.

27 GUARD DOGS

Johnny's two new hires reported to the site where they were using the claw excavator and asked them where they should stay to guard the heavy equipment. The foreman was alerted of some guards coming to watch the equipment overnight and they had a spare wooden office building, so they let them use it to stay warm.

There was a microwave oven, a refrigerator and a freezer that worked. There were yard lights that were kept on all night. They brought one of the Akita pups to alert them if anybody came into the building site. The Akita pup stayed in the office with them and would bark if anyone came into the work area.

Shortly after midnight the dog barked so Dominguez who had a 410-shot gun walked outside the office hut and noticed some people in the yard. He fired one shot into the air, and he noticed a couple of people running for their lives. He checked all the equipment and found nothing suspicious.

Dominguez came back into the office and said they

were all gone. The rest of the night was quiet, so they went back to sleep.

At seven in the morning when the workers arrived the foreman asked Dominguez if anybody came to the work site and Dominguez said the dog barked so he went outside and saw a couple of people in the yard, so he fired his 410-shot gun and they disappeared.

The foreman wondered if they came to steal any heavy equipment so he told his boss about the incident and the boss said I will have some cameras put around the yard and a siren installed as well today. Dominguez said we are going to leave now and left and reported to Johnny what happened last night.

Matt showed up during the day and talked to the foreman said I understand that there was some excitement last night. The foreman repeated what Dominguez told him and Matt asked if there was any damage to any of the equipment. The foreman said none that we could tell. Matt said thanks and walked to his claw excavator and noticed a welder welding on the flat drive plate. Matt asked why he did that and the welder said we do this on all of old equipment to build up the plates so they can climb up a small hill more efficiently.

When Matt went to visit Johnny, he said I need two preppers back because we have a few more cars to paint. Matt said I will talk to the guards and see if they can spare a few men.

When Matt got to the guard compound, he saw a customer just leaving with an Akita after he paid the guard three thousand dollars in cash. Matt asked what that was for and the guard said we train perimeter guard dogs now this was the second one that we sold his week.

The guard continued to explain how they trained

the dogs, and they were more efficient than human beings and were cheaper to hire than humans. Matt asked how many more trained dogs he had left. The guard said we only have two left now. Matt said don't sell the two that you still have left, and I have a job for you tonight. The guard said yes sir and I will tell Captain Santa Anna that you came in today.

He went back to Johnny and said I found a replacement for your painters, so they don't have to go back to guard the heavy equipment anymore. Johnny said thanks because I now have several cars that need painting.

He went back to the construction site and told the foreman that he was going to hire professional guard personnel and they will be here tonight to take over the guard job.

That night the guard showed up in a uniform with two dogs and introduced himself and explained how the dogs were fully trained to do perimeter patrol and that they had small infra-red cameras on their vests that took pictures continuously and transmitted what the cameras saw directly to the guard as well as to the San Luis police station where they monitor the cameras as well.

The foreman was impressed with what the guard told him and immediately called his boss and told him of the improved security that they now had. The boss said I may show up tonight to see how the new security system works and make sure that the guard knows that I am coming so I won't get shot.

28 SALE OF GUARD DOGS

The next night the really big boss from Monterey was also in the guard house with the guard in uniform watching the screen showing what the dogs recorded on their patrol. They saw the screen stop for a minute and saw a couple of suspicious looking men with some tools in their hands. When they came within seven feet from the doges there was bright flash and the cameras on the dogs took clear pictures of the intruders. The intruders had a surprised look on their faces, and they dropped their tools and ran off.

A minute later the San Luis police department called and said we will send a patrol car to the area and see if we can catch the two men and bring them in for questioning.

The big boss from Monterey was so impressed that he asked the guard in uniform if he could buy some of these guard dogs. The guard said we sold two of them this week to a company from Yuma but now all we have left are these two well rained guard dogs.

The big boss said we are losing millions of dollars

to clever thieves in several cities all over Mexico and we can't afford to continue to keep buying more new equipment all the time.

The guard said just go to talk to Captain Sana Anna who is in charge of training these dogs and talk to him.

Matt was back talking to Captain Santa Anna and said you are selling these beautiful, trained guard dogs too cheaply and you should at least charge five thousand dollars an even a partly trained dog. And for more experienced dogs charge at least ten thousand dollars.

Matt and the Captain continued to talk about the cost for food for the dogs and most of all the training that you give to the dogs. The captain said the training is free because the guards love to train the dogs and there is a waiting list for who gets to train the next guard dog.

Matt said they are not free because I buy them new cars from time to time, new uniform, I give them free health care and a dozen of other benefits that no other place in this town gives them.

Santa Anna realized that Matt was right and said we will definitely start to charge more for our trained dogs from now on and we will train more dogs right away. Matt said you will make more money from selling the dogs than you get from me in a few months, and you won't know what to do with all the money and they both laughed.

The next day the big boss from Monterey stopped in to see Captain Santa Anna and said I want to order ten well trained dogs right away and I don't care what you want for the dogs. Santa Anna said I wish I had ten well trained guard dogs right now but all I have left now is the two that are bring used to guard some heavy equipment here in San Luis. The big boss said I want to buy both of them today. Santa Anna said let me call my boss and see if he is willing to part with his last two well trained guard dogs.

Santa Anna called Matt and told him of the man that was so eager to buy both dogs right now. Matt said I will be right down because I am in my motorhome just having coffee. Matt walked into the Captain's office and was introduced to the big boss. They talked for a while and it was close to lunch time so Mat suggested that they go someplace to have lunch.

Ten minutes later they were sitting in the Ritz San Luis having lunch. Matt didn't want to hurry anything, so he ordered some lemonade. The big boss ordered a cocktail and Santa Anna ordered only coffee.

Matt started out by telling the man that his Akitas were the only Akitas that were capable of being trained so well and there was nowhere else in the world where you could find such smart dogs with the exception of buying an Akita from Japan in Akita-ken.

Matt said what if I just let you rent one of our dogs for ten thousand dollars a month and that would be so much cheaper for you. The man said I saw how your guard dogs operated last night and I am willing to pay whatever you want right now. Matt saw Santa Anna looking surprised and asked him if he had enough personnel to guard his excavator for a while.

Santa Anna said that is a huge machine so If you remove the keys at night, it would be difficult for anyone to steal it. Matt said O.K. I'll let you have my best guard dogs than for a hundred thousand dollars apiece.

The man said I will go to the bank and withdraw two hundred thousand in cash and I will meet you at the guardhouse. They all shook hands and left.

Next morning both dogs were cleaned up and fed and were ready to be taken by the man from Monterey and were waiting for them. Matt said for two hundred thousand dollars maybe you should assign a dog handler to go with the dogs so he can show them how to take care of the dogs. Santa Anna said good idea and he will ask for a volunteer to go with the dogs.

29 MONTEREY

Early next morning Matt showed up with a large white delivery truck that he found at his junk yard and brought it to the guardhouse. Santa Anna had the guard that volunteered for the job of accompanying the dogs who had family from Monterey start to load everything that would be needed for the dogs for their trip to Monterey. He put two large dog cages lined with bedding for the dogs to be comfortable on the trip to Monterey. There was food and water in the cage. He loaded a box of pressure-cooked soup bone in the van and a couple of sacks of high-quality dog food in the van as well.

He asked Santa Anna if there was anything else that he should load in the van. Santa Anna said I will send another guard with you to keep you company until you get settled in Monterey and he can fly back when everything is all taken care of. Francisco the guard from Monterrey said great I will have someone to talk to them as I drive.

An hour later the man who bought the dogs came

with two boxes containing two hundred thousand in cash. The guards opened the box and lined up all the money on a large metal table and they started to count the cash. There were several guards helping, so it didn't take too long.

Matt was there also and said looks like everything is in order and shook hands with the man who bought the dogs who went by Montedento de Semenenko, but he told everyone to just call him Mandy for short.

Mandy said looks like we are ready to roll then and told everyone to just follow him in his sleek sports car. Halfway to Monterey Francisco the driver of the white van stopped to check to see if the dogs needed to relieve themselves and took the dogs out of the cages and the van and walked them around the side of the highway and they went into the woods where the dogs pooped and peed. When they came back, he gave them a treat and told them that they were good boys.

The man who bought the dogs was watching Francisco realized how well he handled the dogs.

This time they made it all the way to Monterey, and they parked at a large compound where there was a lot of expensive heavy equipment. Mandy went into the office for a while and came back out and said let's have some lunch. Francisco said I will stay with the dogs because this is new place for them and until we have a permanent place for the dogs he will just stay with the dogs.

Mandy took all of them except for Francisco who stayed with the dogs and had a nice lunch. During lunch Mandy asked the other guard who came with Francisco why Francisco was so protective of the dogs. The guard said that Francisco was the one who cared for the dogs ever since they were puppies and that was why he was so careful with their needs. Mandy said then they were just like humans. The guard said Akitas are the most faithful dogs in the world, and they will save their master's life before they even think about saving their own life. The guard then asked Mandy if he ever heard about Hachiko the Akita dog who lived in Shibuya and always waited for her master to come back from work every night at the train station. One evening when her master didn't come back from work the dog continued to wait for her master at the train station every evening and she kept it up for seven more years until the dog finally died and the towns people built a stature of Hachiko and if you ever go to Japan you can still see the statue of the famous dog.

Mandy gained a lot of respect for Akita dogs after hearing that story and even thought about getting an Akita puppy and raising it himself.

After lunch they all went back to the warehouse where Francisco was staying with the dogs and he was sleeping with his head on one dog and both dogs guarding him.

After that Mandy said we should take care of Francisco now and he should get some lunch himself. The other guard said let him sleep because he looks comfortable being with his dogs for now. The other guard who went by Franky said Matt sent a lot of food and other supplies for the dogs and wanted to know where to store them. Mandy said store them in the warehouse for now and we will figure out where to put them later.

Franky said I should get back to San Luis now and asked Mandy if he needed anything else from him. Mandy said it looks like you're all done here so drive the van back to San Luis and tell Matt and the Santa Anna thanks for all the help. Mandy looked at the white van and said you probably will some money for gas on that clunker so here's a hundred for gas money and hoped that Franky will make it all the way back to San Luis.

30 DINNER

The original Akita named Shogun that sired all the litters that the guards raised was now fifteen years old and the guards decided to give him a retirement. His eyes were failing so they had a meeting. One guard said perhaps he should be euthanized but the rest of tr guards didn't like that idea.

One guard said why don't we remove his collar and just let him roam free and go wherever he wants to go like old humans do when they get old and travel the world. Shogun and the female dog that had most of the puppies were very close and she was getting old also, so they took off her collar and let them both roam the countryside together like an old, retired couple.

At first, they only stayed away from the guard complex only a few days at a time where there was always food for them near the guardhouse. But each time that they ventured away from the compound their visits became more spread apart and finally the quit coming back altogether. It was possible that the female became a good hunter and found enough food for the both of them

like lionesses do in a pride of lions.
They were too old to have more puppies now so that was not a problem. One of the guards decided to go look for them but he couldn't find them, so he gave up and hoped that they were happy in their final days of their lives.

Mandy talked to his wife and asked her if she still wanted to keep up the maintenance of her old house which had three bedrooms and she said with no one living in any house vandals will come in and destroy the place. Mandy said we need a better place to house the new guard dogs and Francisco to live in so why we don't just let him stay there with the dogs. Mandy's wife said that was a great idea and we will keep the maintenance man and the housekeeper, so they won't become unemployed. Mandy said Francisco would be busy with the dogs so we should hire a cook for him so he wouldn't have to go shopping for food all the time so the problem of what to do with the old house was now solved

Mandy bought a van for Francisco to carry the dogs with him whenever he had to go buy more dog food or other things for the dogs. Mandy's wife Ruth said I never got to see the Akita dogs yet so let's invite Francisco and the dogs for dinner soon. Mandy said he liked the idea because he was planning to buy an Akita as a house pet for himself.

Francisco came to Mandy's grand house for dinner on a Saturday afternoon because Mandy didn't work on weekends. Francisco told the dogs to stay by the van and guard the van. The back door of the van was left open so that the dogs could either stay in the van or leave to relieve themselves.

Ruth came out to see the Akitas, but she couldn't see them because they were in the van. Francisco called

Poncho and he came out and sat in front of them. Francisco said Friend and pointed to Ruth, so Poncho came up to her and offered paw. Ruth said what a wonderful dog Poncho was, and she was now thinking about getting a puppy for herself.

Ruth said we are going to have an early dinner today so let's see how the cook is coming with the dinner, so she invited Francisco to come into the living room. Francisco told Poncho to stay with the van guard the van.

When they got into the living room Mandy was reading a newspaper and saw Francisco and asked where the dogs were Francisco said they were outside guarding the van. Mandy told Francisco to bring one of them into the living room so we can get a good look at one of them. Francisco walked to the front door and called GAISHA GIRL. She got out of the van and sat next to Francisco. Francisco told Geisha Girl to follow him into the living room. Then he told Geisha Girl to go sit by Ruth and pointed to her and said FRIEND. Geisha girl went to Ruth and offered her a paw. Ruth shook the dog's paw and told her what a good dog she was. Francisco said I normally reward the dogs when they do a good job by giving them a small treat. Ruth went into the kitchen and came out with a small piece of roast beef and gave it to Geisha Girl and the dog carefully accepted the roast beef from Ruth and then he laid down by her side.

The cook came out of the kitchen and said dinner was now ready to be served. Francisco called Geisha Girl and opened the front door of the house and told her to return to the van.

31 MADHOUSES

Mandy called Santa Anna and asked him if he had any Akita puppies for sale, he said we are completely out of all Akitas for sale at this time and told Mandy to try again in six months. Mandy didn't want to wait six months, so he called Francisco about the problem. Francisco said there is a place just south of Monterey where there is an Akita kennel, and she sells Akitas there.

Mandy said bring your van and I want to visit the kennel now. Francisco said yes sir and I will be right there. Mandy told Ruth that he was going to look at some Akita puppies and might buy one. Ruth said I will go with you.

Thirty minutes later they were all looking beautiful white Akita puppies.

Mandy asked Francisco how you tell which ones are the smartest ones. Francisco said it's hard to tell at this age so the best thing to do in to buy all of them then start to train the smartest ones as guard dogs. Mandy said fine I will do that.

The lady who owned the kennel came by and

asked if Mandy decided which puppy he wanted to buy today. Mandy said I will buy all of them. The lady was surprised to hear Mandy say that but was happy to make a sale in that the puppies were getting almost too big for little girls to handle one.

Mandy asked the lady if she sold dog food here as well and she said we have all types of dog food here. She got on her cell phone and called Susan her assistant to take Mandy to the building where they stored dog food. Susan came in a small jeep and said I will drive you there because it is in far end of the back lot. Mandy hopped in the jeep and they took off. Meanwhile Ruth had already decided which puppy she wanted for her own. She was carrying the puppy, but the puppy got too heavy, so she put on the ground.

They were now in the main store and another customer came in to buy some treats for her dog that she was training. The lady bought several different kinds of treats and paid for them using her credit card. Ruth asked why she bought so many different kinds of treats and the lady that owned the store said dogs are just like us we get tired of eating the same thing all the time so that was why the customer bought so many different kinds of treats.

Susan came back with Mandy and they had the jeep loaded with dog food. The lady who owned the store went by Liz told Susana to just leave all the dog food in the jeep and told Susan to count how many bags were in the jeep and record the price of the bags. Suzy said Yes boss and took a pad and started to write down all prices on the bags and made a list.

Francisco came into the store and said if the store sold handy dog leashes. Liz pointed to a rack of fine leashes and told him to pick out what he wanted. Liz was adding up all the purchases that Mandy made and realized that Mandy already owed her fifty thousand dollars for the five dogs, so she told Mandy that the dog food was on the house as well as the other small purchases and said to come back whenever any of the dog cut a foot or any other problems because she was also a veterinarian. Mandy said thanks for your help. Mandy paid by credit card and it passed the bank.

The trip home was a bit crowded with all the dog food and the five puppies. Ruth held her own puppy on her lap in the back seat of the van and the other four pups were tied together and Mandy was holding on to their leashes and trying to keep them from jumping on him.

When Francisco pulled up to Mandy's fine estate, Francisco took all the puppies for a walk so they can relieve themselves.

Mandy called his cook and told her take two bags of dog food to the kitchen and store them there. The cook called the gardener and asked him to bring a hand cart and take two bags of dog food the back porch.

Ruth took her puppy by the leash took her inside the house along with the treats. Mandy picked his puppy from the group and led his puppy in the house as well.

Mandy came back out and told Francisco to take the three remaining puppies to his house take care of them there along with all the dog food that they now had. Francisco said yes boss and left in the white van.

Mandy's mansion was now a madhouse with the two active puppies chasing each other and they were jumping on the furniture and knocking things over. Mandy said we need to start to train these puppies before they destroy the whole house.

The housekeeper came into the living room and built a crib in the living room and put one of the puppies in the crib and told the puppy to stay in there. The puppy started to wine so after the housekeeper left, he went to the crib picked up the fat white puppy put him on his lap. He was trying to figure out what to name his new puppy. The housekeeper put two large pans of water in the back yard and said I should give them some water and took both dogs to the back yard showed them where the water was. The entire estate was fenced in, so she let the dogs run around and chase each other. Before long the puppies were completely worn out and they were now sleeping on the back porch.

The housekeeper saw them and brought out two old comforters and put them over the sleeping puppies.

32 TWO MORE DOGS

Francisco called Mandy and said we should bring the three puppies that he was taking carc of two Captain Santa Anna and have them trained by his squad of guards because they had the extra manpower already knew how to train Akitas as guard dogs. Mandy realized that training three active Akita pups was too much for Francisco, so he told him to take care of that.

Francisco drove only the three pups in the new white van was in the guard compound in two hours. The guards were happy to see three new Akita pups and asked Francisco what he wanted them to do with the pups. Francisco said he had orders to have you train these dogs as guard dogs and he will pay you for the job. The guards were happy to hear that and said we start to train the dogs right away. Francisco said I will try to come here from time to time to see if you need anything else and he left.

When Francisco returned to Monterey Mandy asked him what the best way was to start to train his puppies. Francisco said there should be a lot of dog training schools in Monterey so join one of them start to train them yourselves. Ruth liked the idea so said I will try to find a good school join them as soon as I can. Mandy said I don't have time to take time off my business, so I want you to do that for me. Francisco said I will be happy to do that for you.

In San Luis the company that borrowed Matt's large excavator finished with the excavator brought the excavator back to Matt's pain store where they originally got it from. Johnny was there to receive the excavator and said thanks for bringing the excavator back. Johnny noticed that the tracks had been welded with strips of metal to improve its traction and marveled at how they did that. He noticed that the excavator looked a little dirty, so he called his prep team get the high-pressure machine and clean up the excavator.

After they were done, he noticed a few scratches on the excavator so he told the preppers to take care of the scratches, but you don't have to spend too much time on it because every time that we rent it out it will always have a few scratches on it when we get it back. But the simonizing job is always helpful so simonize it after the patch up paint dries and do that.

One of the preppers found a note in the excavator and gave it to Johnny. The note said that the trailer that the excavator was a gift for Matt for letting them use the excavator so he can have it. Johnny thought this would be very handy for the next company that may want to rent the excavator.

Mandy got a call from Captain Santa Anna asking where he found these fine Akitas and wanted to know if the female of the puppies was for sale. Mandy had the phone number of the kennel that he bought the puppies from and talked to the owner and asked if she had full grown female white Akitas for sale. Liz said I have a couple that I can sell you so come and look at them.

Mandy didn't have time to do that, so he called Francisco to go look at the white females for sale and buy one if he thought that she was a good dog. Francisco said I will do that right away.

Francisco was shown two beautiful white female Akitas and the lady said I will sell you both of them for only ten thousand dollars. Francisco said let me call my boss and ask him what he thought. Mandy picked up right away and asked if you found one. Francisco said he is looking at two of them and they are both for sale for ten grands for the both of them. Mandy said go ahead and buy them both and bring them back here. Francisco said the boss said he will buy them both.
Liz knew that Francisco wouldn't have ten grand on him so she said go ahead and take the dogs and ask your boss to send me a check for ten grand. Francisco said I will do that and let my boss know what you said and left with the two female white dogs.

Liz knew that most of her customers wouldn't be too interested in buying full grown female Akitas, so she was happy to have sold the two females Akitas.

Francisco brought the two females Akitas to Mandy's office and he came out and looked at the two dogs and assumed that Captain Santa Anna wanted to bread them. Mandy said they look good enough so drive them to San Luis give them to the Captain and while you are there see how they are coming with the training of the three Akitas that we left with them to train. Francisco yes boss and left for San Luis.

Two hours later Francisco delivered the two

females Akitas to the Captain and said these are perfect for what we need and asked Francisco how much he owed for the dogs. Francisco said settle that with my boss. Santa Anna called one of his guards and told them to give Francisco a couple of soup bone to him to take back to Monterey. Francisco said thanks for the bones and left.

33 MEAN DOGS

Six months later Captain Santa Anna and the guards had twenty-one healthy beautiful Akita puppies. They borrowed Sierra and Matt's Shogun to sire the new puppies. Every one of them looked exactly like Shogun.

People who heard about the cute puppies wanted to buy a puppy but none of them would be for sale until they are at least seven months old and had all of their shots. People were allowed to put their names on a waiting list so they will be next in line to purchase a puppy.

In Monterey, Ruth finished her first course of dog raining for Geisha Girl and was given a certificate of completion. Ruth could now tell the dog such commands as SIT, WAIT, STAY, COME, and as dozen more simple commands. Now Geisha Girl cold stay with Ruth in the mansion without there being any danger of the now much larger dog knocking anything over in the house. Geisha Girl learned how to open the back door in the kitchen whenever she wanted to go outside.

All the help in the mansion was happy to live with

such a well-behaved dog.

Francisco also finished the same school that Ruth took Geisha Girl and also got a certificate for Buster, Mandy's personal Akita. Buster stayed with Mandy when he was at work in his office got to ride in Mandy's sports car. Mandy never had to worry about anyone bothering his sports car when he parked his car to do business with his clients.

Francisco was sent to several construction sites with his two white Akitas to serve as guard dogs for expensive construction equipment. The dogs were equipped with infra-red cameras attached to their bodies so the guard in his station can see everything that the guard were looking at and the same images were also relayed to the closest police department in case the dogs fund any intruders came in the construction site.

The guard usually allowed the dogs to make a round at least once an hour but not in any way that an intruder could figure out when the dogs would be on patrol. Mandy got a lot of requests for his guard dogs and rented his guard dogs to a company for a good fee whenever he wasn't using the dogs himself. There were requests to buy the guard dogs, but Mandy always refused to sell his well-trained guard dogs.

Ruth always took Geisha Girl with her whenever she had to go anywhere and also never worried about anyone ever bothering her as long as she had her dog. She could even go out at night and always feel safe. At first, she allowed Geisha Girl to sleep in bed with her but soon they got too big to be in bed with Ruth, so the dog lay on the floor next to her to her bed to sleep.

Francisco was always sent with the guard dogs on any guard job to teach the guard who will be with his dogs to train the new guard how to use the guard dogs, but this only took a day.

Instead of sending both dogs at any one time to guard a site Mandy was now thinking about buying a couple of younger dogs to accompany the well-trained dog and the new dog would catch on to the routine. He sent Francisco back to Liz who sold Mandy the dogs when they were puppies to buy two more dogs to be trained by the more experienced dogs when they went on patrol. Liz had several smart dogs and Francisco looked at all of them. Carefully. Francisco had a lot of experience working with dogs and could tell a smart dog from on that was not too smart. He didn't care what the dog looked like, so the selection was now easier.

Liz now had several Akitas too old to sell as pets for little girls and was willing to part with them at a much cheaper price than the Ten thousand dollars that she charged Mandy for his white puppies.

Francisco asked Liz if he could bring back any dog that he didn't train well and return the dog to Liz. Liz asked what you mean by not fit for your needs. Francisco said he wasn't interested in a dog that was too friendly with strangers. Liz said in that case I will take back any dog that you feel was too friendly.

Liz had five dogs too old to be puppies and a few that were actually too mean to sell to any customer, but they were young and could be trained by a good dog handler like Francisco.

Liz had five dogs that she wanted to get rid of so she told Francisco take all five of them and if any of the dogs were too friendly to strangers, she will take them back and refund him the two hundred and fifty dollars for any dog that was too friendly to strangers. Francisco never expected Liz to sell any Akita for less than ten thousand dollars, so he said It's a deal and took all five Akitas. Francisco had five hundred dollars with him so he handed her five and said I will have Mandy mail you check for five hundred more by mail. Liz wasn't even worried if Mandy never sent her any money because she was glad to get rid of the five Akitas and especially really mean looking ones that she would never be able to sell to anyone.

34 MEETING

Mandy got an odd request from Columbia requesting guard dogs for protection of their property. He called Francisco told hm to come to his office. When Francisco came to Mandy's office Mandy's dog wouldn't let Francisco into Mandy's office. Mandy got up from his desk and saw that it was Francisco and told Thunder that Francisco was friend and the dog backed off.

Francisco said you have a great guard dog here and didn't even try to pet the dog. Mandy told Thunder to go sit on his bed and the dog did that. Mandy told Francisco that he got a request from Columbia and said they are willing to pay a half a million dollars for our services and wondered what you thought about the idea of sending them a couple of our dogs.

Francisco said he didn't want to send our best trained dogs because the job sounded dangerous. Mandy said half a million is a lot of money. Francisco said ask for a million and see what they say about that. Mandy had his secretary send them that message. The people from Columbia came back immediately and said we will send a plane to you to pick up your guard dogs today.

Mandy said they certainly seem desperate to use our guard dogs. Francisco said I will return home and take care of the dogs now and if they show up call me and I will be right over. He went home and fed all the dogs and gave them all fresh water. He looked at the two really mean dogs and realized how ugly they looked. Both of them were already on patrol and had some training from Francisco's older dogs.

He called the ugliest one who was named UGLY, and he came to the gate. Francisco asked Ugly if he wanted to go for a walk and the dog wagged his tail. Francisco put the dog on a leash and walked the dog and gave him some commands and the dog obeyed him. Francisco said you are a great dog and gave him a treat. Ugly sat down and looked like he wanted more so Francisco gave him two more treats then walked him back to his cage and put him in and removed the leash.

Francisco had lunch and took a nap. He had a dream that Ugly found an intruder and tore the man to pieces. After he got up Francisco took a shower and went back to sleep again and this time, he didn't have any more dreams but slept soundly.

He was woken up by his phone ringing and it was Mandy, and he said the men from Columbia were here and wanted to have a meeting and told him to come to Mama Josefina's restaurant.

Francisco got dressed and went to the restaurant and found Mandy talking to two men dressed in a suit. Mandy saw Francisco and introduced him to Alvarez and Mr. Camacho who looked like a gangster. They were all having dinner and asked Francisco if he was hungry. Francisco hadn't had anything to eat since breakfast, so he said he was ready to have dinner.

Camacho told the lady who owned the cafe to bring the young man the best dinner that she can come up with and she went back into the kitchen

Mandy said Columbia looks like a dangerous place now and was thinking about backing off from the generous offer. Camacho said the first day we will put you in a small inn that they own and put the dog handler and the dogs there until the dogs get recuperated from the long trip on a jet that we own.

Mandy said why don't you just hire a couple of men with machine guns and take out the bad guys yourself. Camacho said it isn't that easy and if they get captured, they will torture my men and they will eventually talk and then they will kill them. After my men finally talk, they send an army of thugs and come after me.

Mandy said we have a lot of money invested in our guard dogs and they are not replaceable. Camacho said we will leave a retainer of a million dollars and if either one of your dog's get killed you keep the million. Camacho said after a month and the cartel doesn't figure out who messed them up, we will then send you a bonus like no one ever saw before in your life.

Mandy said let me talk it over with my dog handler and we can meet again tomorrow morning. Francisco was done eating by now and he was ready to leave.

35 COLUMBIA

The next morning Francisco and Mandy had a private meeting at his home. The cook served them some breakfast. Mandy said a million dollars is a lot of money and we could train a lot of guard dogs with that kind of money. Francisco said who will take care of all our dogs at my house while I am in Columbia. Mandy said I will call Santa Anna and have him send me a couple of his guards to take care of our dogs until you get back.

Mandy got on the phone and asked Santa Anna to send two guards to Monterey take care of Francisco's dogs while he went to Columbia. Santa Anna said I will have Charlie fly two guards to you in a few hours.

While Mandy and Francisco had breakfast, they talked about the ramifications of the request by Camacho. Mandy said after you get there, and you feel that it a was too dangerous you can always back off and I can send you money to fly back to Monterey. Francisco finished his breakfast and figured that it won't hurt to at least go see Columbia.

Mandy gave Francisco a thousand dollars in cash

and told him to keep it in case he just wanted to come back home.

Mandy told Ruth that he was going to his office and took Francisco with him. Mandy got a call from Camacho and said are we ready to talk. Camacho asked where Mandy was now. Mandy said I'm at work in my office and you can come here if you like, and I have a private office so we can discuss a plan right here in private.

Camacho arrived with Alvarez but didn't dare to enter the office with Thunder standing guard, Mandy told Thunder to go to his bed and stay there. Thunder did as he was told. Camacho started to walk in but was nervous with Thunder looking at him. Camacho said let's go back to the cafe that we went to last night and have something to eat.

Mandy said fine and told Camacho that he will meet him there. Francisco said did you see how nervous Camacho looked when he came in and saw Thunder. Mandy said If I didn't know Thunder, I would probably be nervous as well.

Francisco got in Mandy's sports car and drove to the cafe to meet Camacho. Thunder was sitting in the back seat with the wind blowing over him and looked happy. When they got to the cafe, Mandy told Thunder to watch his car, but he didn't have to tell him that because Thunder would never let anyone within a few feet of the car. He never had to bark because he was an Akita and Akitas rarely bark. All anybody had to do was just notice Thunder sitting in the car and they would freeze. People would walk as far away as possible from the dog to get to where they wanted to go.

Camacho and Alvarez were already seated at a

table, so Mandy and Francisco sat with them. Camacho and Alvarez already and their food and was just waiting for Mandy and Francisco.

Camacho said you already have our one million dollars as a retainer and when you manage to kill a couple of El Toro's men mysteriously, I will pay you another million and your work will be done. Francisco thought that that shouldn't be that hard, so he told Mandy that he was willing try to do that. Mandy said if we lose either one of our valuable dogs, we there will be a surcharge of $250,000 for the dog if he gets killed. Camacho said no problem we can handle that. Camacho asked if you can be ready to travel in twenty-four hours. Francisco asked if the dogs had nice place to sleep on the jet. And Camacho said its first-class jet we can provide a good place for them to stay on the jet and the trip should take less than five hours. Francisco said I can be ready by tonight then.

Camacho said our jet is in a hangar at the Monterey Airport so we will meet you there in a few hours.

Francisco went home and told the two guards what the plan was and asked one of the guards to help him get Ugly and another dog ready for travel on a jet that will take about five hours. Mendosa said I should come with you to help you with the dogs. Francisco said sure I can always use some extra help. They put each dog in a separate cage with some padding in the cage in case they ran into rough weather and put the dogs in the cages. They covered the cage with a blanket so that the dogs couldn't see where they were going.

When they got to the Airport Camacho was waiting for Francisco with the crew. Francisco and

Mendosa carried one cage together because the cage now weighed almost two hundred pounds and carefully put the cage in the cargo hold which also had the same air pressure as the passenger had in the main cabin. They put the second cage next to the first cage so the dogs would know that they were next to each other.

A stewardess came by to strap Francisco and Mendosa in their seats. There were no other planes waiting to take off, so the tower told Captain Domngo that he was free to take off whenever he was ready.

Ten minutes later they were on their way to Columbia.

36 THE RAID

Five hours later the cabin lights came on and Francisco and Mendosa woke up. The stewardess came by to make sure that they were both securely strapped in their seats. The landing was smooth as silk and the jet taxied directly into a private hanger and the hanger door was closed.

There were several Limousines in the hanger and all the passengers got into a Limousine and they went their own way. Francisco and Mendosa were put in a separate limousine with the dogs and the driver followed Camacho and Alvarez in their own limousine.

Ten minutes later they were in a fancy motel and placed in a big room with the two dogs still in their cages. Camacho told Francisco to get some rest and he will be back that afternoon. After Francisco and Mendoza were alone, they took the blankets off the cages and took the dogs for a walk outside the motel, and it was still dark. Both dogs relieved themselves in the woods and they came back, and Francisco and Mendoza put them back on a leash and brought them back into the motel. They gave the dogs some water and some food. They left the cages open, so the dogs went back into their cages and went back to sleep.

Francisco and Mendoza took a shower and also went back to sleep. At ten in the morning there was a knock on the door. Francisco went to the peep hole and there was a man outside. The man said we came to take you to breakfast so Francisco said give me a minute and we will be ready to join you.

First, they woke up the dogs and put them on a leash walked them to the back of the motel so they can relieve themselves. The limousine was waiting for them, so they put both dogs in the back of the limousine and told them to stay there. Ten minutes later they were sitting in a fancy restaurant and having breakfast. Camacho said first we want to take you to a ranch so you can get the dogs acclimatized to this part of Columbia for a few days.

The ranch had a fine bungalow with cooks and maids and a few cars. There were other dogs in other pens, and they looked well taken care of. Camacho told Francisco to pick a dog pen and his ranch hands will feed them and give them water while we make a plan of attack. Francisco and Mendoza said fine. They were shown to their sleeping quarters and were told where the mess hall was.

Camacho showed Francisco and Mendoza a map on the whole area and showed them where the El Toro gang was camped out. Camacho said we know that there were at least a hundred of them at the camp and they had an armory of high-tech weaponry. Mendoza said let me call my Captain and he might have some suggestions on how to take care of them without getting killed.

Mendoza called Captain Santa Anna explained the impossible situation. The Captain said you look like you you're a snowball in blast furnace you will be melted or vaporized before you even get started to take them down. The Captains recently we had an invasion rats coming from the South looking for food and they were eating wild game and even managed to kill some young children.

We sent one of our guards to Mexico City to buy the most lethal poison available on the market and instead he came back with three bombs guaranteed to kill anything within a hundred yards of the detonation site but it's not the explosion that kills the rats but the highly radioactive waste that the bombs were filled with.

Death is not instantaneous like an explosion but a slow painful process that dives the rats crazy until they finally die. Santa Anna sad we will fly you our biggest bomb because it is too dangerous to use around here but in a jungle like where El Toro has his army camped out it will only kill his men and not you if you stay away from there until the radioactive material is dissipated.

Mendoza said that may do the trick for us because his army is three times bigger than anything that we can muster up here in Columbia. Mendoza told Francisco what the Captain just told him and now they had a plan. Francisco asked how many gangs operated in Columbia other than El Toro. Camacho said there is a small gang south of El Toro's camp, but they are scared to death of El Toro and if they even come close to his camp they will be executed on the spot. Camacho said that the only reason that El Toro lets them exists is because they pay him a percentage of what they make from their own business. Francisco asked and what about the other gang.

Camacho said I would imagine that it was the same as the gang on the South of them otherwise El Toro would take them out in a day.

Francisco said take me to the gang in the South of El Toro and take Mendoza to the gang on the North and we will try to talk them into attacking El Toro from two different fronts and kill them. Camacho thought that Francisco was crazy but what the hell maybe it might work.

Camacho said El Toro has scouts all over the jungle so we will air drop you into the camps of the two gangs and you can talk to them.

The plan was now made and all they had to do was to wait for the bomb to arrive from Captain Sana Anna. Francisco and Mendoza were air dropped to their respective camps and they talked to the gang what was planned. The gang leaders were happy to hear that they had a lethal bomb that will cripple the El Toro's army and was willing take part in the venture and quit paying Homage to El Toro every month. The bomb arrived in Camacho's camp and there were two guards in full uniform with the bomb.

The guards said we were here to help you take out El Toro and wanted to know if Camacho had a good airplane with a skilled pilot to take them to El Toro's camp and drop a bomb on their camp. Camacho said when do you want to do that. One of the guards said sooner the better and said we would like to do this just as the sun starts to set and to fly in from the west side of the camp so that sun will blind anyone trying to shoot the plane down.

Camacho said good idea and called his best small plane pilot who used to be a crop duster by the name of

Billy Boy. It was noon so they all had lunch at Camacho's ranch. The guards explained how the bomb worked and said that there wouldn't be big explosion but that it only contained radioactive material that will make them sick, and it will take time before they finally die a terrible death. Billy Boy said just like crop dusting job and I can come in flying low and drop the bomb right in the middle of the main building. Every detail was now figured out and the pilot studied the map that showed where the El Toro's camp was.

It was still a little after noon so Billy boy asked Camacho if he had a high-flying jet that would be out of range of any rifles and he wanted to make a final check before evening flight in a duster plane. Camacho called his jet pilot and told him to take Billy Boy in the jet so he can get a good look at El Toro's camp.

Billy Boy had a good look of the entire surroundings of the camp and noticed that there was huge glass window on the west side of the big building. There were no high hills on the west side of the building so with a duster plane he could fly low just over the small trees just like he was dusting a crop and drop the bomb through the window and the deadly nuclear waste material will be contained within the building.

The people inside may not even know that they were bombed. Billy Boy said thanks to the jet pilot and went to the couch and laid down and mentally went through the sequence that he will take that evening. Soon he was sleeping like a baby.

At five P. M. he got up and took a shower and had a small snack. He walked up to the duster plane and the bomb was already attached to the duster plane. He checked all the wiring and the several explosive squibs that will detach the bomb from the duster plane, and it looked perfect. The reason that there were several detachment squibs was to insure that at least one of them worked and the timing of the bomb release will not be changed by a delay and miss the target.

He put on his jacket and goggles and got into the plane. He started an automatic engine starter, so he pushed the button and the engine started right up and the propeller started to turn smoothly. He made several short runs on the airfield and then got out of the cockpit to check the squibs on the bomb release system, and they were still fastened as they should be.

He was now ready, so he gently guided his duster plane into the air and drove to the west side of the El Toro's camp. As he cleared the trees there were no people on the grounds, so he figured that it was supper time, and they were having a good dinner. He aimed for the large window then activated the squibs that released the bomb, and the bomb went right into the middle of the large window that had many small glass panes. He heard an explosive noise, so he knew that the bomb did explode. Billy Boy took one last flight from a higher altitude and noticed one man came out of the front of the house and he was throwing up. Maybe the dinner didn't agree with him. He flew back to Camacho's camp and reported that everything worked out just like clockwork. Everyone else already had their dinner so the cook came out and made him a special dinner. Francisco and Mendosa sat by him and Billy Boy explained how the flight went. Mendoza said not everyone will get sick all at the same time, but it depended on how much radiation they were exposed to when the bomb exploded. Mendoza said some of them might even go to bed that night and have a nice sleep but within a few days the effect of the radiation will get to them and they'll get sick. He described how the rats in San Luis go sick it took some of them a week before they died. Mendoza said the rats were first affected in their brain and they went crazy first.

Everyone knew what will happen in due time, so they went about their business as if it was just another regular day. Both teams of rival gangs approached the camp, one from the South and another from the North were now halfway to El Toro's camp and they were still far enough away from the camp, so they were not approached by any of El Toro's perimeter guards.

Two days later they were looking at El Toro's camp and it looked quiet. They even thought if he moved his camp so one of the gang members went closer to the building looked through a window and saw a lot of dead bodies on the floor. He reported back to this team leader and told him what he saw. The team leader remembered Francisco said about using some kind of poison gas, so he assumed that the gas worked.

Some of the younger men didn't want to wait so they walked into the house and came out with some valuable loot. Others saw the loot, so they went into the house to get their share as well. It was more comfortable in the house than outside of the building so some of the men went inside and slept in a nice bed. Next morning one of the men that slept in the building said that he felt nauseous, and the team leader said maybe all the deadly gas wasn't all dissipated yet to his men not to go into the house for a while.

A team of Camacho's men arrived at the El Toro's compound and found both gang members camped outside the building they set up camp here. The team leaders told them what they saw in the house and for now they were just staying outside where it was safer to be there. One of Camacho's men that came there that day said I will return to Camacho and report back to the boss what was happening at El Toro's camp.

Francisco said maybe some of the perimeter guard of El Toro still didn't know what happened to El Toro so he will take his guard dogs and scout the woods to see if there were still some of El Toro's men still in the woods. Camacho said bring a squad of men with rifles and go with the dogs to root out any stragglers still left in the woods.

37 RETURN

The team from the North had to return to harvest his crops before they started to spoil so he told everybody I'm glad we don't have to pay El Toro any money anymore and told them that he was going back home now.

His men already stripped the house of anything valuable, so it was now empty. They used the expensive vehicles to haul all their loot back home with them

The team from the South did the same and the house was now stripped clean of any valuables.

Mendoza and Francisco were planning to stay in El Toro's mansion but there was no furniture or anything else that they can use to be comfortable.

They drove back to Camacho's compound and told him that the place was stripped clean of any valuables and there wasn't even any furniture for them to stay there so they decided to go back home and take the dogs back with them.

When they got back to Camacho's compound, they told him of their plan to leave with the dogs and

Camacho asked them if he could buy the dogs. Francisco said that the dogs were not his and you will just talk to Mandy. Camacho said wait just a minute and I will call Mandy. Mandy was in his office, so he picked up immediately. A few minutes later Camacho said Mandy sold the dogs to him but if you need a ride back to Monterey, I will fly you back in my jet and it will be more comfortable that way. Francisco and Mendoza said thanks and waited for the jet. that way they were happy that they didn't have bring the big dogs back to Monterey with them because it would be such big job to do that.

Captain Santa Anna and his guards had another litter of new puppies to train now and the were busy. They were still selling the fully trained dogs for $25,000 but the untrained puppies were dropped in price to only ten thousand dollars each. They sold a lot of the cute puppies and were making fortune by selling the Akita dogs.

Sierra took another Akita puppy for herself and decided to train the puppy herself and brought it home to her motorhome with her. The puppy was so cute she couldn't help cuddling the puppy. When she was through playing with the puppy, she put the puppy in Shoguns soft bed with Shogun and he made sure that the puppy didn't wet his bed.

Back at the guard compound Mendosa was pumped for information about the raid and he answered all their questions as beast as he can, but he said that the big bomb was the most useful thing that they had. Mendoza asked if any more rats came back to kill more small animals and one of the guards said that he checks the location once week and so far, thy never came back.

Back in Monterey Mandy said that he sold both

guard dogs to Camacho for a hundred thousand dollars each. Francisco said that's probably a world's record for any guard dog. Francisco asked Mandy if he could take leave without pay for a short time because he wanted to return to Columbia and raise a few Akita dogs there. Mandy said I will call Matt and maybe he might want to come with you now that El Toro was now gone.

Mandy called Matt and told him of Francisco's plan. Matt said I've never been to South America so maybe I will go with him take a few Akita dogs with me.

38 PARTNER

Matt and Francisco took up residence in El Toro's old compound and started to refurnish the house with new furniture, housekeepers, cooks a yard crew and a few more new personnel. They also brought five new Akita puppies with them also and hired a dog handler to feed them and even train them if they can do that.

Francisco told Matt that it was strange that no one ever found any large stash of money in the house when it was raided by the two smaller gangs. Matt said maybe the gangs found some money and took it with them along with all of the valuables in the mansion. Francisco said I'm not talking about thousands of dollars but more like the billions that El Toro must have had insofar as he was, he was dealing with opium.

Matt said there's a small backhoe still on this lot so I will start to dig around and see if I can uncover anything.

Francisco said I can help you if you show me how to operate a backhoe. Matt said while you are at it clear a strait section where we can have our own private airfield.

With all the help in the mansion now the place was the most comfortable place that anyone could possibly live in.

A week later Francisco found a buried chest containing rare rubies, gold bracelets and some diamonds. He called Matt and they both were able to pull the chest out of the ground. Matt said this chest looks very old and looks like it could be something that a pirate berried a long time ago. Francisco said this place could have a lot more buried treasures all over the place.

Mat said I can't spend too much more time here so you can dig around and I should get back home to take care of my own business.

Francisco said I want to fly back with you and the staff can handle the daily chores here without me.

When Francisco visited Santa Anna, they were having trouble with rats coming into the Southern section of their land. Instead of using the radioactive waste product bombs they were using Pythons who seemed to love to eat the fat rats. One of the guards said that he checks the area once a week and the pythons seem to have things under control.

Francisco asked can you train some Akitas to dig up buried treasures. One of the guards said we never tried that, but it might be interesting to try that.

Francisco had Charlie fly him back to Monterey to see how Mandy was now doing. Mandy was in his office with Thunder who was a lot bigger now and he also had a cute little Akita puppy sired by Shogun and the puppy looked just like Shogun. Mandy asked if Francisco was back to stay. Francisco said I'm still working down in Columbia but just came back to visit you and Ruth to see how you were doing with the dogs.

Mandy said I'm almost done here so wait here and we can go to lunch soon. Thunder kept looking at Francisco, but he didn't seem to be too protective with Francisco sitting in the office with Mandy, maybe he still remembered who Francisco was because when he was a puppy Francisco was the one who trained Thunder.

Half an hour later they were back home having lunch with Ruth who also had a new puppy. The puppy was allowed to roam the entire house and the maids and cooks loved to play with the new puppy.

Francisco asked how his old house was doing now. Mandy said we have three dog trainers living there now and fifteen new puppies and we are going into the guard dog training business ever since Camacho gave me a million dollars for Ugly and his partner. Francisco thought that Mandy will never be able to repeat that Scenario again but didn't say anything.

Mandy asked Francisco if he was comfortable living in Columbia all by himself and asked Francisco if he ever thought about getting married. Francisco said I'm too busy trying to make my first million right now. Mandy said he bought a Cessna 180 and hired his personal pilot to take him to the many work sites where he is building structures and it saves him a lot of time.

Mandy asked what's keeping you down in Columbia when all your friends are up here. Francisco said when we took down El Toro and killed his army, we couldn't find any great amount of money in the house so he was sure that there must be a lot of it buried somewhere close to his mansion that he was now living in. Mandy said since he was the most notorious drug dealer all of South America and dealing in opium you may be correct about the money. Mandy then asked

Francisco if he was looking for a partner. Francisco said I've known you a long time and you always treated me well so if you want to join me in my gamble you are always welcome.

39 BLASTING

Mandy said I have some business in Cancun so I will fly you down partway to Columbia and from there you can take a commercial flight from Cancun to Columbia.

After Mandy finished his business in Cancun, he said I've never seen the Yucatan peninsula from the air so let's take a look at the site where giant asteroid hit the planet and caused total darkness of the planet and killed the dinosaurs by starvation.

The pilot made several circles around the depression and one could see how large asteroid must have been that hit the Earth only sixty million years ago. Of course, man didn't inhabit the planet yet and all the great accomplishments by man came after that. Francisco was thinking how new we are to this planet.

At Cancun Mandy put Francisco on a Delta flight to Columbia and gave him some cash for him to use after he got to Columbia.

Two hours later Francisco was talking to Camacho and having lunch. Camacho said I built a small landing strip south of El Toro's compound so we can fly there by plane and the trip will be quicker. Camacho said the forest near El Toro's camp grows so fast that it was difficult to keep the dirt road clear of trees.

Francisco said that was nice of you to do all that. Camacho said you look like you needed better furniture, so he had new furniture put in the house as well. Francisco said thanks for all your help. After lunch Billy Boy flew Francisco back to his house using his Duster plane.

Matt never liked to waste time, so he hired a well-established construction company from Bogota to expand the rough landing strip by Francisco's house. As Matt was talking to the construction foreman, he said I think t that we have another job in the same area as where you want the landing strip extended so let me call by boss.

The boss's name was Alfredo de Santa Fe and said we have job request to build a castle only ten miles from your landing strip and we can use a lot of good gravel as a byproduct of extending your Airstrip.

Next day there were surveyors with theodolites looking over the entire area around Francisco's house. The foreman said the best way to extend your airstrip is to blast through the small hill to the south and we will have straight shot to build your airstrip.

Francisco said I will move my dogs to Camacho's compound so they won't get frightened, and you can start blasting tomorrow. Francisco called Camacho and told him that he wanted him to take care of his young dogs for week or so. Camacho said I will have my men come to get your dogs today.

Next day a team of dynamite experts came to Francisco's house and said we are going to start blasting and just wanted to let you know. Francisco said thanks for letting me know and make as much noise as you want. That afternoon people in Francisco's house could only hear a faint noise of what could be blasting. Everyone in Francisco's house went about their business just as a normal day. A week later the blasting noise gradually got louder. Francisco said the noise might get louder so if you want to take a short vacation you can do so starting today. The help was happy to hear vacation, so they started to prepare the house to close it up. Francisco never visited Bogota, the capital of Columbia so he decided to go visit Bogota and spend a week or more there.

40 TRAINED DOGS

Ten days later when Francisco came back to his house things were back to normal, all the maids and cooks and yard men and dog trainers were back to work. The airstrip was paved with Asphalt and smooth as silk. Francisco wondered what the construction company did with the dirt and gravel that must have resulted from the removal of the mountain. He got in his truck and drove down the airstrip and noticed that there was another airstrip that extended to the ocean perpendicular to the longer airstrip. It too was paved.

What he couldn't figure out was what happened to the mountain that disappeared.

There was dirt road along the coastline, so he got on that and finally came to another construction site where they were building up the land with a lot of gravel. He finally figured out where the mountain went.

He stayed in his truck for a while and noticed a no trespassing sign, so he turned around and left construction site.

When he got back home, he got on the computer

and sent a message to Matt telling him that the new airstrip was completed and paved with asphalt. The cook asked him if he was ready for lunch and he said he only wanted a big salad.

He could see out the window that the dog trainers were busy with the dogs.

One-week later Matt showed up in a jet with Sierra. Matt asked Francisco if the construction team found any more hidden treasurers and Francisco said that he was in Bogota for ten days because of all the blasting that they did to remove the mountain. Matt said that they certainly did a great job on the new airstrip which was true.

The housekeeper showed Matt and Sierra to their rooms. When they came back Matt said I brought back two dogs supposedly trained to find buried treasure back with me. Matt went outside and looked at the dog cubicles where they had five cute dogs in a fenced in yard. He talked to dog trainers and asked them to put his two new dogs in a different pen and take care of them for him.

At dinner Matt said if El Toro was the biggest drug dealer in all of South America, he must have at least a hundred million dollars stashed somewhere around here. Matt said tomorrow I will take the dogs that I brought with and see if they really are capable of finding hidden treasures.

Matt took his two dogs for a walk around the house, but they could find nothing. He came back and told Sierra to take the dogs for a walk after lunch and see if she can find anything.

An hour later she came back with a lunch box that had a dog bone in the metal lunch box. Francisco said I was trying to train his dogs to find hidden treasures so knew as the one that planted several of these boxes but none of his dogs could any of them. Matt said then these dogs are actually trained to find things buried in the ground.

After dinner Matt decided to try again and took the dogs to the wooded area farther away from the house. Both dogs started to sniff the ground and started to dig the ground, but the roots of the trees made it more difficult for them to dig too deep. Soon it was getting dark so he came back and told Francisco and Sierra that the dogs might have found something, but it was getting dark, so he decided to wait until tomorrow morning to take the small backhoe and dig deeper.

Sierra was the first to get up so after breakfast she went on her own and took the backhoe and found the place where the dogs started to dig a hole. First, she removed all the small trees that were growing near the hole which had roots spreading all over the ground then she hit something solid, so she stopped and looked down the hole and it looked like an old trunk.

She went back into the house and had some coffee. Matt and Francisco came down to have some breakfast, they stayed up late to watch a movie. After they were seated and waiting for their breakfast Sierra said that she went out earlier this morning and dug around the hole where the dogs started to dig and found something that looked like an old pirate's trunk. Matt said after I finish my breakfast, we should go look at what you found.

An hour later they were able to pull up the old trunk partly rotting and found it full of gold bracelets, diamond rings, rubies and a lot of silver candlestick and the trunk was almost full of them. They all grabbed a few things and went back to the house to examine them more carefully. Francisco said that the trunk looked too old for El Toro to have buried the trunk so it must have been someone else that berried the trunk a long time ago.

But now they knew that the dogs were trained to find things buried in the ground.

41 PLASTIC BOXES

Matt had things to do back home so he told everybody that he was going back home and asked Sierra if she wanted to go back with him. She said I think I will just stay here for a while and maybe visit Bogota while I'm here.

Matt gave her fifty thousand in cash and said if you get tired of this place you can always take a commercial flight home anytime because you have your passport with you now. Matt said goodbye to Francisco and hugged Sierra goodbye and left on his jet for home.

Francisco took Sierra to Bogota and spent a week there. While she was there, she bought a new computer and hired a company to install a state-of-the-art internet system in Francisco's house. Now she could look up more information about the area that El Toro's old house sat on.

When they got back to Francisco's house he went back to where he buried the trunk and it looked like no one had bothered it. He got the backhoe and moved a small tree and planted on top of where he buried the chest. If the chest was buried for who knows how long it wouldn't hurt to be buried a few more years.

The dogs loved to go looking for buried stuff, so Sierra always took them out at least once a day to do that. One day she took the dogs to an entirely new area they never went before and just turned the dogs loose to hunt for treasures on their own. After an hour she decided to go try and find them.

Half an hour later she found them digging a hole in a different part of the forest. She marked the spot with tree branches that looked like a teepee. Sierra told the dogs to come home with her, and she will feed them.

She put the dogs back into the pen and made sure that they had clean water and a lot of food. She went into the house and found Francisco on the Internet

At dinner Sierra told Francisco that the dogs found another spot and they were digging a hole. Francisco said I will go with you tomorrow morning we will look at the place.

Next morning Sierra showed Francisco the spot and he said I will get the backhoe and start digging around the hole. Francisco said I think that I heard something, but it wasn't metallic sound. Sierra said be careful and just dig around the area until we can see what it is.

Francisco was very careful this time and saw a plastic box. He made the hole big enough so he can crawl down there, and he was able to lift the plastic box all by himself and he slid it on the ground above him. He looked at the plastic box and there was a padlock on the box. He found a rock and hit the lock and the lock opened right up.

Both Sierra and Francisco looked into the box and

noticed that the box was filled cash neatly stacked with one-hindered dollar bills put in bunched of a thousand dollar in each strapped bundle. He removed two bundles and handed them to Sierra and said I will be right back. He had a large canvas tarp and covered the plastic box and put some dirt around the edges so the canvas tarp will stay in place.

They walked back to the house and looked for private place to inspect the money more carefully. The only place that he could think about was to go to his bedroom so they both went there and closed the door. Francisco gave one bundle to Sierra and told her to take it into her bedroom and inspect the cash make sure that they were not counterfeit money.

Sierra did the best that she could, but she was not an expert at examining hundred-dollar bills, so she hid them under her bed covers and went down to the living room to look for Francisco, but he wasn't there.

Half an hour later he came back and whispered into her ear that he reburied the plastic box in a different place and covered it up with dirt and planted a tree on top of where he reburied the plastic box.

The next morning Francisco and Sierra were in the First National Bank of Bogota talking to the bank manager. Francisco handed the bank manager his bundle of one-hundred-dollar bills and asked him if they were genuine paper money.

The bank manger took a closely at one of the hundred-dollar bills and said it these were counterfeit bills they were the best ones that he ever saw. He said if you really are worried about them let me have one of the bills x-rayed and he should have a result in a week. Francisco said thank you and left with Sierra.

They went to a fancy restaurant had an expensive dinner and paid for it with a hundred-dollar bill. The cash register lady rang up the bill and gave him some change.

When they returned to Francisco's home, they had enough information that the bill was either genuine or the best counterfeit money in the world. Sierra e-mailed her father Matt and told him of the large amount of money that they now had and asked him to fly down talk to us.

Two days later Matt was looking at the large plastic box and asked how much money was in the box. Francisco said we didn't count it all and he didn't want any of his help to see him with so much money. Matt understood and said I will take some of this money to cover my expenses for getting the area improved and you can keep the rest hidden for the time being. Matt brought several suitcases and filled them up with cash, but it hardly made a dent in the large plastic box.

Then Matt asked what ever happened to the old trunk with the all the gold coins and rubies and other stuff. Francisco said they are still buried in the ground for now. Matt asked Francisco if he wanted any of it and he said with all the money he now had he wasn't interested in keeping any of that junk. Matt said if you could help me get it loaded in my jet, I will sell some of it and send you some money for it. Francisco said don't bother because all I want to for now is to figure out what to do with all the cash in the plastic box.

Matt said I'm sure you will figure it out soon and said I will be leaving tomorrow morning with Sierra.

42 BACK HOME

After the jet was safely returned to the hanger and the hanger door closed. A guard came to the hanger with a van and helped Matt load the old chest and the suitcases in the van then drove them to back the motorhome. The guard helped Matt unload the van put everything on the ground and left. Matt told Sierra to find the keys to the motorhome and unlock the motorhome.

They were now in their secluded area on top of a large hill, and they went into the motorhome and made some tea. Sierra said I feel more relaxed in the motorhome than in any fancy hotel and Matt agreed with her. Matt asked Sierra what we should do with all the stuff that we brought back from Columbia. Sierra was thinking but had no great ideas so she couldn't answer.

Matt carried the three suitcases into the motorhome and told Sierra to put them somewhere where they won't get in the way. Matt said I'm going to town and find some smaller boxes to transfer the stuff from the old chest and he will be back soon.

Sierra was looking out the motorhome window and she could see the guard compound and see a lot of cute little puppies running around and they looked happy. She could see the hanger and noticed the stewardesses coming back with what looked like groceries. They looked happy with their lives as well because they weren't always not having to fly all the time to help the airlines make more money. Her father was a great manager and made sure that everyone who worked for him was well paid and given more benefits than any large company in the world.

She reminisced about the time that she worked for Diamond fence company and the boss gave her a raise made twenty dollars an hour and it was twice what most teenagers made at that time. She was thinking that she lived a wonderful life and was happy that she wasn't a waitress working for tips just to get by to pay her rent.

She wondered why she never found someone that she liked enough to marry him. She thought about Isabella who married Shunjiro and now had nine kids and she was happy. She knew if it wasn't for her Shunjiro would still be struggling to make enough money to feed himself and his mother but now thanks to Sierra he was a millionaire and Isabella didn't have to even leave the house or even have to go shopping for food because her cook did all that for her. Sierra came to the conclusion that having a lot of money was better than being poor.

Just then she was woken from her revelry when Matt came back with lot of wooden boxes. Matt asked her what she was thinking about and she said I was just thinking how lucky I was to have such a wonderful life. Matt went out and started to transfer the contents from the old chest into the small wooden boxes and Sierra helped him.

The wooden boxes were strong, so Matt started to

put them under the motorhome. Matt put the empty trunk on his GMC and was now ready to have some lunch. He asked Sierra where she wanted to go for lunch. Sierra wasn't sure. Matt said let’s have Charley fly us to Monterey and we can visit Mandy. That sounded like a great idea, so they did that. When Charley landed at the Monterey airport there was a car waiting for hm because Charley had already alerted Mandy that he was coming with Matt.

The driver who worked for Mandy said Ruth was fixing lunch, so he was instructed to drive Matt and Sierra to Mandy's house. A maid greeted Matt and Sierra at the door and showed them into the living room and they sat on a couch. A cure puppy came in and jumped on Sierra's lap. Sierra hugged the puppy and the puppy loved to be hugged.

A maid came into the living room and showed the to the dining room table and Ruth and Mandy were already sitting at the table.

First the maid brought them a small salad, so they started with the salad. Mandy said that Camacho gave him a hundred thousand dollars for each of the guard dogs and Matt was surprised to hear that. Matt asked how Thunder was doing now. Mandy said he developed arthritis, so he is now living at the dog farm and he gets to struggle around wherever he wants to go at night he gets to come in the house with the guards and he sleeps on the rug of the floor in the living room.

Sierra said that she read that big dogs have more trouble when they get older and usually don't last as long as the smaller sled dogs in Alaska. Matt said Charley is waiting for us at the airport so we should be heading back home.

Just then Matt noticed that he still had some jewelry from the old trunk and told Ruth that this was for her from Francisco. Ruth picked it from Matt and said these are very heavy and they look like they should be in a museum. Matt said we think that they are relics from the Mayan Empire when the Conquistadors invaded the new world and forced the Mayans into slave labor and a lot of them died of starvation.

But evidently the Mayan priests were able hide some of these and the Conquistadors didn't get all of them. Ruth said he rubies on the necklaces look huge and there is a lot of heavy gold used in these necklaces Matt said maybe you should start your own museum store them there.

The driver came to pick up Matt and Sierra to take them back to the airport, so they all said goodbye and left.

43 CASTLE

Matt brought a handful of ancient jewelry to Maria and gave it to her and told her that we found these in Columbia. Maria looked at them carefully and said these are very unusual. Matt said we think that they were made by the ancient Mayans when the Spanish conquistadores invaded the new world, and this was what was left of them then Matt left.

Matt went back to the motorhome and found Sierra just storing all the small wooden boxes under the motorhome and she came back into the motorhome.

Matt said I just stopped by the guard compound and gave them a couple of bundles of strapped one-hundred-dollar bills. Sierra had some tea, so she gave Matt some tea. Matt had a taste of the tea and asked what kind of tea this was. Sierra said they are the ones that Rose orders from Monterey, and they are reported to be good for all kinds of ailments and that she drinks them all the time.

Matt asked Sierra what she wanted to do next. Sierra said I might just go back to Columbia and look for more buried treasures. Matt said I will go with you then.

A week later they were all in Francisco's house having dinner. Matt said I had Constantine package up some Ume trees and he will ship them to you by freighter and they should arrive in a month or less. Francisco knew what Ume fruit was like, so he was happy to start to plant some of the trees.

Matt asked if Francisco found anymore buried treasure and he said I still haven't decided what to do with all the money I already found. Matt said start investing them in CD;s and deposit some cash in different small banks all over Columbia.

Matt asked Francisco if he was ready for a vacation. Francisco said I've been on a vacation ever since I came to Columbia. Matt said maybe you should go visit Mandy your old boss and bring him a present. Francisco said like some cash. Matt said you can do that but what about those two candle sticks on the Mantle.

Francisco said maybe I can bring back a few more dogs so I can train them here. Matt said you can leave here with no one watching your house. Francisco looked at Sierra and asked her if she could stay here for a week and watch the house and he will be back in a week. Sierra said you have maids and cooks here so I should be comfortable for a week.

Matt and Francisco left on the jet the next day and they were now back to Mexico.

Matt had the guard drive him to his motorhome and Francisco was brought to the guard compound. Francisco noticed that there was another litter of Akita Pups. He talked to Captain Santa Anna and gave him a bundle of cash and said I want to buy five pups so I can train them in Columbia.

The Captain called one of his guards and told him

to count the cash.
Meanwhile the Captain took Francisco to look at the new litter of Akita pups.

When they came back inside that guard said there was close to three million in cash here. Santa Anna was surprised to hear three million. The Captain said we are currently selling our pups for fifteen thousand each now but if you take ten of them, I will give you he ten pups for $125,000. Francisco said fine and asked the Captain to get them ready to ship to Columbia by jet in a week.

Francisco asked if he could spare a guard to drive him to Monterey. The Captain said I will assign Freddy to drive you there and he will stay there with you all the time that stay in Monterey.

Sierra took the two dogs to the North side of the house where no one ever goes and turned them loose to find more buried treasures then she went back to the house to have breakfast

After breakfast she went back to look for the dogs. Ten minutes later she found dogs digging under some small trees. She let them dig and went back to get the backhoe.

The dogs looked tired, so she told them to take a break and she started to remove some small trees. The whole area was full of small trees, so she cleared a larger space to place the small trees and now there was a larger space to work in. she didn't want to get the dogs get in the way and get hurt so she walked them back to the dog compound and told the dog handler to take care of them.

She went back to the house and e-mailed her father that she might have found more buried treasures. Sierra knew that if she went back and continued to dig where the found the spot it could be another plastic box full of cash and it would be a lot of work to get it out of the ground and if it did contain a lot of cash like the first one, she wouldn't be able to get the box out all by herself.

She remembered that in only a few days Francisco Will be back, and he can do all the heavy work. Besides she and Matt already had more gold still buried where the old outhouse used to be and there were more than several billions of gold still buried there .

She really didn't need any more money so why she was doing looking for more buried treasures . She had a fine motorhome that was perfect for her needs and a fine house in Mikame where Shunjiro and his family was living and taking care of the place. She decided to just leave the possible buried treasure stay where it was buried and when Francisco comes back, she can talk it over with him and they can decide what to do with it later.

There was still three days left before Francisco was due back, so she decided to explore the South side of the house and see what was down there. She got in Francisco jeep and traveled to a place that she never explored before.

Sierra drove on the new airfield that was paved with asphalt and drove all the way to the end of the airstrip. There was a dirt road that went west so she took that road.

Then she found another road that was fully paved, so she drove south for a while. The road ended and there was a huge sign that read for sale. She drove to the beautiful gate and found an intercom by the gate. She pushed a button and said hello into the speaker. Sierra said I don't speak Spanish but was interested in seeing the castle. Someone else came on the intercom and said something in Spanish again. \

She just sat in her jeep and hoped that someone would come to the gate. But to her great surprise the gate opened so she drove to the castle and stopped by a drawbridge hanging over a moat

The drawbridge lowered so she drove over the bridge and came to a huge wooden door that looked like it weighed a hundred tons. The door opened from the inside, so she drove into an open courtyard. Two guards approached her dressed in uniforms and spoke to her in Spanish. She raised her hands and said I can't speak Spanish. One guard got on his cell phone and talked to someone in Spanish.

A few minutes later an older guard came to the jeep riding on a white stallion and said I am the captain of the guards and I can speak some
English. Sierra said I am interested in buying the castle. The Captain invited Sierra to come into the castle where they can talk.

44 A PURCHASE

Matt and Francisco arrived by jet and unloaded ten new puppies and put them in the dog pen. Francisco unloaded some coked soup bones and brought them into the kitchen and found Sierra eating lunch.

Next Matt came into the kitchen and sat down. Matt asked what was with the new discovery of possible buried treasures. Sierra said I just left them there because what would I do with it if it was full of cash. Both Francisco and Matt thought she was right.

Francisco asked what was with the new Castle that she went to look at. Sierra said I talked to the people in the castle, but we never talked about price. Matt said let's all go visit them now and talk to them.

Francisco went to his hiding place and pulled out a bundle of cash and put it in his inside coat pocket. When they got to the gate Sierra knew the routine and she went to the gate, then to the drawbridge, then to the huge wooden door to the Castle and now they were in the open courtyard. The same Captain of the guards came to greet them and asked what they wanted.

Matt said we were interested in buying the Castle,

so the Captain invited them to come inside the Castle. A maid brought them some coffee and some fresh tortillas and some fresh salsa. Francisco didn't want to fool around with niceties and pulled out his bundle of cash from his inside vest pocket and put it on the table

The Captain said that they put the Castle up for sale before for a hundred million dollars and no one was willing to pay that much money for a place so isolated where it would be difficult to protect the castle. The captain kept looking at the bundle of cash and then said if we lower the price to only seventy million and you can have the Castle right now.

Matt, Sierra and Francisco had a huddle and decided to accept the offer. The captain asked how much money was in the big bundle sitting on the table. Francisco said I didn't count the money so maybe we should count the money now. The bank tape was removed, and cash now expanded some and everyone separated the bundle.

Francisco separated the pile into four stacks told everybody to start counting the cash. Fifteen minutes later they were done counting their own pile of cash and the total came out to be exactly a hundred Million dollars. Francisco gave the Captain seventy million and said that this was for the Castle.

Everyone was surprised to see how fast the transaction went. Matt said we have to leave now but we will be back tomorrow to talk to you some more then left with Francisco and Sierra.

45 SECURITY

During dinner of the night that they purchased the Castle they discussed the possibility of the Castle needing some important repairs like a new sewer system, a better electrical supply system and a few more important things. Sierra said everybody there looked clean so they probably had enough water, and the sewer system must have been adequate for their use

Matt said what we should do is for us to actually live in the Castle for a while and we will learn more about the Castle. Matt said I'm not sure if I want to eat tortillas all the time so maybe we should bring our own cook with us.

All three of them drove in separate cars and returned to the Castle. A lot of the security measures were changed and made simpler, and Francisco liked that because the old system too much of their valuable time.

After they were in the Castle the housekeeper came to greet them and showed them to their rooms. Their rooms were cleaned, and everything looked fine, so they went back down and sat in the great room. The cook came in and asked if they were ready for lunch. It had been a while since breakfast, so they were ready for lunch. A maid showed them to the dining room, and they were seated. The maid said lunch will be ready in ten minutes and she left.

Another maid came by and brought them some water. Francisco spoke to the maid in Spanish and asked where the Captain of the guards was. She said he was offered a new job, so he left with some of his guards, and they were now gone. Francisco said "Muchisimas Gracious" and the maid said "de Nada.

Matt stayed at the castle for a week and decided that the sewer system needed improvement, so he hired a company to build a new system. The electric supply system was inadequate, so he ordered a nuclear power system to supply an unlimited amount of electrical power. Everyone in the castle was happy because they no longer had to be careful not overload the electrical grid for the Castle. The cook was happy because the water system in her kitchen now worked a lot better.

Gradually the Castle became a more comfortable place to live. Sierra started to stay in the Castle more often.

Sierra used her state-of-the-art internet system and found some twenty MM cannons for sale, so she ordered five of them with the explosive shells that came with the cannon.

The guards were busy training Akita pups to become perimeter guard dogs. They set up their guard post right by that main gate and they stationed a guard there. No one as allowed to come to the Castle without a complete background check or permission from one of the three members of the Castle who now owned the Castle.

Francisco found flack ammunitions left over from WWII so he ordered a lot of them that can be fired from the twenty-millimeter canons.

Matt heard about the over-the-horizon missiles invented in Okinawa and ordered the entire system to be installed at the Castle

The shipment of Ume trees arrived so Francisco had some of them planted by his house and the rest of them planted at various locations around the Castle.

Sierra hired more maids and cooks to help in the Castle.

A new guard post was built near the end of the paved runway where the new paved road was used to come to the Castle. No one was allowed to advance any further without permission from the main guardhouse by the main gate. The whole area was becoming more secure by the week.

46 BACK TO THE CASTLE

Matt flew back to San Luis to check on how things were coming there. He told Captain Santa Anna about the Castle that they bought and all the security that they were planning for the Castle. Santa Anna said I would like to go see the Castle myself when I have more time. Matt asked if there were any intruders coming to this area anymore. The Captain said no since started to use our roaming guard dogs and they were better than human guards for the perimeter work.

Matt said why don't you fly back with me to Columbia, and you can train my dogs how to do perimeter patrol. Santa Anna said I can do that, and I will bring one of my best trainers with me.

Matt drove to the new Ritz and the place looked like it was doing great business. He drove all around the small town and noticed that there were more smaller eating places now open.

He drove back to his motorhome spent the night there. In the morning he checked the area around his motorhome, and nothing was disturbed. He drove to Rose's hotel to see how she was doing. Rose said we get a few customers from time to time but things are quiet most of the time. Matt asked if Rose had a lot of Ume pits for sale now and she said I will call Junko and she usually has a lot that she sells to the Korean stores so she can send me all you want.

Matt said tell her to send you three cases of the frozen Ume pits and keep them frozen until I fly back to Columbia. Then he asked what you have for lunch. She said how about some Yaki Soba and Matt said fine.

Matt drove back to the guard compound and the Captain getting ready to fly to Columbia and he looked anxious to leave. Matt didn't want to make the Captain wait too long so he made plans to leave as soon as possible.

He drove to town and bought large block of frozen dry ice and had Rose pack the frozen Ume pits in the Styrofoam boxes and told her to bring them to the guard house. He called his pilot Takashi Kato and told him to prepare to fly back to Columbia.

He checked his refrigerator to see if there was anything that might get spoiled if he stayed in Columbia too long.

Two days later they were all sitting in the jet ready to leave San Luis. The stewardesses came by to check their seat belts. The head stewardess told the Captain we are ready now. The captain alerted the guard house that the jet was now leaving the airstrip.

Twelve hours later they were all having dinner in the Castle. The cook served all of them home made Tamales and a lot of fresh salsa. After dinner they were all shown to their bedrooms.

Next morning the cook had a makeshift menu and there was choice of bacon and eggs with hash brown potatoes or a Mexican breakfast. Most of them ordered the bacon and eggs but Matt decided to take a chance with the Mexican breakfast.

When the maid brought Matt his Mexican breakfast, he was amazed how tasty it was. There was a cake of Masa Harina cake with a lot of Tomatillo sauce that was similar to salsa Verde but touch sharper in taste. Matt was now thinking about having more of the Mexican breakfast from now on and it looked healthier that the bacon and eggs.

47 VISIT

Captain Santa Anna took charge of the guards at the Castle and completely re-organized the guard set up. He fashioned the new guard complex after what he had in Mexico. He ordered new wool gabardine uniforms for the guards because in humid weather they hold their press better. He also ordered two sets of fatigues for the guards. He ordered red chevrons for the guards that they can sew on themselves or take it to a shop where they can do that.

The new guard complex was run like a military unit except for the pay which was three times what any military unit could pay them. As such, there was long waiting list for young men wanting to join Captain Santa Anna's guard company. There was an inspection of the quarters every morning and a lieutenant did the inspection.

The living quarters for the guards were top notch and the mess hall served great food. Fridays was steak night, and the mess hall served the best steaks like in a gourmet restaurant. Life couldn't be better for any young man who was lucky enough to pass the entrance exams and allowed to join the special guard unit, the emblems on the lieutenant's lapel were real gold and they sparkled.

Matt was impressed how quickly Captain Santa Anna transformed the new guard complex.

Sierra took charge of all the people who worked in the castle. For any person who worked in the Castle who was getting too old she gave them a good retirement program so they can live on the retirement for many years. She modernized the kitchen with state-of-the-art kitchen equipment. Once a month she had a well-known chef come from Bogota come to demonstrate his best dinner. All the cooks loved that because it increased their knowledge of cooking fancy dinners.

Francisco finally cleaned out his big stash of money from the plastic box and invested in Bonds, C.D's, and other annuities. He would never have to worry about money ever in his lifetime

Matt had other business back in San Luis, so he left to take care of his businesses.

Captain Santa Anna wanted to see more of Columbia, so he stayed on in the guard compound to make sure that everything went like clockwork.

Sierra decided to go visit Francisco to see what he was doing to keep himself from getting too bored. When she walked into the living room, he was taking a nap on the couch. She didn't wake him up right away but walked outside to where her dogs discovered a possible hidden stash. The tree that she planed over the spot was now getting taller.

She visited the special dogs that were trained to hunt for hidden treasures and noticed that they were getting a little fat. Apparently, the dog handlers weren't taking them out enough, but it was not their job to do that. Their job was only to make sure that they were well fed and well taken care of. She thought about borrowing them so that she can take them back to the castle and she can go with them for meaningful exercise. She decided to take them back with her to the Castle and let them run around in a new area and she will get some exercise at the same time.

Sierra walked back to Francisco's house and this time he was up. Francisco was happy to see an old friend and invited her in to have lunch. Sierra was curious to see what kind of food Francisco was eating lately so she said she will have lunch with him.

Lunch turned out to be frozen Tamales that Francisco heated up in the microwave oven. He also had salsa in jars in his refrigerator put it on the table. Sierra was surprised to find out that the lunch was actually tasty. During lunch Francisco told Sierra that he cleaned out the big plastic box and invested the money in C.D.'s and other annuities.

Sierra said that was wiser thing to do because the money will now earn interest and only grow as time goes by. Sierra said I think it is now time to dig up what her dogs found, and it may just be some old dog bones, or it may even have some cash in it.

Sierra said I should get back now, and I will be back again tomorrow morning.

48 EMPTY BOX

Captain Santa Anna's dog trainers finished training four dogs for the perimeter patrol, and they sent two dogs go on patrol by themselves. The dogs had miniature cameras attached on their collars which stuck over their heads and the guard in the guard house could see everything that the dogs could see. They were much faster than a human being because they travelled by trotting.

Half an hour later they were back at the guardhouse and they were rewarded. They still had ten half grown Akita dogs and one of the guards suggested that we let two untrained dogs go along with the trained dogs one of these days and see if the untrained dogs will be automatically trained by the trained dogs just by going on patrol with the trained dogs.

Even if the untrained dogs don't get fully trained by the trained dogs, they might at least lean the route and it would be a great help for the guards to do final training.

The cooks at the castle were learning a lot of new recipes from their monthly visits from the great chefs from Bogota and they were becoming very creative. Sierra was usually the only person being served dinner at night, so she let her chefs decide what to make for her every night. Her chefs would spend half a day just studying what to make for Sierra and Sierra always loved what they made.

Next morning Sierra left early with two large suitcases and drove to Francisco's house. She found Francisco having breakfast and he offered her some breakfast as well. This morning there was a cook in the kitchen and the cook asked Sierra what she wanted. Sierra said just make me a traditional Mexican breakfast.

Sierra said I brought two suitcases with me just in case there was any money in the second plastic box.

After breakfast Francisco got the backhoe and started to dig around the small tree that Sierra planted over the spot where the dogs started to dig. Twenty minutes later Francisco had a trench around the plastic box. He didn't even scratch the plastic box. He guided the bucket of the backhoe and pushed the small tree into the trench.

When Francisco got down into the trench to try to pick up the box it was so light that he thought that the box was empty. He grabbed a handle on one side of the box and flipped it right out of the ground and it lay on the ground above the hole.

Sierra grabbed a rock and hit the flimsy lock and the lock opened right away. She opened the box and said that there was only about a hundred million in cash in this box and handed the cash to Francisco.

Francisco went back to the house and brought back only one suitcase and Sierra put all the cash in the suitcase and they went back to the house to have coffee.

Francisco asked why the box was so empty and Sierra said maybe that was all the cash that they had left. Sierra said I will divide the cash in two and you can have half of it, and I will take the other half back with me back to the Castle. Sierra already had breakfast with Francisco so she said I will head back to the Castle and hide my cash in my bedroom and the cash may come in handy one of these days.

Francisco reburied the empty box and put the tree back on the top of the dirt where the box was now buried.

49 TO SPAIN

Captain Santa Anna promoted one of the lieutenants to captain and gave him a good tutorial on how the best way to run an efficient guard team.

He called Matt and said he was ready to return to Mexico. Matt said I will be there in a few days to pick you up and you can fly you back to Mexico

Francisco heard about the jet coming to Columbia, so he wanted to fly back to Mexico with Santa Anna. He gave everybody in his house a vacation and closed the house down. He drove to the Castle and joined Sana Anna to fly back to Mexico.

Captain Takashi Kato came with Matt in the jet to pick up Santa Anna.

Santa Anna and Francisco boarded the jet and flew back to Mexico. Matt stayed with Sierra to get caught up on what was going on in Columbia. The cooks were happy to show off their cooking skills, so they put on a grand feast for Matt and Sierra.

Next morning Matt and Sierra drove to Francisco's house to see how it was being taken care of. The place looked closed up, but Sierra knew where the spare key was so se got it and they were able to get in. Sierra made some coffee and they sat at the kitchen table and had a good talk.

Sierra told her father that when they dug up the plastic box it was almost empty and only had several hundred million in the bottom of the box. She said that we divided the money, and I brought my share back to the Castle and put it in my safe in my bedroom. Matt asked if there was nothing in bottom of the plastic box. Sierra said nothing but the wooden floor of the box. Matt knew that many suitcases had hidden compartments in the bottom of the suitcase and mentioned this to Sierra.

Sierra said maybe we should go back and check it again then. Matt got the backhoe and dug up the plastic box again. Matt looked inside and said it looks like there is no secret hiding place on the bottom of the box. Then he turned the box on its side and kicked the bottom of the box and the wooden bottom fell out. Sierra crawled in and removed some paper and showed it to her father. The paper was written mostly in Spanish but there were a few words written in English as well. Matt noticed the word Bearer Bond and was convinced that it was indeed a Bearer Bond.

Matt took three of the Bearer Bonds into the kitchen to examine them more closely. In the kitchen in better lighting, he was able to make out the words in Spanish "Banco de Madrid de Espania" Matt said we are going to take a trip to Spain.

Matt went back to the plastic box and returned the bottom of the box like it was originally. He buried the plastic box back up and re-planted the small tree on the ground where the box was buried. He checked all around the area and it looked like it was not disturbed. After they went back into the kitchen Sierra cleaned up the kitchen and put everything back like it was. Sierra locked up the house and returned the key to its original hiding place.

Matt drove back to the Castle and had lunch at the castle. He called his pilot Takashi to come and get him and make sure that the jet had enough fuel to travel to Spain.

Takashi called Matt from the airstrip and told Matt that he was ready to take Matt to Spain now. Matt and Sierra had a guard drive him to the airstrip boarded the jet. The guard waited until the jet was in the air and then he returned to the guard compound.

50 MADRID

In Spain Mat and Sierra went directly to the Banco de Madrid asked to talk to the bank manager. When the bank manager came out Matt showed him one of the documents that he was sure that it was a Bearer Bond. The bank manager took only one look at the Bearer Bond and asked Matt and Sierra to come into his private office. After they were seated the bank manager ordered some coffee for all of them

The bank manager filled them with some history of Spain when the Spanish Civil War took place. He said that General Francisco Franco was in need of tremendous amount of money just to fund his war against the Insurrectionists. He even had several countries from all over the worlds to help in the war. He said even many Americans volunteered to help. Paper money was worthless by then and the only thing that the Bank of Spain could use was gold. There was an old well-known family that had ancestors who went to the new world and brought back a lot of gold from the Mayans and it was rumored that they still had a lot of gold. The president of our bank back then pleaded with the Conquistadores family to lend the bank some gold so the country can survive. The conquistador's family relented and loaned the bank a lot of gold.

This Bearer Bond that you brought in with you this morning is the result of the loan in gold to the bank. Since the amount of gold loaned to the bank was so huge the bank president created this special bearer Bond that you brought in the morning and it has the unique feature that the longer that the bond holder does not try to cash in on the bond the bond will continue to gain interest on the Bond at the rate of One percent a year.

Now we are past the mid-century more than half of the of the twenty second century so the interest alone on this bond is tremendous so you should try to not cash in on this bond as long as you can. Matt asked the bank manager to give him a minute and we will come to a conclusion. Sierra said we don't need any money right now. Matt said maybe we should just cash just one of these since we seem to have box full of them still in Columbia. Sierra said fine let's just cash one of these in right now and see what it will bring us.

Matt told the bank manager that he would like to cash this bond now because we have more of them still in Columbia. The bank manager said we can do that and give us a few hours while our comptroller figures out what the interest is on this bond. Matt said we will be back in a couple hours then and left with Sierra'.

One block from the bank they saw a fine restaurant named El Clair de Lune. Matt knew that his international credit card had enough money to order any kind of dinner he wanted so they went into restaurant and the place was magnificent. They had a couple of hours to kill so they took their time ordering their meal

When they finished their meal, they went back tit the bank and talked to the bank manager again. The comptroller finished his calculations, and everyone was surprised how large the interest was. The bank manager suggested that the bulk of the money be invested in C.D.'s and the rest of the money invested in annuities. Matt said that was fine but he would like to open a new credit card with this bank so we can use it in Europe. He also said I would like to have a hundred thousand in Spanish Pesetas.

The bank manager said that will be easy to do and called in his head teller to take care of that for Mr. Nations. The bank manager thanked Matt for doing business instead of going to a rival bank and said come back anytime you are back in this part of the continent

Matt and Sierra followed the head teller to her office, who took care of Matt and Sierra in her office. Fifteen minutes Matt and Sierra was now all done with the bank, so they left the bank checked into the best hotel in Madrid.

51 DINNER PARTY

Francisco started dating a beautiful girl from Monterey by the name of Susan who was one-quarter Korean who introduced Francisco to her parents. Her parents owned a fancy Korean restaurant in Monterey, and they invited the whole clan.

During the dinner one of Susan's uncle asked Francisco if he was interested in going in partners with him to start a Korean grocery store in San Luis de Colorado. Francisco was already thinking about investing in a real business instead of just keeping his money n C.D.'s. Francisco said I will be glad to join you in a business venture. They decided to meet the next week to discuss the details of the business.

Matt and Sierra removed all of the Bearer Bonds from the plastic box and re-berried the box and put the tree back where it was. They had Billy Bob fly them to Bogota and the put ten percent of the Bonds in a safety deposit box in Bogota. Matt had Captain Kato fly them back to Madrid and deposited ninety percent of the bonds into a safety deposit box in the Madrid Bank where they already had an account. They figured that it was the best place to store the bulk of the Bearer Bonds.

Both Matt and Sierra were multi-millionaires, but they didn't mind being a multi-billionaire as well. Their goal in life was to help enterprising young people get started in making their own mullions.

Francisco's house was still unoccupied, so they decided to go find out what was taking Francisco so long to get back to his house in Columbia.

When they got back to San Luis de Colorado, they found him running a Korean grocery store. Francisco said he was just helping out today but normally his partner was here to run the store because he wasn't too familiar with all the products.

Francisco said he was dating a beautiful part Korean girl who lives in Monterey and asked Matt and Sierra if they would like to meet her. Matt said sure we would be happy to meet her

A few days later Matt and Sierra took residence in one of the best hotels in Monterrey. Francisco invited his girlfriend to dinner at the Nuevo Concepcion Hotel to meet his friends. Both Matt and Sierra bought new clothes in Monterey and were waiting in the dining room of the hotel.

Francisco's friend Susan and a few other friends arrived in the restaurant and Susan introduced her friends to everyone. Most of them were Spanish looking except for one young girl who looked more Korean.

They all had interesting stories to tell as they had their dinner. During dinner an older man saw Susan and came to the table to say hello to Susan. Matt was curious to know who he was, so he invited him to join him. The man said that he was in the business of fishing for tuna and was doing fine.

The young Korean looking girl who went by the name of Saatchi said she was working in her uncle's grocery store selling groceries. Everyone had a story to tell and after the dinner was over Francisco noticed that Susan left the restaurant with older man who said that he was in the tuna business. Matt noticed that too and thought that it was unusual.

Francisco had a chance to talk to the Korean looking girl and asked her if she had ever been to San Luis. The girl said she heard a lot of good stories about the place and wouldn't mind getting chance to see the place. Francisco said I am part owner of a Korean grocery store in San Luis, and I can use more help.

Sachiko said my aunt from Japan arrived in Monterey to visit her and we are living together now in Monterey. Sachiko said I have a week of vacation time coming up so we will take a bus and come and visit you in San Luis soon.

Matt said don't bother with a bus because I have a large van and I can drive you there myself in my van. Matt asked Sachiko if she can leave tomorrow. Sachiko said I will let my boss know if she was sure that he will let her start to take her vacation right away.

Matt got Sachiko's phone number and her address and said I will be at your apartment tomorrow at eight in the morning.

52 JAPAN

Francisco showed Sachiko his Korean grocery store and her aunt who was with them looked all around the store and she asked why he didn't sell Japanese foods as well. Francisco said that he was just a business partner, and his partner was a Korean man that ordered all the merchandise for both stores.

Francisco said let's go find a place have some lunch now. The closest place was the fancy restaurant that had a lot of different foods on the menu. A waitress showed them to a table by a window and the place was not crowded because it was before lunch. Matt noticed that his friend Thomas who owned the restaurant was not in the restaurant and was the one to always came to greet him because Matt was the one who lent him the money to start the restaurant.

When the waitress came back Matt asked the waitress where Thomas was. The waitress said ever since his wife died, he became depressed and rarely showed up to the restaurant anymore.

The waitress brought them a menu, so they all

studied the menu. Sachiko's aunt who went by Kiyoko noticed that there as a tiny section of the menu that served a few Japanese dishes. Kiyoko decided to have the Sashimi dinner. Sierra notices it so she decided to have the same. Matt liked Sashimi also, so he ordered Sashimi as well.

The Sashimi order took some time because the Tuna was frozen and had to be thawed out carefully. Thomas came into the restaurant just to see how business was and noticed Matt sitting at a table, so he came by to say hello. Matt asked him to join him at the table and Matt introduced everyone to Thomas as his good friend.

Thomas called his waitress and had her bring some green tea. Thomas asked what he ordered, and Matt said we ordered Sashimi. Thomas said that the tuna was frozen so it may take a long time to get it thawed correctly. Thomas said I still owe you a lot of money from when I first bought this restaurant and you have never pressed me for the money. Matt said I never worried about you not being able to pay that debt and I am willing to just forget about it .

Thomas said I am all alone now since my wife died and was thinking about just retiring . Matt said why don't you do that, and I will buy your restaurant from you right now. Thomas said are you sure because he hasn't been keeping up with eh maintenance of the restaurant and it will take a fortune just to get it back up to what it was a year ago .

Matt said I can write you a check for a million dollars now and we can call it even. Thomas said that was too much money and you are just doing that just to help me out. Matt said I found an old Bearer Bond and it is worth more than a hundred billion dollars so don't worry about me with not having enough money to do anything that I want to do with money.

Thomas said I really do need a long vacation and If I ever get back on m my feet, I will pay you back. Matt said if you try, I will only donate the money to some charity and that will be the end of that.

Thomas said I never visited Japan and I hope to do that soon. Thomas said I also own a small house in the woods, and you can have that if you want because the place is isolated, and vandals may come in and ram sack the place if I leave the place too long. Matt said don't worry about you place because I will the guard the house using guard dogs to watch your place.

Matt said I have a jet so why don't I fly you to Ja[an tomorrow morning and you won't have to bothered with trying to fly on a commercial airplane. Thomas said that will be great and I will be ready to fly, and I will take a taxi to your private airport and meet you there.

Matt said I will alert my pilot to have the Jet ready to fly to Japan tomorrow morning then.

Sierra, Sachiko, Kiyoko heard that Matt was going to fly Thomas to Japan, so they said that they would like to join the flight to Ja[pan.

Next morning everyone going to Japan was gathered in the hanger waiting for Captain Kato to finish the final inspection of the jet. The stewardesses came to seat the passengers into the jet.

Ten minutes later the jet was now on its way to Japan.

53 IN JAPAN

The jet landed in Narita International, and Sierra gave everybody a hundred thousand dollars each for spending money. She bought a first class ticket for Thomas to fly to Okinawa and told him to go the Onsen and improve his health. She bought first class tickets for Kiyoko and Sachiko to go check on their family back in Shikoku.

She told everybody if they needed any help to call her and bought everybody a new cell phone that worked better in Japan. She programmed her own phone number in each of their cell phones and she already had their phone numbers programmed in her own cell phone.

Back in San Luis Matt already had a team of contractors rebuilding Thomas's restaurant. The first thing that Matt did was to buy the empty lot between the restaurant and the old Korean grocery store. While he was doing all the remodeling his business partner stopped by to tell Matt that he wanted to sell his stock on the old Korean store.

His partner said that he was now just going to

concentrate working in Monterrey because it was too difficult to try and keep up with two stores so far apart. Matt gave his partner a hundred thousand dollars and asked him if that was enough for the merchandises in the store. His partner was happy to get rid of the Koreans store in San Luis and said good luck with trying to run the store all by yourself. They shook hands and parted as friends.

Matt closed the Korean grocery store because he was planning to change its set up as well. The empty lot between the restaurant and the Korean store was cleaned up of all the junk on the ground and taken to the dump. Matt had the empty lot paved with Asphalt and it looked like a great parking lot.

The contractors finished changing the entrance to the restaurant from the street where there was no parking space and change it to the side of the restaurant where the new parking lot now was It was a much better arrangement for the customers because they no longer had to park on the street to come into the restaurant.

Every day more improvements were completed to the restaurant. A different construction company was hired to completely rebuild the old Korean store with sleeping quartered upstairs for its employees.

Sierra went to Okinawa and found Thomas enjoying the Onsen. He now had a new friend and was enjoying her company. Sierra asked him if he needed more money and he said I have more than I can spend in a couple of years as long as I don't buy anything too expensive. Sierra said I will be back to check on you in a week or more then and said goodbye.

She next flew to Shikoku to check on Kiyoko and her niece Sachiko. Sierra found them in an old farmhouse discussing what to do with the farm. They were just having dinner, so they invited Sierra to join them.

The farmhouse was big, so they gave her a place to sleep. Kiyoko had two brothers and a sister, and they were not making any money on the farm. Sierra said we have a large plot of land with fertile soil, so she invited all of them to come back with her to Mexico to look at the large farm. She said that her father had a jet, and I can have him fly you all to Mexico in two days and you can go explore a new land. This sounded exciting to all of them, and they said that they would like to go see the new land.

54 MODEL MAKING

The first night Matt put all of them in the new San Luis Hotel. They had a long flight so after a big meal they all went to bed in the hotel.

Next morning Matt drove them to Tomas's old house. They all looked around noticed how large the land was. One of the guards started a vegetable garden and the vegetables looked like they were growing fast.

Kiyoko's family from Shikoku brought some seeds with them one of her sisters said I want to plant these seeds and see how they take to this soil. Matt said I am remodeling an old restaurant and I would like to show you the place.

All of them got back in Matt's van and he drove to the construction site. The second construction was now done with the Korean restaurant and showed them the Korean store. They all walked into the store and looked around and noticed that there were no Japanese foods for sale. Kiyoko asked why this was so. Matt said the store used to be a Korean store and he hadn't had time to restock the shelves yet . Matt said there are several sleeping quarters upstairs so any of you wants to run this store and live upstairs and start to restock the shelves with Japanese merchandise.

Matt then took them across the parking lot and showed them what the contractors were working on in the restaurant. Kiyoko's oldest brother Ichigun used to work in a fancy restaurant in Tokyo and was very interested in the new construction. Ichigun asked Matt if he could make some suggestions to the contractors and Matt said off course and I want to make you the manager of the restaurant when it is completed. This was the best news that Ichigun heard since he was young working in a fancy Tokyo restaurant as a dishwasher.

That night they all went above the Korean grocery store and slept there. Next morning Ichigun was the first to get up and had a small breakfast and he was looking in the restaurant and already thinking about making some suggestions. Matt hired an interpreter for Ichigun to help him with the language. The interpreter was a young college student from Monterey and was happy to get the job who went by Francesca. Ichigun and Francesca sat at an empty table and Ichigun started to tell her what he wanted. Francesca took notes and listened carefully.

When the contractors came to report to work that Friday morning Matt told them o take a break because we are going to make some changes to the interior of the restaurant and to report back here on Monday morning. The contractors were working long hours for a long time and could use a little break, so they were happy to take a break.

Matt took Ichigun to a model making shop and they bought a lot of light balsa wood to make a three-dimensional model of what they wanted for the interior of the restaurant. The clerk also showed them some miniature people made out of plastic they can be bent like gum balls.

When they got home, Matt told Ichigun to make a model of what he thought the interior of the restaurant should look like. He spent all day Friday making models of the interior of the restaurant. Saturday morning at about ten in the morning a high school boy noticed the new restaurant and was looking for a job doing anything just to pick up a few bucks on a part time basis. He saw Ichigun making a model and told him that you are doing that all wrong. Off course there as a language problem but Ichigun was just trying to make a model of the interior of the restaurant, and they were already in the restaurant.

The boy spoke primarily Spanish and was studying English in Hight school. Ichigun spoke primarily Japanese and also took English in high school himself. By doing a lot of pointing and a lot of charade type movements Ichigun was able to actually communicate with the boy. By noon Ichigun was hungry so he took the boy out to lunch and they had tamales. The boy actually had a lot of good ideas like building the model in modular form so that you can rearrange the model easily.

At three p.m. Ichigun was tired so he told the boy that he was going to quit for the day and come back tomorrow morning and we can continue the model making job in poor English as best he can. As he left, he told the boy who went by Jose to close the door so that animals won't come in and make a mess.

55 A NEW JOB

Matt came into the new restaurant to see if anyone was thcrc yct. Hc saw thc young boy slccping by thc model. Matt woke him up and asked him what he was doing sleeping in the restaurant and the boy said that he was working with Ichigun making this model and pointed to the model.

The boy looked like he stayed all night working on the model and was probably hungry so he said I will take you to get some breakfast somewhere and they both left in Matt's van.

Ten minutes later they were sitting in the truck stop across the street and there were a lot of truckers having breakfast. Matt was ready for a good breakfast, so he ordered sausage and eggs with hash browns and a glass of orange juice. The boy ordered the same. While they were waiting for their order Matt had a chance to talk to the boy and he found out that he didn't have a father and his mother was working nights cleaning up offices just to make a living for herself and her son.

The boy said that he was in high school taking

Japanese and that was the reason that he was able to talk to Ichigun and they worked together making the model. The boy's name was Jose and told Matt that he talked Ichigun into making model in a modular fashion so they can change the model easily. Matt could tell that the boy was a smart and said what do you do after school. He said that he helps his mother clean up offices at night during the week, but he was free on weekends so that was the reason that he was able to work with Ichigun.

Matt knew that cleaning offices didn't pay too much so he asked the boy what she really liked to do best. The boy said that she liked to cook and liked working in a grocery store because she wouldn't have to work late at night and sleep during the day in her brother's house with all the small kids and she never got any good sleep.

Matt said it looks like you need a better place to live, and I have several little cabins close by and you and your mother can stay there for free until you decide to go somewhere else.

The boy couldn't believe what he was hearing and thought that Matt was just joking. Just then their breakfast arrived and they both started to eat. The boy noticed that the truckers left nice tips for the young waitresses and he wondered if he could also work in the trucker's diner.

An hour later Matt and the boy finished breakfast. Matt left a hundred-dollar bill for the waitress as a tip and the boy couldn't believe his eyes. Matt went to the cash register and paid his bill and they got back into Matt's van.

Ten minutes later Matt was showing the boy several empty cabins and they were fully furnished with nice furniture. Matt told the boy to take his choice of which cabin he wanted for himself. The boy asked Matt it he could get his mother to come with him and she can decide on which cabin to choose. Matt said of course we can go do that right now.

The boy directed Matt to a slum like area of San Luis and they parked on the street where there was garbage in the yard and a dog was eating the garbage. They walked into the living room and found the boy's mother changing diapers on a crying baby. The boy's mother was a young lady, but she had dark rings around her eyes from lack of sleep.

Matt asked where his bedroom was, and he said we sleep in the living room because it is the best room in the house. Just then a man walked into the living room and told the boy's mother that he will take the baby up to his room so you can get some sleep before you have to report to work tonight. The mother said thank you for rescuing me and tried to sleep on the couch.

Matt knew that the mother could never get any good sleep in a madhouse like this and suggested that they all get in Matt's van and leave right away.

When Matt got back to his old compound where very few people lived there anymore the boy's mother was sound asleep in the back seat. The mother looked so comfortable that Matt didn't want to disturb her at this time. He got on his cell phone and called the guard house to come to the compound to help him with some people that needed some help. He couldn't call Sierra because she was still in Columbia in the Castle.

The guard came in uniform and they helped the mother get out of the van and they took her to one of the cabins and put her to bed. The cabin had two bedrooms and showed the boy where he can sleep. Matt said I have some things to tend to now, but I will be back before too long and left in his van. He asked the guard to stay in the cabin because the lady may be confused when she got up and you can explain how she ended up here.

The guard was happy to be of service to the big boss and gave him a salute.

Matt drove back the restaurant and found Ichigun looking at the model. Ichigun saw Matt and told Matt that the boy was a smart boy and did a great job of finishing the model. Matt said I met the boy this morning and he was sleeping here so I took him to breakfast, and he looks like a nice boy.

Matt asked how everybody else in the Korean grocery was doing and Ichigun said that Kiyoko found some old movies upstairs and we all watched them until two in the morning. Matt said they must be pretty tired then. Matt said the contractors will be back tomorrow morning so you can tell them what to do. Ichigun said that they all speak Spanish so it would helpful if you could get the boy to talk to them.

Matt said I will ask him if he can skip school tomorrow then. Matt was sure that with the three-dimensional model Ichigun could handle the job all by himself. Matt walked to the Korean store, but the place looked quiet, so he drove back to his old compound and went to the restaurant that Sarge was still running. At the restaurant Sarge came out to talk to Matt and said maybe we should close the restaurant up for a while because no one comes here anymore.

The boy's mother woke up from her sleep and she thought that she died and went to heaven. The bed that she was sleeping in certainly looked like heaven. There was a bathroom next to the bedroom, so she took a long hot bath and almost went back to sleep in the tub.

When she got out of the bath, she dried herself with a clean white towel and found a white bathrobe, so she put that on and walked to a closet and found some clean clothes that fit her perfectly . She picked one out and put it on . In the bedroom there was dresser with a mirror and found some makeup, so she put some on even if she no longer used any make up lately.

In the dump that she lived in until today. She looked in the mirror and realized that she really didn't look like an old woman anymore. She walked down to the living room and found the guard reading a magazine.

The guard saw her, and said you're up. The boy's mother asked where she was now. The guard said that you fell asleep in Matt's van, so we brought you in the cabin and put you in bed. The boy's mother said that she had the best rest that she had in a year and I felt much better now.

Matt walked into the cabin and saw the boy's mother and asked her if she wanted a new job. She was now all rested up, so said I will like to go interview for a new job. Matt took her across the street and brought her into Sarge's restaurant and they sat down.

Sarge said you must be the new hire to help me while I will be away for a while. Sarge showed the lady to the kitchen and said we don't have too many customers at this time, so working here in the kitchen should be easy. He showed her where everything was and said after a day or two, I will leave the place all to yourself.

The boy's mother said you don't have to wait a day; you can leave right now because I know a lot about kitchens, and I can take it from here.

Sarge said are you sure that you don't want me to stick around at least for a day in case you need anything. The boy's mother said whatever you want. Then she asked Sarge if he wanted to have something to eat. Sarge was curious to see what she can cook so he said sure, have at it and I will be in the dining room talking to Matt while you make me something .

The lady found some Masa Harina and made something that looked like biscuits, then she made some fresh salsa, she now had enough to bring to Sarge. She found a cart on wheels, so she put the biscuits and the salsa on the cart and brought it to Sarge and said try this for now.

Sarge was surprised how fast the lady prepared the meal. He put salsa on the hot biscuits and ate the biscuits. After only one bite he told the lady that this was a great breakfast and complimented her on how fast she was able to make the meal. He then asked her if there was more biscuits and salsa left. The lady said if you like it, I will bring the whole bowl of salsa and the hot biscuits and be right back.

Matt could smell the hot biscuits and the salsa, so he dug in as well and ate some. Matt said this is really great salsa and asked Sarge if she passed the test. Sarge said she certainly made the grade, and I may stay here one more day to see what else she is capable of creating.

56 OLD MAN

Kiyoko's older brother told everybody that he was going back to Shikoku to either sell the old farm or rent it out to someone that wanted to use the place. Francisco heard him say that and said I will go with you because I never have been to Shikoku.

Francisco called Matt and told him that he wanted to fly to Shikoku with Kiyoko's older brother who had some business to take care of there. Matt said come to the hanger and I will have Captain Kato fly you there.

Ten hours later Francisco and Kiyoko's brother Tetsuo landed in Narita International waiting for a jet to fly to Shikoku. Francisco booked first class tickets to Shikoku and now they were just waiting to board a plane.

The flight to Shikoku took only one hour. The plane landed in Matsuyama airport and Francisco rented a car to drive to Tetsuo's farm. When they got to Tetsuo's farm no one was there to greet him. Francisco thought that the farm looked deserted. Just then a young man came out of the farmhouse and recognized Tetsuo and bowed to him and asked him to come into the farmhouse. The young man's wife prepared some vegetables and white rice and they had dinner.

Tetsuo asked the young man how he was doing, and he said we are doing as good as we can but without better farm equipment, we can only produce a small amount of produce. Francisco could understand most of what they were talking about because he studied Japanese in high school.

Francisco asked in poor Japanese what was the sign next door written in Japanese. The young man said that the man that owned the land was old, and he didn't want to do all the back breaking job of growing vegetables anymore. Francisco was thinking about approaching the old man to find out more about his farm when he got a chance.

Next morning Tetsuo and Francisco got up and the young man's wife made them some Miso Shiru which wasn't that bad. Francisco wanted to help the young couple, so he asked where the closest farm equipment store was. The young man who went by Sango said its downtown about three miles from here . Francisco said let's all go there and see if they have anything on sale today.

After breakfast they all piled into Francisco's rental car drove downtown. At the farm equipment store there was snotty looking kid who might have been the boss's son came out and said what are you looking for today. Francisco said we are looking for some good farming equipment. The kid directed them the most expensive tractor that they had. Francisco looked at the price tag and decided that they were charging too much. Francisco didn't like the kid so he said go fly a kite in English and kid couldn't understand English and looked confused.

Francisco wanted to get out of the place, so he said let's have lunch now and he took them to a fancy restaurant, and they had lunch.

After the experience with the kid, Francisco wasn't interested in looking for more farm equipment anymore so he drove everybody back to the farmhouse and told them that he was going to visit the old man with the sign.

When he drove up to the house a housekeeper came to the door and asked Francisco what he wanted. Francisco said I came to see about the sign. The maid said follow me to the solarium and Francisco followed her.

The solarium was a beautiful place with all types of tropical plants and the temperature in the solarium was at least ninety degrees. Francisco removed his coat and looked around for a place to sit down. The old man pointed to a folding chair, so Francisco got it and sat in front of the old man.

The old man said you don't look Japanese. Francisco looked at the old man and introduced himself. Now they had something to talk about. Francisco asked what was with the sign outside by the road. The old man said that was mistake and he was going to take it down. Francisco wanted to ask he old man how old he was but that would be impolite.

Francisco said we went to town to buy some farm equipment but he didn't like the snotty looking kid so I decided not to do business with him/ The old man said I know his father and he didn't raise the kid up right and he will have a lot of trouble with the kid the rest of his life.

The old man was actually glad to see a foreigner and liked Francisco. The old man asked Francisco if he knew how to play Shogi. Francisco said isn't that something like chess and he said I was the chess champion in my high school in Monterey Mexico. The old man said why don't you visit me soon and we can play some Chess or Shogi. The old man said and the next time I will a have a better chair for you to sit in and a cotton bathrobe and you can think of the solarium as a sauna.

Francisco said thanks and said I may do that soon. The old man said thanks for dropping in and come again. Francisco asked the old man what he can bring him. The old man said I don't need anything right now. Francisco said goodbye to him in Spanish and the old man said something in Portuguese.

Francisco actually liked the old man and planned to comc to scc him again.

57 JUNK EQUIPMENT

The second in command lieutenant of the Castle guards approached Sierra and asked if anyone was using Francisco's old place. Sierra said Francisco has a couple of guard dogs there and a guard handler takes care of the dogs once a day to feed them and give them some food. Lieutenant Domingo said in other words the place is not being lived in. Sierra said that was correct. Domingo said I can pay Francisco some rent if I can be allowed to just live there and commute to work on a daily basis.

Sierra said you don't have to pay rent just make sure that the dogs are well taken care of and the dog handlers will be happy to know that you are also there to watch the dogs. Domingo said thank you to Sierra and left. Sierra was thinking about taking the dogs out more often and she can get some exercise at the same time.

Back in Shikoku Francisco told Gunzo that he was returning to the farm equipment store again and try again even if he didn't like the snotty kid that waited on us the last time and told Gunzo to come with him.

At the Farm Equipment store the kid was not there

so Francisco and Gunzo walked into the display room where all the newest equipment was being displayed. No one came to the display room so Francisco and Gunzo walked into the shop and talked to one of the mechanics and told him if they can buy some used equipment. The mechanics name was Makunouchi and said I can help you in that case and walked them to the back lot where there was a lot of junk equipment. Makunouchi said around here I just go by Meccano because it was shorter so just ask for me by that name whenever you come here again in the future.

Makana said I am in charge of cleaning up the back lot in exchange for my work I was given permission to sell anything in the back lot because it will save money at the dump where we have to pay by weight when we take our junk there.

Makana showed Francisco the first lot where the mechanic was still working on old equipment on weekends during his time oof. Then he pointed to a small lot where he said we will eventually have to shell out some money to get rid of that pile.

Francisco and Gunzo was getting a good tutorial on how the used equipment was being run. Francisco asked Meccano if he had anything that actually ran right now. Mekano showed them a two-ton dump truck and said I can let you have this one for a hundred dollars and the trailer comes with it. Next, he showed them a beat-up diesel truck with manual transmission and said you can have this truck for two hundred dollars.

Francisco asked Mekano how I should pay for the junk equipment then. Mekano said I only deal in cash because I am not part of the main company that sells the new equipment. Francisco took his wallet out and gave him five one-hundred-dollar bills and said if you can deliver what I bought today the two hundred is yours.

Mekano realized that his was even easier than fixing old equipment so he said it's a deal and said give me a minute and I will follow you now.

Half an hour later Mekano was at the old farmhouse and asked where Francisco wanted the everything parked. There was a flat spot behind the farmhouse, so Francisco said just park it there.

Francisco drove Mekano back to the Farm Equipment company and Mekano got out of the rental car. The big boss saw Mekano and said you did a good job of getting some of the old equipment out of the lot and gave Mekano a ten-dollar bill and told him to take the rest of the day off. Mekano said thanks to the big boss that rarely came to this store.

After that show, Francisco said how would you like to have lunch with me now that you have the rest of the day off and I may have a proposition for you.

Mekano could use a good lunch because he skipped breakfast and said sure I am ready to have lunch with you now. They found an Udon shop where it was quiet and Francisco told Mekano of all the possibilities that were an available to him in getting rid of all the used equipment quickly.

After lunch Francisco brought Mekano back to the Farm Equipment Company and told hm to come and see me in my farmhouse and I may have a surprise for you then.

58 SHOGI

Jose, the boy that made the model for the restaurant finished high school and Matt hired him full time as a do it all to fill in wherever he was needed. He used the red truck that was left at the cabin to run all the errands.

His mother who now ran Sarges restaurant was doing such a great job that Sarge decided to go to Columbia and help Sierra run the castle. Sierra was becoming more athletic and was model of good health.

On one of her outings with her dogs, the dogs found a small wooden trunk filled with ancient Mayan artifacts. She already had similar artifacts stored under the motorhome so she called Francisco in Shikoku if he could use some of the artifacts. Francisco said I'm having fun in Shikoku helping a young couple trying to run a farm.

Sierra said I will fly down to Shikoku to check my friends in Mikame then I will come and visit you as well. Sarge took over the running of the Castle while Sierra went on her trip to Shikoku and enjoyed being treated like royally. He also visited the guard complex and noticed that they were doing great job. Sarge wanted to know more about the specially trained dogs that did the perimeter guard business and got involved in that.

Sierra brought one of her guards from the Castle to help her carry and guard the small trunk all the time as they traveled by jet. When she got to Mikame she was surprised that Isabella now had eleven children and the oldest boy was now a captain of the second tuna fishing boar. Shintaro, Isabella's husband no longer had to go out to sea as often because his son did most of the fishing in a newer boat. Sierra still had her bedroom upstairs, but the house was getting a little crowded with so many kids in the house. She went the Shikoku First National Bank that had a branch office in Mikame and rented the biggest safety deposit box that they had, and she put ninety percent of the ancient artifacts in the safety deposit box. She had to rent a second box because the small trunk held more than the first box could hold. She put about three percent of the original contents of the ancient box back into the trunk. And had her personal guard carry that for her.

After three days she told Isabella and Shintaro that she wanted to go to Matsuyama and visit Francisco. The cook made some Sashimi that night from unfrozen tuna and Sierra enjoyed the Sashimi.

The next morning Shintaro drove Sierra and her guard to Yawatahama, and she took a train to Matsuyama where Francisco was staying for now.

Sierra liked the young couple who ran the farm and she stayed with them in the farmhouse for three days. she removed a gold bracelet from the trunk and gave it the Shingun's wife as a present.

Francisco told Sierra about the old man that liked

to stay in a hot solarium and asked Sierra if she wanted to go visit him someday. Sierra said why don't we do it today then. Francisco told Sierra how hot the solarium was so Francisco took Sierra to town to buy some light cotton clothes.

When Francisco brought Sierra to visit the old man, the old man ordered cold lemonade for all of them. Sierra noticed that the old man had a Shogi set on the next table and asked the old man if he liked to play Shogi. The old man said that he attained the rank of San Dan when he was younger, but he couldn't find anyone to play the game with anymore so was probably getting a bit rusty at playing the game.

Sierra said I have time right now, so she suggested that they play the game now. The old man who went by Constantine called his maid to come into the solarium and make space for Sierra so she can be comfortable playing Shogi with him.

After Sierra was comfortable Constantine asked Sierra if she was ready to start. Sierra said now is a good a time as any and she was starting to sweat from the heat. The old man you can start first which gave Sierra a slight edge. Sierra made her first pawn move and Constantine remembered that it was a standard first move. Five minutes later they took a break and Constantine complimented Sierra on how good a player she was. The maid brought more cold lemonade and they had more lemonade.

Constantine asked Sierra if she was ready to start playing again and it was Sierra's turn. Five minutes later it was checkmate and Sierra said she had fun playing the game even if she lost the game. By this time her cotton dress was soaking wet, and she said thanks for playing the game and she said I will be back tomorrow to play again then she left.

59 MATT

Makunouchi showed up to the farm and he had a large cultivator with him and asked Francisco if he wanted to buy it. Francisco asked Makunouchi if he could demonstrate how the cultivator works, Makunouchi drove the cultivator to the back of the farm and plowed a small strip of bare ground with no problem. Francisco asked how much and Makunouchi said a hundred dollars. Francisco said you should charge more.

Makunouchi said it would have cost us two hundred if we brought it to the city dump because it was so large, and I could have just given it to you for free and I would still be ahead. Francisco said how would you like to work for me a few days a week and I will match what you make as a mechanic working for a whole week. Makunouchi said let me finish cleaning up the back lot first because the big boss is really anxious to get the lot cleared up as soon as possible.

Francisco said O.K. And I will find a better place to put all the junk equipment.

Sierra went back to play Shogi again with Constantine and she brought an ancient gold coin with her to give to Constantine. Francisco and Sierra found Constantine as usual in the solarium, so she handed him the gold coin and said this a present for you for my losing the shogi game yesterday. Constantine took the gold coin and a said this should be in a museum. Sierra said I will go back to Columbia find more and bring more back to you from the Castle. After Constantine heard the word Castle he became very interested to know more about the Castle in Columbia. Francisco said I have access to a jet, and I can fly you there and you can see the castle for yourself one of these days when you feel like you want to travel. This planted a seed in Constantine's mind, and he was thinking about going to see the castle.

Francisco said what I really want to talk to you today was to ask you if can rent some land behind the trees so I can store some farming machinery there. Constantine said you don't have to rent it I have not used that land for so long so why don't use you as much of that land as you want you don't have to pay me a penny for using the land.

I will be happy if someone can make use of it. Francisco said I will buy some guard dogs to watch the place, so we won't have to worry about kids coming around and messing with the equipment. Constantine said I like big dogs so buy me one also. Francisco said I will do that.

Francisco knew that there was a lot of stuff stored in the back lot of the Farm Equipment Company and it will take Makunouchi forever to get all of it out of there, so he hired a moving company that specialized in moving heavy equipment had them remove everything from the

Farm Equipment Company and bring it to the Farm.

The company had huge flatbeds and they managed to move everything in just one weekend. When the big boss came to inspect the store on Monday morning, he was surprised to see how fast Makunouchi got the job done. He promised to give him a big raise soon.

Matt showed up in Shikoku to check on Francisco and they had a long talk about what to do with the old farmhouse. Francisco said I want you to meet an interesting old man that lives next door to me, and he stays in a solarium.

The next day Francisco brought Matt to visit the old man. Sierra was already there playing Shogi with the old man. The old man saw Francisco and he invited them to sit at the next table and he will order some lemonade for them while he finished playing shogi with Sierra. It didn't long before Constantine, the old man finished checkmating Sierra. Sierra was getting better and knew that she will beat the old man in his own game soon

Matt said I understand that you are interested in seeing the Castle in Columbia and I have jet that can fly you there in nine hours. This sounded like a great adventure to Constantine, and he never even left Shikoku ever before and he was getting older so when Matt offered to fly him to Columbia in only nine hours, he said I will love to have the chance to see the Castle in Columbia.

60 CHANGES

The living room in the Castle was converted into a special living place for Constantine and he loved all the attention that he was given. He especially liked the special foods that the cooks prepared for him every evening. Sierra gave him two loving Akita dogs to stay with Constantine all the time as his guard dogs. The Akitas even slept with Constantine in a huge bed to keep him warm at night. The dogs loved sleeping with Constantine, and he loved the dogs sleeping with him at night because the dogs kept him warm.

He started to sleep better than he ever did before and his health got better as well. It could have been the different diet that he started to eat made by the Columbian cooks in the Castle or maybe it was the Ume fruit Sierra gave him from time to time. The increased physical exercise that he got walking with his dogs improved his blood circulation and he no longer felt cold anymore. He could even work up a sweat from a short jogging that he did early in the morning before breakfast with the dogs.

Sarge returned to San Luis on the same plane that brought Constantine to Columbia from Japan.

Jose finished his first year of college and could now speak better Japanese. He sometimes worked in the kitchen if they got too busy and he learned to be a good cook.

The restaurant was renamed Tokyo Inn and the name caught on quickly. Even people from Yuma heard about the Tokyo Inn and started to frequent the restaurant more. Before long there was waiting list for reservations just to get into the restaurant. The restaurant was officially only open from Five in the evening to Ten in the evening, but in the afternoon, they opened the side room for local people to come in and have a simple lunch. None of the fancy Japanese foods were served during the afternoon hours but only the simple dinners that were easy to prepare so that the customers could come in and see the beautiful Restaurant.

Jose's mother expanded her menu in Sarge's old restaurant, and she hired more cooks and waitresses.

The guards were the ones that frequented Sarge's restaurant the most and sometimes they brought their girlfriends with them.

Sierra noticed how Constantine's health was improving so she started to eat more Ume fruit and started to go jogging with him in the mornings. She didn't lose too much weight but became more muscular and she had to buy different clothes.

The girl that was working on her post doctorate degree in anthropology finished her thesis and it was published. She spent more time with the lieutenant that rented Francisco's house and they were even talking about getting married. Clementine's house in Shikoku was now empty. Francisco called Constantine and asked him what he wanted to do with his old house. He emailed back that as far as he was concerned, he may never come back there ever again. Francisco emailed back that the house needed some repairers so he asked Constantine if he can fix it up and live there. Constantine said you can have the place and that he was thinking about permanently leasing the Castle for his personal use from now on. Francisco said talk to Matt, and he may even sell it to you if you have enough money to buy the place.

Makunouchi was promoted to be a full-time heavy equipment salesman. Salesmen work only on commission so they can either show up for work or depending how they felt. The Showed up for work whenever the other salesmen didn't show up. He spent a lot of time at Francisco's farm repainting old equipment. When customer showed up that didn't have enough money to buy a brand-new piece of equipment, he referred them to Francisco's farm where there were a lot of rebuilt equipment. He made more money selling the equipment that he fixed than he made selling brand new equipment that only large companies could afford to buy. He was trying to figure out how to disengage himself from selling new equipment altogether.

Gunzo's wife's sister finished high school and came to the farm to work with her sister. She was a young girl and had a lot of energy so was a great help to her sister.

Francisco completely rebuilt Clementine's old house and it started to look more like a normal house. He still kept the solarium but decreased the temperature from ninety degrees to seventy degrees and planted things that were more favorable to a lower temperature. Francisco liked the solarium, so he started to sleep in it most of the time in warmer weather.

He hired housekeepers and a cook to take care of the new house. He hired carpenters to rebuild the old farmhouse to make it more efficient for the young couple and the new sister.

61 NEW YEAR'S EVE

Sierra decided to return to San Luis to visit because she heard of all the changes there. She told Constantine if he ever got tired of the Castle to come and visit her in San Luis.

Francisco married Sachiko, who was the Gunzo's wife's younger sister and took residence in Constantin's old house where he had several maids and a cook.

Jose got his degree in Japanese and was made the manager for the day shift of Tokyo Inn.

Sarge decided to retire and turned over his restaurant to Jose's mother and now she was the boss of the entire restaurant.

Matt and Sierra were back living in their old motorhome where they found it always comfortable. They always had their breakfast in the motorhome and sometimes even had lunch there. They were on a health kick and they always went jogging before breakfast.

Mandy had a stroke and went to the hospital. Ruth made the foreman of the Mandy's business the new boss and he was doing a good job of running the business.

Matt suggested that they should go visit his youngest daughter in Long Island. When they got there, they were surprised that both Howard Johnson Senior and his wife had passed away and they sold the family business. All their kids were grown, and they had their own careers. Their oldest son Howard Johnson the third became a banker in Manhattan and was promoted to assistant manager of Chase Manhattan bank which was huge responsibility. The CEO of Chase Manhattan Bank lived in Connecticut and invited all his bank managers for a grand party in Connecticut every New Year's Eve and it was always a grand event.

Matt found a good hotel in New Haven and they went there a few days earlier to see the town of New Haven where Yale University was located. Harvard University was also not that far.

At the party there were several young people there, but Sierra stood out from the rest of the debutantes because she was not a spoiled girl like the rest of the debutants. The CEO's son immediately noticed Sierra started to talk. The CEO's son's name was Christopher Grey, and he immediately took a liking to Sierra because she was not a debutant.

Sierra was not dressed all fancies up like the other young girls who were dressed to kill. Sierra was only dressed in a modest light-colored dress. While they were talking in one corner of the dance floor, one of the debutants saw Christopher and came over to him and demanded that he dance with her. Chris knew the girl, so he had no choice but to relent and be polite to the beautiful girl. As they were dancing another Debutante cur in one her and demanded a dance with Christopher. Chris was sort of a bookworm and had a degree in

Japanese and really didn't like the spoiled Debutants that he grew up with.

When he finally got away from the mob of beautiful Debutantes Sierra was not where he left her. Chris continued to look all oven the crowded dance hall and finally found Sierra talking to the Dean of far Eastern Studies and they seemed to be having a serious conversation.

Sierra felt like she didn't really fit in with these a very rich people so she told her dad that we should leave. They were able to sneak away without anyone noticing them mainly because they were not important people.

Matt called a taxi and went back to their hotel sat in the lobby near a fireplace where it was quiet. But now it was getting close to midnight and the revelers would soon be back mostly drunk, so they decided to retire early.

He found the Dean and asked where Sierra was. The dean said he didn't know but he said that Sierra was the most intelligent young girl that he ever met and was trying to offer a position in his department of Far Eastern studies and make her an assistant professor and he almost had her convinced to join the Yale Faculty.

62 ENGAGEMENT PARTY

Savana's mom took an extended vacation from the Onsen in Okinawa and flew to Long island to be with Savana who now had seven children but all of them were now grown up except for the two younger ones that were still in high school. She spent a couple of months with Savana and got to know her more.

Sierra started teaching at Yale University as an assistant professor of Far Eastern Studies. She didn't want to teach basic Japanese because that was such an intensive job and there were many great professors already at Yale who were doing a great job of doing that. She wanted to start a brand-new series of classes that didn't take a lot of scholarly expertise.

She met with the board of regents and proposed a class that would be suited for many of the ladies that already had degrees from Universities that could take a class that didn't require a lot of time studying. She already put a lot of thought for the class and for the entire program that she had in mind and presented to the board.

No other University ever heard of any class or

program like this program. New Haven was full of educated fine ladies that had already raised their families and was in need of something new. This program will have very little homework for its members and all that they had to do was to participate in class to discuss the basic culture of the various countries that they will study. Sierra suggested that they start with Japan because it had such a rich history of ancient Japan.

During spring break the students will take a vacation to Japan and stay in the best inns in Japan and visit many of the most famous places in Japan. The board relented and agreed to allow Sierra to try the program on a trial basis. The first class started in the spring semester and it filled up quickly. The University realized the great opportunity to increase its student body with wealthy older students who will become new alumni and they will be a great source of leaving their fortunes to the University.

One board member suggested using the auditorium to hold the classes, but Sierra said she wanted to have more one-on-one contact the with students, so they decided to allow a three-semester hour class with a limit of twenty-five students. The class required no prerequisite, so anyone was allowed to sign up.

The first class filled up quickly mostly by middle aged wealthy women. The class had no actual homework assignments was mainly on a voluntary basis to do research on their own to look up more information of the places that Sierra listed in her class prospectus.

This year during the spring break they will visit the Northern part of Japan first. Anyone who had time was allowed to present a paper after her research and present it to the class. In this way all the class members will know who was doing most of the work. Not everyone was required to present a paper, but it was only on a voluntary basis and who had best research paper would be known by the other class members and have their respect as a result.

On Fridays one person was allowed to present her paper. As the presentations progressed more papers were presented. Each student was given the chance to grade the presentation based on the presentation and they gave a grade on each presenter and gave it to Sierra. By the end of the semester everyone knew who did the best work and therefore was known who was best student.

At the end of the semester there was a party in a fancy hotel, and anyone was allowed to attend. The wealthy students took a collection to reward the top students with a cash award and also a gift from any member of the class.

Some older ladies donated fine jewelry that they that they no longer wanted and had it wrapped up as a fancy gift. There was a first, Second and a third award for each member selected by the students themselves. No cost was spared for this party and the ladies could bring their spouses to attend the party as well.

The newspapers were invited to attend the party and television crews were also invited. Anyone could become an instant celebrity if they were chosen by the students to be the best student.

During the summer there was an extended trip to Japan, and anyone can join the trip as long as there was space left for the trip.

The class became the most popular class in all of Yales classes.

That summer the CEO's only child proposed to

Sierra and they got engaged. Chris's mother took the opportunity to hold a mid-summer party for her son's engagement party and it was held outdoors because she invited all of her sorority friends.

There was a great estate that came up for sale and Matt bought the estate. The estate had over a million acres with a lake and several bungalows and a grand house that needed some repairs. There was a beautiful lawn area near the lake, so Matt had it landscaped and put-up white tents I case it rained. Matt told Chris's mother that she can take charge of the engagement party and she planned to invite all of her friends and then some.

Chris's mother selected Mid July for the outdoor engagement party because July was the dry season in Connecticut.

Matt hired food caterers to provide all the food for the party and there were more than ten of them with their own food stands. There were newspaper teams to covet the event and several television companies to cover the event for the evening news. The party started at noon, so a lot of people came early to claim a spot. There were several sailboats in the lake so anyone who wanted to try using a sailboat could do that . No motorboats were allowed because they would be noisy and be a distraction. Several live bands were hired by Matt and they took turns on the bandstand to perform throughout the entire afternoon. There were also several well-known opera singers to perform for the party.

The entire afternoon was a series of great performances. There was a temporary dance floor near the band stand so young people could dance on the temporary wooden floor. At three o'clock Sierra and

Chris got on stage and made their appearance and then they walked down to the wooden dance floor and did a waltz.

Other young people joined them . By six in the evening most of the older people started to leave the party. There was no hard liquor served at the party but only soft drinks and fancy non-alcoholic cocktail s for the kids.

By nine the band went home, and more people left the party

That evening the television was full of scenes from the party with many ladies dressed in their Sunday best. News commentators got on the television to describe how the party went and all the different food stands were shown in detail and it was great advertising for the different food venders.

By ten in the evening all the tents were removed, and the grandstand was dismantled and hauled away. Clean-up crews came in to clean up the entire area and by morning the place looked normal except for the grassy arca that looked a little worn.

63 THE WEDDING

After the summer engagement party just about everybody in Connecticut knew that Chris was now engaged so the debutants started leave him alone except for those that might have plans to take him away from Sierra because there was still a whole year to do that before they will finally get married.

The million acre estate that Matt bought was a beautiful place but Matt new that the mansion itself needed a lot of work. He hired Carpenters, Masons, and the best Architects to completely rebuild the mansion and make it a sparkling place in only one year.

He knew that Sierra had a lot of friends that will want to attend the wedding next summer, so he selected a wooded area behind the mansion where he planned to build a lot of cabins for his guests from San Luis and other places all around the world. He built deep outhouses in the compound where his guests can use it for more than a week before the wedding actually came about. He built a Tori Mon near the lake before the long wooden pier so some people can come to the wedding by boat. The lake was connected to the Atlantic Ocean by means of lakes and deep natural channels where even a moderately large boat can come into the lake with no trouble.

He planned to have a beautiful stage in front of the lake to hold the wedding. He had everything planned to the last detail for the wedding that was still more than three months from now.

At Yale University, Sierra had three different classes each week to teach the same Japanese cultural class that was so popular during the spring semester and most of them were already filled up before the fall semester even got started. This class was a huge success for the University because it will eventually bring in a lot of donations for the University when the wealthy older people make their wills.

Sierra didn't plan to teach all three of the fall classes all by herself, but she had the University hire two more highly qualified assistant professors to help her with the Far Eastern Cultural classes.

Christopher spent more time in the bank helping his father so that he will be ready to take over the duties at the bank m as the CEO when his father decides to retire.

Chris's father held his year-end New Year's Eve party as usual at the Ritz New Yorker where he was a member of the board of directors for the hotel. Chris's mother started to make a guest list for her son's wedding nine months before the wedding and mailed them out to her favorite friends so that they can start to make reservations at the best hotels in New Haven.

Matt hired wedding planners to start to plan for the wedding six months before the wedding and told them not to worry about the coast because he already put a deposit of fifty million dollars for the wedding. The wedding planners had a lot of time and they were happy for the large retainer.

Matt had his own list of guests for the wedding, and they started to prepare for the wedding as well.

Sierra finished the spring semester with flying colors and the three different groups planned to meet in Japan for the expensive cultural tour. Only the well to do students could afford go on this tour unless one of the younger students had a rich relative that could foot the bill for them. Even some of the Debutantes that took the classes made it on the tour.

Many alumni made pledges to the University that they will include the University in their final wills.

By June most of the best hotels were fully booked for the forthcoming wedding to be held in July.

Two weeks before the wedding Samuel Grey the Bank CEO's best buddy from Harvard University who was also his roommate back then arrived in a fancy yacht and parked the yacht in the lake near the pier. Every night he had his own party long before people were ready to start to attend the wedding.

A few days later several more yachts appeared on the lake and it started to look like an armada of fine yachts and boats there were even a few fancy house boats on the lake as well. Matt had ordered a large amount of lake trout to be put in the lake so the guest can do some trout fishing on the lake.

There were parties every night on the yachts and you could hear music coming across the lake. By the end of the first week most of the guests on the lake became old friends now. Sierra was frequently invited to these parties, but she never indulged in drinking any of the fine wines because she never drank any alcoholic beverages.

The bank CEO took a week off from working at the bank and started to attend some of the parties on the lake. He spent a lot of time with his college roommate Samuel Grey on his yacht gave him some advice like retiring while he was still young and enjoy life more.

The bank manager's wife had her own parties starting a week before the wedding in her grand house with her own college friends and sorority sisters.

By the first week before the wedding just about everyone already knew each other like they never left each other so many years ago.

Three days before the wedding all the food venders were all set up and some of the guests came on shore and ordered food that was free.

Matt' friends had their own parties in the campgrounds behind the trees and had their own parties starting a week before the wedding.

By noon of the wedding day all the guests were seated in comfortable chairs under the clear blue sky, and they didn't need the tents after all.

The wedding ceremony began by Matt walking his daughter down a wooden walkway to the alter. The groom was waiting for his bride with his best man and other college friends, the left side of the wedding party was taken up by Sierra's friends mostly from San Luis.

The right side of the wedding party was filled with the groom's side of the family and his mother's college friends. It was nice that the tent wasn't needed because it was a beautiful warm day and there was a gentle breeze that kept everybody cool.

Matt didn't want a long-drawn-out wedding

because the weather is always unpredictable even I July in Connecticut .

The wedding ceremony went smoothly and before anyone realized, it was all over and now it was time for the reception party to start.

Chris and Sierra cut the huge, beautiful cake and everyone had a piece of the cake with fresh coffee. There were many round tables where people can sit together and talk as they were served New York Strip Sirloin steaks grilled on an open pit with all the trimmings to go with the stakes.

The waiters were dressed in white tuxedoes and brought the dinners to all the tables located all over the lawn where the guests can start eating before the steaks got cold. Also, a vegan dinner was available for those that were on a vegan diet.

The dinner lasted about two hours and ended with vanilla ice cream as a desert. An army of waiters were busy removing the empty plates and waitresses came by to clean the white table with wet towels. The orchestra continued to play soft music. The outdoor dance floor was open for dancing for anyone wanting to dance. As the sun started to dip below the horizon of the hills behind the lake Japanese lanterns were turned on the and the dancing continued .

Sierra was obliged to dance with her guests on the smooth wooden dance floor because it was normal tradition in the United states.

She changed from heals to dancing shoes for the dancing because it was more comfortable. Many older guests left as soon as the sun went down but many younger guests stayed to dance on the wooden dance floor. At eight P.M. the band closed shop and the music was switched to music provided by a recording .

But after the live band left most of the people left the wedding party as well. People who had yachts returned tit their yacht to retire for the night there. Some guests continued to party on their yachts late into the night and you could hear music coning across the lake. Sierra and Christopher returned to the mansion to rest there after a busy day.

Next morning the bride and groom took off on their honeymoon. But that didn't bother some guests still at the wedding party and they continued partying for two more weeks until it finally fizzed out and the lake got quiet again.

64 YACHT TRIP WITH SAM

Two weeks after the wedding, the bride and groom returned home to the mansion that Matt gave them as a wedding present. They were all rested up by now, so Christopher returned to the bank to resume his job as assistant bank manager.

His father's old friend Samuel Grey was back with his yacht and wanted Christopher's father to go on a trip with him to see the world. The father mentioned this to his son and asked him what he thought about the idea. Cristopher said things are quiet this time of the year at the bank and besides we have many fully trained sub-managers working here at Chase Manhattan Bank so you might as well spend some time with your old college friend. Christopher's father said maybe I should do that then.

During the wedding Sierra's mother and sister hardly had a chance to sit down really have a good talk with each other. Serra's new house had thirty-one bedrooms so everyone could have their own bedroom. That might have been why they didn't get together to talk as much as they should have.

But now that the wedding was over with, and things were quiet they could talk in the kitchen at breakfast, or lunch or at any other time that they felt like talking. Sierra asked her Mom, Kari, if she was going back to Okinawa and work at th e Onsen again. Kari said I liked working there and loved the great soaks in Onsen, but I stayed there so long that I missed out on watching Savana's kid grow up and now they're all grown up and I really don't know them.

Sierra said now that I am married, I may be having some kids myself one of these days and you can stay here and watch them grow up. Kari said that I may leave here and then I will come back here and live with you again.

Matt still had a few more ideas about the mansion so he didn't leave for San Luis right away. He thought that the housekeepers, cooks, yard men and anyone else that worked in the mansion should have their own place to live close to the mansion but not necessarily in the house itself.

He called the architectural company that redesigned the mansion told them what he wanted. The architectural company sent some planners to the mansion and took some photographs of the area around the mansion then said we will be back in a week to present you with our suggestions. Matt said fine I'll see you in a week then.

Kari returned to Okinawa talked to her boss Yuki who still looked too young to be her boss. Yuki said you know the hotel staff pretty well so start to train some of them to replace you and as soon as you are done doing that, we will have great going away party and you can leave after that.

After Matt approved the plan that the architects presented him, he told them to go ahead with the plan and he will be back in a month to look at the final results.

Matt flew back to San Luis to checked on all of his business ventures there.

Christopher Templeton, the CEO of Chase Manhattan Bank was now enjoying the carefree cruise in the fancy yacht with 'Samuel Grey his old buddy from the old Harvard college days. With very few other people left on the yacht now they were able to have a more serious conversation. There were no young girls roaming all around the yacht anymore except for Sam's favorite girlfriend who was too young for him. But she wasn't with Sam all the time so Chris could talk to Sam about more serious things.

The first thing that Chris asked Sam was why he didn't get married after his third divorce. Sam said it was nice while it lasted but in a few years all marriages get old we get bored with each other, so we end up in divorce. Chris was quiet for a while but then he asked did you have any kids from any of your former wives and he said we were having so much fun that they we never got around to having any kids and he said his young wives always on the pill, so they didn't get pregnant.

Sam thought that that was probably a good thing for Sam. Chris then asked Sam what you are going to do when you get old. Sam said I saw my parents get old and it was no fun for them when they got old, so he was not going to get old. Chris wasn't too sure how to answer him on this one.

Just then his young girlfriend came back and said I'm getting bored and wanted Sam to come with her back to their cabin.

Chris was now by himself and he had time to run through everything that he and Sam talked about that morning. He even thought that maybe Sam was doing the better thing by changing girlfriends whenever they got tired of him or the other way around fell back to sleep on the deck of the yacht.

He had a dream about him as an old man and he had no one to talk with. In the dream he was rich like Sam but now that he was old, he couldn't attract any more young girls. He had another dream, which in this dream, he was not rich, and he was living in a rescue mission eating rotten food with bed bugs in his bunk and he had red marks on his body, and he was miserable.

In the dream he went out every day to panhandle for small change and he was so miserable that the only thing that drowned out is misery was to get stinking drunk and he was sleeping in a dirty alleyway and dogs came by and peed on him.

Sam came back to see how he was doing so he shook him back out of his dream. When he woke up, he was glad that it was just a dream, but he couldn't' stop thinking about the terrible dream. It was dinner time, so Sam took him to the dining room and ordered a fine meal.

His girlfriend's name was Candy and she looked sweet but shallow and nothing at all like his son's new wife who was well educated and an intelligent young lady

After dinner Sam said that tomorrow, we are going to drop anchor in Biscayne bay in Bermuda and spend a few weeks there. Chris was still thinking about his dream but managed to say great I would like to see Bermuda and finished his dinner.

After dinner he had a full stomach and told Sam that he was going back to his cabin and retire early. Chris took a long hot bath and almost fell asleep in the tub. He got out of the tub then brushed his teeth and got ready for bed. After a few hours he was awaken up by another dream where he was with this wife and they were now both old and living in a nursing home and being well taken care of. In the dream his wife had Alzheimer and her memory was starting to fade. But Chris had many memories of her when they were younger and realized that he still loved her.

He fell back to sleep and didn't wake up until the yacht pulled into St Georges Harbor on the Eastern side of Bermuda where the large cruise ships didn't go there. Sam came to wake Chris up and said let's go ashore and have breakfast on shore. His girlfriend was still asleep because she drank too much the night before, so it was only the two of them again.

Sam took Chris away from the main drag and found a small shack to have breakfast. The shack was small, and Chris and Sam were the only customers at this time of the morning. Sam ordered the traditional breakfast that the locals ate on the on island and it was simple but not bad.

Sam noticed that Chris was quiet and asked him if he had a bad dream. Chris told him of the last dream where he was old and with his wife and they were living a in a nursing home and his wife had Alzheimer and she started to forget things. Sam said I probably won't have to worry about getting old because I will be dead before he got too old and laughed like it was a joke.

Chris said I left my son in charge of the bank, so it was time that I return and help him out at the bank. They agreed to meet again every ten years and catch up on each other. They said goodbye then Chris said I will catch a plane and return home now.

65 VACATION PLANS

Chris's father Alfred, made it back to Connecticut and he took a few days to stay homc and talk to his wife Gwendolyn. He told his wife about his friend Sam who owned the Yacht and told her what he thought about his lifestyle. He told Gwen that we should spend more time together before we get too old and let his son Christopher take more responsibility of running the bank.

Gwen had many friends that waited too long before they went on vacations themselves with their spouses and some of their spouses died before they had a chance to go on vacations. Gwen said I think that you are right about taking vacations before we get too old to travel.

Gwen suggested cruise ships to her husband, and he said I looked at some fancy cruise ships and all they are a just huge floating hotels and sometimes they have an outbreak of some kind of a disease and everyone on board is trapped on board and they get quarantined for two weeks.

Alfred said we have enough money so we can

design our own special vacation every year and our son's father-in-law has his private Jet that he can fly us to anywhere in the world with no problem.

Al said he frequently flies to Long Island where he has his own private airstrip and a hanger so I will invite him to dinner some time and ask him if he has some ideas as to where go for two weeks 'vacation soon.

Sierra decided to take a break from teaching at Yale University for a while because she was now pregnant with her first child. She was always interested in researching where the Japanese language originated and so far, there were no good decisive research done on that subject and she can do that research right from home even being prenatal with a child.

She already had an army help to take care of the large house and she didn't have to do any cooking or cleaning because the staff took care of all of that. She wouldn't even have to go the University and go to the library because she can find all the research material right on her computer on the Internet.

When Gwen found out that Matt was visiting his daughter Sierra, she invited them to dinner at her house in Connecticut. Matt and Sierra and her husband drove to Connecticut to have dinner with Gwen and Alfred. Dinner consisted of the Barron of Beef which her cooks prepared for them.

Alfred suggested a fine wine with the dinner and Matt and Sierra declined because she was now pregnant. Chris decided that it wouldn't hurt so Alfred ordered some red wine. The conversation quickly went to where to go for a short vacation. Matt said that we have a Castle in Columbia and asked Alfred if he would care to go see the castle.

Gwen said off course we would love to see the castle. Matt said how about next week and you wouldn't even need a passport because he will fly you in his private jet and we have an airstrip close to the Castle. Matt said that the Castle is fully staffed with guards, cooks , and housekeepers and they will take good care of you all the time that you are there.

Alfred said we will plan on going with you then in one week. Sierra said I won't v be going with you because she was now pregnant so she will just stay in her house with her husband and do some research on the Japanese language.

Matt suggested that Alfred and Gwen drive to Sierra's house the day that they wanted to leave for the trip to Columbia and Matt will have Sierra's chauffeur drive us to Long Island and we can board the jet from there.

Everything was now all set for the trip, so all Alfred had to do was to get ready for the trip. He told his son that he was going on a two weeks'vacation to Columbia and told his son that you will be in charge of the bank while he was gone. His son Chris said I did that before so don't worry about the bank and just have fun on your trip.

66 CASTLE

Alfred and Gwen were being treated like royalty in the Castle. The Castle was not a hotel or any other public place, but it was now a secret resort only for members of Matt's extended family or special friends. The staff at the Castle were always excited when anyone came to the Castle because the Castle was not used enough.

Whenever the Castle was not being used by any member of Matt's extended family all the hired staff at the Castle felt like they were on vacation because they had nothing to do except keep the Castle clean. The headmaster of the Castle staff was a towering man with a deep voice that can rattle the dishes in the kitchen where all the staff members had their meals. The entire castle staff was run like a military compound and anyone who didn't do their duty would be immediately dismissed for one year and sent home and then they would have to find employment for half of what they made at the Castle if they were lucky to find employment. This happened several times before. Those who were older sometimes couldn't find employment went to a rescue mission and died there.

The headmaster of the servant's unit looked just like Mr. Carson in the British movie series called Downton Abby that ran for seven seasons was a hit all over the world. His name wasn't Mr. Carson but he had a Spanish name by El Senior Carso-nacho who was younger than Mr. Carson but still had the same booming voice that could intimidate any of the servants in the Castle. Carso-nacho ran a tight ship and people were afraid of being let go end up in the streets and starve to death.

When Alfred and Gwen arrived in the castle it was a chance for every member of the Castle staff to do their best and stand out. Carso-nacho was multilingual and could speak some English. He hied a few other Castle staff that could speak English as well and they were there to help Alfred and Gwen.

Gwen studied Spanish in College and could speak some Spanish, so she took advantage of her Spanish speaking knowledge and became a hit with the Castle staff.

They had their breakfast in the drawing room and had lunch in the library, but dinner was always served in the great hall and they always had a wonderful dinner. A musician came to the Castle to perform for Alfred and Gwen after the evening dinner. They could never have this kind of service an any great hotel anywhere else in the world.

During the day Alfred could take the dogs out for a walk around the castle and inspect all the fine trees and the landscape. One day one of the dogs who was trained to look for hidden treasures started to dig near a small bush and Alfred could see a small casket that looked like a pirate's stash.

He had no shovels or any other small tool, so he planned to come back the next day to dig the casket out of the ground. Two days later he finally managed to dig the small casket out of the ground the casket was empty except for a few pieces of gold coins and a ring with a huge ruby. He put the coins and the ring in his pocket and covered up the casket and put it back into the ground just like he found it.

That night after dinner and he was back in bed with Gwen, he told her what he found and showed her the ring with the huge ruby. Gwen said when we get back home, I will take the ring to a reputable jeweler and have it appraised.

Before long their two weeks' vacation was over and Matt came back to take them back to Connecticut.

67 BANDITS

Seven years after Alfred and Gwen visited the Castle Alfred decided to retire and turn over the Bank to his son Chris to manage the bank. Alfred and his wife have already been to Egypt, all the major attractions in Europe and even been to Japan twice.

Sierra had five children now and the youngest was two years old. Matt decided to have a grand reunion of all his extended family and meet in Okinawa and stay in the original Onsen in Okinawa where it was no longer being used so much anymore because the new Onsen was much bigger and newer. They all decided to meet in Okinawa when they were able to go there.

Matt and Sierra and all of her kids and her mother were the first to arrive in Okinawa and took residence in the original Onsen hotel and its entire complex. Kari resumed her old job as the general manager of the entire Onsen complex and hired new help. Alfred and Gwen showed up next and before long the entire extended family was now all living in the old Onsen-Hotel complex.

Sam grey heard about the reunion and he went to Okinawa as well with three new young ladies in his yacht. Okinawa was the perfect place for the reunion because there were already so many of Matt's old friends there as well.

Thor still kept his original lumber mill open, and Shinzo was managing it well. Odin was still the Mayor of Little Sicily, but he no longer had too much to do. He sometimes went with Thor's oldest son to go to Ume island and harvest Soft shelled crabs sold some at the farmer's market.

The new visitors to Okinawa who were now staying in the original Onsen and some of them joined him and went deep sea fishing with Thor's oldest son.

Thor's three Engineers came to the Onsen to join in on some of the parties.

There was so much to see in Okinawa in the Theme park and all of its small inns and attractions so there was never any time to get bored. Savana caught up with her old friend Kasha and spent a lot of time with her in her studio and started to paint again. Yuki planned another auction in the Crystal Palace in nine months. Yuki told Kasha to paint three more Edward Hopper painting for the auction.

Gwen signed up for Japanese classes for forefingers and started to learn some Japanese. The University had a pre-school program for young children, so Sierra signed her two oldest boys to attend pre-school there.

Kiyoko's retirement home next to Little Sicily was not being used so Alfred rented the place for himself and Gwen to live there while they were in Okinawa and it looked like he had no plans to return to Connecticut any time soon. He hied a housekeeper and a cook from Little Sicily to come in every day starting at noon to do the cleaning and the cooking for Gwen and they left after the evening meal and retuned to Little Sicily.

Matt asked Thor if he ever went back to the new volcano to check on the giant titanium obelisk. Thor said he hadn't been there so long that he was not even sure that he could even fine the place. Thor said that Shinzo sill had his private stash of gold, so on weekends he goes there to cut a small piece of gold and takes it to the Sumitomo bank to exchange it for cash and his daughter Techiko who was now married to the assaying manager always took care of him.

Matt asked if he was busy lately and Thor said he was actually retired and just taking it easy with no more kids living in his house because they were now all grown up doing their own thing.

Matt said let's go visit the new volcano one of these days and see if we can find the obelisk again. Thor said I am an old man now but after I took Yuki's advice and started to eat sourer Ume fruit, I feel twenty years younger, and I can probably do the physically taxing job of climbing up the volcano and look for the old Platinum Obelisk.

Thor's motorboat was still available, so they stocked up with food and fresh water and some fuel for the generator and travelled to the new volcano. The cabin looked like no one bothered the place, so they went in and brought all the supplies that they brought with them in the motorboat and restocked the cabin. Thor went out to the generator and filled the generator with gas and started it and the generator started to recharge the banks of storage batteries. After a few hours Thor went back out and shut the generators off because they were noisy and switched to the bank of batteries to supply electricity for the cabin.

They had a small supper of rice balls and green tea and went to sleep for the night. Next morning as soon as the sun came out Thor fixed some breakfast and after they had coffee, they were ready to hike up the volcano to look for the obelisk.

When they got to the old cave Thor checked it put and it looked just like it was several years ago. They rested at the cave for a while until they regained their energy, then walked South around the volcano to look for the obelisk. When they got there, Thor remembered where the obelisk was. He then noticed some activity by the shore and there was a small boat and it looked like some people were staying in the old cabin that the lady used to live in where she used to grow the small egg plants. Thor got his binoculars out and looked at the cabin and It looked suspicious.

He handed the binoculars to Matt and he studied the cabin and noticed a man with a rifle, and he was looking around. They stayed there at their vantage point and studied the cabin for an hour and Thor came to the conclusion that there were at least five young men.

Thor and Matt saw enough for now, so they returned to the cabin and tried to decide what to do next. Thor said we should go back now and decide what to do after we get back to Thor's house.

The house was now practically empty with no kids living there anymore and it was just for Thor and Tomiko and Matt. Thor suggested that Matt stay in one of the rooms above the three-car garage and we can make plans to figure out what to do with the men with the rifles.

They didn't want to let the bandits or whoever they were that they were discovered so they didn't go back there again until they had a plan on how to take them out.

Tom was an old man now so he couldn't go with them to look at the cabin because it was too much of a physical job for an old man but a least, they can tell him at him at University and get some advice.

They planned to do that soon.

68 BANDITS KILLED

When Thor and Matt went to the University to talk to Tom, he reminded them of Stephen Hawking the famous British physicist who was able to use a computer to continue his work by using special plastic pointer that he held in his mouth and tapping the special monitor that allowed him to write on the computer.

Tom wasn't as bad as Hawkins, but he was severely handicapped. Thor suggested that he start to eat some Ume fruit, but he didn't seem to be interested.

Thor said what we really need is a way to take out some bandits who are living in a small cabin on the south side of the new volcano. Tom got on the intercom and called his team of students who were working on a new system to kill bad people.

The students came in with a mechanical snake and explained how it worked. Thor described where the bandits were living, the students were anxious to try out the new snakes.

It was Friday afternoon so Thor said I can take you there tomorrow and show you where they were staying in a cabin. The students said we will be ready to go with you tomorrow morning.

First Thor took them to his cabin on the west side of the volcano and drew a map showing where the bandits were staying. One student took the map and said I will go check the area out now. When he came back, he said it looks like the job will be easy and said we can do it in daylight right now. All the students put the mechanical snakes in their backpack and headed off to the site where the bandits were staying. One hour later they were back and said we think that the bandits are all dead now. Thor and Matt were thinking that they were going there to only look at the site but never expected them use the snakes in broad daylight .

The students explained how they guided the snakes into the cabin and when they were inside, they activated them, and it immediately saturated the cabin with deadly poisonous gas, and it was all over within a minute.

Thor asked how long the gas stayed active and the students said no more than an hour. Thor asked if it was now safe to go there and check the cabin. The team leader of the students said absolutely so we can go there now. Thor didn't want to walk that far so he said we can all go in my boat and check out the place now.

When the boat was a half a mile away from the cabin Thor took out his binocular and studied the cabin and it looked quiet. He handed the binocular to the team leader and he studied the cabin as well. The team leader saw a man staggering out of the cabin and fell down on the ground. He handed the binocular back to Thor and told him to look at the man on the ground. Thor got is high powered rifle and fired carefully shot at the man on the ground and saw the bullet enter his body. He waited a while longer and then he drove the boat closer to the cabin and they all looked at the man on the ground and the cabin. Matt said maybe we should go check out the boat the moored by the wooden dock first. He took the rifle and made sure that it had enough rounds in the chamber to use in case he ran into any more bandits. Matt walked into the boat and found the boat empty.

He came back to report that the boat was empty.

69 THE B & B

Matt came back to the University and handed Tom a check for a hundred thousand dollars. He then asked him where the students were that helped him take out the bandits. Tom said they were in the library having a meeting.

Matt found them in the library and told them that they did a great job and now he had something for each of them. He handed each of them a check for a hundred thousand dollars then left the library.

Matt went back to Thor's house and found Tomiko cooking some vegetables. Thor asked Matt if he had lunch yet and Matt said not yet. Thor told him to sit down and join him for lunch. As Matt was eating lunch, he asked Thor if we should go back to the volcano try to figure out where the Platinum obelisk was again. Thor said I'm not interested in going back there because my leg is bothering me again.

Matt said we'll wait until it gets better before we try to go back to the volcano then.

Yuki found Sierra in the restaurant and asked her

how she liked living in her old house next to the restaurant. Sierra said it was the perfect place for her at this time. Yuki asked Sierra if she could borrow her youngest girl for a while to live with her. Sierra said off course and she will like the extra attention.

Chris decided to rent out his parents' house now that they were living in Okinawa loving the place. He talked to his next in command and asked him how he liked living in Wilmington Arms. He said that it was O.K. But his mother-in-law moved in with them and it was a little crowded now.

Chris asked how much the rent was and he said it was two thousand a month. Chris said I am planning on taking more trips to Okinawa and I don't need a big place like I am living in now so how would you like stay there rent free. This sounded like a god send to his second in command and said I will like that, and I will take good care of the place for you until you want it back. So that was now settled.

Chris went back to his father 's house and told all the helpers that he was closing the place up until his father comes back from Okinawa so you can start to put everything away and leave after you are done and gave them all a nice going away present.

Sam Grey decided to sell his yacht, so he approached Alfred his old buddy from college days and asked him if he wanted to buy his Yacht. Alfred said I don't know the first thing about yachts and besides how could I afford to pay all the crew members that you have working on the yacht. Sam said I'm going to be a land lover from now on, so I don't need the yacht anymore.

Alfred said go see my son-in-law and maybe he might want to buy your beautiful yacht. Sam said I'll go talk to him then and got off the phone. Sam called Thor at home because he knew that Matt was now living there and asked for Matt.

Matt got on the phone asked what can I do for you to Sam. Sam said I decided to sell my yacht and wanted to know if Matt wanted to buy it. Sam said how about three million dollars and you can keep the same crew that I have on the yacht because they know everything about the Yacht. Matt asked where the yacht was now, and Sam said that was the other problem and that he didn't have a permanent mooring spot for the yacht yet.

Matt said find a good place to moor the Yacht and I will buy your yacht.

Chris went back to his father's estate and found that the help did a good job of closing the place up so the next day at the bank he saw his second in command and gave him the keys to his father 's estate and said the place is all yours now. His second in command Doctor Hunter was there and said thanks and promised to take good care of the estate.

Chris then went to Wilmington Arms and looked all the available apartments and found them cold looking so he left.

Chris drove around the area and found a small B&B with a sign that space available. He knocked on the front door and an old man came to the door and asked him in. Chris asked him if he had any rooms for rent. The man said we used to have three rooms, but it was too much work for his wife and me, so we redesigned the house and now we only have one large apartment and asked Chris if he wanted to see the room.

Chris said sure and they walked up to the third floor and it was a beautiful room a with a panoramic view of the harbor. Chris liked the apartment and said I'll take it without even asking how much the place cost.

The old man said we also have a two-car garage, and you are welcome to use that also. Things started to sound better all the time. He removed his wallet and asked if he took credit cards and the man said we prefer cash if you can manage that. Chris asked how much cash he wanted. The man said if you pay for the first and last month right now it was two thousand dollars a month for you. Chris said I will be right back with the cash and left.

Half an hour later he was back with two thousand dollars in cash and gave it to the old man. The old man was surprised that Chris agreed to rent the room without trying to talk him down on the rent but was happy to get the money. Chris said I will be back later to get my clothes and will see you then.

70 CONVERTING BONDS

Sam found a marina to moor the yacht just south of thc old Onsen and rented a space to put the yacht. The place looked a little run down, but it was a handy place so called Matt and told him that he found a handy spot for the Yacht. Mat said I'll be right down to see you. Sam said I'm in the restaurant now so I will be here waiting for you.

Matt found Sam sitting at a table having coffee so he joined him. Sam said the marina doesn't look too fancy, but it is a handy place, and it looks like the yacht is he only boat in the entire place. Matt said let's go look at the place then.

Ten minutes later Matt was talking to the owner of the marina and the owner immediately tried to sell the marina to Matt and he was surprised to hear the owner say that he wanted to sell the marina. Matt could see that the marina had a large exposure to the southern coast of the island and basically it was a perfect place for a marina. Matt estimated that the maria could easily hold a dozen Yachts in the marina, so Matt asked the owner how much he wanted for the marina.

The owner of the marina hesitated for a while but finally said I have a cabin halfway up the volcano and if you let me stay there for a year after you buy the marina, I will sell the marina to you for a million bucks. Matt looked at the cabin and it looked like it was a mile up the volcano and realized that the property must be huge. Matt said O.K. You have a deal, and they shook hands and Matt left.

Yuki liked Sierra's youngest daughter and she took her everywhere she went. Yuki decided to name the girl Yuki also after herself because the girl had flaming red hair just like Yuki did when she was a young girl. Before long everyone just assumed that the little girl was Yuki's little girl. Sierra didn't mind as long as her daughter was happy.

Kari offered Sam a job as the manager of the hotel so that Kari can concentrate on running the restaurant and the Onsen. Sam immediately accepted the job because he was looking for a place to put his third girlfriend to stay away from his other two girlfriends. The first one had a bungalow in one of Tony's new housing complex on the south side of the island and the other one had a place in one of Kiyoko's upscale housing units by Pizza Parlor NO. 2.

Now there was Little chance that the three young ladies will ever run into each other and find out that Sam was taking care of all three of them.

Matt wasn't hurting for money, but he didn't just want his billions in bearer bonds to just sit in a safety deposit box in Madrid and just rot there. He flew to Madrid and removed one of his billion-dollar bearer bonds and cashed it at the bank where the bond was originally made out a long time ago. The bank manager was happy to have Matt cash in the bond because it will quit earning more interest on ne bond. Matt put the proceeds from the bond into three different kinds of investments.

One was in a checking account, another was in long term C.D.'s, and the last one was in a savings account that he can withdraw easily by only a phone call or an email to the bank. Now he can spend as money as soon as he needed, with no problem.

Next Matt flew to Bogota Columbia and went to the bank there that he deposited ten of the billion-dollar bearer bonds there. He went to the safety deposit box in the bank in Bogota and removed one of the ten bearer bonds from there and cashed it in the bank in Bogota. Since the bearer bond was for a billion dollars and it was not issued by the bank in Bogota it would have to cleared by the bank in Madrid and it may take up to a month before it will clear the bank.

Next, he flew back to Connecticut to check on his mansion that he bought for sierra as a present when she got married. It was still being well taken care of by a staff of caretakers so he advertised the mansion for rent and so somebody can make use of the fine estate. He stayed in the estate and he was the only one being taken care of by a full staff of staff members. He stayed in the mansion and enjoyed the place and spent a lot of time with this son-in-law Chris who was now the CEO of Chase Manhattan Bank who was staying in a B&B that was close to the bank.

When they went out to dinner one night Matt asked Chris why he stayed in a B&B when he could just stay in his father's big house that was just sitting there.

Chris said the house was too big for him and he was wasting too much time just coming to work each day at the bank and the B&B was just a block away and he can just walk to work each day and even get some exercise.

Matt complimented Chris for making such a wise decision and the asked what happened to his father's large house. Chris said I let my second in command manager live there for free because his mother-in-law came to live with him to be with her grandchildren now that she was getting older.

Chris said he no longer has to pay all the staff at his father's house anymore because the new tenant is now living there and doesn't need such a large staff of people just to take care of the big house and everybody is saving a lot of money. Chris added '"A PENNY SAVED IS A PENNY EARNED" Matt complimented his son-in-law for being such a smart manager.

Chris said that he second in command manager is so grateful to him that he tells me to take more time off because he can handle all the extra work all by himself so now, he was planning to take more short vacations to go to Okinawa visit his wife and his kids more often. Matt told him you certainly got everything under control and said that you should do that.

Matt asked Chris if the bank had a private jet for the bank managers. Chris said we have a heliport on top of the bank, but we don't have private jet at this time. Matt was thinking about just buying a private jet for the bank so that his son-in-law could fly to Okinawa every weekend and be with his daughter .

It turned out that the marina had a natural hot spring halfway up the volcano and that was the reason that the man who sold him the marina wanted to stay in the cabin. He approached the former owner of the marina and made him a proposition to build him a new place higher up on the volcano and he could stay there for free for as long as he wanted to in exchange for letting Matt redesign the natural hot string as an Onsen. The former owner who went by butch immediately agreed to Matt's proposal and said I would like to be the manager of the Onsen for you for free in that case.

Now that that was settled Matt went to his Yacht and told them that he was going to build them a fine place to live right in the marina and you wouldn't have to live on the Yacht all the time and that he was thinking about building dry dock for the Yacht and have it completely gone over for any necessary repairs. All the members of the Yacht crew were thrilled to hear what Matt proposed and asked if they could also leave the marina to go see the rest of Okinawa. Matt said I will give you all three months paid vacation and you can have a ball.

71 COUNTRY CLUB

Ivan who was now managing the new Onsen on the new volcano had a strange request from a team of well-dressed guests in his new hotel. Ivan immediately detected their accent as Israeli. The team leader of the group asked Ivan if the hotel had any boats for rent. Ivan said not here but I will call a man with a motorboat and see if he can accommodate you and asked them to give him a minute. he went to the back room and called Thor who had a motorboat and told him that he was sure that they were Israeli men and may be dangerous and told Thor not to give them too much information but be polite to them.

Thor said I will be right over with my motorboat in ten minutes or less. Thor walked into the new Onsen hotel and Ivan introduced him to the five Israeli men. Thor looked like a fisherman and he didn't look intimidating to the Israelis.

The men dressed in fine suits told Thor that they wanted to go to the South side of the new volcano where he and the archers took out five armed bandits. Thor took them to the site where the cabin was still there and parked the boat offshore from the cabin. The men already had color photographs of the cabin and compared the cabin to the photographs. One of the men said this is the place alright.

Another man took photographs with his cell phone and said this was the place and asked if they could go see the cabin. Thor already informed the archers of the mysterious men and the archer and his father who were living in the cabin were ready for the Israeli men. The Israel men were invited into the cabin and they started to take some pictures there with cell phones. The Israeli man asked how long the archer and his father was living in the cabin and they said about a year because the cabin was empty, and it looked like a nice place to fish.

The Israeli man asked if they ever saw any men near the cabin and the archer said not that they knew of. This seemed to satisfy the Israeli men and they said thank you and said goodbye and returned to the boat with Thor.

After Thor returned the men back to the hotel handed one of the men gave Thor a hundred dollars for his service and said thank you.

The next day the Israeli men were gone. All guests coming into the new Onsen hotel were automatically photographed by the hotel's by their hidden cameras and recorded in the hotel database. Ivan told Thor that he was going to turn over the ruining of the Onsen Hotel to his assistant and said that he going into the spying business.

Matt got a call from Sotheby's Real Estate Company saying that they had several offers for his ten-thousand-acre estate in Connecticut and wanted him to come to Connecticut. Matt said I will take a jet and be there the next day. They met at Matt's ten-thousand-acre estate and had a meeting there.

One man offered ten million dollars for the estate and the real estate agent was sure that Matt would accept the offer. Matt didn't need any more millions because he already had many billions in bearer bond stashed away in the safety deposit box in Madrid as well the nine more bonds in Bogota Columbia. Matt said that the estate was only being offered for lease and not for sale. The real estate agent looked disappointed knowing that six percent of ten million dollars was $60,000.00.

The man who offered ten million for the estate told Matt that he wanted to have a secret meeting with Matt that afternoon and Matt agreed to meet him.

The marina on Okinawa was completely renovated with an Onsen that was managed by the former owner and there were ten new bungalows built near the Onsen and all the member of the Yacht crew were house there. The Yacht was still in dry dock at the new marina, and it too was completely being renovated with new features.

Sam was promised to be hired as the captain of the yacht as soon as the yacht was finished with its many new features.

Matt donated a new jet for the Chase Manhattan Bank so that it's CEO cold use it to travel to different locations. The bank already had a heliport on the roof of the bank and all Chris would have to do was to have the helicopter take him to Long Island where the Jet was permanently housed in a secure hanger with guards to watch the jet and there was also a maintenance crew that was housed there to attend to any repairs for the new jet.

When Matt got to his Estate in Connecticut, he had a meeting with the man who asked for the meeting. The estate was still fully staffed with cooks, gardeners, and all the help that Matt had for Sierra when he gave the estate to Sierra when she got married.

The meeting was held in the veranda of the mansion and the kitchen staff served cold non-alcoholic drinks for Matt and his guest. Matt and his guest by the name of Theodore Appleton talked for about three hours about the estate and the fact that Matt would have to pay so much taxes if he sold the estate to anyone in addition to the six percent fee to the real estate agent who managed the sale. Theodor now understood why Matt didn't want to sell the estate to anyone.

The meeting now switched to the possible lease of the estate. A hundred thousand acres of prime land so close to New York City was a perfect place to have a several golf courses and a few riding stables. Ted explained the great possibilities of his plan to Matt and offered him a partnership in the new venture if Ted could lease the estate for twenty-five years and he showed how the new venture could make enough money to pay off the loan in less than ten years.

They both had a pad with calculators and did a lot of figuring and Matt came to the conclusion that a lease of twenty-five years would be a great investment even if he never visited the new country club it will have a hotel as well as the fact that he could stay in the hotel for free for two weeks every year. Ted or Teddy then said I will have my attorneys draw up a contract for the lease and it will be ready to be signed in less than a week. Matt gave the address of the hotel at the Onsen and asked that the finished contract be sent there, and he will have his lawyers review the contract and mail it beck to Ted after that .

Both men were happy with the decision to lease the estate and were looking forward to start building the new country club.

72 YACHT REUNION

The Penthouse at the old Onsen Hotel was turned into a place for kings with all the time and money that Sam spent with Matt's money. He agreed to give it up in exchange for him living in the yacht as if the yacht was now his personal yacht, but it was only for show for Sam, and he was happy for the trade .

The Penthouse was mainly for Yuki or for Matt who financed all the cost of its transformation. Sometimes Yuki will take her new borrowed girl to the Penthouse whenever it was not being used and spend a night there. Yuk's borrowed daughter was getting used to the wonderful life with Yuki.

The Penthouse was also available for rent to anybody foolish enough to pay the extravagant price for the penthouse, so it was seldom ever rented out to any customers.

The contract for the lease on Matt's estate was completed and it was a long and complicated document, so he brought it to Yuki to have her personal attorneys to review the contract or Matt. Yuki said that her personal attorneys will study the contract carefully and she will report back to Matt when they were done examining entire complicated contact

One weekend Chris the new CEO of Chase Manhattan Bank showed up in Okinawa to visit his wife Sierra. Yuki told Sierra to use the Penthouse for the weekend and stay there with her husband.

Sam sometimes brought one of his girlfriends to the yacht and they spent a night on the yacht without the crew in the yacht because they were not going out to sea and just spending the night there. This made big points for Sam with his girlfriends, and they had a nice time on the yacht for the night.

After Sierra and Chris spent a few days in the penthouse Matt transferred them to the yacht so they can spend week on the yacht. It was now time for another family reunion, so Matt arranged to have everyone come to the yacht. Sam was hired to be the captain of yacht for this occasion. Even Yuki said she will come to the yacht for a couple of days for the reunion.

Yuki's personal Lawyers completed the review of the lease contract and made a few changes to the contract. They said that the contract was basally fine, but they wanted to add a few more small items that the other lawyers would certainly consider them to be just peanuts

The first change was a clause that stated that after the first twenty-five years a new contract will have to be made.

The next clause was that Matt can have a week and stay at the country club for free for a week each year, and if it was not used in any particular year, it will automatically be added to the next year for him thereby increasing his use for the next year.

There were a few more clauses that would not amount to a hill of beans, but it may be advantageous to Matt in the long run.

After the attorneys explained every detail to Matt, he then signed the contract and gave it back to the lawyers to finish it up and resubmit the contract to the lawyers in New York City

The reunion was a great success on the yacht and even Yuki was impressed at how things went on the yacht. Sam asked if he could bring one of his girlfriends to the reunion, but Matt said that it was only for his extended family members.

The yacht was not a huge cruise ship, so it was cozy, and everyone got to know each other. All of Chris and Sierra's kids were on the yacht and got to know to know their relatives.

After the reunion was over with Chris flew back to New York to resume his duties at the bank.

Little Yuki was a great hit of the reunion and everyone loved her because she was so cute and smart.

After the reunion things settled back to normal and Sam got to stay in the yacht again like it was his personal home.

73 ALFRED'S TRIPS

Ivan set up his spy office in Cairo with a team of highly trained operatives. They managed to uncover a huge amount of information on the Moesha Haddine group and found out that they were for hire to anyone or group that had enough money to hire them to have someone killed or kidnapped. They already did that several times in Iran when they took out some of their best scientist and leaders. Off course the Iranians suspected the Israelis, but they couldn't prove anything.

After a few months Ivan had all the information that he needed so he closed shop in Cairo and returned to Okinawa. He told his mother that he wanted to start his own investigating company right here in Okinawa and Yuki said do whatever you want because she wanted her son to be happy. The new Onsen hotel could be managed by other managers.

The B&B that Chris was staying at had to close because the couple that ran the place got too old to run the B&B. Chris offered them a handsome retirement plan with large amount of money for the B&B so they can retire in style.

For a while Chris just lived there like it was his personal home but it was too large, and he couldn't keep up with all the work, so he gradually started to hire some help for the old B&B.

The lawyers from Yew York approved the new contract and the deal was closed for the next twenty-five years. Chris invited his father Alfred who used to be the CEO for Chase Manhattan bank to take a vacation back to New York just to see how the bank was doing now. After spending three days in the bank, he realized that he was lucky to be out of the place. Matt put him in the new Country Club complex for a week, but he got tired of that as well and he never liked playing golf anyway and thought it to be waste of valuable time. He missed watching his grandkids grow up, so he returned back to Okinawa where all of his family was now living with the exception of Chris who was his only child.

He loved to spend as much time as he can with his grandchildren and gave them a lot of good advice about the banking business.

One day he went to the Okinawa branch of the Sumitomo bank in Okinawa to open a new bank account there and noticed some foreigners having trouble talking to the bank teller about the complicated business of C. D,'s and other investments so he stepped in to explain to them how it worked in English. The manager noticed how helpful Alfred was to the foreigners, so he approached Alfred and offered him a job as clerk to help forefingers. Alfred didn't need any money so he said I can do that for free because I am a retired man and I already have all the money that I need. But I would love to be of service to your bank and I would like to know how the banking business is done in Japan.

The manager gave Alfred a tiny office in the lobby where he can help foreigners and he was able to help many foreigners who came into the bank for help

One day the manager found out that Alfred was the CEO of Chase Manhattan bank in New York City before he retired so he invited Alfred to join him in the yearly New Year's Eve party in Tokyo for all the branch managers in Japan. At the party many of the other managers heard that Alfred was the CEO of the Chase Manhattan Bank in New York City so everyone at the party wanted to know more about the famous bank.

He was seated at the big round table and he was mobbed by many of the other branch managers, the enjoyed getting so much attention and made a lot of new friends. He was invited to come to various small places in Japan and visit the other banks all over Japan whenever he wanted to that and take his wife with him to see all the quaint towns and small villages.

74 KIDNAPPING

Matt went to the marina to look for Sam who was living on the refurbished yacht, but he was not there. He went to the crew's quarters and asked them if they have seen Sam. The pilot of the yacht said that the last time that we saw him was more than two months ago and he was walking with two tall men in suits, and they left in a black car.

Matt asked if there were any customers who came to the marina to rent the yacht. The pilot said Sam was the one who handled all the requests for the yacht because he was the one who lived on the yacht and was in charge of making all the arrangements then he will call us when to get ready for another cruise.

Matt said two months is a long time and told the pilot to call him if Sam ever shows up again. The pilot asked Matt if he was a customer because everyone at the marina assumed that Sam was the big boss

Matt left the marina and went to talk to Yuki and told her about the mysterious disappearance of Sam. Yuki immediately called her son Ivan to come to the restaurant to have a meeting with Matt.

At the meeting Matt told Ivan of the mysterious disappearance of Sam and no one has seen him for more than two months Everyone agreed that that was a long time and Ivan said he has a detective company that can look into cases like these, and he will have his men immediately start to work on the case.

Ivan called Matt and said all three of Sam's girlfriends were also missing and Ivan said we think that we may have a lead and will get back with him as soon as we have more information.

Chris came back to Okinawa and spent another week with Sierra who was now living in Thor's new lumber mill after two of his engineers retired and the lumber mill was converted to an upscale grand living quarters for Sierra and two of her kids. Sierra's youngest daughter was still living with Yuki and loving it. The two oldest boys were in school making progress in their studies.

One of Ivan's operatives said we have a photograph of Sam in Beijing with two armed guards, and he was hand cuffed. Ivan said we should call Matt and show him the photograph. This time the meeting was held in Ivan's private detectives' quarters and he asked Matt what was so special about Sam that they will kidnap him and take him to Beijing. Matt said Sam liked to act like he was the boss of the marina and in a way, he was but his lifestyle made him look like he was the boss of the whole island and he lived high the hog.

Ivan said that the Chinese were interested in securing some of the precious Tungsten carbide Gold colored metal for their military needs and who else to get a hold of the metal other than the big boss himself. Matt said but Sam doesn't know the first thing about the tungsten carbide metal so why would anybody want to kidnap him.

Ivan said if the Chinese figured that if he was the head man in Okinawa, they would certainly figure out that he had access to all the information that the Chinese wanted. Ivan said the only way that we can be sure of why Sam was kidnapped was to send one of my operatives go to Beijing and infiltrate the Chinese military compound.

Matt said that seems like an impossible task and asked if Ivan had any operatives that spoke Chinese as his natural language. Ivan said we have access to a lot of money, and we can setup a clandestine team in China and train new Operatives to infiltrate the Chinese military. Ivan said with enough money just about anybody can be bought.

75 GOBI DESERT

Ivan went back to China the same way he did with Masa when he went to china to learn how to speak Chinese and even took Masa with him again. The old couple that they worked for the first time that went to China retired and no longer lived in the old house and the place was up for sale. They weren't asking too much for the farm, so Ivan bought the farm and started to harvest the Shiitake mushrooms again. He hired a few men to do the hard work of growing Shitake mushrooms.

Ivan expanded the farmhouse and had his operatives come to live in the farmhouse to get used to China as he started to make plans on how to infiltrate the interrogations compound in Beijing.

He found out that only after a few months in Beijing most prisoners were taken to a prison to be reeducated and possibly be made to be useful to the Chinese government. There was this case of Peter Humphrey who was an American who was married to a Chinese lady while he was still living in the United States and after his prison sentence and was released, he talked about how the Chinese prisons were run.

He remembered running into Sam and Sam told him how they tried to get information from him on how to get the precious Titanium Carbide Gold colored metal, but he didn't know a thing about the metal, so they put him in the same prison camp as Peter Humphrey.

He said during the interrogation process they brought in his girlfriends and tortured them as he was forced to watch them die. He said that all three of his girlfriends were killed and only after that did the Chinese determined that he really didn't know anything about the Tungsten Carbide that the Chinese wanted.

After that he was transferred to a secret prison camp in Central China where no one leaves there alive. This prison camp was an unusual place where there were no fences around the prison except for the fence in the interior of the prison where the water and the food were prepared for the prisoners. Each prisoner was allowed only one cup of water a day and a gruel made from a cactus that grew close to the prison and it tasted so bitter that none of the inmates wanted to eat it. But it was eaten to keep them from starving to death.

All the prisoners were free to leave the place whenever they wanted to leave but the North side of the prison was a place with huge sharp basalt that extended for ten miles to the North. The prisoners weren't given any shoes or clothing and basically, they were naked.

In the Gobi Desert it was freezing cold at night and baking hot in the day. The only way that the prisoners could keep from freezing to death was to huddle together at night to keep from freezing to death.

During the day when it got warmer some prisoners ventured out to the desert and were free to leave. But with no water and all of them starved to the point of looking like walking corpses they were lucky to last half a day before they collapsed, and the snow leopards would come to eat what was left of the emaciated thin bodies. The snow leopards had to eat a lot of dead bodies to even get a small meal, but it was easy pickings and all they had to do was to wait until more prisoners ventured out into the Gobi Desert. In this way the prison never got overcrowded.

The escaping prisoners could have eaten the bitter cactus growing in the desert, but they were so bitter that they extracted more liquid from the escaping prisoner's body than they had, and they died a painful death. The snow leopards didn't mind eating the dead corpses because it was basically free food.

There were a few Desert Camels, but they always were in groups and were able to ward off the Snow leopards and sometimes the leopards would get injured d by the dangerous camels.

Ivan found out about the prison from the guards that worked there who was allowed to leave with a small bonus after five years of service at the prison. They could also leave anytime that they that they wanted to leave but they would not receive any money.

The Chinese government wanted the outsiders know how difficult it was for anyone to leave the prison and anyone who came close enough to be able to see the prison, they could be shot by twenty-millimeter canons and if they were using a vehicle or a camel, they were stuck in the Gobi Desert and they too will perish in the desert. No one in their right mind would ever think about going to the prison to look at the prison in the Gobi Desert.

After Ivan learned all this from the retiring guards, he decided not to risk any of his operatives to travel to the Gobi Desert to check for themselves. Besides there was very little chance that Sam was even still alive in the prison, so he closed shop and they all retuned to Okinawa and reported o Matt what they found out in China.

76 NEW YEAR'S EVE

Matt promoted the Pilot to be the new Captain of the yacht and they resumed taking customers out to sea for excursions. Everything else was the same as when Sam was running the marina, and no one seemed to miss Sam.

There were no more kidnappings in Okinawa, and it looked like the Chinese simply gave up trying to obtain any of the highly prized tungsten carbide metal. There were rumors that Thermodynamics was selling various military components to the Chinese and they were making some money.

Instead of Chris flying to see Sierra once a month Sierra flew to Connecticut to be with her husband. Sometimes she stayed in the old B&B that Chris bought for himself because it was located just behind the Chase Manhattan Bank in New York City where he reported to work each workday.

This gave him an extra two hours each workday and he can even go to the gym and get some exercise. But most of the time he just left his car in the garage at the B&B and had a nice walk to the bank. Sometimes he would get to the bank before it opened at ten in the morning so he will walk to a coffee shop or a nice place to have a nice breakfast.

When Sierra visited Chris in New York she usually stayed at the B&B with her husband Chris, and did the same thing with Chris as he did when he went to work. Chris had already rented his parents estate to his next in command because he had two children and the mother - in-law was also living at the estate. Off course Chris's second in command didn't use the entire staff that his father had as well as Chris had when he was still living in the grand estate to cut down on the expenses to run a large estate. But the second in command by the name of Clifford made sure that the estate was still well taken care of.

On weekends Chris and Sierra will book a room at the country club where Matt had an agreement that any of his immediate family members could stay at the country club for free for two weeks or fourteen days scattered throughout the year as they pleased which was more to the liking of the country club because there were always members of the club coming and going all the time from New York City.

In Pasadena where the president of Thermodynamics had his grand mansion where he held his yearly New Year's Party for his top managers and other important friends on New Year's Eve things went well as they did each year.

Next morning When his wife woke up, she noticed her husband was not in bed with her. Sometimes her husband Mr. Gregory Grey will stay up late talking to his friends having a night cap and just sleep in the den, so it didn't bother his wife.

But when her husband Greg didn't show up for breakfast she started to worry, and she called his office at Thermodynamics to see if he might have stopped in his office after the party. The phone in office rang for a long time and finally a security guard pick up the call from his station and said hello.

Cynthia Grey told the guard that her husband was missing and that she couldn't find him anywhere on the estate. The guard said I will call the police and they will come to talk to you as soon as they can.

Ten minutes later a detective and his assistant showed up at the Grey's estate and Cynthia invited them in. They asked her a lot of questions and said that they will send a quad to come to the estate to review all the security tapes from their security system.

The Grey's estate became a beehive of police activity. After three days the detective said we will continue to monitor the case from their office in Pasadena and report to Cynthia as soon as anything surfaced. Cynthia said thanks to the detective Rasmussen and he left with this crew.

Cynthia was now all alone again in the huge estates except for the staff that ran the estate. She called her son Martin who worked at a bank and told him about his father's mysterious disappearance from the estate on New Year's Eve. Her son said I will try and find a good private investigator that specialized in missing persons and that he will get back to his mother as soon as he can.

77 PASADENA

Almost two years have now gone by and there was still no clue about the disappearance of Mr. Gregory Grey. The detective agency that Cynthia's son hired said that he couldn't continue to keep spending any more time on this case, so he backed off from his investigations.

The detective agency in New York City said that we have done everything that we can possibly do so they quit taking money from Cynthia as well.

When her son Martin from Los Angeles who worked for a bank came home for thanksgiving dinner, she showed him a mysterious letter that she got from Mexico City. The letter said that if you send ten million dollars in cash, they will look for Mr. Grey. Cynthia said that letter looked like s scam, so she never bothered to answer them. Her son looked at the letter and agreed.

Her son said that there was a detective company in Okinawa who specialized with important people being kidnapped and that they had a good reputation. Cynthia asked her son to try and get a hold of them and see if they were willing to take on the case. Martin said I will do that.

Back in Okinawa Ivan had few more assignments involving women who disappeared, and he was able to find them and bring them back unharmed. None of them involved dealing with the Chinese. He still had his outpost in Southern China where they grew Shitake mushrooms, and they were actually making some money from that venture.

Ivan received a letter from Pasadena California requesting his help in locating the president of Thermodynamics. Ivan did some research on his computer and found a lot of information about Mr. Gregory Grey. He now knew as much about Mr. Grey as the Pasadena police department did. Ivan also knew that there were some students from Okinawa that were hired by Thermodynamics a long time ago.

Since Ivan was Yuki's son, he had Yuki fly him directly to the Pasadena municipal airport in a small jet. In Pasadena he rented a room in the Four Seasons Motel and called Mr. Gregory Grey's house from the motel. Cynthia picked up the phone and found out that it was the investigator from Okinawa and asked Ivan where he was now. Ivan said that he was in the Four Seasons Motel. Cynthia said I will send my driver to get you in ten minutes and told him to check out of the motel and wait in front of the motel.

Ivan thought that that was a reasonable request and did that. By the time that he checked out of the motel and was now standing I front of the motel a limousine pulled up and the driver asked Ivan if he was the person from Okinawa. Ivan said yes and the driver pushed a button the back door of the limousine opened, and Ivan got in. Fifteen minutes later, Ivan was sitting in grand living room of Cynthia's house.

Cynthia asked Ivan if he had breakfast yet and Ivan said I just arrived in Pasadena and he didn't have time to go anywhere to find a place to have breakfast. Cynthia said my husband's disappearance was a complicated story so she suggested that they have a breakfast, and she can tell Ivan everything that she knew.

Breakfast consisted of French toast, orange juice and a basket of fresh fruit. Ivan guessed that Cynthia was a vegan.

After breakfast they talked for another half an hour and then Cynthia realized that Ivan must be tired from his long trip from Okinawa and had her housekeeper show him to his room. Cynthia said after you have a nap come down and have lunch. Ivan was actually a little tired, so he said thank you to Cynthia and followed the housekeeper to the guest room.

Her guest room was huge with a bathroom attached to the room, so he took a hot bath and fell asleep in the tub. When the tub got cooler, he woke up and put more hot water in the tub and scrubbed himself clean.

There were toiletries in the bathroom, so he shaved and no longer had a morning growth of beard on his face. There were extra clean clothes on a dresser for him to use so he put them on and walked downstairs to meet Cynthia.

At lunch the detective that worked on the case when Mr. Gregory Grey disappeared was also there for lunch and Cynthia introduced the detective to Ivan. After lunch the detective who went by Martinez said I will drive you to my office in Pasadena and show you what we have in our files there. Ivan thought that that would be helpful, so he agreed to go with Martinez and go to the Pasadena Police station.

78 MEETING WITH SHUNJIRO

After a week talking with Detective Martinez Ivan and the detective could find no reason why anybody would want to kidnap the president of Thermodynamics, Mr. Gregory Grey. Ivan said thanks to Martinez for all his help and returned to Cynthia's house. He told Cynthia that he wanted to visit Thermodynamics and talk to some of their employees.

Cynthia said go see my mechanic in the garage and he can give you a car to use while you are working on the case here in Pasadena. The mechanic showed Ivan several cars in the garage and suggested the old Buick that still ran well. Ivan asked the mechanic he had a smaller car that would be easier to park.

The mechanic said let's go in the back lot where we keep our old cars that we are no longer using. There was a red Subaru that needed a paint job and Ivan asked it that Subaru still worked. The mechanic said Subaru's last forever and asked him to wait until he could find the keys for the Subaru.

When he came back, he said I can't find the keys

for the Subaru in the normal place where we keep keys for the old cars. Ivan said maybe the keys are still in the car and walked to the Subaru and sat in the driver's seat and noticed that the keys were still in the ignition. He turned the ignition key on, and the Subaru started right up.

The mechanic said I will drive with you to the office and drop you off there and bring the Subaru back with me so I can change the oil and make sure that everything is still in perfect running condition. And when you are ready to come back just call the house and I will come and get you.

The Mechanic dropped Ivan off at the front door by the lobby and Ivan walked into the lobby and talked to the receptionist. The receptionist asked him if he wanted some coffee and Ivan said sure and he was directed to a comfortable chair by the window. A young lady came with coffee and a donut and left it there with Ivan.

The receptionist came back to Ivan and asked him who he wanted to talk to. Ivan said many years ago there were some students that were hired by the president of the company from Okinawa, but he didn't know their names but wondered if any of them still worked here. The receptionist called the personnel office and a lady picked up and the receptionist handed the phone to Ivan.

They talked for about five minutes and lady on the other end of the phone said I think that Shunjiro can help you told Ivan that Shinjiro will be right down to talk to Ivan.

Shinjiro was no longer a young man but now a man in his thirties and dressed in a grey suit. After five minutes talking to Ivan Shunjiro said I will call my supervisor and tell him that I want to take rest of the day off and we can go somewhere more private to talk. He said I want to go back to my office and get my briefcase and I will be right back then left.

Thirty minutes later they were in a little Mexican restaurant eating Tamales. Ivan asked Shinjiro if the company ever manufactured anything using the rare Tungsten Carbide metal at Thermodynamics. Shunjiro said we did for a few years but after we were not able to get anymore of the metal, we switched to a sister metal, but it was never as good as the original metal.

Ivan asked Shunjiro if they ever shipped any of the original Tungsten Carbide material to anyone out of the country. Shunjiro had to think for a while and then said we once had a Chinese man come to our company to talk to the president and they talked for a long time.

This sparked an interest in Ivan but only said thanks for your time and said I may come back again to talk to you again. Shunjiro said I am all done for today and asked Ivan if he needed a ride somewhere. Ivan asked if Shunjiro knew where the presidents house was and Shunjiro said I'm going that way so I will drive you there and continue from there.

Twenty minutes later Ivan was at the main gate and talking to the guard. The guard got on the phone and called the mechanic and told him that there was a man at the gate waiting to talk to you then hung up. A few minutes later the mechanic came to the gate and picked up Ivan in the old Subaru and drove him back to the house and dropped him off at the front door. A maid came to the door and invited Ivan back into the house .

By now it as supper time and Cynthia told Ivan to go back up to this room and change for supper. Ivan couldn't understand why he should have to change for supper, so he went up to his bedroom to clean up and put on better cloths then he came back down, and he sat in the living room.

Martinez walked into the living room and sat by Ivan and they had a small chat. Next the maid came into the living room and asked them to come into the dining room and Cynthia was already sitting at the dining room table. Cynthia said we are going to have the Barron of beef tonight and she said she hoped that Ivan liked red meat. Ivan was glad it wasn't going to be another vegan dinner, so he was more than happy.

At dinner there was some small talk but after Ivan had his fill of the Barron of Beef, he said I might have some interesting stories to tell everyone as the maid drought them some ice cream and coffee. Ivan told everyone about the kidnapping of Sam at the marina and it was a long and convoluted story but the finally got the whole story told.

Cynthia asked if Ivan could go back to China see if he can go rescue her husband. Ivan told them of the unusual prison where the inmates could walk out into the desert anytime that they wanted to but after only an hour or less and would die from the extreme cold if it was night or be baked by the sun in the Gobi Desert and no one ever got out of there alive.

Ivan had some ice cream and drank some coffee and then said that the only people that he thought could get into the prison without getting killed would be the Mosha Haddin who operated out of Israel. Martinez said I can have my team try to contact them and we can have a meeting.

The dinner was over now so they all broke up and everyone left the dining room table. Ivan said my work here in Pasadena was now over so he told everyone that he will be returning to Okinawa in a day or so.

79 HELICOPTER

When Ivan returned to Southern China to check on his Shitake mushroom farm the place was humming with activity. One of his workers told him that they built a helicopter pad right across the border from China in Viet Nam and they were flying the mushrooms directly to Mian Mar where they quick dried them was selling the dried mushrooms all over the word and now they were making more money than they knew what to do with all the money.

Ivan was glad to hear that they were doing so well. Then he asked if there were still any guards from the Gobi Desert prison that stopped by. The team leader said we see them come by from time to time and that we give them a place to rest and in return they help us with the harvesting of the mushrooms.

The next time that one of them stopped by Ivan was planning on talking to them about the prison. The next time that a helicopter stopped by to pick up more mushrooms he caught a ride back with them and had them drop him off in Saigon.

The war with Viet Nan was long over by now and many Americans came to visit Viet Nam. Their favorite hangout was Soo Chi Ming where there they also had rooms for rent. He rented a nice room and studied the crowd that came to the restaurant from the upstairs balcony above the restaurant.

Whenever he saw anyone that looked interesting to him, we went downstairs to listen to them and see what language they were talking in. One day he ran into three young men who looked like Americans, so he joined them and bought them a round of the best Vietnamese beer that the restaurant sold.

He found out that they were recently discharged from the army and just wanted to see Saigon where one of his fathers talked so much about. He told them that he was a Shitake mushroom farmer and that he was using a middleman to fly the mushrooms to market in Mien Mar where they had a quick drying plant and sold the mushrooms all over the world and even to Japan where they were so popular and asked them if they would be interested in working for him for a while.

The men were young and adventurous and willing to see more of the area in South East Viet Nam. He said I was planning on buying a good helicopter and asked one of them who used to fly a helicopter which one would be the best to buy. The young man asked how much Ivan was willing to spend and he said that he had a lot of backing so he can buy the best helicopter on the market.

Ivan said I 'have a room here above the restaurant so come and see me whenever you want then gave each of them a business card showing his Shitake farms with his name and phone number on the card.

A week later the young man who knew a lot about helicopters came to talk to Ivan and said that he might have a good deal on a helicopter. Ivan said I can leave now, and I can rent a car and go talk to them. The young man who used to fly helicopters went by Flying Frank and they talked as Ivan drove the rental car to a small hut where there were three men staying there.

They parked the rental car in the thick Vietnamese jungle and caught a ride with a Vietnamese farmer carrying a load of vegetables to market. When they were a couple of hundred yards from the hut where the men who said that they had a helicopter Ivan got off the wagon and asked Frying Frank to go first to talk to the men and that he will stay here until you find out more from them.

Flying Frank went to talk to them, and they talked for abut ten minutes and he came back to Ivan. Frank said I think that they are in the American military and just doing some business on the side and maybe they are stealing things and selling them on their own. Ivan asked if they looked armed and Frank said I think they are just armatures. Ivan was well armed, so he walked with Flying Frank to talk to the men himself. Flying Frank introduced Ivan as his boss, and they started to talk about price.

First man said how about a million dollars. Ivan knew that a good helicopter would certainly cost that much so he said I can write you a personal check for a million dollars now and we can take the helicopter with us now. The young man who looked like the team leader said we only deal in cash. Ivan already suspected that the helicopter was stolen but didn't mention that.

Ivan said I own a ranch close to the Chinese border

and if you fly me there now, I can give you a quarter of a million cash right away.

The three men had a small talk among themselves and finally agreed to fly Ivan and Flying Frank to Ivan's farm. One man stayed behind as if he had something to guard and two of them and Ivan and Flying Frank were brought into a hanger where the brand-new looking helicopter was stored.

They all pushed the helicopter by hand and now they were outside. Flying Frank volunteered to fly the helicopter and the team leader said go ahead. Frank checked all the gauges and asked if they had any more aviation fuel around here. The team leader told the other man to get two cans of aviation fuel and bring it to the helicopter. Frank removed the black plastic cap from the square can and took his pocketknife to cut the thin seal on the can and pulled it off the can then started to pour the fuel into the tank of the helicopter.

He went through the normal start up procedure for helicopters and the blades started to rotate as they should. Frank asked it everyone was strapped in and everyone said yes. Ivan was in the front seat of the helicopter and telling Frank which way to fly. Half an hour later Ivan pointed to the helicopter pad and Frank landed the helicopter on the pad.

Ivan called his men on the farm and had them to bring two vehicles to the helicopter pad. They left the helicopter on the pad and Ivan drove them to his Shitake farm and fed all of them. He came back with a suitcase and told them that it and it had cash in the suitcase.

After everyone was fed a good meal Ivan asked Flying Frank if he wanted to go back to with the men that he bought the helicopter from or if he just he wanted to stay on the farm for a while. Franky said I will go back with them and return the rental car back to the hotel for you. Ivan said I am paid up for a whole month at the restaurant so you can use my pad as your own until the rent runs out and handed Franky ten thousand in cash for him to use as he pleased.

Ivan said you know where the farm is now so come up and visit me whenever you want. Ivan said goodbye to the two young men that sold him the helicopter and told them that they were always welcomed at the farm and said goodbye.

80 LEAVING CHINA

Many people passed the porous border in southern China in Quang Ninh province and no one ever checked on who was coming or going from that area. Many of the guards from the Gobi Desert prison knew about Ivan's farm where you can get a fine meal and a place to rest in exchange for harvesting Shitake mushrooms.

Some of them only stayed a few days and others stayed for a month or more because Ivan was not stingy with the pay. Ivan learned to recognize the guards from the Gobi Desert prison and when they were comfortable with Ivan, he would show them a photograph of Mr. Gregory Grey and ask them if they ever saw this man in the prison. Some of them were regulars that worked there many times and none of them ever saw Gregory.

Ivan came to the conclusion that Gregory Grey was never sent to the Gobi Desert prison and wondered if he was still in Beijing.

Ivan kept in touch with the Mosha Haddin group from Israel and he relayed all the information that he managed to get from the guards to them. After Ivan had a hunch that Gregory was actually helping the Chinese, He sent some of the guards to Beijing to see if they can find out anything in Beijing about Gregory.

A month later one of the guards sent word back to Ivan that they found Gregory living in the outskirts of Beijing and he looked perfectly well. He relayed this information to the Mosha Haddin group in Israel and they came to Ivan's ranch in Southern China to make plans to kidnap Gregory and take him out of China.

Ivan could speak enough Chinese, so he decided to go to Beijing and talk to Gregory. Ivan had two Mosha Haddin operatives dressed like Chinese peasants to come with this to serve as guards in case they ran into any problems in Beijing.

The Mosha Haddin operatives found out where Gregory was staying, and they reported back to Ivan and told him that he looked relaxed and had a nice place to live.

Ivan volunteered to go to where Gregory was staying and try to talk to him in person. At first, he went there as a farmer trying to sell fresh vegetables to the cook and go to know the cook. On the next trip he got to know the housekeeper and his knowledge of Chinese was good enough to pass their inspection. On the third trip he handed the housekeeper a note written in broken English saying that he had some information for him and asked him to meet him in a small noodle shop close to his house

He set the time told him to look for an old man who looked like a farmer. Ivan was surprised when he saw Gregory show up at the noodle shop. Ivan suggested that they go to the back of the noodle shop so they can talk in private, and Ivan was still dressed as an old farmer. Outside under a tree sitting at a small table where the cooks cleaned vegetables Ivan talked to Gregory and asked him if he was here in Beijing on his own will.

Gregory said sort of as long as he was able to feed the Chinese government a lot of valuable information. Ivan asked Gregory if he would like to leave Beijing and get back to Pasadena and be with this wife again. Gregory said that would be nice, but he couldn't figure out how that would be possible.

Ivan said that he has a helicopter and has two highly qualified guards that can protect them in a gunfight if need be but that would probably not be necessary because he we can stay on the outskirts of the Gobi Desert and avoid the Chinese radars and be in Viet Nam in one day.

Ivan said don't carry anything with you and meet me tomorrow night here at the noodle shop at ten in the night and we have a car that can drive us to the helicopter, and no one will ever know that you were gone until the next morning and by then we will be next to the Vet Nam border.

Gregory said I will be here tomorrow night at ten then.

The next day Gregory went about his business at his home like usual and straightened out his room. He dressed in his usual dress when he reported to the Chinese government. At nine in the evening, he left the house from the back of the kitchen and walked across the yard into the neighbor's yard and walked to the noodle shop to meet Ivan. The noodle shop was just closing so they walked down an alley and there as a car waiting for them with two men in the car. Ivan told Gregory to sit in the back of the van with him and they drove out of town to an isolated farm. Ivan's operatives were already there and Franky was waiting for them in the camouflaged helicopter.

Ivan stored the car in the barn and closed the barn door. Franky flew the helicopter towards the Gobi Desert, and he flew low on the flat land and soon they were in the Gobi desert. From the desert if was easy going as he flew around the outskirts of the Gobi Desert and they landed on the helipad in Viet Nam. Franky refueled the helicopter and then they flew to southern Viet Nam and boarded a jet for Okinawa.

Ivan said thanks to Franky and told him to go to his Shitake farm whenever he needed money and they have instructions to give him money.

Two hours later they were all in Thor's lumber yard where there was a nice living quarters and they rested there for a few days.

81 PICKING A SITE

Gregory Grey was happy that he made it out of China without getting killed. Ivan advised him not to go back to Pasadena for at least seven years. He suggested that he bring his wife Cynthia to Okinawa where it was a beautiful place and start a new business there.

The Mosha Haddins were given a chunk of Platinum worth more than a hundred million dollars for their help in getting Gregory out of China. They didn't have to resort to violence when they sneaked Gregory out of Beijing but in the event that there was any violence, they could have taken out a dozen men in less than a few minutes, but they were just lucky that no one noticed Gregory being moved.

If it wasn't for Shunjiro Ivan would never have a clue as to who ordered Gregory to be kidnapped so Gregory made him the CEO of Thermodynamics at least for the time being. Shunjiro was surprised to hear that he was being made the CEO of Thermodynamics, and he was going to try do the best job that he can.

Ivan went to the University of southern Okinawa and gave the University a huge amount of money to start a program to study and design small helicopters to be used in Okinawa, primarily on the new Volcano where there were no roads on the volcano yet.

The difficult thing was how to be able to land a helicopter on the inclined slope of the new volcano. The University had a lot to think about in designing such a helicopter for Ivan. Thor footed the initial finance for the new helicopter branch of the University to get started.

Cynthia rented her estate to Shunjiro now that he was the new CEO of Thermodynamics and with his increased wages and other benefits, he was able to hire a staff to run the estate. He didn't have a girlfriend yet because he was working hard ever since he came to work for Thermodynamics in Pasadena but now, he started to think about that.

He started to hold parties for the many managers of the company in his estates and even held picnics in the summer for the entire company members down to the last maintenance workers. He became a sought-after young man that any young lady would love to latch onto and live in the grand estate and be a queen of the company.

Shunjiro was a good-looking young man so there was no shortage of young ladies wanting to get to know him better. Of course, he was a hard-working young man, so work came first. Sometimes the security guards would find him in his office working late hours into the night. He also liked to swim so he spent a lot of time in the swimming pool on the estate swimming both in the one indoors and the larger one outside on one side of the estate.

He bought Taylor made suits for himself that fit him show off his slender swimmer's frame.

Ivan didn't waste any time starting his new

company for building small helicopters and sent for Franky to come to Okinawa to help him in his new company. Franky had never been to Okinawa and marveled how nice the island was laid out. He also noticed that there were no really poor people living on the island and hence no crime on the island.

Ivan decided to build his engineering firm right on the new volcano and it was determined that the new volcano was now stable.

Ivan found a fairly flat section of land on the West side of the volcano and claimed it for his new engineering company and the factory that he was planning to build as soon as the University came up with some good designs for the small helicopter.

82 SAM

Franky decided that he wanted to be the test pilot for the new helicopters. Of course, there were no helicopters for him to fly yet, but he had a lot of models that he built with light balsa wood. Franky had a room next to his office where he could build small models.

Young women also entered the engineering curriculum and in Okinawa where there were no discriminations against having young women enter the field.

He hired one young lady who was energetic and also was good at model building. Ivan gave her own desk in the spare office, and she worked part time because she was still taking classes at the University.

Matt was still living above the three-car garage at Thor's house and had lunch and dinner at Thor's house because they were the best of friends. Thor asked Matt if he wanted to visit the Platinumobelisk again. Matt said that he was getting older now and didn't want to exert himself climbing up any old volcano. He added he still had some bonds in a bank, and he wanted to cash one out and make something new.

Thor asked him if he knew about Ivan trying to start a new company designing small helicopters to use on the new volcano. Matt said I'm no engineer, but I know that helicopters can crash and kill people more easily than airplanes can.

He went to visit his daughter Sierra who was now living in Okinawa most of the time. He was going to ask her if she wanted to take a trip to the states but after noticing her busy schedule, he decided not to ask her. Besides she was now married and had several kids and some of the boys were already grown up. Matt realized that Sierra was now a grown woman and not like the old sidekick that she used to be when she was still single. Matt liked it best when she was a young kid, but he couldn't reverse time and he knew it.

Matt noticed a teenaged girl who would be his grandchild and started to talk to her. He noticed that she spoke mostly Japanese was very poor in speaking English. Matt asked Sierra why she wasn't teaching her how to speak English because if Sierra waited too long, she would never learn to speak a new language.

When Matt's granddaughter Samantha or Sam for short walked into the living room she didn't even acknowledge her grandfather Matt and went directly to her computer and started to work on her computer. Matt asked Sierra how old she was, and Sierra said that she was sixteen going on seventeen, but she skipped a few grades when she was young so just finished high school.

Matt asked Sierra if his granddaughter would like to go om a trip with him sto the states. Sierra said lately she is on some rebellious mood and sometimes won't even talk to her mother or father anymore. Matt said he heard of many teenagers that get that way and it takes something new for them to really get interested in something and then they will snap out of it.

It was lunch time now, so Sierra fixed a salad for lunch and Matt and Sierra started to eat the salad. Matt's granddaughter walked by the table and she pulled up a chair and started to have some salad herself. She didn't say anything but was just listening to Matt and her mother talking about helicopters and Matt was talking about going to the states to talk to some of the best helicopter's manufacturers.

Matt said I want to convert one of my trillion-dollar bearer bonds and take a trip to the United states and have them design and make me a small helicopter for me and I want to start to spend the proceeds from the bonds. Sierra's daughter still didn't say a word, but she was listening to every word that her grandfather was saying. Her real name me was Samantha but she went by Sam most of the time. Matt said I will talk to Yuki to have her fly me to the United states so I can interview a couple of helicopter companies and I may leave in a couple of days or as soon as Yuki sets me up with a jet.

Sam wasn't hungry anymore, but she didn't want to miss out on the interesting things that her grandfather Matt was talking about. Matt thanked Sierra for the salad and told Sierra that he was going back to Thor's house to let him know that he was going to leave Okinawa in a few days as soon as Yuki gets a jet ready for him to fly.

He got up and hugged Sierra and said goodbye as he left Sierra's house. Matt didn't say anything to Sam and acted like she was a nobody.

83 CALIFORNIA

The next day Matt was sitting in the kitchen of Thor's house and having a rice ball and some tea. He heard someone knocking on the kitchen door so he went to the back door and saw Sam standing there. Matt said nice to see you and asked her to come in and have a seat at the table.

He asked Sam if she liked rice balls and she said yes so Matt went to the refrigerator and picked out a rice ball and put it in the microwave. As soon as it pinged, he went and removed it from the microwave oven and put it on a plate and told Sam to be careful because it may be hot.

Sam picked it up and started to eat it. After a few bites Sam put the rice ball and asked her grandfather what the United States was like. Matt said it was very different from Okinawa and said you might like it and asked her if she wanted to go with him to talk to some helicopter companies.

Sam finished her rice ball and said thanks for the rice ball and said I'm going to ask my mother if I can fly to the states with you then she left.

Matt thought that Sam wasn't all that bad on this visit and wondered what came over her. He went back to eat more rice balls and was just thinking about Sam's visit. Half an hour later Sierra called Matt and said that her daughter told her that she wanted to fly to the states with him in a few days and wanted to know if that was O.K. With him.

Matt said that she visited him, and we had some rice balls, and she was very well behaved and that he enjoyed her short visit. Sierra said as long as you are O.K. With her going to the states with you I can't see where it would be a problem then. But if she starts to act up just put her back on the jet and send her back to me. Matt said I think that she will be just fine and maybe she might learn how to speak English better as a result of going to the states with me.

Matt asked if she had a credit card in case she got lost or decided to leave on her own. Sierra said she has, and I will get her a passport as soon as I can. Matt said I don't think that we need one because we are flying on a private jet, but it never hurts to have one.

Sierra asked her father if he will come to the house to pick up Sam on the day of the flight and Matt said I will do that.

Two days later Matt came to Sierra's house to pick up Sam and it looked like Sam was all ready to travel. Sierra handed Sam's suitcase to Matt and Sam gave her mom a big hug and even kissed her on her cheek. Sierra looked surprised that Sam did that but was happy that she did.

After Matt and Sam left Sierra had tears in her eyes.

Soon they were at the airport and ready to board the jet. Captain Tsukinoue was the Captain of the jet today and he introduced himself to Matt and Matt introduced Sam to the Captain as his granddaughter. A stewardess came and showed them to their seats and strapped them in and made sure that the straps were tight.

Captain Tsukinoue announced that we will be leaving in a few minutes and told the stewardesses to strap themselves in as well.
The take-off was smooth, and Sam could see her island disappear beneath some low clouds. Ten minutes alter the jet reached cruising altitude the stewardesses came to ask Matt and Sam if the wanted anything to drink. Matt ordered some hot coffee and Sam ordered some lemonade.

There were several magazines on a table between them, so Sam picked one up written in Japanese and stared to flip through it. The flight was uneventful, so Sam fell asleep. And a stewardess came by to make sure that she was still strapped in her seat.

Matt took a nap himself and woke up five hours later. A stewardess came by and asked Matt if he was ready for lunch. The stewardess named two different entrees and asked which he wanted. Matt chose the Japanese entree and she left.

When the stewardess came back with Matt's lunch Sam woke up because she smelled the food. She unstrapped herself and went to the bathroom and then came back. The stewardess saw her and asked Sam if she was ready for lunch and read of the two lunch options. Sam chose the American entree. Sam watched her grandfather Matt eat his lunch.

After Matt finished his lunch, the stewardess came and picked up his empty paper plate and drought him his coffee. Matt noticed Sam still eating so he picked up a magazine written in English and started to browse through it. Before long Sam finished her lunch and the stewardess came to pick up the empty paper plate. The stewardess asked Sam if she wanted anything to drink and Sam asked what she had. The stewardess said we have cranberry juice, orange juice and a soft drink. Sam asked what kind of soft drink and she said we only have cream soda. Sam asked for the cream soda and it came in a can.

Matt didn't want to push any Unwanted conversation her way, so he continued to read his magazine. After the cream soda Sam went back to sleep and the stewardess came by to make sure that she was still securely strapped in her seat.

The next thing that they knew the jet was descending to a lower altitude and Sam's ears popped and she woke up. Captain landed in Glendale airport because it had a secure place to park the jet and he went there before . He called the tower in Glendale and asked for a private hanger to park the jet. The tower told him that Hanger C-3 was available, so the Captain taxied the jet to hanger to C-3.

They all got out of the jet and the Captain filled out all the paperwork for the jet to be put in the hanger for two weeks. The Captain told Matt that we like the Holiday in and suggested that Matt go there as well so that they can make plans to where to go next.

Matt said good idea, so they all went to the Holiday Inn to check in. Matt put Sam in a room next his room and told her to get cleaned up and meet him in the dining room of the hotel in because we're going to have a good dinner tonight .

.	Half an hour later everyone was assembled in the

Holiday Inn restaurant having dinner. Matt said he was going to contact some well-known helicopter companies in the L.A. Basin and wanted to talk to them first. After dinner the flight crew went to their rooms and the jet crew was tired from their long flight from Okinawa, they went to bed early.

Matt and Sam already slept on the plane, so they stayed in the restaurant to have some desert. Sam was more talkative now, so Matt and Sam had time to talk one on one.

Matt told Sam that he never finished high school, but he did very well in life and made a lot of money. He said on the other hand your mother has a PhD in Japanese and is a very well-educated lady and asked Sam if she planned on going to college. Sam said not right away because she wanted to find out what she really wanted to do with her life first.

After a couple of hours of talking Matt suggested that they retire to their rooms and meet the next morning in the restaurant again.

84 SHUNJIRO

After breakfast Matt had a meeting with the flight crew and told them that he was going to look for a helicopter manufacturing company and wanted to talk to them. He gave the stewardesses five hundred dollars each and told them to enjoy themselves. One of the stewardesses said I may go to Disneyland and check that place out.

Captain Tsukinoue said if you are going to talk to helicopter companies, I may just go with you and learn something about helicopters.

Matt found a branch of the Sikorsky helicopter in Glendale so Matt, Sam and the Captain went to talk to them. Matt asked if Sikorsky could design and build a small helicopter for him. The sales manager said why not just order one of our smallest helicopters and it will save you a lot of money and time.

The man was a good salesman and said our smallest model currently sells for just under half a million dollars but if you buy three of them, I can give you three of them for only a million.

Matt talked it over with Captain Tsukinoue and the

Captain asked if he can I test drive one of them first. The salesman asked if the Captain was a licensed helicopter pilot and the Captain said no. The salesman said if you come back here in two days, I will have our best small helicopter here so we can take you for a test-flight and you can see what the helicopter can do.

Matt said fine we will be back in two days then have you take us for a test flight.

Glendale wasn't that far from Pasadena, so Matt decided to call Thermodynamics and talk to Shunjiro who Matt heard that he was made the CEO of the company. Matt and his granddaughter Sam rented a car and drove to Pasadena to find Shunjiro.

When Matt got to Thermodynamics the receptionist told Matt that he left early today and went home. Matt asked her how he can get a hold of him and the receptionist asked Matt if he was a friend of the big boss. Matt said I think he should remember me even after all these years. The receptionist said give me a minute and I will call his home and see if he is there.

Shunjiro's wife picked up the phone and the receptionist talked to his wife. His wife said wait a minute and I will get him for you. A few minutes later Shunjiro was on the phone with the receptionist who asked him to wait a minute. The receptionist handed the phone to Matt and said the boss wants to talk to you personally. Matt was on the phone a long time taking to Shunjiro then handed the phone back to the receptionist.

The receptionist told Matt that that a limousine will be here soon to pick you up so please have a seat and someone will be here to pick you up.

A chauffeur showed up in uniform and asked for Mr. Nations. Matt got up said that he was Nations. The uniformed chauffeur directed Matt and Sam to the limousine, and they got into the limo. The chauffeur said the boss's house is close by so we should be there in seven minutes or less.

When the Limo got to the gate the guard checked his I.D. and lei him pass through the gate. When the limo got to the house Shunjiro was standing by the door and invited Matt into the house and a maid came to seat them in the living room where they sat down. Shunjiro said I was swimming so I will be put on some proper clothes and be right back.

A maid brought Matt some coffee and some lemonade for Sam. Shunjiro asked Sam if she liked to swim, and Sam answered in Japanese that she didn't know how to swim. Shunjiro was surprised to hear a young girl with flaming red hair speak so fluently in Japanese.

Matt said that Sam was his granddaughter and she just tagged along with him to come to California while I talked to some helicopter manufacturers. Shunjiro asked why are you interested in helicopters and Matt said it was long story and when you have time, I will fly you back to Okinawa and my friend will explain why we are interested in helicopters.

Shunjiro said I went to school in Okinawa and was hired by Thermodynamics to come here a long time ago and I've been here ever since.

Matt said I have a jet in Glendale and when I am done talking to the helicopter people, I can fly you back with me and you can visit your old school. This sounded like a great opportunity to Shunjiro so he said I might just take you up on your offer.

85 SAM STAYS IN PASADENA

Matt, Sam, and Captain Tsukinoue were back at the Sikorsky dealership and the sales Manager was ready with the latest model of the smallest helicopter. The Sikorsky pilot was making his final checks on the helicopter.

When he saw Matt and his small group, he came over to introduce himself and he said my name is Butch McConnell and I am your pilot, then asked everyone if they were ready to have a test flight on the helicopter.

Matt said we are ready, and they all walked to the helicopter and got in. Butch made sure that everyone was securely strapped in. Then he said hang tight, and the helicopter got off the ground like it was a feather in the breeze. When Butch was high enough, he did a loop, and everyone could have fallen out the helicopter if they weren't securely strapped in.

Butch did all kinds of maneuvers and Sam felt sick. The helicopter had been in the air over half an hour, so butch flew back to the Glendale sales landing pad and neatly brought the helicopter on the ground.

Sam immediately got off the small helicopter and

threw up on the ground. They all walked into the sales office and the sales manager asked Matt what he thought about the helicopter. Matt said that he was impressed. The Sales manager asked Matt if he was ready to close the deal and Matt said sure.

Meanwhile, Tsukinoue was talking to the helicopter pilot and they got back into the helicopter and they flew of the ground again. After they were high enough in the sky the helicopter pilot let Captain Tsukinoue take control of the helicopter and did a few maneuvers but not the loop.

Eventually, the helicopter landed again and Tsukinoue came back to the sales office and saw Matt and the sales manager shaking hands. Matt signed a lot of papers after he looked them over carefully.

Sam was now sitting in a chair looking a little pale, but she was all cleaned up again, but she was not smiling. Matt said we are all done here now, so they all left. Matt dropped Tsukinoue off the Holiday inn and told him we may be leaving California in a few days to alert him so he can get the jet ready to fly again.

Matt and Sam drove back to Shunjiro's mansion and the guard knew Matt by now, so he let Matt pass through the gate. Matt parked the car in front of the house and the chauffeur came to move his car into the garage for Matt. Matt thanked the Chauffeur and walked up to the front door and a maid came to the door and let them in.

The maid said her boss was back in his office, but he usually came back for lunch and his wife was taking a nap upstairs.

It was a beautiful hot day in Pasadena so he asked the maid if he could use the pool. The maid said go to the cabana and there are different sizes of swim trunks and swimsuits for Sam as well.

Sam was cleaned up some, but she still smelled of vomit, so she got into the cabana and changed into a swimsuit and she carefully walked into the light blue pool that smelled a little like chlorine but only slightly. She stayed on the shallow side of the pool and did some dog paddling and was able to move around the pool on her own.

Matt went to the deep side of the pool and plunged in and did a few laps. He was out of shape, so he got out of the pool and sat on a lounge chair in the sun it felt great. Sam got out of the pool as well and sat next to Matt, but Matt looked at her snow-white skin and knew that she would get sunburned, so he told her to sit under the umbrella and stay out of the sun. Sam soon fell asleep in the shade and Matt did the same.

The maid came out and woke Matt up and said we are ready to have dinner now and asked them to get dressed and come back in. Matt asked the maid if they had some clothes that would fit Sam because she needed a change of clothes. The maid told Sam to go back into the cabana and told her that there was some change of clothes there.

Matt went up to his room and changed clothes as well and came back down and sat in the living room. Half an hour later Shunjiro's wife came down to the living room and started to talk to Matt.

She was an attractive blond girl, and her given name was Gibson but after she went to Japan, she acquired the name of Michiko and her students in Japan called her Michiko-san when she taught them English. Matt was getting the full background of Shapiro's wife

Gibbs, or Gibson, and understood why Shunjiro and Gibbs got along so well.

Gibson said that she and Shunjiro talked it over about Matt's offer to fly them to Japan his jet and they decided to take him up on his offer, and that her husband was at his office now closing up his office and assigning two managers under him to run the company while he went to Japan.

Matt thought that was fast but didn't say anything. Sam came down to the living room and she looked all cleaned up and dressed in pretty girl clothes.

Shunjiro came home and said I'm ready to travel now. They talked in the living room for a while and the cook came in and asked if they were ready for supper, so they all went into the dining room started to talk there while the cook finished making the dinner.

Shunjiro said we can leave in two days or even tomorrow if that was O.K. with Matt. Sam said I want to stay here longer and learn how to swim better. Sam was already seventeen and finished high school, so she was not a child. Matt asked her what would you do if we were in Japan for oven a month. Sam said you could enroll me in a private school, and I can learn how or speak English better. They all talked it over about Sam attending a private school and Gibson said we have a chauffeur, and he can drive her to any private school in Pasadena and pick her up after school and the maids and the cook could spoil her silly if she wants.

Sam was listening carefully and liked the idea of having the whole mansion all to herself while her grandfather and the other adults went to Japan. Matt said if you get bored, I can come back and bring you back to Japan anytime that you want. Sam had a big smile on her face.

86 TITANIUM FLEXON

Three Sikorski helicopters arrived in Okinawa, and Matt brought one to the University for the students to study. He brought the second one to Thor's new lumber mill on the new volcano. He kept the third one at the airport so that Captain Tsukinoue could use it for special customers who needed to fly to difficult places like high on a volcano.

Thor and Matt used the helicopter to look at the giant obelisk where no one went in a long time. Matt uncovered the red fireproof rubber material and the gauges on the large tanks still showed that they were still almost full. Matt looked in the deep hole and didn't see any small animals making it a home.

Thor stood back in case the Platinum splattered after Matt started to melt the Obelisk. First, he cut the left side of the obelisk then he switched to the right side of the obelisk and the obelisk move slightly. Thor told him to stop, and he climbed up to the left side of the Obelisk pushed the top of the obelisk with his feet it tilted a little more. Then he braced himself against the side of the volcano used both feet and pushed it as far as he could, and the obelisk was now hanging only by a thin ropelike member.

Thor asked Matt what he thought about cutting the last remaining part. Matt looked at it and guested that it will roll all the way down the side of the volcano and end up in the sea. But there was large beach where it was flat, and it may not roll all the way into the ocean. Thor said what the heck go ahead and cut the last restraint. Matt said O.K. here we go.

He cut was irregular in shape so there was no way to predict which way it will roll. It started to roll and bounce around each time it hit a boulder then gained speed and both Matt and thought that it will end up in the ocean then it would be much more difficult of a job to retrieve the huge chunk of the obelisk that cold weigh more than a ton. Finally, it smashed into a huge boulder and the boulder dislodged and the boulder rolled into the sea. But the obelisk was now wedged between two boulders and it was stopped in its tracks.

Matt rolled the hose of the cutting torch and neatly placed it around the large acetylene bottle and then he wrapped the red rubber mat around the bottle with the hose on it and retrieved the rope that was on it originally secured it tightly. After they checked the area, they decided that the place looked like it was except for the missing top of the giant obeisant. Matt found some small trigs and put them over the remainder of the obelisk and now no one could ever tell that there was anything there.

They carefully made their way back down the volcano using the same path that the huge chunk of obelisk made and looked at the Platinum ball that was now wedged tightly between the two large builders. There was no way that they could dislodge the Platinum without using dynamite or something even more powerful. Thor and Matt gathered the smashed boulders laying near the Platinum and covered it like if was some kind of a god. Matt found a small sapling and stuck it between two smaller boulders and hoped that it will start to grow someday. They walked around the west side of the beach until they found Captain Tsukinoue in the cabin, and he like he was napping.

They let him sleep for a while longer and made themselves some coffee and as far as they were concerned their day was done and they were ready to go back home.

Carrying boulders to cover up the Platinum was hard work for older men, so they took a nap as well.

Thor's men who worked at the new volcano found a new vein of strange looking metal but this time it was not golden in color but silver like Titanium. They were able to curt a small piece of it off and Thor said that he will bring it to the University to have it analyzed.

At the University Doctor Edonouchi was no longer there because he retired years ago but now there was a new head of the metal analyzing department by the name of Doctor Ziegler who specialized in unusual metals. When Thor gave the Doctor the small piece of metal, the doctor said this is not Titanium because it was light as a feather. Thor didn't say anything but just asked the doctor to analyze it and he will be back in a few days to find out what the lab found out about the new metal, then they left the lab.

87 FEATHERWEIGHT HELICOPTERS

Sam really liked swimming and she became very fast with her special style of kicking which was twice as fast as the normal style of moving her feet from her ankles. Her style consisted by using only her feet from her ankles .

Nataly who just came home from college was staying in her parents' home who were now in Okinawa for the summer. She approached Sam and told her to come with her to UCLA where there were some girls practicing for the summer Olympics in Japan.

The UCLA pool was a regulation Olympic sized pool, and she used the pool whenever the girls from the Olympic team were done using it. One day the coach of the Olympic team noticed a red headed girl swimming in a completely different style using her feet that he never ever saw before.

Without even using her arms she was swimming as fast as the girls on his Olympic team were swimming. He walked down from the glassed in observation room and waited until Sam was done swimming. When Sam got out of the pool, she wasn't even breathing hard. He asked Sam where she learned to use her feet like that. She said it just came naturally because when she was growing up if she got restless, she just raised her foot on her toes and vibrated her foot until she got caught by the teacher and she had to quit for a while. The Olympic coach was a lady about forty years old and said If you use your arms when you swim you could swim twice as fast as you swim now.

The coaches name was Veronica Lakeside who looked like the famous movie actress of the past century by the name of Veronica Lake. Veronica asked Sam if she would like to join the US swim team and go to Tokyo this summer and even compete if one of the other fully trained swimmers got hurt and couldn't take part in any of the many swimming events.

Sam said I would love to go back to Japan because I haven't been there in a long time. This sounded strange to Veronica coming from a pretty young flaming red headed girl that was just standing in front of her.

Veronica asked Sam what her name was and a phone number that she can get a hold of Sam. Veronica said I will call you in a week and let you know if the committee approves my taking you on as a supernumerary for the Olympics and warned her that she probably will not be able to actually take part in any of the games unless one her girls got sick or injured and only then, would she be allowed to swim in an actual Olympic event.

Sam said at least I will be able to watch the other girls swim and was not the least bit disappointed of what the Olympic Coach told her.

Back in Okinawa the University students completely disassembled the Sikorsky helicopter and remanufactured each piece using the new Titanium colored metal that was even lighter than the gold-colored metal.

The new helicopter was now so light that a strong wind could easily blow the helicopter off its pad it wasn't to tied down with a steel rope to keep it from blowing away. Once people got into the new helicopter it will be heavier and it won't blow away in a strong breeze.

Matt's team also started to copy the Sikorsky helicopter in Thor's lumber mill building close to where the titanium-colored metal was mined. Their replica was also extremely light and also has to be secured with steel rope to keep it from blowing away in a strong breeze.

The only difference in Matt's design was the large plastic enclosure around the passenger and pilot cockpit that was made with heavy plastic. In Matt's model, Matt reduced the thickness of the plastic to one half the original design and the helicopter became even lighter.

After the few experimental flights, the engineers decided that the mainframe and everything else used on the new helicopter didn't need to be as thick as they made it the first time, so they completely redesigned the new helicopter making all of tits structural members even thinner.

The landing skis under the helicopter was so thin they will flex whenever the helicopter landed with a full load of passengers, but it never broke because it was stronger than the original steel rails that the Sikorsky helicopter had.

Thor started to manufacture many of them in a new assembly line factory. They found out that when the helicopter fell into the water it floated like a light piece of wood and the never had to worry about it ever sinking in the water.

The new feather-weight models were sold for ten times as the same price that Sikorsky sold their own models as when they were sold on special sales. There were now more than seventy of these new feather-weight models in Okinawa. So far, there were no accidents except when a customer jumped from the helicopter, and an sprained an ankle but that was not due to any design defect of the helicopter but just a misjudgment of the customer that jumped, and the may have been overweight to start with, and would even sprain his ankle if he jumped off a pickup truck.

Many of these new helicopters were used for delivering food and other things that would be hard to deliver where there were no toads.

Whenever any of the customers wanted their helicopters upgraded, they can always bring them back to the factory and Thor would upgrade any part or even replace a part for a fee for them.

88 OLYMPICS

It was the week before the opening of the official Olympic games in Tokyo and Sam was with her team practicing in the official swimming pool. One of the girls on the swim team sprained her ankle so she was sidelined until she recovered which could take up to a month. There as now a good chance that Sam could actually swim in some of the swim events and maybe even win a bronze medal if she was lucky

Veronica the coach, spent more time teaching Sam how to use her arms to get more speed. After each practice, Sam got faster on all of her swimming events, and there was good chance that she will be a great help to the swim team from the USA.

At the opening ceremonies of the Olympics every member of every country was in the parade except for Sam who insisted on getting more practice.

The first few days of the Olympic events, more attention as given to the track events and the Nigerians made the best show in that event. Some of the men's track team from Japan won some silver medals but no gold.

The women's swim team had to take second fiddle to the men's team who were faster and one of them even won a gold medal.

Finally, it was the women's chance to show off their skills. Sam got to be in the short hundred-meter event and she came in first which would mean that she will be given a gold medal at the end of the women's swim events.

Next day it was day for the two hundred meter race and she came in first by a whole meter which would win her another gold medal.

Next day it was the longer five-hundred meter swim but she had a whole day to rest, but it was still trying for her. She was trailing behind a German girl who looked like a gorilla but after first two hundred meters she started to slow down, and Sam finally caught up to her.

Sam's feet were flipping so fast the that it was hard to see how fast they were flipping, but this was her best skill and she did this all her life. She slowed down her arm movements because she knew that she couldn't keep it up forever and just made sure that she stayed even with swim machine from Germany.

To her great surprise the German girl started to lag behind her so in the last lap Sam gave all she had and used her arms that would certainly wear her down but it was the last lap, so she gave it all she had and won by a full swimmers length. Even Veronica was surprised to see the little red headed Sam beat the great swimmer form Germany.

Fortunately, there was a whole day before the relays were stared and this event took longer because there were more girls in a relay event. Veronica put Sam to be the final swimmer to bring up the rear because Veronica felt that she had enough rest to handle that task.

The last event was the longest event and Sam was swimming behind the German team and it looked like Sam would not be able to make up the difference in this event. When the baton was handed to Sam, she did her darnedest to catch up to the German girl who led her by a full body length.

Instead of waiting for the second lap Sam started to use her arms more and caught up with German girl and now they were neck and neck.

In the final half of the last lap Sam gave it all she had, and passed the German girl by only a second.

The race was so close that the officials had to play the cameras several times to make sure that the American team actually beat the German team by a whole second.

This was a big event because it meant four more gold medals for the winning team. Veronica was thrilled with Sam's great effort. Sam arms were so tired and was so weak that she didn't even try to get herself out of the pool and she just stayed in the pool. Her teammates mates came to help her get out of the pool, she just lay on the side of the pool and trying to recover from the final sprint of the final lap. But with the help of her teammates, she was helped to her feet and she was led to a bench where she could rest.

Fortunately, there were no more relays and Sam wasn't sure if she could take another relay no matter which position she was placed in.

At the final day of the women's events, she stood on the top platform three times and the relay event she was one of the four who was given yet another gold medal.

During rest the Olympic games she mostly stayed in her room watching the T.V. Because her arms hurt so much.

But by the final closing ceremonies she recovered enough that she could take part in the parade and she enjoyed being in the final parade. Her arms still hurt so she passed the honor of carrying the American Flag to one of her teammates and all she had to do was walk in the final parade.

89 CHEMISTRY

After the Olympics Sam decided to stay in Japan and not go back to America and take place in the grand reception for all the athletes that won medals and be a big hero in the United States. She could have been given many opportunities to travel all over the country for a year making speeches and be honored at many different banquets as she made speeches.

But she still hadn't mastered the English language well enough to speak in public which would only make her look like a stupid girl.

Sam went back to Okinawa and stayed with her mother in her modest home where her father came to visit her mother once a month.

Her grandfather Matt and his friend Thor decided to take a big chance see if they can dislodge the one-ton chunk of Platinum themselves but when you're dealing with something worth more than a trillion dollars too many people will get involved and that would start a Platinum rush to the peaceful beach where the Platinum was still stuck between two huge boulders.

They flew to Alaska where Matt used to work for a

mining company and talked to blasting experts that Matt knew. One of them was an old man who quit doing dangerous work after he got is fingers blown off by handling blasting caps. He liked to hang around the Oasis bars on University Avenue talking to his buddies about the good old days when he was a young man.

Matt found him in the Oasis bar and steak house having dinner. Matt asked him if he still recognized him when he was a foreman at the Fort Knox mining camp and old Smithy squinted his eyes and couldn't believe how young he looked.

It was such a long time ago and asked Matt if he was Matt's son. Matt merely said that he changed his diet got on a health kick and his health improved dramatically. He didn't mention the Ume fruit that was responsible for his transformation because there were no Ume trees in Alaska.

When Smity finished his meal at the counter, they switched to a small table away from the crowd at the bar and Matt asked him how he was getting along. Smity said he was now on medicare and was still getting some money from the mine for getting his fingers blown off, so he was doing just fine.

Matt described how he found a huge chunk of metal stuck between two huge boulders and wanted to dislodge the metal ball. Smity asked Matt a lot of questions like if the place was in a populated area and many more questions involving zoning and the like. Matt said that it was on a beach where nobody lives and was at least ten miles from where anybody ever visited.

Smitty said in that case it was easy but then he asked if he wanted to save the metal ball. Matt had to think about this for a while being that he really wanted to save the valuable Platinum.

Matt said that the ball was made from some special metal and he wanted to only retrieve some small pieces of metal and make something from the small pieces. Smitty put what was left of his fingers on his whiskered and thought for a while.

Finally, he said if you really were interested in the metal itself the best thing would be is to pile a lot of rocks on top of the ball so that when you blast it, it won't get blown all over the beach and it will take you forever to find the smaller pieces after the blast. Smitty asked if Matt was going to use Tri-nitro-toluene or dynamite to do the blasting. Matt asked what was Tri-nitro-toluene and Smitty said that as a common liquid that they use in oil fields to snuff out burning oil wells which works the best. Smitty said it usually goes by the name of TNT. Now Matt understood what Smitty was trying to tell him.

TNT couldn't be found in a place like Okinawa, but dynamite might be available. Smitty said do they use fertilizers near the beach and Matt didn't know. Smitty said fertilizers are usually made from a compound of nitrogen and used in fertilizer and it is cheap and readily available almost anywhere. Smitty said go to a library and look up compounds of nitrogen and you should be able to find all the information you need to make a big explosion.

Matt said thanks for the information and gave Smitty five one-hundred-dollar bills and said goodbye and left.

When Matt go back to Okinawa, Matt and Thor went to the University and talked to the chemistry department to have them look up compounds of Nitrogen that were used in fertilizers. Matt found out how dangerous nitrogen was, and he heard of a fertilizer factory in Beirut that blew up and destroyed half of the town where the fertilizer factory was. Matt said let's just forget about trying to dislodge the Platinum for now and get on with other projects.

Two days later a young man who was a chemistry student approached Thor and said that I understand that you were interested in blowing up some rocks. The young man's name was Kondo, Thor was interested to find out more of what he did for a living. Kondo said that he works for his father on a farm and they grow a lot of vegetables and they use a lot of fertilizers and he makes his own fertilizer himself to save his father a lot of money because fertilizer had become more expensive lately.

Thor gave the young man some hundred-dollar bills and asked him how he can get a hold of him. Kondo said the best place would be at the University Chemistry lab where he did most of his research because he was trying to get a degree in Chemistry. Thor said thanks and told him that he may come to see him soon.

90 A SMALL EXPLOSION

Matt and Thor were looking at the pile of rocks on top of thc huge Platinum ball that was wedged between two boulders. Thor said moving these rocks off the titanium is too big of a job and said there must an easier way to do that. Matt looked at the Minnie backhoe that was still close to the rocks and said I can do that in less than an hour so let me try

Half an hour later Matt dug down deep enough that he could see a small tunnel under the Platinum. Matt said if we can put the explosive under the Platinum and maybe we can dislodge it and it will be free from the huge boulders.

They left everything just as it was and went back to the University to talk to Kondo again. Kondo was working on his Doctorial theses on Titonite which was a new element to be added to the periodic table of elements that was never discovered until now. This new element was an element between Lithium and Beryllium, and had unusual qualities that no other element had.

It was ten times lighter than Titanium and ten

times stronger than Tungsten Carbide, and worth more than Diamonds by weight. The only person that found any of this rare metal was Thor, and the had almost an unlimited supply of Titonite. Thor sold a cubic centimeter of the Titonite for a million dollars. Only people who wanted to try to replicate the rare metal would pay that much money for the Titonite.

People already succeed in replicating Diamonds, but it cost almost as much to replicate the Diamonds than it did to just buy natural Diamonds.

Thor and Matt asked Kondo the problem that they had in trying to dislodge the huge ball of Platinum that could be worth more than a billion dollars.

Kondo came up an explosive device that he thought could be used to dislodge the Platinum. Kondo came up with a plastic bag that can be shoved under the Platinum and be filled using a nitro-glycerin small pipe then detonated by a dynamite cap a long fuse.

Matt made a drawing of the two boulders and showed how the Platinum was wedged between the boulders. Kondo asked where the Platinum was now. Thor said that it was on the volcano on the south side of the volcano and no one lived anywhere close to the site. Thor said I have a small boat and we can be there within an hour.

Kondo had an idea and said if we transport the liquid nitrogen separately, then feed it in the bag tube carefully, then feed the glycerin by a tube without giggling anything it would be safe, then we should be able detonate the bag.

Kondo went back to the storage room and brought out a container containing liquid nitrogen and carefully put it in an insulated Styrofoam box. Then he brought out some tubing and a hand pump and several other devices. He said this may not be enough, but I just wanted to see if it would work.

An hour later Kondo was done assembling everything and told everyone to get behind the back for protection in case some rocks blew out of the wedge as I figured that it would. He lit the fuse with a match and watched as it burn and sparkle towards the Platinum. There was no loud explosive noise but just a soft muffled noise and the Platinum rolled free from between the boulders.

Kondo waited a few minutes longer just in case there was a secondary explosion but there was none. Kondo walked up to the huge Platinum ball that was resting on the sand with the side that had green moss still growing on top of it. Kondo asked Thor if this was what they wanted to dislodge from between the boulders that were still where they were and Thor said yes.

Thor went back to this boat and brought back a canvas tarp and covered the mossy titanium ball. Thor said I want to come back later with different tools to work on this later, but this ball can sit where it is tonight and told everybody to get back on his boat.

Kondo gathered what was left of his stuff and got back on the boat. Matt said we should celebrate the great success of Kondo's experiment. And after Thor parked his boat back into the new Marina, he took everyone to the Onsen restaurant, and they had a fine dinner.

After the dinner, Thor asked Kondo if he wanted to go back to the University and Kondo said just drive me back to my mother's house.

Kondo's mother was in her garden picking some vegetables for supper. Kondo introduced his mother to

Thor and Matt and she invited them into her small hut to have tea.

Thor asked Kondo if he was going to stay here for the night, and he said yes. Thor said I would like to be back here in an hour or two to bring your mother some things. They bowed and then left.

As they drove back in Matt's car, he said how are we going to reward Kondo for all of his great work today. Thor said I will think of something soon.

91 SASHIMI DINNER

Two hours later Thor and Matt were back to Kondo's mother's house. Thor asked Kendo's mother what she liked to eat best. She said she liked Sashimi the best but lately rt was hard to come by and it was very expensive now.

Thor said there is a new volcano to the South and there I saw some beautiful tuna swimming there and if I can catch one, I wall bring you one. Matt said what do you want to be called when we talk to you. She said just call me Sachiko. Matt said O.K. We will call you Sachiko-san from now on then. Sachiko said I can't handle a whole tuna and I don't even know how to prepare such a delicate fish.

Thor said in that case let me take you to a restaurant where they prepare Sashimi, and we can all go there now. Thor drove to Kiyoko's new restaurant that just opened where there was a large parking lot and after Thor parked his van, they walked in. It was still early so the place was empty.

Momosan who was in charge of the new

restaurant came out and invited them to come in. Momosan asked Thor if he wanted to be placed in the western style part of the restaurant or if he preferred the Japanese in style better. Thor said he wanted the Japanese style room better.

Momosan led them to the left side of the restaurant where there was a sign in English that read reserved only for special guests that had a reservation sign in large letters. Momosan unlocked the sliding door and there was a genkan where they could change from street shoes to house slippers, and they were seated in a nice room with a brand new Tatamis on the floor.

Momosan said that her Japanese waitress wasn't here yet so she asked them to be seated and she will bring them some green tea and some sembei. As they were seated in the private room, Thor asked Kondo where his father's farm was. He said that his father and his mother were separated more ten years ago, and they were happy doing their own thing. Thor didn't probe anymore after that.

Finally, the Japanese waitress arrived and said sorry for the delay but we don't usually have costumers ask for Japanese section of the restaurant so that is the reason that we keep it locked so Westerners don't walk in here with their shoes on. Now they understood why the place was kept locked up.

The waitress said I will bring you a menu, but before she even finished Thor said don't bother, we came here for the Sashimi dinner. The waitress said good choice because we just got a shipment of fresh tuna it hasn't been frozen yet then she left the room and closed the door again.

When she came back, she had a young man carry

a large wooden tub of steamed hot rice and he put it in the middle of the low table on the tatami.

Next a girl brought in some beautiful pickled vegetables and put several plates all around the table and she said go ahead and start to eat the rice and pickled vegetables because the cook still has to cut up the large tuna which may take a while.

By now everybody was hungry, so they helped themselves to the hot rice and the pickled vegetables and started to eat. When Sachiko tasted the tiny pickled eggplant she said I have never seen such cute little eggplants ever before. Thor said that a lady was growing them on the south side of the new volcano, and they grow so fast because the soil is so full of fresh nutrients that she can't even harvest all of them quick enough.

Thor said I will take you there tomorrow and you can buy some from her.

The Sashimi finally came and there were two huge plates of fresh Sashimi on each plate. Everyone was surprised how thick the Sashimi was. When Sachiko picked one up with her chopsticks and put it in her mouth, she said I've never tasted such tender Sashimi ever before. Thor said that was because the tuna was never frozen before. He said the next time that you come here the tuna would have already been frozen and it won't be so buttery.

Sachiko said " "Ah so desu ne" and had another Sashimi except this time she put some fresh wasabi in the small dish with soy sauce and had another thick slice. No one else was talking because they were all eating the Sashimi.

The waitress noticed that one of the pickled eggplant plates was now gone, so she came back with another fresh plate.

Half an hour later they took a break rested before they went back and had more Sashimi and pickled Eggplants.

They all took their time eating until all of the Sashimi and the eggplants were all gone.

The waitress came back and asked them if they wanted more Sashimi and pickled eggplants. Sachiko said if I have any more, I will burst, and everyone had a silent chuckle.

A waiters came in and removed the empty tub of rice and all the empty plates and the table was now cleared again. The waitress came back with a sake-zuki and some tiny sake cups and said that his was on the house and said that it was just the house-sake and nothing too special. Matt had a small sip of it and so did Kondo. Kondo had several more tiny cups and the Sake was now empty.

The waitress came back with more green tea and it was the perfect aperitif for the evening.

Thor said I should drive you back to your house now and Matt led them to the van as Thor went to pay the bill.

92 OLD LADY

Next morning Thor and Matt were looking at the one-ton chunk of pure Platinum and both Thor and Matt realized that they didn't really didn't need to cut up the chunk of Platinum. It was too heavy for the Minnie backhoe to pick up and they didn't have a boat big enough to be able to carry such a heavy load.

Matt said why don't we just burry this thing right here and worry about it later. Thor said I agree. The backhoe was still there so Matt started it up, started digging a deep hole. Half an hour later there was a hole six feet deep and Matt looked at Thor and he nodded indicating go ahead.

Matt tried to push the huge chunk of titanium with the bucket, but it didn't budge an inch. The sand was too soft. Matt then drove the backhoe to the opposite side of the hole and started to dig a channel from the Platinum ball to the hole. Now there was smooth path for the Platinum to roll into the hole if it were a perfect sphere, but it wasn't and it had an odd shape to it.

Matt tried to cup the Platinum from the opposite

side of the hole but he couldn't reach the heavy ball. Matt then backed the backhoe and drove it to the other side of the Platinum Ball and pushed the irregular shaped titanium and it finally moved a few inches. Thor was watching Matt and said what if you back up more and extend the bucket arm all the way out and use it like a battering ram. Matt said what if I break the backhoe. Thor said try it anyway, so Matt drove the backhoe back until the tracks were now on more solid ground. He slowly cupped the bucket back down so that the bottom of the bucket it touched the platinum and started to push on the ball.

This time the heavy Platinum ball started to move down the channel. A few minutes later it was now on the very edge of the deep hole and Matt stopped and told Thor that if I let the heavy Platinum drop into the hole, Matt said do you realize how hard it will be to get it out of the hole later.

Thor said I don't need the money and asked Matt if he needed the money. Matt realized that he still had all those billion-dollar bearer bonds and said I don't need any more money for as long as I live. Thor then said O.K. Let it go then and Matt gave it the final push and there was a thud and the ground shook.

Twenty minutes later the beach was perfectly smooth over the buried Platinum. Thor said in a year or two we would never be able to know exactly where we buried the titanium. Matt looked at the huge boulder still where they left it and went back to retrieve it and pushes it with the backhoe and put it right over the middle of where the Platinum was now buried.

After all that, they both felt like they solved a big problem. They got back into the motorboat and drove to the south side of the newest volcano.

The boat was now parked close to the shore, so Thor dropped anchor so that the ocean current won't drift the boat out to sea.

The Minnie eggplants were now growing wild, and it looked like no one was now living there anymore. Matt said maybe we should go check just in case the lady fell down and died in the cabin.

Matt removed his shoes and socks tied the shoestrings together hung his shoes around his neck and rolled up his pant legs up as high as he could. Matt moved to the front of the motorboat and carefully put one foot down until his bare foot touched the firm sand under his feet. Thor watched Matt until he got on dry land and watched Matt put his shoes back on.

He then decided to do the same thing and also ended up on dry land. They saw no animals in the area, so they walked up to the cabin and noticed that the cabin door was halfway open. Matt yelled into the cabin saying is there anyone here, but no one answered. The cabin looked empty until they found the bedroom where they saw an old woman laying halfway on the floor with one leg caught in between two vertical bed tubes at the end of the bed and she looked dead. Matt leaned down and put his hand on her wrist, and he thought that he felt a weak pulse. Matt looked at Thor and said I think that she is still alive.

They carefully put her back on the bed and everything stank of urine, so they covered up their nose with clean clothing from a drawer and covered their faces. Matt found a jug of what looked like clean water and he took a sip of it make sure that it was water.

He found a cup and put a small amount of water in

it and brought it to the lady on the bed. He found a clean small hand towel and dipped one corner of the towel and then put it on the lady's lips which were dry as paper.

Matt saw a tongue come out of the mouth and it licked the wet towel with her tongue. Then they found some pillows and propped her up and Matt brought the cup of water and the lady started to drink some of the water and she fell back to sleep.

At least they now knew that she wasn't dead. Both Matt and Thor cleaned up the cabin as well as they can. There was a larger plastic container with some water and Matt found a small cup and tasted it and it tasted O.K.

An hour later they heard a soft grown coming from the bedroom and the lady had her eyes open now. She saw the two men and she said did I die and am I now in heaven. Thor said no you didn't die but you are awake now and we have to get you some nourishment and get you back in better shape.

They gave her more fresh water and let her recover some more. There was comfortable soft chair close by and they asked her if they can move her to the chair. They managed to get her in the chair, and they removed the dirty bedsheets and carried them to the beach and let the ocean waves wash the dirty bedsheets.

Thor found a package of dried miso soup mix, so he put some water in a sauce-pan and heated it up then mixed the dry miso soup mix into the pan and mixed it up. He found a clean towel and put the soup in a bowl and brought it to the old lady. The old lady was too weak to hold the bowl, so Thor found a wooden ladle and put a small amour of soup into it and lifted it to the lady's lips and she closed her eyes and drank a small amount of the soup then fell back to sleep. Matt covered her up with a thin blanket and let her sleep even though it was a warm day.

Matt and Thor and wondered what to do next. The only thing that they could think about was to go back to Okinawa get Sachiko, Kondo's mother and have her come here to help the old lady recover. Matt said the old lady is sleeping now so I will watch her, and you can get Sachiko, and bring her back here to help the poor old lady.

Two hours later the old lady woke up and this time and she looked much better. Matt asked her if she was ready for more misoshiru and she nodded yes. Matt went back to the kitchen heated the soup in same sauce-pan and heated the pan again.

Matt put a small amount of the soup in a bowl and brought it back to the lady. The lady was now strong enough now to hold the bowl herself and feed herself. Matt watched her eat the soup and she ate the whole bowl up this time.

Matt took the empty bowl and the wooden spoon and brought it back into the kitchen and when he returned, he found the old lady sound asleep again. He covered her up again and let her rest.

An hour later Thor returned with Sachiko and Kondo was with his mother. Thor brought them into the bedroom and showed Sachiko the old lady sleeping in the couch. The bedroom still smelled like urine but not as bad as when the dirty sheets were still on the bed.

Thor and Matt brought Sachiko and Kondo back into the kitchen explained how they found her almost dead but how it looked like she might survive. Sachiko said I will stay here and clean up the cabin and Kondo said I can help.

Thor asked Sachiko what she needed to take care of the old lady and Sachiko gave him a long list of things that would be handy to clean up the cabin and a lot of food for the lady. Thor asked Sachiko if she would be fine for now and said I will be back in less than an hour and left with Matt.

93 READY FOR THE OLYMPICS

Sam was washing the dishes in the kitchen when her older brother Anderson walked in and told everyone that he was accepted to join the Olympic swim team for Japan. He was six feet seven inches tall. He said that he was swimming in the University pool when a man saw him and approached him if he wanted to join the men's Olympic swim team because it was summer, and they had a contract with the University of Okinawa because they were cheaper than anywhere in Tokyo and all they had to do was to help pay for a new Olympic length pool.

This surprised both his mother Sierra and her daughter Sam who just finished with the dishes and was putting them away. Anderson, or Andy, to his family said I don't need a pool in Okinawa in the summer because we have pristine beaches here in Okinawa and I can start practicing in the ocean.

Andy looked up at the wall and said if you could win four gold medals I can win twice as many in three years in Germany where the next summer Olympics will be held. Andy said I might even start to study some

German so I can go to Germany early and practice in their Olympic pool.
Sierra said I don't think that they even started to build their Olympic pools in Germany yet. Just then their grandfather, Matt walked in and joined the conversation. After he found out what Andy wanted to do he said I have nice spot on the south side of the second volcano where no one lives there, so i can build you a nice cottage there and you can practice swimming in the ocean.

Sierra said My husband Chris can get a loan from his bank to pay for the house on the beach. Matt said he doesn't need to get a loan I can handle all of it myself. Then he asked everyone how many rooms should I plan to have before I start to build a cabin. Sierra said I wouldn't mind living on the south side of the volcano where it will be sunny in the in the winter and I can rent this place to someone else.

Matt said fine you will have at a cabin on the south side of this volcano in a month.

Thor made another trip to the newest volcano where Sachiko was now living and taking care of the old lady who was getting better each week. Each time that he went there the whole place looked more organized and Sachiko's husband was also there, and he said gave up his old farm and decided to move there because the soil was so full of nutrients and things grew so fast.

Thor bought him a fishing boat so he can go fishing and use the boat to transport his vegetable to the farmer's market in Okinawa. He had a young man living with him in the boat and they were comfortable.

Thor said I will have my men come from my lumber mill to add on this house and you will all be more comfortable. Kondo took up spear fishing because there were so many fine fish in the ocean near the beach. Sachiko always loved to cook any new fish that Kondo caught, and served some for lunch.

Matt made sure that that there was an abundance white rice for them, so Sachiko served them white rice and a variety of pretty small fishes. Off course she also had the pickled Minnie eggplants that both Thor and Matt liked. It was still summer, and the eggplants were still growing all over the hill above the cabin and there were more than she could pickle.

Thor said I will find you some help and you can pickle a lot of it for me and I will keep them in my large refrigerator at home.

One week later, the carpenters finished the temporary cabin including all the modern facilities and Andy and his sister Sam moved in to start practicing swimming in the ocean.

The temporary cabin was built close the spot where Thor and Matt buried the huge one-ton ball of Platinum.

Andy started swimming five miles in the morning before it got too hot and again in the evening because of his fair shin that comes with being a red headed young man. Sam tried sun-screen but it didn't last too long in salt water so she joined Andy when he went for his swims.

She didn't have the endurance that Andy had so she concentrated on short burst of swims in the ocean. She noticed that the ocean had more buoyancy, and her body flew over the surface of the water more quickly than in fresh water like they use in the Olympics.

She noticed that small flying fish liked to swim

next to her in the ocean and when she was too slow, they will fly over her head and end up a yard ahead of her and wondered how they did that

As each week went by, she noticed that her shoulder muscles were getting stronger, and she could even do the butterfly now. She still had three years to practice so there was a good chance that by the time that the Olympics came around, she will be in top shape.

Sam and Andy's father changed his working schedule from coming to Okinawa once a month and changed to staying an entire month because his two oldest boys were now taking over the banking management business.

Chris now had more time to take up swimming in the ocean with Sam and Anderson. Whenever Thor's oldest son caught a large tuna, he cleaned the tuna right on his fishing boat and quickly saved only the best part of the large tuna and let the bones and entrails fall back into the sea. He had a huge cooler on his fishing boat and kept the tuna just above freezing temperature so when he distributed the tuna it will be the best tuna for Sashimi.

He drought a good supply to his mother and father, then some to Sierra and to Sachiko every week so they can nave fresh Sashimi at least once a week. Thor finished the new addition to the cabin for Sachiko and now they had all the room that they wanted. The old lady recovered fully, and started making a lot of pickled Minnie eggplant.

When she had more than the extended family can possibly eat her son brought them to the farmers market and he sold out within the first hour.

People were getting so healthy they all ended up being in better shape.

94 TRAINING

Another year passed and Sam's shoulders got even stronger. She kept racing with the flying fish and now could be above the surface of the salt water for a second which would cut down the tremendous surface tension drag that was caused by having any part of her body partially in the sea water. Off course, in fresh water it may be a different story. But she still had another full year before the actual Olympics in Germany.

Matt flew to Germany close to where the summer games will be held and looked for a place where all of his extended family could stay the next year when the Olympic games in Hamburg will be held. All the best hotels were already fully booked for the Olympics.

The closest town to Hamburg was Luneburg which was only thirty miles from Hamburg which was the size of Fairbanks Alaska. Matt found an old abandoned leather factory with a small stream for sale, with a large farm nearby. Matt knew if he had a whole year to fix up the old factory it could be used for all of his family and even some friends to stay there and drive to Hamburg for the summer games or he could even have one of his helicopters to fly his family back and forth from Hamburg.

He hired local masons and carpenters to immediately start to work on old factory convert it to a five-star hotel. He interviewed local people to work in the old leather factory as soon as it was converted to a grand hotel.

He had the grounds cleaned up and had all the discarded vehicle and other rusted trucks hauled to the dump and the place started to look a lot better. He heard of the man who was a manager of the old factory and hired him to oversee the entire job and offered mi a handsome salary. He was already on the German social security system so he was not starving. He had a few grown children that could help him oversee the rebuilding of the old factory.

By April, the old factory was completely rebuilt so Matt returned to Luneburg to check out the old factory and now it looked like a grand mansion. The staff for the mansion were local hires and they reported to the mansion by car or bicycles if they lived close to the mansion.

. Maximillian turned out to be a great manager and Matt was even thinking about keeping him on even after the Olympics to run the mansion for special clients.

Sierra and her husband Chris were invited to the mansion early to have time to visit Hamburg before the summer Olympic games by which time Hamburg would be a mad house. Sierra told her Dad why don't you build a swimming pool here since there is so much room on the estate with a beautiful stream running through the estate. Matt said great idea, so hired a concrete company to build an Olympic sized swimming pool on the estate.

A helipad was built in front of the mansion so people can fly to Hamburg in less than five minutes using Thor's new lightweight helicopter.

Matt had Sachiko make a lot of pickled Minnie eggplant treats for his family when they arrived in Germany in less than two months.

The Olympic team in Tokyo had their own plans for their best swimmers and they were getting ready for the summer games as well. Newspapers and news commentators already started to post which countries will win the most medals. On top of the list was Germany and Russia. Next it was the United states and a few other large countries in Europe. At the very bottom of the list was Japan with their smaller number of athletes but no one knew about the two dark horses of Sam and her brother Andy who was developing their new style of swimming since they were training in the ocean in Southern Okinawa where no one could see them.

Matt moved Sam and her brother, Anderson to Jonesburg where the new mansion was already built. They can now start to practice in fresh water instead of in the salt water that gave them more buoyancy where they could fly over the water like flying fish when they swam with in the ocean.

Both Sam and Andy were a bit surprised that that they couldn't just fly over the surface of the water like they did in the ocean in salt water which was denser. After the first week of practice in the fresh water both of them started to regain some of their original speed of flying over the surface of the water but there were other advantages in the fresh water that they didn't know about before. They capitalized on the new advantage and continued to practice in fresh water.

The lesser accomplished Japan swim team also joined them in Julesburg to practice with Sam and Andy. Sam and Andy gave them some good advice on how to cut down on the surface tension of the water which would slow down any swimmer. The less accomplished Japanese members of the team miraculously picked up some of the stroke moves that Sam and Andy were using and improved their speed.

A week before the opening ceremonies, Matt brought the team who were living in his mansion to Hamburg so they can spend a day looking around the great city. Off course, the city was overcrowded with touristed from all over the world and was even difficult to find a place to eat in Hamburg but at least they got to see the beautiful city before the games. Maybe after the games some of them can stay in the ne mansion and visit Hamburg some more after most of the tourists were gone.

After the day trip to Hamburg, they all returned their training in their own private pool at the mansion. They all liked the Japanese food preferred by the Japanese cooks who gave them Sashimi once a week and the white rice that wouldn't be served in the Olympic mess halls for all the athletes who came from all the countries from all over the world.

By the week before the opening ceremonies, they were as well trained as they could be, so they took a day off from training and watched some videos from previous Olympic games and watch the best swimmers and their tactics of winning a gold. They watch Sam from the last Olympic games held in Tokyo and complimented her on winning four gold medals.

95 OPENING CEREMONIES

On the morning of the opening ceremonies, Matt drove all the swimmers that were training in his mansion to Hamburg by bus and they got ready to take part in the long parade to be held in Hamburg. There was a lot of standing around and Sam and Andy almost thought about skipping the parade in the opening ceremonies go back to the mansion-hotel but they were already in Hamburg, so they stuck it out and marveled at all the great athletes from all over the world.

The beautiful new stadium in Hamburg was completely filled with spectators but Matt made sure that everyone who wanted to attend the games still had a chance to be there for the opening ceremonies.

The United States had one of the largest number of athletes in the parade as did Russia and Germany. Some countries had only one athlete who carried the country's flag followed by a couple of his important people.

Sam got to carry the Japanese flag for Japan because she won four gold medals in the previous Olympic game which was held in Japan and her great-

great grandfather happened to be Japanese who was Firmin Murakami. Andy was in the very back of group of athletes from Japan and he stood out like a candle being six feet seven inches tall and with flaming red hair and looked completely out of place.

The opening ceremonies lasted forever but it was worth staying up to see it all. After the ceremonies were over it was late in the evening and Matt had the bus waiting to take all the Japanese swim team that were staying at his mansion brought back to the Hotel restaurant and they had late night snack and they all went to sleep after a long soak in the bath.

The next day was the beginning of the games and it started with the track events, but the swimming events didn't start for another three days so the Japanese swim team that were staying at Matt's mansion did a few more days of intensive training.

Three days later when the short sprint events in swimming started Sam took place in the one-hundred-meter race and won a gold. The silver and bronze were also won by Japan. More people started to pay more attention to the small group of Japanese female swimmers.

The next day was the three-hundred-meter race and Japan took all three of that event as well. This surprised people even more including the other half of the Japanese swim team.

The day after that, at the five-hindered-meter race Sam got the gold and her teammates took the silver and bronze.

The final event for the girls' swim team was the long relay and Sam brought up the rear, and barely came in first. This event involved four swimmers, so

Japan won four more gold metals.

After that event Sam and her teammate were all done with the swimming meets and they became spectators of other Olympic game and enjoyed watching all the great athletes who came from all over the world. What surprised everyone was that Jamaica took all the medals for track even being such a small country. There were other surprises that no one would want to miss.

The Olympics lasted a little over two weeks and Sam and her teammates tried to attend most of them but many of them were held simultaneously so seeing all of the was impossible.

At the closing ceremonies Sam and her teammates were honored eight gold metals and the men's team from Japan won several more golds and silvers.

What surprised everyone at the games was that Russia didn't win a single Gold medal even with their huge contingencies of great athletes. Maybe in four years when the games will be held d in Russia things may be different.

After the closing ceremonies were over people stated to leave Hamburg and the city started to look like a ghost town.

All the Japanese athletes from Japan had to return to Japan to Tokyo to take place in their own parade for their great athletes. Anderson, or Andy won nine gold metals and that was a record for all the Olympics games so far.

Matt's hotel restaurant was kept open, and people came there frequently to enjoy the great mansion.

96 POP THE QUESTION

After the Olympics, life itself was like a balloon that was losing all of its air and everything was settling down to earth from somewhere high up in the sky.

This would be natural, after all the excitement of competition was now over with and it will take a while before Sam can get used to a quiet life. She went back to her house that was her home for three years until the Olympics where she and her brother started training hard in the ocean for three years looking forward to the Olympics where they will either win or lose not really knowing until their actual encounter with their competition.

But now, it was all over with. Now she would sometimes go back into the ocean and have a swim and the only company she now had were the flying fish, but she no longer tried to outdo them.

Anderson went back to college to continue his study with no great goal in sight. Sam wasn't ready to go to college. She needed quiet time to unwind from the three years of intense training and wasn't even sure if she wanted to go to Russia in four years to compete in the Olympics again.

` But that was a long ways in the future. In the meantime, she just planned to drift along like log in a stream and see where she will eventually end up.

Sachiko was back to harvesting the wild mini eggplants and pickling them and taking them to the farmers market where she was making new friends. Sometimes her son Kondo would go with her and give her a hand. He seemed to not be interested in anything particular after he got his degree in Chemical engineering and even took a job in Tokyo but as soon as he got there, he hated Tokyo because the place was always a madhouse and people were working such long hours trying to outdo each other and never had time to make new friends. Maybe he wasn't the competitive type.

Kondo went back home to help his mother on her farm and ended up being a big help to her. He certainly didn't need a Chemical Engineering degree to do that.

When Matt went to visit his granddaughter Sam, he noticed that she looked like she no longer had a purpose in life. He gave her one of the lightweight helicopters which was safe and taught her how to fly it.

Sam liked flying the helicopter because it was easier to use on the sandy beach where she lived than trying to use a car where there were no roads to begin with. She was a good enough swimmer to visit different parts of the volcano just by swimming but flying a helicopter was more exciting and even handier than driving car on the sand and getting stuck. She started to explore all over the old volcano as well as the newest volcano and she noticed an old lady harvesting the mini eggplants, so she landed the helicopter on the beach and gave her a hand.

The lady's name was Sachiko, and she was a kind lady and Sam liked her. Sam learned how to pickle the small eggplants and enjoyed eating them and they were healthy to eat with white rice.

Once a week Thor's oldest son brought some tuna to Sachiko so she can have Sashimi and Sam loved Sashimi. Sam started to spend a lot of time with Sachiko and visited her frequently which was easy using her personal helicopter.

Her Mom Sierra and her father Chris spent more time going back to Connecticut and sometimes she was all alone in the big new house by the beach. She always went swimming once a day instead of taking a bath because it was simpler than using the bath tub and she wouldn't have to clean up the bathtub after a bath. Off course, she still take a hot bath once in a while and loved that as well. Life was now so much simpler for her.

One day when Sam flew her helicopter to visit Sachiko, she found her son Kondo helping her harvest the mini eggplants. She parked her helicopter on the beach and helped them harvest the eggplants.

After they were all done harvesting the eggplants, Sachiko invited Sam to stay for dinner. While Sachiko prepared hot rice and some Sashimi Sam and Kondo had time to talk to each other. He told Sam that after he graduated, he took a job in Tokyo but he couldn't stand the place, so he came back home and just helped her mother and they made enough money to live comfortably. Sam didn't dwell on her spending three years training for the Olympics because she was sure that he watched the news and Sam was on the front page of every newspaper for a long time.

Sam just talked about how peaceful it was living on the beach and taking it easy. They seemed to both be happy with their simple life and in due time they became good friends.

Sam even showed Kondo how to fly a helicopter and he took to it quickly. He even thought about buying one for himself to fly pickled eggplants to the farmers market with her mother. Sam liked how he always helped his mother and wondered if she should help her own mother, But, her mother Sierra was not the type to need much help.

Sometimes Sam would use her helicopter to take Sachiko's pickled mini eggplants to the farmers market and found it was fun selling the small jars of eggplants and watching how fast they sold. Sometimes after the farmers market they would go someplace to have dinner instead of going back home and making their own dinner.

There was a new place in Okinawa where they sometimes had a kabuki performance by local performers and at other times it would be a live performance by local people they got better as time went on.

Each time that Sam spent time with Kondo and his mother she felt more relaxed mostly because Kondo was not a competitive person.

When her mother Sierra, came back from her visit from Connecticut she told her how much she like the easy-going manner of Kondo and she wanted her to meet him and his mother. Sierra had nothing else to do when she was back in Okinawa, so she was wantrd to meet Sam's new friend.

At first Sam took her mother Sierra to Sachiko's farm and sometimes she would help her harvest the mini eggplants and after that Sachiko would fix everyone a simple dinner which was always healthy. Before long Sierra was spending more time on Sachiko's farm and having fun. Chris sometimes returned to the bank to see how his two sons were managing the Chase Manhattan Bank and during those periods she would be all by herself or with Sam who was now spending more time with Kondo.

One day when Sierra was alone with Sachiko they started to talk about their children where none of them ever got married and she mentioned this to Sachiko.

Sachiko said she only had one child and now he was a young man, and she knew sooner or later he will find someone he liked and then he will start his own family. Sierra said I wouldn't mind having some grandkids someday and Sachiko said that might be fun and she could show them how to harvest the wild eggplants and even take them to the farmers market with her when they got old enough to do that.

Now the seed was planted and all it took was for their seed to take root and end up in a grand wedding. They both started to have dreams about having wonderful grandchildren. In the meantime, Sam and Kondo were becoming close friends and sometimes they went out together by themselves without an adult chaperon.

One evening after a nice dinner out Kondo popped the question about them getting married. Sam thought how nice life would be being married to Kondo so she said Let's do it.

97 WEDDING PLANS

Sierra already met Kondo and even his mother and couldn't think of a better person for her daughter Sam to get married to. Sierra's husband was back from Connecticut and they started talking about what kind of a wedding they should have for their daughter Sam. They talked to Sam's grandfather Matt and they had a serious meeting.

Matt said I could cash in one of my billion-dollar bearer bonds and we can have the biggest wedding that Okinawa has ever seen and we could use the Crystal palace to have the wedding. They decided to take Sam out to dinner soon and ask her what kind of a wedding she wanted to have.

The dinner was held at the new Japanese restaurant with the private room where they can discuss things in private. Sam's soon to be her husband wasn't there because the was in Stockholm Sweden being honored with a Nobel prize at this time. But Sam knew him well enough that he was easy going enough that he would never object to any kind of plan that Sam came up with.

Sierra said I would like to invite all of my friends, Matt said I would like to invite all of my friends as well. Already there would be more people at the wedding than the Crystal Palace could hold. Also, there would be Kondo's mother who certainly would want to have many of her friends attend the wedding.

Sam said if we have the wedding in the summer, we can have the wedding outdoors on the beach, and it can be right in front of our house on the South side of the volcano where it is a beautiful place to have a wedding and we could use the entire beach because we are the only people living there.

This sounded like great idea, so the place to have the wedding was now agreed upon. The beach was ten times larger than the Crystal Palace and they could invite as many people as they wanted to, and no one would be put out by not being invited. The idea of having a formal wedding was now out of the question if the wedding was going to held on a beach.

None of them wanted to have a religious wedding so the wedding itself could be simple and they could concentrate on the reception which could also take place right after the wedding they could provide the best food that was ever served at any wedding reception in the world.

Sam said if we had the wedding next summer it would give us nine months to prepare for the wedding and even the invitations could be sent out six months in advance Everyone agreed to that suggestion as well.

Matt said I will handle the food part of the reception and no one would have to leave hungry. There were other considerations like sanitation for a big crowd on a beach and Matt said I will handle that also and all that you will have to do was to decide who you wanted to invite to the wedding.

If the invitations were sent out six months in advance it would certainly give all the guest plenty of time to figure out how to get to Okinawa and they can figure that out on their own. Now the wedding sounded a lot simpler except for the sanitation question that Matt said he would take care of also. It looked like Matt had the hardest job of all of them and he was happy to take on all of these tasks for his favorite Granddaughter Sam and he had nine months to prepare for that.

Matt spent the next month staying in the house on the beach where the wedding would take place and he invited the best wedding planners on the island to come to the beach and look over the beach

He talked to Sam and asked her how fancy of gown or dress she would like to wear for her wedding and she said it really didn't matter that much but she thought that it would be fun being that it would be summer if she could immediately remove her gown and jump into the ocean and take a good swim and cool off in the ocean and we could let the guests know that that would happen and they can dress accordingly and join her in the water.

This may even solve some of the sanitation problem so now all Matt had to think about was to provide handy places for all the guests to take a poop after eating a great amount of food.

Matt decided to have fancy portable outhouses that would only be used for a few days and then they would be removed from the beach after a few days after reception

Matt didn't want the usual green tall green

commercial outhouses so he was going to have the fanciest and cleanest out-houses ever made and put several of them all over the beach and maybe some behind some trees that he can plant a few trees on beach for the more modest guests like the older ladies. These outhouses will be painted pink for the ladies and sky blue for the men folks who were too shy to pee in the ocean in their swimsuits.

Matt would have barges on the beach to handle all the food scraps that may result from everyone eating on the beach. One barge will be reserved for clean food scraps. This barge will be pulled out to sea and the left-over food can be fed to fish which will make them happy as well. Paper waste will be put on a separate barge and taken to Ume island and incinerated there and remaining ashes buried or put in the sea where no one lived on Ume island .

If there were any fancy plates that the food venders brought with them to serve their food to the guests, it will be returned the food venders who provided the food, and their staff can handle that job.

It looked like all the bases were now covered and he will have another meeting with Sam and her mother, and they may have some ideas to add to what Matt had already planned for the wedding and the reception that would follow.

98 PRACTICE

July was the month when the actual wedding was to takc placc, but Matt wanted hold practice wedding one month earlier to make sure that he didn't overlook something. June was not necessarily the driest season, but it was dry enough to hold a practice wedding.

Matt had white tents put up just in case there was a shower anyway. When he got to the beach by helicopter, he noticed three beautiful yachts moored off the beach already and it looked like they were already starting to celebrate the wedding.

He used his motorboat to approach the biggest yacht and his son-in-law greeted him said welcome aboard. Matt said I don't have time now because we are going to have a practice wedding today and you are certainly welcome to join us. Chris said I invited a few of my friends and they are here on the other two yachts and asked if Matt wanted them to attend the practice wedding ceremony as well.

Matt said off course, because it will look more authentic. There was a small white plastic cover over the podium where Thor was to be the marriage magistrate the marriage. There were several guests seated in folding chairs ready for the practice wedding to start.

Thor had a Microphone and there were several speakers around entire beach then he said we are now ready to start the ceremony. Everyone quit talking and it go a bit quieter except for a small breeze that rustled the plastic cover.

Thor read the full name of the bride Samantha Lynn Grey and Sam nodded her head. Next, he read the groom's name Takashi Kondo and he nodded. Thor read we are gathered here today to witness the joining of the bride Samantha Lynn Grey to the groom Takashi kondo in holy matrimony.

This sounded like what a priest would say, and Thor probably that he saw on the internet, but it served the purpose well enough. The best man stepped up and handed Takashi the platinum wedding ring to Takashi and he took it in his hand. Thor asked Takashi to repeat after him as he read "with this ring" Takashi repeated "with this ring" Thor had a few more lines for them to repeat after Thor and when that was over with Takashi and Samantha both said "I do"

Then he ended the ceremony by saying I now pronounce you as a married couple and the practice wedding ceremony was over

It was the shortest wedding ceremony that all of the guests ever witnessed, but it did the job, and everyone clapped and congratulated the young couple even if it wasn't the real wedding.

Thor then said we are now going to start the reception party and Sachiko served them all some hot rice and some pickled mini eggplants and some of them ate the rice and pickled eggplants.

Then the bride and groom removed their outer garments and now they were in swim suites and they walked into ocean and took a quick swim. Thor was still on the microphone and told assembled guests they can join the bride a groom for a swim also. No one had their swim suites on, so they couldn't join them.

Beside it looked like it was going to rain, so all got under the tent and waited there until the quick thunderstorm passed over them. Thor got on the loudspeaker and again thanked everyone for attending and said that in a month we will have the real wedding.

At least everyone got a glimpse of what the real wedding ceremony will be like. Chris invited everyone present to come on his yacht and we will continue the party there. Some people went with Chris but most of them went back home.

After that, a crew of men came to remove the tents and store them until they will be used again for the real wedding and the beach was clean as a whistle again. Thor and Matt retreated to Sierra's home on the beach, and they had another meeting. Everyone had a few suggestions and Matt made a note of all of them.

99 WEDDING

It was the beginning of the week of the actual wedding, actuality, it was nine days before the wedding day. There was an armada yachts and beautiful boats anchored in the ocean offshore and you could hear music coming from the yachts and the boats. There was a beautiful houseboat that Takashi rented, and it was fully staffed with cooks and maids to help any of Takashi's special guests.

On the beach there were many small tents where young people camped out and were enjoying all the free food served by the many venders on the beach. There were several uniformed guards with guard dogs patrolling the beach who checked the people on the beach to check if they had an official invitation to the wedding. If anyone didn't have a proper invitation the guards took their photographs and registered them as an uninvited person. They were told that if there was any funny business, they will be escorted to jail and left there for a month, but Okinawa really didn't even have a real jailhouse.

Couple of them looked like homeless people but as long as they were well behaved the guards didn't hassle them. The guards told them to stay away from the wedding guest and not to bother them or ask them for money. If any of them were caught doing that they would be removed from the beach and taken to a temporary jail. The few homeless people stayed hidden during the day and only came out as the venders were closing shop and the venders would give them some leftover food that would otherwise go to waste.

The real guests never saw the homeless people during the day because they stayed away from the beach during the day, and they only came out late at night.

The day of the real wedding finally arrived, and it was a hot July day and most of the guest were dressed in swim suites and seated under umbrellas over their tables.

The actual wedding ceremony went smoothly and Sam's father also with flaming red hair walked his daughter to the alter and Thor officiated as before. The actual wedding went pretty much the same as the practice wedding and there was no rain this time.

As soon as the wedding ceremony was over the bride and groom ran to the beach and removed their outer garments and dove into the ocean. A lot of the guests who were already dressed in swimsuits also joined the bride and groom and tried to keep up with the bride who was an Olympic gold medal winner.

Half an hour later the bride was all cooled off and returned to the beach and joined the many parties that were going on.

After the wedding the bride and groom stayed around to make sure that they had a chance to meet all their friends that came to the wedding.

Three days later the bride and groom thanked everyone that were still left on the beach and left on their honeymoon.

100 FIVE YEARS LATER

Five years flew by since Sam and Takashi Kondo got married and they now had two healthy boys.

Takashi's mother Sachiko hired teen aged high school girls to help her with the mini-eggplant business. All the wild eggplants were replaced with neat rows cultivated eggplants and they were held up off the ground by wooden sticks that she got for free from Thor's lumber mill. Sachiko's new eggplant farm now looked like a well-kept grape orchard with the plants no longer laying on the ground.

With the new sticks, the eggplants were now growing off the ground on elevated vines and all the eggplants were perfectly uniform in shape had no flaws and all of them were perfectly shaped.

Harvesting these new eggplants became much easier compared to when they grew wild and laid the ground and frequently ended up growing in odd, twisted shapes. Also, the girls didn't have to bend down so far to pick them and made the job easier and faster.

Most of the girls were high school girls looking to

earn an easy buck and they came to work after school was out and only worked a few hours each day except Saturday during which time they could pick more boxes.

Sachiko paid them by the box which she preferred because in this way she didn't have keep track how long they worked and on which day they worked if she paid them by the hour.

The girls weren't all the same age, and the older ones were faster and ended up making more money.

Anderson took the job of flying the girls from high school to Sachiko's farm by helicopter for a dollar a trip and it only took him a few minutes to transport them by helicopter and he was going that way anyway because he was free every afternoon and all of his classes were in the morning. Andy also took the job of flying Sachiko to the farmer's market on Saturdays to sell her mini eggplants there and it saved her a lot of time and if Andy was willing to spend a few hours she gave him a percentage of her sales which was quite a bit.

At the farmer's market she quit selling pickled eggplants and just sold fresh eggplants because it took too much of her time to pickle them

Matt built himself a small cabin three hundred yards west of Sam's house and he stayed there from time to time when he was in Okinawa.

On the East side of Sam's house Matt built Sam's mother Sierra and her husband Chris a second house for them to stay in when they didn't want to stay in their first home. Chris was now fully retired now, and his two oldest boys were co-CEO's running the bank.

When Chris and Sierra stayed in their second home next to Sam's home Sam took them swimming and showed them how to swim faster. Both Sierra and

Chris's health improved dramatically with regular exercise and eating healthy food and started to look younger each year.

Sachiko planted a grove of Ume trees halfway up the volcano and they flourished in the new soil and plentiful sunlight.

Sam won five gold medals in the Russian Olympics and Anderson, or Andy won eight golds in Russia. In that Olympic games he met a German girl and they hit it off right away. Her name was Gretchen Gunderstatt, and she was majoring in Far Eastern Languages which included Japanese.

Thor's second oldest boy started fishing after Thor bought him a brand-new fishing boat and he frequently caught some tuna, and he had his deck hands process the tuna at sea put the fresh tuna in a cooler until he came back home and gave some to all of his immediate family and also to Sam and Takashi because they were related as well. Once a week everyone had fresh Sashimi and hot white rice which was easy to prepare, and the tuna was never frozen.

In one of Anderson's visit to Germany Andy proposed to Gretchen and they were now engaged. A wedding was planned for the summer after Gretchen graduated from college In Hamburg.

Matt still had his Hotel mansion in Julesburg, which was only thirty miles from Hamburg, so he started to make plans for a possible wedding in Germany for Anderson who was Sam's older brother.

101 GERMANY

Andy and Gretchen's wedding took place in June and it was held in Hamburg because Gretchen's family lived there. She had one younger sister and one older sister and an uncle who also lived in the same house.

The Gunderstatts were a well-established family in Hamburg, and they had a lot of relatives that lived nearby and many of them were farmers.

Gretchen's father was a Doctor, and her mother was a nurse. The wedding was planned for late June when the weather in northern Germany was the best.

The wedding was planned to be held in a German Gothic Church and the reception was planned to be held on one of the Doctor's brother's farm which was close to Matt's huge Mansion and temporary hotel. Andy, the groom started to take residence on Matt's hotel-mansion starting in late May and in early June and took advantage of the good weather in Northern Germany in May and June.

Most of Matt's retired relatives came in May and stayed in Matt's mansion and took trips to neighboring small towns and took short day trips there by car or helicopter. Even Sam's mother-in-law Sachiko was there, and she visited the local farms to see what kind of crops were grown in Germany.

The wedding took place on a Saturday afternoon in the German Gothic Church, and they sang a lot of German songs during the wedding.

After the wedding, everyone met at Gretchen's uncle Hans's farm where the reception was held. The weather was dry in late June in Northern Germany, so the reception was held outdoors and there was lot of tasty food at the reception. Sachiko was seated next to Gretchen's Uncle Masa whose mother was Japanese, so he spoke some Japanese and Masa and Sachiko spent the whole evening talking to each other. Sachiko told Masa about her beautiful farm in Okinawa and invited Masa to come to visit her in Okinawa. Matt was sitting next to Masa, so he heard Sachiko and Masa talking about their farms, Matt told Masa that he owned a jet and invited him to fly back to Okinawa in a week. Masa said thanks and said he might take Matt up on his offer.

There were three kinds of sourcrout and a lot of fancy sausages that Andy's family never saw before. Of course, they were delicious, and everyone enjoyed eating them. There was no rice but a lot of different kinds of wonderful breads that Andy's family never saw before except for some of the guests that arrived early who went traveling out to the neighboring small towns while they were staying in Matt's mansion.

The reception ended at ten in the evening when it finally got dark. All of Andy's side of the wedding returned to Matt's mansion was in bed by midnight.

Next day Masa came to Matt's mansion driving an

old truck and came to take Sachiko out to see his farm. Sachiko stayed at Masa's farm all day and didn't return until late at night and Sam was a little worried, but she did come back and looked happy.

Masa came back to the mansion every day until the day before Matt was ready to leave Germany and Masa asked Matt if he was serious about his offer to fly him back to Okinawa on his jet. Matt said we have a lot of room, so you are welcome to join us.

102 PROGRESS

When Andy and Gretchen came back from their honeymoon Gretchen's father gave Gretchen a letter addressed to her from Japan. The letter was from her uncle Masa and it contained a document showing a transfer of title which left uncle Masa's farm to Gretchen as a wedding present.

When Doctor Gunderstatt came back from his office that day he said let's go see Uncle Masa's old farm. There was a farm hand plowing a field and there was a housekeeper in the house. The housekeeper invited Doctor Gunderstatt into the house, and he asked her if she knew that Masa gave his farm to his daughter as a wedding present, and she said that he called and told her that he was going to do that'.

The housekeeper said let me show you all the rooms in the house and she led the way. It was a big house, but it looked like it could use some upgrading. The housekeeper said that the house may not look all that great, but the farm was huge, and it extended all the way to great mansion on top of the hill. They could see the mansion from the back window, and it looked like it was ten miles away. Doctor Gunderstatt asked how large the farm was and she said that she was not sure, but she said that it was a little more than ten thousand hectors. Doctor Gunderstatt never heard of such a large farm so close to Hamburg but it was not in Hamburg so he figured that the land may have been cheaper at the time that Masa inherited the farm.

Doctor Gunderstatt said thank you to the housekeeper and said we may be back this weekend and left.

Back in Okinawa Sachiko and Masa were busy working on Sachiko's eggplant farm. The farm was great, but Masa said we should rebuild the old farmhouse one of these days.

When Matt heard that Masa gave his farm to Andy' and his wife as a wedding present he started to think about his big estate mansion in Germany and wondered if he really wanted to keep it. He was already thinking about selling the place, but he didn't need the money.

The next time that they all went out to dinner Matt drought up the idea of giving Andy his mansion in Germany to Andy and his new wife as a wedding present. Chris who was already retired said wouldn't that be a great responsibility for such a young couple. Matt said maybe I should go back to Germany and talk it over with Doctor Gunderstatt and asked him what he thought about the idea.

Matt then asked if anyone wanted to join him on another trip back to Germany. Most of them were retired anyway so they all said great idea and they planned to make another trip in a month.

In Hamburg Doctor Gunderstatt was getting older

and he started to think about retiring. Also, his right eye was getting weak, so he went to see an eye specialist by the name of Franz Eichmann. He was a young man and a specialist for eye problems in older people.

After he examined the Doctor, he said there are more people with your same problems with people getting older and in Berlin they are experimenting with a new treatment. The young man said as soon as I can find a place to start my own practice, I plan to take a trip to Berlin and talk to them.

Doctor Gunderstatt said you can use my practice and use it as your own because I was thinking about retiring soon. This was great news to Franz Eichmann and said I will be willing to pay you some rent. Franz said I will leave this weekend and be back in a week.

Matt and his entourage made it back to Germany and stayed in Matt's mansion again. Masa and Sachiko was also with the group and they brought some mini eggplant starters and some Ume trees with them on Matt's private jet so they bypassed the problems with the agricultural department who will prevent any new species of plants to enter Germany without a year of quarantine before the plant can be released into Germany. Masa's old farmhouse was still there, and Andy and Gretchen didn't move in yet so they said we will just stay here and do some planting.

Matt then drove to Hamburg and found Doctor Gunderstatt packing his things in his office. The doctor said I'm renting this place to a young specialist dealing with eye problem and was thinking about just retiring.

Matt said you're too young to be retiring so maybe you should move to a town where there are no doctors and just be a Family doctor and you can retire after that,

Matt said I have a huge hotel where you can use a part of it for your office. Matt said I can have it remodeled for your office and you can open your practice there. Matt said I am going there now so why don't you follow me there and you can look the place over. The Doctor said I still have whole week to clear my things from this office so I can follow you now. Gretchen who was helping her father said I will join you and called her husband to meet her at Matt's Mansion.

When they all got to the mansion Matt showed them the entire mansion and Doctor Gunderstatt said that the left wing of the mansion will be the perfect place for a small practice. Matt said I can have some masons build you a new entrance coming directly from the parking lot and your customers can park in the parking lot and walk directly into your office. The doctor said that would just great.

Matt said it is close to lunch time so let's go have lunch now. They all walked through the rotunda and ended up in a large dining room and sat down. A waitress dressed in a black and white uniform came to the table and gave them a menu. The menu had the traditional German dishes, so they ordered what they wanted.

Andy walked into the dining room and said I notice that the Olympic style swimming pool is still here, and it looks like no one is using it now. Matt said he closed it soon after the Olympics in Germany and it was never used after that but if you can use it, I can have it restored and it won't be that big of a job.

Andy said I still think that if I practice, I may still have a couple of more Olympic gold medals waiting for me in the future. He joined the group at the table and ordered his lunch when the waitress came back to the table with water.

After this morning there was a million things to plan for now and Matt always liked to be in the one to be in charge of things when there was a lot of progress to be made.

The next day a team of masons was knocking a hole on the left wing of the mansion and they started build the new entrance to the Doctor's office.

Another team of concrete contractors were repairing the Olympic sized swimming pool . Another team of iron workers were building an aluminum frame over the huge outdoor swimming pool and glazers were busy installing double insulated glass plates onto the aluminum frames. Matt estimated that whole swimming pool be ready in three weeks.

Masa and Sachiko finished planting the mini eggplants and the Ume trees and they were watering them.

A team of rice farmers were planting short grained rice originally developed in Sacramento California and they were planting them in the shallow water where there was already wild rice growing along the banks.

Things were happening so fast that most of them couldn't keep up with all the rapid progress.

One of the Masons walked into the doctor's half completed office and said my son has a bad cough and he wanted the doctor to have look at it. Doctor Gunderstatt got his instruments out of his black bag and examined the boy. Doctor Gunderstatt then wrote out a prescription for the boy and gave it to the boy's father who was the mason. Doctor Gunderstatt said that all you need was to get this precondition filled he would be fine in three days.

The masons said we don't have a pharmacist in this town. The doctor said in that case you will have to drive to Hamburg and get the proscription tilled there. The mason said thanks to the doctor and left .

The next time that the Doctor ran into Matt, he told him that what this town needs a pharmacist.

103 ANOTHER FIVE YEARS LATER

Five years later, Andy took part in two more Olympic gamcs. The first one was held in Argentina, so it had to be delayed half a year because Argentina is in the Southern Hemisphere and their summer is in December. Andy won eight golds in that Olympics

He lost his red hair on top of his head, so he just decided to shave it off. Some people that didn't know him started to think that he might be a member of the new Neo-Nazi group that was gaining more members in several different countries.

Doctor Gunderstatt eyes were corrected so he decided to continue his practice a few more years before he finally retired. His first receptionist got older, so she retired and now the Doctor hired two young ladies to help him in his office. He took in a young Doctor to help him in his practice and took more time off.

The rice fields down below from their home started to do so well that Andy started to harvest the rice. Gretchen opened up a health food store in downtown Julesburg where she sold only health foods. She even carried Japanese foods in her store and a lot of oriental people from Hamburg came to her store to by oriental food items.

All three of Andy's boys looked just like Andy when he was a child with their flaming red hair. Andy started to teach them how to swim in their family Olympic sized pool which was covered and heated in the winter.

By the time that they become teenagers they could try out for the Olympic games themselves.

Masa and Sachiko returned to Germany once a year to see how their mini eggplants were doing and harvested some and sold them at Gretchen's health food store.

Whenever Chris came to visit his son Andy and his wife in Germany, he always took one of the boys back with him to Okinawa to stay with him and his wife Sierra for several months each time. Apparently, that was what retired grandparents liked to do. Sierra taught them a few words of Japanese during these visits. Children who learn words when they are young will remember them all their lives.

Sometimes Masa and Sachiko will bring them some of Sachiko's pickled mini eggplants and they loved to eat them with hot white rice. When Thor's son caught a fine tuna, they will give the boy some Sashimi and he learned to love that as well.

When the boy's vacation was over, she sent cases of pickled mini eggplants back with the boy so they can all enjoyed eating them at the mansion in Germany. The boys will always have fond childhood memories of Okinawa and they will remember them all their lives.

Thor and Tomiko finally got old, and they passed

away. Thor's oldest boy took over all of Thors businesses and he ran them with the help of his brother. Yuki for some reason didn't change much and continued to look like a teenager probably because she continued to eat the sour Ume fruit.

Her borrowed daughter that Sierra and Chris loaned her as a baby was now a teenager and frequently came to visit her real mother and they had they had time make up for years of lost time.

104 BACK TO GERMANY

As soon as Anderson's three boys became teenagers Andy talked the German Olympic committee to recruit them as swimmers for the Olympics. They started to swim from the time that they were three years old in their own Olympic sized swimming pool and now they were as tall as Andy. They all had the six feet seven-inch arm span and they had great shoulders and already one of them could out-swim their father who was a gold medal winner in five previous Olympic games all over the world . Andy was now thinking about retiring from the Olympics and just concentrate on continue training his three son's full time.

Matt was getting older now and he chose his favorite granddaughter to continue his good work of helping people succeed in life. He had Yuki's lawyer's draw up a will that will be given to Sam only after he passed away.

But while he still had the chance, he took Sam to all the places that he had trillions of dollars-worth of Platinum and Gold buried in the ground and also took her to Madrid and to Bogota where he had the billion-dollar Bearer Bonds in a safety deposit boxes. Matt registered Sam as the co-owner of all the Bonds.

When Matt brought Sam to Germany to meet her cousins living in the big house, she visited all over the small town of Julesburg. Sam liked to go to the Gretchen's health food and always bought some pickled mini eggplants for herself. At the health food store, she noticed a huge lot next to the store that was for sale. It was a perfect place to build a Japanese Inn, so she bought it using the proceeds from one of the billion-dollar Bearer Bonds from Madrid.

All she had to do was to email the bank in Madrid and give her password and her account in Madrid would automatically show up in the Banks computer system and she can withdraw any amount she wanted from her account in Madrid.

The empty lot next to the Gretchen's health food store was for sale for half a million dollars so she went to the real estate office that was handling sale and bought the land which was still filed with some rusted cars and other discarded junk.

This would be her first project that she had a chance to dive into and it was the most exciting thing she ever did. Her first job was to hire a company from Hamburg who specialized in big clean-up jobs that had a lot of heavy equipment and they had the huge lot completely cleaned up in a matter of only a few days.

She went back to Gretchen's health food store and asked her if she sore had a place to stay at the store. Gretchen said that there was an apartment upstairs and no one was using now so it was all for Sam's to use.

Sam set up the apartment like a command center

and hired some young girls who knew how to use a computer and they set up shop in the apartment.

Sam ordered food from the health food store and a clerk brought them their order from next door. After a busy day Sam treated the girls to a fine dinner before they went home to get some rest. After only a week the girls had photographs of the fanciest Japanese Inns in Tokyo and Sam hired an Architect from Japan by the name of Toshio to oversee the construction of her new Japanese Inn. He also brought his mother with him so she can see Germany for the first time in her life. His mother Ichiko

used to work in one of Tokyo's most famous Japanese Inns and was familiar with how the best Japanese Inns were built and run so she was big help to Sam and her son.

Sam was in Germany for more than a month and she had other responsibilities in Okinawa so she asked Toshio if he could handle the construction of the inn while she returned to Japan and left him with in charge of a bank fund of a ten million dollars. Toshio said you will be surprised when you come back and see how fast I get the job done.

Sam gave Toshio the keys to her office above Gretchen's health food store and said I will be back in a couple of months.

When Sam got back to Okinawa, she told her grandfather Matt, what she was working on in Germany and he was surprised how fast Sam was catching on with getting things done. Matt told her don't be too conservative with spending money because we have more than we could ever spend in several lifetimes because the bonds are accruing more interest faster than we can spend the money.

Matt went to see Yuki to have her lawyers set up a will that will leave all of Matt's holdings to his granddaughter Sam.

Matt decided to go to Germany to see what his granddaughter Sam was working on. When he got there, he was surprised how well it was designed and complimented her for doing such a great job.

Off course the Inn wasn't completely finished but he could tell that it will be a beautiful Japanese Inn.

Matt walked to the South side of the Inn and noticed that there was a lot of heavy equipment working about a half mile to the South next to a large lake and noticed how beautiful the lake looked like as the sun was just setting.

Matt drove down the construction site and talked to the road engineer who was in charge of the construction job. The road engineer said that the state was planning on building a superhighway starting from Hamburg to the next town West of Julesburg, but it would bypass the main part of Julesburg, but people could get to Julesburg by a ramp that will take them to the West side of Julesburg, and it would be good for the people of Julesburg as well because it will cut the travel time by half.

Matt asked the engineer how he could buy some of the land next to the superhighway and the engineer said there will be at least three hundred yards on either side of the highway because it will be reserved for maintenance use and the department of transportation was going to build a steep concrete wall all the way up the hill and probably no one will be allowed to build anything near that area for at least a half a mile.

The engineer said however sometimes the state will lease the land under some conditions as long as they didn't build anything too close to the high wall which a structure could roll the down the long incline and end up in the superhighway. Matt was now getting the picture, so he decided to lease the long piece of land next to the Japanese Inn.

Yuki named her adopted daughter, also named Yuki after herself and a will was already made out in her name as the sole benefactor of everything that her adopted mother owned. The new Yuki will have to learn everything that her adopted mother learned in three lifetimes of her long life and that may take three more lifetimes to learn all of that.

Yuki brought her in her office and gradually started to give her more responsibilities for running her grand dynasty scattered all over Okinawa. The new Yuki was smart and energetic just like when Yuki the adopted mother a young girl and she was enjoyed the responsibilities given to her.

Before long the new Yuki was running the entire enterprise all by herself. The old Yuki took more time off and tended to her Ume grove by her house.

Masa and Sachiko got old and passed away and were buried halfway up the volcano where they can watch the mini eggplants still growing down below.

One of the high school girls that used to work for Sachiko got married and she took over the running of the mini eggplant farm. She was a good manager and she also hired young high school girls to harvest the mini eggplant just like she did when she was a high school girl.

She sold most of the mini eggplants at the farmer's

market, but she was more ambitious, so she built a small factory to pickle the mini eggplants right on the farm and sold them all over the world which made her a rich young lady. Her husband used the lightweight helicopter to bring the Mini eggplants to the farmer's market and the preserved pickled eggplants to the airport to be shipped all of over the world.

She sent ten cases of the pickled mini eggplants to Julesburg to Andy's mansion where he distributed them to different places in Julesburg to be sold. There was a standing order to ship ten cases of the pickled mini eggplants to Germany for Andy's wife to sell in her health food store in Julesburg. Most of them were sold in her wife's fancy health food store and people from Hamburg came to her store just to by the pickled mini eggplants.

Thor's three boys didn't have to train all the time, so Andy decided to show them how to harvest the eggplants now growing wild on his farm down below that were growing wild that Sachiko and Masa planted decades ago.

Andy had the new owner of the new eggplant farm to come to Germany to get his boys started on how to pickle the mini eggplants and make their own pickled eggplants right on their own farm. It took a while, but they did start to make some good mini eggplants. They weren't the best tasting pickled eggplants, so Andy flew to Japan to hire the best vegetable pickling experts to come to Germany to show his boys how to pickle all sorts of fine of vegetables and they got better at it and at first, they ate most of them in their home.

One of the pickling experts was a young girl from Shikoku and she and the oldest boy Gustave got along great because she was also a student at the University taking German as her Major. Her name was Akiko because she was born in the fall and she was a beautiful Japanese girl who was also very tall for a Japanese girl.

Before long they were engaged, and they had big engagement party at the Mansion. Sam bought a jet from a company in Hamburg and had a hanger built for Andy on his large estate for his to use whenever he felt like flying anywhere in the world. One of his sons went to flight school and became a pilot and now he could be a co-pilot under a seasoned captain for the jet.

Andy flew his new jet to Shikoku to bring Akiko's family to Germany for the engagement party. Akiko had several sisters and two brothers who were farmers.

105 LITTLE TOKYO

With so many customers coming to Gretchen's health foods store Matt decided that she needed a larger store. There was huge empty lot North of the health food store, so Matt bought the land and built a much larger store three times larger than the Gretchen's current store. Gretchen still kept her first store open while the second store was being built because it was far enough to the North, so it didn't bother her business while they built the new store.

Matt started to landscape his newly leased five-mile-long strip of land next to the superhighway and planed a grove of Ume trees along the side of the steep incline down to the superhighway where the ume trees wouldn't block the beautiful view to the large lake. The South side of the Japanese Inn was expanded to make a veranda where customers could sit and enjoy the beautiful view of the lake on the other side of the superhighway which was several hundred yards down the from the Inn so no one could hear the traffic of the cars and trucks passing far beneath the Inn.

Matt figured that this would be the perfect place to hold the wedding for Andy's oldest son and his fiancée Akiko. But that was still nine months from now, so he had plenty of time to plan for that.

Sam opened the new Japanese Inn to the customers to see how the restaurant did for the clients and see if they liked the new Inn. The Inn wasn't in the middle of the town so it was difficult for the customers to get to the Inn but those with cars could come to the Inn and have a Japanese dinner.

At first not too many customers came to the Inn and she wondered if she made a mistake by building the Japanese in where she did. But so far, she didn't advertise the Inn and she knew that if people really liked the Inn, they would spread the word and maybe eventually more customers will come to the restaurant.

If there was a good place right in the middle of the town, she would have built the Inn there but there was no land big enough for the large Inn that she had in mind. For now, she could only cross her fingers and hope for the best.

Matt built himself a nice bungalow along the five-mile-long strip next to the Inn but far enough away from the Inn so that the noise would not bother him. He just wanted a quiet little place where he could retreat and be comfortable like this Motorhome that he still had near the small town of San Luis de Colorado. He called Captain Santa Anna to send him two Akita dogs to keep him company and also be guard dogs for his small bungalow.

Toshio and his mother were still with living above the new Inn where she had a great view of the large lake on the other side of the superhighway and his mother who ran the Inn. With very few customers coming to the

Inn she had a lot of time to figure out what type of food to serve at the Inn.

So far, the Inn opened starting at five in the evening and closed at ten at night. Therefore, the running of the Inn was simple. One of Akiko's uncles from Shikoku used to work in a fancy restaurant in Tokyo as a cook, so Sam hired him to be the cook for the new Japanese Inn and the food became better after he took over the kitchen.

Word got around town of the new Japanese Inn and more people started to come to the Inn. Toshio's mother hired a dish washer and a couple of local girls to be waitresses for the Inn.

Gretchen's new health food and grocery store was completed, and it was three times as large as her first one and it also had two stories to the building.
On the second floor there was a delicatessen where customers could get a quick lunch of healthy food.

The entrance to the health food store was switched one-hundred-and-eighty degrees so the entrance to the store was now on the South side of the store instead of the North side of the store. The North side was changed for a place as a loading docks where the farmers could drive up and deliver their fresh produce every morning usually before the store even opened

The second floor also sold Japanese rice bowls, special chopsticks and fancy Japanese dinnerware that could not be bought anywhere else in Germany. Even people who weren't even part Japanese started to come to the new store and started to buy all sorts of Japanese merchandise.

Gretchen had to hire more help to run the store and she also hired a manager for each division of the store.

The old store was removed, and it became the middle of a huge new parking lot between Gretchen's store and the new Japanese Inn, which was a quarter mile away, so the new parking lot was the best kept parking lot in all of Julesburg. The new Japanese Inn also was gaining more popularity and more customers came to eat there at night.

Andy's boys were now so busy harvesting the mini eggplants that Masa and Sachiko planted so many decade ago that they cut down on the pickling part of the of the mini eggplants and sold at Gretchen's at wholesale prices because they had so much of the eggplants.

Across the street from the grocery store and the Japanese Inn where previously there was only large wheat field before small shops started to pop up and one of them was a place where they started to pickle the mini eggplants that were being sold wholesale across the street at Gretchen's grocery store and selling the pickled mini eggplants back to Gretchen's store and now everyone was making more money.

Some people started to call the new area “LITTLE TOKYO” and it caught on.

106 DRY RUNS

When Matt flew back to see how the wedding will be done, he went to the City Hall to find out how they handled the marriage license of even if it was necessary. He couldn't help overhearing some men talking about incorporating the new businesses where Gretchen's super store and the new Japanese Inn was located so he immediately left and went to talk to Doctor Gunderstatt about what the men were talking about.

Doctor Gunderstatt said that the sewer system was getting old and needed rebuilding and that the electric grid was inadequate for the old town so that was the reason that City Hall was thinking about incorporating more areas around the town. The Doctor said before long we may be incorporated into their web and we will have to start to pay more taxes also.

Matt told the Doctor about what happened in Okinawa when the same thing happened, and Yuki decided to simply declare the new rapidity developing part of Southern Okinawa into a new principality like Monaco and beat City Hall to the punch and they didn't know how to handle the new principality. Matt said that Yuki even donated some money to old City Hall ad they quit trying to overthrow the new principality.

Matt said that settles it and have a simple fence built around any place that didn't want to tax and put up a sign that said KLEIN TOKYO. At first no one thought much about it, but when they found out that the New Principality had no income or property taxes more people wanted to be included in the Klein Tokyo community and avoid paying any taxes at all.

The current property taxes were only nine persent of estimated value of the property but it would be much better if they didn't have to pay any taxes at all.

Matt had a Nuclear Power Plant built and supplied the entire town with unlimited power and blackouts stopped happening. Even old City Hall was glad that Matt did that. Next, Matt started to rebuild the sewer systems all of the new developments and they had no more sewer backups, and the citizens were happy about that too. Next Matt built a reverse osmosis filtering plant at the big lake to provide clean fresh water for anyone that wanted to hook into that system.

By this time, it was impossible for City Hall to make any complaints about what Matt did and was grateful that Matt accomplishes all that without City Hall having to pay even a penny. Matt arbitrarily appointed Doctor Gunderstatt as the mew mayor of Klein Tokyo.

The wedding of Andy's oldest son to Akiko was still three months from now so Matt switched all his attention to prepare for the wedding. The wedding was set for July during the dry season in Northern Germany, so Matt decided to have the reception outdoors in the large parking lot between Gretchen's superstore and the new Japanese Inn.

Matt built an impressive nine-foot steel fence around both the Superstore and the Japanese Inn and the entrance to both businesses was in the middle of the large fence with a steel gate that could be automatically opened and closed from the guard compound inside the parking lot. At night there were perimeter Akita guard dogs that patrolled the entire compound and it was one of the safest places in tall of new Klein Tokyo.

Two weeks before the wedding Matt had a practice reception in the parking lot and invited some local guests to see how the reception would play out. There were white tables and chairs arrange all over the parking lot where people could sit and have their dinner. For this dinner it was only tubs of white rice grown in Andy's farm and pickled mini eggplants prepared by the new mini eggplant manufacturing store across the street from the compound.

Akiko and Andy's oldest son Gunther got to meet some of the local people at the practice reception that they would otherwise have time to meet at the real reception.

107 MATT DIES

In the North Atlantic Ocean, the blue-finned tuna came back and seemed like to hang around the Sargasso Sea where it was reported that all the eels in world were hatched there and then migrated from there and spread to the rest of the world and eventually ended up everywhere.

These blue-finned tunas were very smart, so they developed a plan how to disturb the huge mass of eels then the eels which would scatter from the Sargasso Sea and the tunas had free pickings of the delicious eels.

The tunas also ate other sea life as well, but the eels were their favorite meal. Whenever they saw a huge factory ships, they had sense enough to stay far away from them. They knew that nets meant death, so they stayed away from them as well.

No one could figure out why they were so smart, but they were, so they propagated and multiplied and continued to feast on the eels. Only rarely would a fisherman catch one using a handheld fishing pole from a small fishing boat, and that was the reason that they knew that they were back.

When Andy's son Gunther and Akiko got married, Matt gave them his cabin by the Japanese Inn as a wedding gift and he moved back to Okinawa.
Matt liked Okinawa the best and spent most of his time there with his great-great-randdaughter Sam whose kids were now getting older.

Sam liked living in her modest home on the beach and the house to her left of her was now empty after her parents passed away. The house on the right was also empty now. Sam's three boys were now teenagers and had a lot of energy, so she told them about the one-ton chunk of Platinum still buried on the beach, but the stone marker was now gone so they had to look for it on their own.

Sam knew that Thor and Matt buried it close to her home but that was so long ago that it would be a miracle if her boys ever managed find it. For now, it was just something that the boys can get together and gain some camaraderie between themselves that would last them the rest of their lives even if they never managed to find the one-ton chunk of Platinum worth more than several hundred billion dollars.

On the next volcano to the South where the Minnie eggplant farm was it was still flourishing, and people were still using the lightweight helicopters for transportation because no one wanted a lot of people coming to their private beaches and making a mess of the place so there were no roads built on the beaches and they wanted to keep it that way as long as they could.

In Germany all the new maps no longer showed Julesburg on the maps. Now it was all Klein Tok. The last part of Tokyo was dropped because it no longer mattered. Someday someone may get curious and find out that there was a town called Julesburg but for now it was just Klein Tok.

Gunther and Akiko now had three boys and were still living in the cabin that Matt gave them as a wedding present, but the cabin was now too small for a family of five. Gunther and Akiko decided to rent the cabin to someone that worked at the Inn or the superstore because it was so close to those two places and they can walk to work from the cabin.

The old Mansion on the hill which was still owned by Andy was still available with many empty rooms now that another of Andy's boys got married to a German girl and her father gave her daughter a farm with a nice house to live in. The farm had a lot of livestock and the farm made a lot of money. Sam's husband still worked at the University teaching graduate students who were working on their master's degrees. It was an easy job for Toshio because he only had to be at the University three days a week for only a few hours at a time.

One day, Matt didn't wake up from his nap and just kept sleeping for three days. When he finally did wake up, he no longer could remember anything and even lost his ability to speak. This was a common occurrence with older people who contracted Alzheimer's disease, but usually they got the disease gradually but in Matt's case it came on suddenly which was rare.

Matt was Sam's favorite great-gteat-great-grandfather, so she was not going to trust having him put in a nursing home and rot away. Sam brought Matt home to her own home and gave him a comfortable room and took care of him herself with loving care.

At first Matt slept eight hours then got up and ate

something and went for a walk on the beach which was the safest place in Okinawa. But as the weeks went by, he continued to sleep longer each time and was now sleeping more than twenty hours at a time. Sometimes when he did wake up at midnight while everyone was still sleeping. He never bothered anybody but just went out on the beach an took a long walk.

Eventually, his sleeping schedule became more regular, and he started to wake up a ten in the morning and go back to sleep at two in the afternoon. Sam's youngest daughter Sukiko was nine years old now and was always at home so she always walked with her great-great-great Grandfather Matt on the beach, and they became great pals even if Matt could no longer talk.

Sometimes Matt will get a shovel and try to dig in the sand on the beach but that was too slow. He found some tools and started to fix the old mini backhoe which was now just a relic but sometimes Matt would get it going and he showed Sukiko how to operate the mini backhoe, but it quickly kept breaking down, so they finally quit trying to use it. Sometimes Matt would make a drawing in the sand and it looked like he was trying to tell Sukiko something.

One day Matt didn't wake up and didn't get out of bed for two days. Sukiko tried to wake Matt up but she couldn't wake him up, she told her mother and Sam come to check on Matt and Sam found that he was not breathing. Sam tried to wake hm up, but it was no use because he was now dead. They had a small family funeral for Matt and tried to decide where to burry Matt. Sukiko wanted Matt buried close to the cabin up on the volcano where Matt could see the beautiful beach, they agreed to have Matt buried where Sukiko wanted him buried.

Sukiko brought Matt food and other things to Matt's grave because the Japanese had that kind of tradition. Sukiko would spend a lot of time at Matt's grave talking to Matt who was buried there. Sukiko kept this up for three years just like Hachiko the famous Akita dog in Shibuya train station who waited for her master for eleven years until the Akita finally died and the people of Shibuya honored the Akita dog with a statue of Hachiko at the train station.

Sam was worried about her daughter Sukiko, so she asked Sukiko what she wanted for her birthday present one day, Sukiko said she wanted a mini-backhoe. This surprised Sam so she talked it over with her husband Toshio and they finally decided to buy her what she asked for.

Every day after school Sukiko practiced on her own and got better at operating the backhoe.

108 THE WILL

The reading of the will prepared by Matt was done at thc family house on the beach and it was private. The will left all of the billion-dollar Bearer Bond for Sukiko, but she will have to wait until she reached the age of twenty-one before she could have control of those Bearer Bonds.

The Castle in Columbia was left to Sam's oldest son as well as Francisco's cabin where they found the Bearer Bonds. Originally.

All the property and businesses in San Luis were left to the second son to do as he wished with his businesses along with a hundred million in cash deposited in the Sumitomo Bank of Okinawa.

Another hundred million in cash was deposited in the bank was also left for all of Sam's sons because they may need it to fix up the properties that they inherited.

Matt also left a million dollars in cash for the new girl that took over the mini-eggplant farm. The Motorhome in near San Luis was left to Sierra and she can pass that to someone else after she passes away when the time comes.

A hundred million was also left for both of Sukiko's older sisters to do as they wished with the money.

This pretty much covered everything stated in the will.

Sukiko finished High School then enrolled at the University and took courses in finances so when her inheritance becomes due at the age of twenty-one, she will be better prepared and not do foolish things with her Bearer Bonds.

After Sukiko finished High School Sam took her on a vacation to Klein-Tok in Germany and they spent a month at the Japanese Inn and got to see all of the town of Klein-Tok. They were invited by all of their relatives living in Klein-Tok and Sukiko was welcomed by all her relatives there. She even took some swimming lessons from Andy's youngest son who was already an Olympic gold medal winner.

Sam's older brother Anderson, or Andy, took over the job of being the new Mayor of Klein-Tok and proposed a tax of three percent of the federal Income tax that was being paid by all citizens of Germany to be paid to the City of Klein-Tok to pay for road repairs, Garbage collection and upkeep of all the parks and recreation parks in Klein-Tok.

The First National Bank of Klein-Tok offered bonds for sale at a three percent maturity gain to be paid at the end of twenty years after full maturity. These bonds were better than C.D.'s offered from the banks in Hamburg which only averaged a little more than one-percent paid by most banks all over Germany. More than half of the bonds were scarfed up by other banks all over

Germany.

When Sam heard about the new hospital Sam donated a hundred million to the Hospital committee and the committee decided to name the hospital Samantha Grey Hospital in her honor.

A few days before Sam and Sukiko were scheduled to fly back to Okinawa the Town's people threw a big party for Sam and Sukiko as a going away party for them. Anyone that wanted to attend was allowed to join the party for small fee of only ten dollars to cover the cost of the party and to keep out the rift-raft coming from neighboring towns to come to the party just get free food.

The party was held at the new addition to the Japanese Inn which was the only place big enough to hold such a large crowd. In addition to the food prepared by the Inn any of the small businesses were allowed to bring their own special food products that served as great advertisement for their business as well and was mentioned in the program.

The newly formed Philharmonic Orchestra of Klein-Tok performed during the party and they did an amazingly good job. There were other famous opera singers and musicians that volunteered to perform at the party as well.

There were television and newspaper crews at the parry recording everything at the party and was broadcast t all over all the neighboring town and villages as well as in many of the big cities in Germany.

Sam was asked to give a speech during the party, and she never expected that her donation of a hundred million dollars to start the Hospital fund would end up with this much attention. The Hospital committee presented Samantha with a bouquet of red roses at the party just before her speech by the president of the hospital committee.

109 SUKIKO

Sukiko received her master's degree in Business Administration at thc agc of twcnty thrcc, from thc University of Okinawa and she returned to her family home on the beach, and they had a small party for her there.

During the party everyone kept referring to Great-Great-Great Grandpa Matt and it became too long to refer to him that way, so they all decided to shorten his title to just Grandpa Matt who passed away a long time ago and was still buried just above the cabin from where they were all sitting.

The oldest boy Ichigun told everyone that after the first year that he went to check on the Castle in Columbia the noticed that the place needed a lot of repairs but even before he started to think about how he was going to tackle the big job a real estate company from Bogota sent an agent to the Castle and offered him fifty billion dollars for the Castle. He said that it sounded like a great idea, but he turned it down because he wanted to think about for another year.

Ichigun did some research and found out that the original owner who built the Castle spent more than twenty million dollars just to remove a large mountain to get the gravel necessary to build the Castle before they could even start to build the Castle.

Then a few decades later Grandpa Matt spent another billion just to replace the run-down sewer system and built a new Nuclear Electric Generator to replace the old system which was inadequate by then. Then Grandpa Matt spent more millions improving the Castle in the years that followed.

Ichigun knew that even if he never decided to live in the Castle himself, he thought that the Castle was worth keeping for future generations of their clan, so he turned down the generous offer made to him by the Real Estate Company in Bogota Columbia.

Next it was Tsuguio's turn to report what he was doing all these years and he talked about the land and holdings in San Luis de Colorado.

After the party Sukiko walked up the volcano to visit her Great-Great-Great Grandfather's grave and she put some flowers on his grave. she liked the grave site because it was quiet there and told him that she finally got her MBA got had a quiet moment at the grave.

110 At the Grave

It's been many years since Sukiko visited her great-great-grand-Grandfather's grave, so she decided to visit the grave again.

No one was living at the cabin on the beach anymore and it was empty. She walked in the cabin and there were cobwebs in the rooms, but it looked like no one ever came here and bothered the place.

Sukiko walked up the volcano to visit Matt's he grave. The grave looked overgrown with weeds, so she cleaned up the grave site. Sukiko told her Great-Great-Great-Grandfather everything that she was doing the past seven years.

There was a slight breeze and a tree branch kept scraping against Matt's grave stone and it kept making scratching noise like It was trying to tell Sukiko something, the noise sounded like "Baackhoow".

Sukiko thought perhaps her Grandpa was trying to tell something, stranger things have happened before like the ancient tales told in the Christion faith.

Sukiko walked up to the backhoe, and the wind blew and it seemed to bow to her. She brushed the dirt off the seat of the backhoe and noticed that the key was still attached to the ignition with the same thin steel line. She turned the key and it made a sputtering noise and tried to start but it died. She figured that the backhoe was either out of fuel or it was too old. She knew that her grandpa always kept spare cans of diesel fuel in the shed, so she went there and found a red plastic can an of diesel fuel.

She came back and put the diesel fuel in to the rusty old backhoe and tried again and this time the backhoe sputtered for a while but then it kept o running and eventually it sounded likes a brand new backhoe.

Sukiko remembered where her Grandpa used to try to tell her where to dig. So she drove the backhoe to the approximate area and started to dig there. After an hour of digging, she needed a break, so she went back into the old cabin and found a box with small bags of green tea. She turned the faucet of but no water came out.

She always carried emergency supplies in her helicopter and retrieved a plastic bottle of clean water and brought it back into the kitchen and finished making hot water. The stove worked on propane so it still worked.

She made hot water and had some tea. She mentally went through all the jobs that she had in the past seven years and remembered that none of them were what she really liked to do as she quit each of them serially.

A cute little squirrel came into the kitchen and made a lot of noise like it was trying to tell Sukiko what are you doing in my house. If she had anything to give to the squirrel she would have, but there was nothing in the kitchen, and squirrel kept on scolding her.

Sukiko liked the cute little squirrel but it was so noisy that she went back outside and returned to the backhoe and noticed that the hole was already five feet deep, and she thought maybe she was just wasting her time. But she was already sitting in the backhoe so she started it up again and started to dig some more. A few minutes later the bucket hit something solid an she could see something shiny in the ground.

She dug more sand out of the hole and now she could go down there and get a better look at the shiny metal. She went to the tool shed and got a chisel and a hammer and started to chip away on the sot metal and soon she had chunk of metal about the size of thumb.

She went back to the house and brought back a plastic table cloth and covered the metal and put some sand on top and a left it there.

She got back on her helicopter and flew back to Okinawa, parked her helicopter, and got back into her car and drove it directly to the Sumitomo bank to have the metal assayed.

She found out that the small piece of metal that she brought in was pure Platinum and it was worth more than a million dollars. The bank manager brought her into his private office and suggested that she set up a new bank account and put most of money in C.D.'s, some in savings, and set up a credit account. Sukiko agreed, and the Bank manager called his head account secretary and asked her to set up everything for the young lady. The account lady walked Sukiko to her own office and explained everything to Sukiko and a half an hour they were all done.

Sukiko walked out of the bank with her new credit card, her new savings account, and bag full of cash. She needed some time to digest everything that happened this morning, so she drove to Pizza Parlor No. Two, and ordered a rice ball and some green tea.

Kill the Bully 111

Sukiko drove back to her apartment that she was renting with her friend and found her with a black eye. Sukiko already guessed what happened and said did Masami find you again and beat you up. It was obvious that he did find her. Tsukiko said I will never be able to get rid of him.

Tsukiko said at first he was nice and wanted her to come back to take care of him again. Tsukiko already did this many times and it was always the same, but with the slightest thing that bothered him he went into a rage and ended up beating her up all over again and it was always the same.

But this time, he broke her new computer and that was the thing that hurt her the most and she would never be able to replace that at least for another year of scrimping and even skipping meals to buy another computer.

Sukiko said you can't stay here anymore because he already knows where you live, and he will keep coming back to you until you end up his salve for life.

Sukiko said just leave everything just as it is and come with me. She drove Tsukiko to the airport and Sukiko bought two first class to Osaka where she used to work for a whole year until she finally quit.

When the jet landed at Kansai airport in Osaka Sukiko hired a taxi and the taxi drove them directly to the Dojo where her old friend taught a class in self-defense to his students.

When they walked into the Dojo, the assistant instructor came up to them and said that the Sensei went out for a while to take a break, but he will be back soon. Sukiko and Tsukiko watched the students in the Dojo practicing their moves marveled how good the students were.

Half an hour later, Tonogun walked in and saw Sukiko and asked where have you been. Sukiko said it was a long story, but she now had an emergency and needed his help.

Sukiko said this may take a while so where is a good place to have something to eat. Tonogun said we are only a block away from the Tenmonji restaurant but that is a fancy restaurant and didn't know if Sukiko was willing to spend that money just for a dinner.

Sukiko said I came into some money and I no longer have to worry about money anymore so let's go there.

Tenmonji was a beautiful restaurant, and they were seated at nice table. A waiter came by and dropped them a menu and left. A waitress came by with cold water gave them water.

While they were sitting at the table, Sukiko

went through the whole story about her friend Tsukiko getting beat up and she was not able to get away from her abusive boyfriend. Tonogun could see the big black eye on Tsukiko's eye and knew that this as a serious matter.

Sukiko said If I give you a million dollars now, could you leave your Dojo for a week and have your assistant trainers take over for a week and you can come with me back to Okinawa and take care of the abusive bully.

A million dollars was a huge amount of money to anyone so Tonogun said fine I will be happy to come to Okinawa and take care of the bully. Sukiko said I will stay in the Osaka Inn and wait for you there until you take care of your Dojo and we can fly to Okinawa with you to show you where you can stay there and wait for the the bully.

Two hours later they were all in Tsukiko's apartment waiting for the bully to show up. Sure enough the bully showed up and saw his girlfriend told her to come with her right now. The Bully noticed Tonogun and asked him who he was. Tonogun said I'm just here to beat you up. The bully was a big boy and weighted more than 250 pounds.

The saw Tonogun sitting in the couch and threw a haymaker at him and caught Tonogun on his upper lip. Tonogun took his finger and touched his lip and noticed blood, which pissed him off.

The bully wasn't done yet and lunged at Tonogun still sitting in the chair.

Tonogun flipped out of the chair, and gave the bully a Karate chop on the back of his neck. This surprised the bully and now the was mad as well. The bully got up and took a stance like hew as going to take out Tonogun and the came after him again.

As the bully was charging Tonogun, Tonogun spun around and caught the bully in his balls and the bent down. Next Tonogun brought his knee up and caught the bully under his jaw and some teeth fell out. Next Tonogun shoved his thumb into the bully's left eye and a split second later the shoved his index finger into the bully's left ear. As the bully was falling down he kicked the bully in his solar plexus and the bully spit of a lot of teeth and more blood. The bully was now unconscious and laying on the floor.

Tonogun grabbed the red table cloth and wrapped the Bully with the table cloth. The Bull's legs were sticking out so the kicked them at the knee stuffed them backwards and stuffed them in the table-cloth. The used a lamp cord and tied the red tablecloth with it and he looked at the ball, then decided to add a couple of cast iron frying pans in the ball and decided it was good enough for now.

The rolled the ball to his van but it was too big to fit in his van. Sukiko said wait here for a while and I will borrow Thor's old red pickup truck with a tailgate lift, and I will be right back.

When she came back, all three of them rolled the heavy ball on the tailgate and Sukiko pushed the button on the side of the tailgate and it lifted up to the level of the back of the truck. They pushed the ball in the bed of the red truck, and she closed the tail gate and told everyone to get into the truck.

When they all got to Thor's old house, Ichimon was just getting ready to go fishing on his boat. Sukiko asked hm if the could give them a ride in his boat to get rid of some trash, and gave him stack of cash with a bank band strapped around the hundred dollar bills.

Ichigun accepted the bundle of cash and said where to, Sukiko said take the boat out to sea and I want to dump the trash there. Half an hour later Sukiko noticed that the water got suddenly bluer, asked Ichigun why the water changed color. Ichigun said we are now over the Japan trench and it is the deepest trench in the world. Sukiko said stop the boat here, and she went back to the back of the boat where the heavy ball of trash or the Bully was tied up and asked everyone to help her dump the ball overboard. The all watched the ball as it sand out of sight. They saw some sharks swimming around and wondered if they can catch up to the sinking ball.

Sukiko went back to Ichigun still at his helm

and told him that we are all done now so we can go back home. Ichigun turned the boat back towards Okinawa.

The New Dojo 112

When they all got back to the apartment they looked around, and Sukiko asked everyone if they wanted to save anything from the apartment. No one could think of anything that they needed except for Tsukiko who wanted to take her brand-new computer with her.

They all got into Sukiko's van and she drove directly to the old Town House Meeting building, and there was a sign on the door that said building for sale for $100,000. The door was broken and the place looked empty. It had a wooden floor and a high ceiling.

Sukiko asked Tonogun if this would make a good enough Dojo to start with. Tonogun said this building is three times bigger than my Dojo in Osaka and ceiling also a lot higher. Sukiko said I can hire some carpenters and they can have it completely remodeled in a week. Inside another sign said to talk to the Mayor if you want to buy the place.

Sukiko knew where the Mayor's house was so they all drove to talk to the Mayor. When Sukiko drove up to the mayor's Mansion the place looked like it needed a lot of repairs. The all walked up the broad steps and knocked on the double door. But none came to the door. Sukiko pushed on one side of the door and the heavy door opened.

An old man finally came to the door and the apologized for taking so much time. The old man said I am the Mayor of Little Sicily and said how can I be of help. Sukiko said we just came from the old Town Hall building and noticed that it was for sale.

The Mayor said please come in and have a seat, and pointed to the broken down couch. When they sat down dust flew up from the couch. The Mayor said my housekeeper got old and left a long time ago and so did all my staff so now I am doing all the work buy myself.

The mayor said I also have nine houses close by and they are for sale as well. The Mayor said this house is too big for me so I was thinking about selling the house as well. Sukiko asked how much the wanted for the house. The Mayor said how about a half a million dollars. Everyone figured that it was $500,000.

The mayor said that there was a lot of land here and there is a of old fruit trees growing here and if you hire a yard man you could pick some fruit and sell the fruit at the Farmer's Market and make some money.

Sukiko was ready to close the deal right now but she wanted to know what everybody else thought about the house. Tonogun asked the Mayor how many rooms the house had and the Mayor said I have ten large bedrooms upstairs I but I usually sleep in the living room because it is too hard for me to walk up those big stairs.

Sukiko said what if I buy the place and hire some good staff to do all the cooking, the house cleaning, and hire a couple of house maids to help you get up to one of the bedrooms and you can say here for free and what do you think about that. The Mayor said don't they make chairs that I can sit on and it can take me up the stairs all you have to do is to sit in the chair. Sukiko said I can have one installed for you if you like and it won't cost you a penny.

The Mayor was happy to hear Sukiko say that and said it's a deal. Sukiko said I will have a bill of sale for you to sign in few days and you can look it over and if you change your mind that will be fine as well. They said goodbye and left all left.

Sukiko took them all to the Onsen restaurant to have dinner to discuss how everything went.

At the Onsen restaurant they all found a nice table and started to discuss everything that went on today. Yuki was sitting at the next table and when she heard them talking about a contract she popped in and said I couldn't help you talking about a contract and I have access to fine lawyers and I will be happy to have my lawyers help you with the contract.

Yuki said I will be here tomorrow at noon with my lawyers we can help you then. Sukiko said thank you to Yuki and said I will be here tomorrow at noon because we are all staying here in the hotel. A few minutes later a waiter came by and handed them all a pass to the Onsen and told everyone that it was from his boss and handed each of them a pass to the Onsen.

After they all had their dinner Sukiko asked the waiter for her bill and the waiter said that his boss already paid for the dinner as well as for the hotel rooms.

This surprised everyone and wondered who the big boss might be.

113 Yuki

Sukiko was waiting for Yuki at noon and Yuki showed up right on time with a couple of her lawyers. They got right to business and the lawyers asked Sukiko to describe all the terms of the contract. After Sukiko told them everything that she discussed with the old Mayor, the lawyers said we will have the contract all written up for you by tomorrow and we will see you here again at noon.

After the lawyers left Yuki invited Sukiko to her table and said let's have lunch. Yuki said I don't think that I have ever met you before and she was curious as to who she was. Sukiko asked Yuki if she had a lot of time, and Yuki said I have all afternoon. A waiter came by and asked Yuki if she was ready to order. Yuki said she already called the cook last night and he was preparing some Sashimi for her, Yuki asked Sukiko if she liked Sashimi. Sukiko said I love Sashimi so that was all taken care of now. Sukiko said that her Great-Great-Great-Grandfather left me a lot of money after the died and now she would never have to worry about money anymore. Yuki asked Sukiko what his name was, Sukiko said his real name was Mathew Nations, but the wanted everyone to just call him simply as Matt. Yuki said I think that I heard of him and said that she heard that he was a good man and always helped people get on their feet and they all did well in life. Sukiko then asked Yuki who she was and why she had access to the fine lawyers

Yuki said my story is more complicated than yours and after we get to know each other better I will tell you more. Just then the Sashimi dinner came and they both had to stop talking to eat the Sashimi.

114 Moving In

Sukiko and Tsukie moved into their own houses which were very nicely furnished. Both units were similar in design where they could cook their own breakfast and lunch there. At night they usually went out to eat somewhere together.

Tonogun and Kamimura came back to Okinawa and Kamimura had his father with him. They all had their own private bedrooms with a bathroom next their bedrooms.

The Mansion was now fully staffed with maids, a cook, three house keepers and three yard men who all reported to work shortly before noon and stared to do their work. All of them came from Little Sicily and they either walked to work, or bicycled, or came by car if they had a car.

The first thing that the cook did was to pick all the vegetables from the front vegetable garden and bring them into the kitchen then put them in the sink to be washed. After that, she moved them in the refrigerator to crisp them up. Only after they were fully cold will she even begin to make the salads which made her salads the freshest and crispiest salads available. Anywhere, these salads ended up tasting different everyday, because she will buy different things to add to her salads everyday. One day it may a sprinkling of blue cheese, and the next day it will be something entirely different. Everyone in the mansion looked forward to their lunch because it was when everyone got together, and they can tell each other what they planned to that day.

The physical exercise class started in the after noon, and lasted for an hour and a half. The purpose of this class was to strengthen the lady's bodies before any serious marshal-arts classes were started because the ladies need to have a strong body before they can do that without getting hurt.

Kamimura and his father will show the ladies what a smaller person can do with the skill that they will teach the ladies after they got their strength up to point to where they can do the same maneuvers. It looked easy when Kamimura and his father did the demonstrations, and the ladies were eager to try the same maneuvers themselves as soon as they were strong enough to try to do them. Both Kamimura and his father will show each lady how to do the maneuvers and they all got a feel for how it could be done as soon as they became strong enough to actually do them.

One night each week, Tonogun will have a special class just for Sukiko and Tsukie how to use the Ninja stars and other Ninja weapons and Kamimura and his father were also there to show them how easy it was to use those weapons. For this class they didn't have be fully built up physically and have their full strength. This class was hidden from view from the rest of the clients who were playing shogi in the front section of the big hall.

After that, Kamimura's father Shizo will join the Shogi group and play any member of the group who wanted to challenge him in a game of Shogi. So far none of them could come close to defeating Shinzo. At the Shogi meetings Shinzo will have a lady serve them green tea in exchange for a free lesson of Shogi or a private Judo lesson for the lady who served the green tea.

Tsukue took classes at the University on creative writing because she was already a good writer, but she could always get good feedback from the professor and her classmates when she presented a novel for review. She always got an "A" on all of her novels.

The old Mayor couldn't be happier with his new housemates who always had lunch and sometimes dinner with him, and he no longer have eat all by himself anymore.

Now they had great conversations as they ate and sometimes the Old Mayor would entertain them with one of his seven Violins and give the history of each of his special violins. Actually, he was not bad at playing the violins even at his advanced at age.

Sukiko had a special house bult over the hole where she had her stash of hidden platinum and whenever she needed any more cash she went down to her basement and cut a piece of Platinum using a miner's mall and a chisel and curt a small piece of it off and brought it to the bank and exchanged it for more money.

In this way she always had a handy supply of cash for small business transactions such as having all of her three cabins remodeled to look brand new, and the carpenters preferred cash even if there wasn't any income tax in the new Principality of Okinawa for some unknown reason. After all the remodeling was done, the cute squirrel came back, and they became good friends because Sukiko always bought the squirrel some great treats and soon the squirrel started to eat his dinner in the kitchen with Sukiko as she had own dinner at the same time. Sukiko even had a special bed for the squirrel in the kitchen with fresh water for the squirrel. Whenever Sukiko was away from her house, the squirrel always guarded the house from intrudes like birds and mice and other small animals.

ABOUT THE AUTHOR

Firmin Murakami was born in 1927 in Los Angeles, CA. After WWII started in 1941, he was sent with his family to a prison camp in Jerome Arkansas. He began to learn how to speak English when he started public school as a young boy. He had difficulty in school because he couldn't understand what his teacher was trying to tell him.

Before WWII officially came to an end, he served in the United States Marine Corps and was honorably discharged with a rank of Sargent.

He currently lives with his wife, Gael, in Fairbanks, AK, along with a cat called Phantom and a dog called Shane.

He lost use of his formally good eye seven years ago and now he only uses his bad eye which is not all that good. He doesn't watch TV because he can't see. He recently bought a large computer screen in order that he can enlarge the letters and make out what he is writing, so he started writing books.

This book is a product of his efforts.

Made in the USA
Monee, IL
27 July 2021